Black Moon Rising

Black Knights Inc: Reloaded

JULIE ANN WALKER

BLACK MOON RISING
Copyright © 2025 by Julie Ann Walker

This is a work of fiction. Names, characters, places, brands, media, and incidents are either the product of the author's imagination or are used fictitiously. Any resemblance to actual or fictional characters or actual or fictional events, locales, business establishments, or persons, living or dead, is entirely coincidental. The fictional characters, events, locales, business establishments, or persons in this story have no relation to any other fictional characters, events, locales, business establishments, or persons, except those in works by this author.

No part or portion of this book may be reproduced in any form without prior permission from the author.

All rights reserved by the author.

ISBN: 978-1-950100-20-0

Cover Art © 2025 by Erin Dameron-Hill

Interior Formatting: Bravia Books, LLC

Published in the United States of America
Limerence Publications LLC

To my father.
This is the first book I've written since you've been gone. But it's certainly not the first book I've written about heroes who look out for the little guy, who believe right is more precious than might, and who value truth and justice above all else.

These things I learned from you. Thank you for always leading by example.

I miss you every day.

Those who do not know the value of loyalty can never appreciate the cost of betrayal.

—Alexander the Great

PROLOGUE

South Riverside Plaza, Chicago, Illinois

Britt Rollins was a stalker.

That's right—a *stalker*.

He hadn't set out to be anything of the sort. It had started by happenstance.

You see, a month earlier, he'd made a trip to the Beverly neighborhood in the farthest reaches of South Chicago to buy King Curve Rhino handlebars from a mustachioed dude selling them cheap on Facebook Marketplace.

As was his tendency, Britt had arrived at the rendezvous point early. And since he'd needed something strong and black and packed with caffeine to take the edge off the sharp hangover he'd been sporting thanks to an engagement celebration from the night before—the celebration was for some friends, not for him—he'd stepped into the coffee shop on the corner.

And there she'd been.

The ineffable Julia O'Toole. All five towering feet of her.

Give or take an inch or two.

He'd known she had a bangin' little bod under her standard-issue pantsuits and crisp, button-down shirts. But he'd been unprepared for... *perfection.*

As The Commodores sang... *Thirty-six, twenty-four, thirty-six. What a winnin' hand!*

Her cutoff jean shorts had passionately hugged her round butt and emphasized her muscular legs. Her ribbed, blue tank top had molded to her breasts and followed the lovely dip of her waist. And her casual plastic flip-flops had highlighted the arches of her dainty feet and the charm of her unpainted toenails.

He'd only ever seen her with her hair pulled back into a ponytail or twisted up into a tight bun. But that day she'd left it loose to hang down her back in a silky sheet.

"Old money blonde."

That's how Eliza, the Black Knights' den mother, on-site chef, and all-around Girl Friday, had described Julia's hair...that warm, honeyed color somewhere between light brown and dark blond. Considering Eliza *came* from old money, who was Britt to argue with her assessment?

Anywho...let's return to the moment I took on the title of Creepy McCreeperson.

Julia had popped the top on her cup of coffee the instant the barista handed it to her. He'd thought she might stroll over to the condiments station to fill her drink with cream and sugar, and he'd been eager to watch the sway of her hips in those Daisy Dukes. But to his disappointment, she'd simply shuffled to the side to allow the next person in line to order before pursing her lips and blowing across the surface of the steaming black liquid like she couldn't wait to get the contents inside her mouth.

Seeing her lips in that perfect moue had done things to him.

If he'd been one of those cartoon dogs, his eyes would have bulged from his head, and his tongue would have unfurled from his mouth to hit the floor. But since he was just a man, he'd stood there stunned. Jaw agape. Heart pounding. Dick...well...doing decidedly dickish things.

When she had turned in his direction, he could have lifted a hand and said, *"Fancy meeting you here, Agent O'Toole."* He could have bobbed his chin and offered her a knowing smile. Hell, he could have shot her a one-finger salute followed by a friendly wink.

All of those things would've been normal. Natural. *Not* stalker-y.

Instead, he'd gone with door number four.

Stepping quickly behind the wide concrete support beam in the center of the room, he'd held his breath as she breezed by him on her way to the front door. He'd felt the air shift as she passed. And his nostrils had flared unwillingly when her perfume's sweet, warm scent wafted over to him.

Thinking back now, he told himself he'd avoided letting her see him because he was a man of secrets—loads of them. And since she was a woman paid by Uncle Sam to uncover secrets, avoiding a run-in with her was instinctual.

Fourteen years of conducting covert operations worldwide had taught him many things. The most important was to trust his gut.

If things had ended there, everything would have been fine. *He* would have been fine and not have become…well…what he'd become.

Things had not ended there.

Before he'd known what they were doing, his biker boots had followed her out the door. Before he could stop them, his eyes had searched the sidewalk and spotted her hopping into her cherry-red Jeep Wrangler. Before he'd thought to convince them otherwise, his legs had carried him to his tricked-out, custom-made Harley chopper.

And the rest, as they say, is history.

He'd followed her turn-for-turn for five full minutes. When she'd pulled into the lot of a small city park, he'd walked his bike to the opposite curb, cut his engine, and leaned his forearms across his handlebars to watch her leap from her Jeep and be welcomed into the group of people gathered around a picnic table.

He'd known they were her family *not* because he had much of his own to speak of. But because he had Black Knights Inc.

The men and women who worked at the covert government defense firm that masqueraded behind the façade of a custom motorcycle shop were his siblings by choice instead of by blood. And the children of the OG group—Britt and the five guys who currently ran missions with him were BKI version 2.0—had become Britt's noisy, oftentimes *sticky*, honorary nieces and nephews.

Being welcomed in the fold at BKI meant he'd easily recognized as goodhearted sibling rivalry the noggin scrubbing Julia had received from one of the big-shouldered men who'd greeted her. He'd pinpointed the motherly love in the eyes of the older woman who'd hugged her before brushing back a strand of hair from her forehead. And he'd identified the squeals from the crowd of kids who'd swarmed her legs as the excitement of children whose favorite aunt had just arrived.

Forgetting about his hangover, Mr. Mustache, and those sweet handlebars, he had spent the next hour covertly watching the festivities in the park. Smiling as Julia pushed a wild-haired boy with a Bluey Band-Aid on his dirty little knee on the merry-go-round—*adorable*. Curling his hands into tight fists while she played a rather harrowing game of flag football with her brothers, a group of men twice her size—*anxiety-inducing*. And sucking in a ragged breath when she wrapped her luscious lips around a hotdog—*talk about shwing!*

Just that easily, Britt the Stalker had been born.

He might have forgiven himself the voyeurism had that afternoon been the sum of it. But like jumping out of an airplane or hanging off the side of a mountain by a pencil-thin safety line, he'd been hooked once he'd tasted that sweet adrenaline.

Now, he made it a point whenever he was CONUS—military speak for inside the continental U.S.—to get up early and grab the table in the far corner of Peet's Coffee in South Riverside Plaza because, Monday through Friday, Julia O'Toole came in at precisely seven-thirty A.M. to order her standard cup of no-frills java.

How had he learned this was her pre-work pitstop, you ask?

To his utter shame, he'd followed her home from the park that first day and watched from down the block as she was greeted by two mangy-looking dogs and one loud-mouthed cat. The picture window in the front of her bungalow-style house had afforded him an unencumbered view of the large, gray parrot that had flown from its perch to alight on her shoulder. And when one of the animals had done something to make her smile, when he'd heard her soft laugh drift out through the screen door, he'd been transfixed.

Captivated. *Enthralled.*

He'd gone *back* the following morning because he'd told himself if he saw her in her boxy pantsuits, if he caught a glimpse of her badge, if he watched her walk into the FBI building, then the spell she'd cast over him the day before would be broken. He'd told himself if he could be reminded she was Agent O'Toole and not the sweet, Southside girl with a soft spot for rescue animals, he'd be able to go back to not dreaming about her when he was asleep and fantasizing about her when he was awake.

Turns out, he thought now. *I lied.*

Before she'd made it to the field office on Roosevelt Road, she'd stopped at Peet's Coffee. And even in her pantsuit, even with her hair pulled tight into a bun and her sidearm poorly concealed in the shoulder harness beneath her jacket, she'd still been…

Julia.

Julia with the kind of face you'd see on the girl next door—the one who always waved as you passed by. Julia with the kind of fresh complexion that was soft and inviting, a natural sort of beauty that needed no enhancement. Julia with that direct, unfaltering gaze…behind which lay a mind as honed and precise as a steel trap.

Far from being freed from the spell she'd cast over him, he'd been hooked.

Hooked on catching a glimpse of her smile. Hooked on hearing the deep, sultry tone of her voice. Hooked on the warm, sweet scent of her perfume that seemed to linger even after she left the room.

Which brings us to this morning and my spot here at the corner table.

He liked the corner table because it was shadowed, hidden behind the condiments station, yet still afforded him a view of the counter, the cashier, and anyone who placed an order.

You know, if he leaned to the side and wasn't thwarted by an idiot in a three-piece suit standing in front of the jug of cream and checking his phone instead of getting on with it and moving the hell out of the way!

Britt glowered up at the man.

When Mr. Three-Piece felt Britt's knife-sharp gaze, he quickly filled his cup with cream before scampering away in a pair of wingtips that probably cost more than the custom chrome exhaust Britt had recently installed on his motorcycle.

"Agent O'Toole!" A deep voice broke through the *hiss* of the barista's steaming wand and the low hum of conversation emanating from the coffee shop's many patrons.

Today's cashier was Britt's least favorite. Maybe because the asshole had hero hair, and any man who spent that much money on product was automatically suspicious in Britt's book. Or maybe because the guy's teeth were so perfectly straight and so blindingly white that Britt felt the need to slide on his sunglasses anytime the dickhead smiled. Or maybe—okay, most likely—because Julia flirted with the twatwaffle.

Case in point...

"Hey you!" Her grin was patently sexy. Britt loathed seeing it aimed at the bastard behind the counter. "Long time, no see."

"I keep telling you twenty-four hours is an eternity between visits." Chaz shook his head. Yes, the bastard's name was *Chaz*. *Oh, the clichés abound!* "I get off at noon. Want to meet me for lunch?"

"You know I don't mix business with pleasure." Julia's dark lashes fell to half-mast so her expression became decidedly...bedroom-y.

Britt gripped his mug so hard he was surprised it didn't shatter in his hands. He wanted to jump up and shout: *Can't you see he's vain and vapid and sporting a micro-penis?*

Okay, so he'd had plenty of observation days to back up his vain and vapid assessment. The micro-penis? Pure speculation.

Or maybe that's just pure hope.

A guy that good-looking must have at least one physical flaw. The universe believes in balance, right?

"But we don't work together," Chaz countered, flashing her a grin that made his dimples wink.

The woman in line behind Julia sighed like an actress in a melodrama, and Britt rolled his eyes so hard that he was surprised they stayed in their sockets.

"In a way we do," Julia insisted. "You're the key to my success. Without you fueling me with caffeine, I'd be useless. And since I hunt bad guys for a living, surely you don't want me off my game."

"Now that's where you're wrong."

Julia cocked her head.

"I *definitely* want you regardless of your game."

An evil expression spread over Britt's face, and at the same time, a blush spread over Julia's. Her heightened color was accompanied by a dreamy look that alarmed Britt more than if she'd launched a grenade in his direction.

Chaz is that guy, he thought, his jaw grinding so hard it was a miracle his molars didn't turn to dust. *The one begging to have all those pretty teeth rearranged by my fist.*

Once again, his legs had a mind of their own. They'd shoved him to a stand before he'd made the conscious decision to move. And since when it came to Julia his ability to control his impulses rested comfortably on the head of a pin, the only thing that stopped him from marching over to the counter and dragging Chaz across it so he could punch the asshat in the peanut pouch was the heavy hand that landed on his shoulder.

"Busted."

Britt blinked in surprise to find Hewitt Birch standing beside him. His shock was partly because they were miles from the former-menthol-cigarette-factory-turned-custom-motorcycle shop that was their home. Partly because Hew was a recluse—when the guy wasn't piloting a chopper in a country half a world away, he was in a corner somewhere with his nose buried in a book. But mostly because Britt hadn't seen Hew come into the coffee shop.

Which meant he'd been so focused on Julia that he'd completely abandoned his training.

"What the hell are you doing on this side of town?" he demanded, feeling a crease form between his eyebrows.

"Watching you watch Agent O'Toole with a broody stare that's all covetous and hot," Hew replied in that thick, Downeast Mainer accent that made most folks think he'd been born and raised in Boston.

If Britt had been the blushing sort, he would've been red from his toes to the tips of his ears. Since he *wasn't*, all he did was retake his seat and sullenly admit, "I'm already hating this conversation, and we're only one sentence in."

Hew snorted and grabbed the chair next to Britt, easily lowering his substantial frame into it.

Where Britt was lean and muscular, Hew was big and bulky. They both spent their fair share of time in the BKI outbuilding packed with gym equipment. But Britt chose exercises that honed his agility and endurance while Hew picked up heavy things and put them down again.

"I couldn't help noticing you've spent the last two weeks sneaking out at the crack of dawn to take the train to the other side of the city for a cup of coffee that's not half as good as the stuff we brew back home." Hew quirked an eyebrow two shades darker than the auburn hair on his head. "Am I right in assuming that's due to one hot-to-trot fed?" He hitched his bearded chin in Julia's direction.

"Never assume, Hew. It makes an ass out of you and m—"

"Yeah, yeah." Hew waved him off. "Stop with the diversion tactics and spill the tea. Or…the coffee, as the case may be." Hew appeared pleased by his own wit. "Are you two secretly dating?"

"*No*," Britt hissed. "And keep your voice down. That accent of yours travels."

"I don't have an accent. *You* have an accent." Hew blinked when he realized they had gotten off-topic. Again. He pointed an accusing finger at Britt. "Diversion tactics! Stop it!"

"Shhh!" Britt peeked beyond the condiments and didn't know if he was relieved or ready to spit nails when he discovered Julia still deep in conversation with Mr. Hero Hair. "And no. Julia and I aren't secretly dating."

"Then what are you doing here besides shooting eye daggers at Captain America working the register?"

"If I tell you, you'll think I'm crazy."

Hew snorted. "Hate to break it to you, brother, but you think jumping out of perfectly good planes is fun. We passed the exit to crazy miles ago."

No use lying. Bitt was caught red-handed. "I've been coming to…uh…see her."

Hew rubbed his hand over his short beard. "Now, see? When you say it like that, it sounds okay. Because when you say you've gone to see someone, people assume that means the person you went to see is seeing you too. But not once has that lovely little blond looked your way." He hooked a thumb in Julia's general direction. "And I can't help but notice you've picked a rather strategic spot over here behind the condiments station."

Britt didn't respond. But he knew his glare was sharp enough to cut.

Unbothered, Hew grinned. Or what passed for a grin on Hew's face, which was more just a quirk of the left side of his lips. "No need to look like someone shoved a cactus up your ass. Just tell me why you're stalking an FBI agent."

And there it was. Said right out loud. The S-word.

"I'm not *stalking* her." The lie fell easily from Britt's tongue. Unfortunately, it tasted like piss.

"To borrow one of your favorite phrases…*bullshit*."

"Okay, fine. But it's not what you think."

"I think she's got a smile that could melt the brass off a doorknob. And I think one look at her makes your boy parts get bigger."

If the Earth's crust had chosen that moment to crack open and swallow Britt whole, it would have been a kindness.

Instead, Britt was left to grit his teeth. "So it *is* what you think. But it's more than that. She…*fascinates* me. She's got all these interesting pieces that don't fit together. And I can't stop myself from trying to solve the puzzle."

Hew's eyes narrowed. "Care to elaborate?"

"Not really. I'd like to forget we started this conversation."

"Humor me anyway. Unless you'd rather I got Agent O'Toole's attention and—" Hew turned in Julia's direction and cupped his hand around the side of his mouth like he was getting ready to shout her name. Britt astonished himself by punching Hew in the arm.

"Don't you dare," he hissed.

Hew lifted an unphased eyebrow. "Then give me a reason not to. I need something to make the trip out here worth it. And if you're not willing to entertain me, then maybe the hottie with the body"—again he hooked a thumb in Julia's direction—"will."

"Fine," Britt spat.

Hew crossed his arms, the picture of indolent interest.

Sighing heavily, Britt decided that maybe if he admitted his reasons for following Julia, it would take away their power. Maybe if he said the words out loud and heard how ridiculous they sounded, her hold on him would loosen.

"She's…tough and no-nonsense, right?" They'd learned that much about her when she'd come into their lives while investigating a mass shooting at a senator's house. "But she's also this tenderhearted thing who collects stray animals like most folks collect Amazon boxes. She's whip-smart, and yet she reads trashy sci-fi novels." His words came quicker as he listed her quirks and qualities. "She pays attention to the most minuscule details when she's on a case, but she's a menace on the road. I'm convinced she's paying attention to everything *but* the fact that she's driving when she's behind the wheel. If there's a pothole, she finds it. If there's a curb, she'll hit it. She's a mystery inside an enigma wrapped in a boxy pantsuit. And all I want is to figure her out."

For what felt like an eternity, Hew remained expressionless. Then he grinned—or, rather, that corner of his mouth quirked. "You like her," Hew said.

"She has more than two brain cells to rub together and is built like a brick shithouse." Britt shrugged noncommittally. "What's not to like?"

"No." Hew shook his head. "You *like* her like her. Like, hearts and flowers like her. Because if it were anything less, you wouldn't be stalking the woman."

"Quit using that word." A muscle ticked in Britt's jaw.

"Which one? Like or stalking?"

"Now that I think of it, both."

"Quit liking her to the point of stalking her"—Hew shrugged as if it was just that easy—"and I will."

CHAPTER 1

You're being paranoid, Julia scolded herself as the coffee shop's glass door swung shut behind her and she was swept into the crowd on the busy sidewalk.

She couldn't shake the feeling someone was watching her, but she told herself the sensations were left over from her fifteen minutes of fame.

After she'd uncovered the culprit behind the mass shooting at Senator McClean's residence—the villain had turned out to be none other than the frickin' senate minority leader—the press had hailed her as the hero of the hour, and they'd spent weeks hounding her for interviews. She hadn't been able to leave her house for a while without some over-zealous reporter shoving a microphone in her face.

But since the news cycle was the news cycle and kept spinning, she'd eventually gone from "breaking news" to "human interest story" to… nothing. And yet, she couldn't shake the sensation she was lined up in someone's crosshairs.

Paranoia, she silently insisted. *It'll pass.*

Scrubbing a hand over the back of her neck, she shoved her disquiet aside and forced herself to take in the day and the city around her.

Chicago…

It was a place of contrasts: both beautiful and gritty, tranquil and chaotic.

A construction site on the corner was noisy, with clanging metal and roaring machinery. But she could also hear an orchestra tuning up in Millenium Park—that green oasis amidst the concrete jungle.

Fall was in the air. The earthy aroma of dying leaves mixed with the fresh, clean scent of the cool breezes that swept down from Canada.

An hour earlier, the sun had peeked its head above the waters of Lake Michigan. Now, it cast its golden glow over the buildings, bathing them in that wonderful half-light that made everything seem magical.

The sidewalk grew less crowded—and more uneven—as she continued south towards the FBI building. The tourists who thronged the streets closer to downtown, standing in line for a bag of Garrett's Popcorn or snapping pictures of the iconic architecture, had no reason to wander this far past the river and—

The buzzing of her phone in her pocket wrenched her from her ruminations. Pulling out the device, she frowned at the screen when she saw who was calling.

Dillan Douglas. Her partner.

Also known as the pain that lives in my ass.

Dealing with him required more caffeine than she currently had onboard. Which meant there was only one solution.

Tipping back her coffee, she gulped down as much of the burning beverage as she could manage before she had to come up for air or risk a scalded esophagus.

It wasn't that Dillan was a *bad* agent. His interrogation skills were average and his investigative instincts were fair. She'd worked with better agents, and she'd certainly worked with worse.

The *problem* was he thought he was god's gift to the bureau.

Which meant he hadn't taken it well when *she* had been promoted to lead agent. And even though he'd managed to get over most of his pique in the handful of months since she'd assumed the position, he still didn't afford her the respect her title deserved.

But what's new? she thought with a sigh of resignation. She'd spent her whole life having to prove herself worthy of the kind of recognition and regard guys like Dillan—guys like her father and brothers—were given as a matter of course just because they had the hair and the height and the jawlines of comic book heroes.

When her phone buzzed again, she took another quick sip of coffee before thumbing on the device. "Hello?"

"Where are you?"

"Good morning to you too, Agent Douglas."

"We've worked together long enough to skip the pleasantries." The annoyance in his tone was palpable.

It took everything she had not to squeeze her coffee cup hard enough to pop off the top and have its remaining contents bursting forth in a geyser. But she reminded herself that the coffee was hot, and she didn't feel like making a trip to Northwestern's burn unit.

Plus, you know, I still need the caffeine.

"Okay. Consider the pleasantries skipped. What do you want?"

"I want you to haul ass into the office. We just landed a new case, and you'll never guess who might be involved."

Her pace quickened at the words "new case," and she took the steps up to the front door of the FBI field building two at a time.

She and Dillan had been given decidedly *low-priority* work after the massacre at Senator McClean's mansion. Their supervisor had said they couldn't effectively work a big case with the press hot on their heels. Then, once the reporters moved on, he'd told them he wanted to give them time to decompress before throwing anything of genuine interest their way.

Not to put too fine a point on it, but she'd been bored off her ass for weeks now.

"I'll bite," she said as she ran her security badge through the checkpoint and nodded to the guard manning the front desk. "Who might be involved?"

"None other than those custom motorcycle builders over on Goose Island. Small world, huh?"

She didn't bother answering as she stopped in front of the bank of elevators because, one, it was a rhetorical question. Two, she hadn't exactly heard it since the moment Dillan had alluded to Black Knights Inc., her mind had tuned out what he was saying so it could fill itself with images of one particular man.

Army Ranger turned motorcycle mechanic, Britt Rollins had become… well…a bit of an obsession. She'd spent many an hour after work—and usually after a glass or two of wine—remembering how absolutely delicious he'd looked in his jeans, biceps-hugging T-shirts, and biker boots.

He wasn't as drop-dead gorgeous as his coworker Fisher Wakefield, or as big and built as the Black Knight who'd introduced himself to her as Hewitt Birch. But there was just…*something* about Sergeant Rollins.

Maybe it was the way the jagged scar across his temple turned his otherwise comfortably handsome face into a visage that was as compelling as it was intimidating. Maybe it was the unique sound of his accent. It wasn't the slow drawl so many associated with the South, but something softer. Something rounder. He avoided the final and middle R sounds in words so that the English language hit the ear the same way tupelo honey hit the tongue.

She'd done some digging on him.

Yes, I used my position within the FBI to pull his records. So sue me.

There had been frustratingly little to discover, however. She'd found out he'd been born and raised in Charleston, South Carolina, which explained the accent since the city's language had been affected by the local African-American Gullah dialect as well as different European influences.

Yes, I looked that up too.

She'd discovered he'd lost both of his parents when he'd been too young to experience such tragedy. And she'd unearthed that his brother was a bit of a ne'er-do-well.

But when it came to his military service? When it came to figuring out what had put that hard glint in his crystal-blue eyes or that tough cant to his jaw?

Nada. Zero. Zilch.

His file had been redacted six ways from Sunday. Which actually told her all she needed to know.

He'd seen action. The hard kind. The bloody kind.

For whatever reason, that just made him even *more* fantasy-worthy.

And boy-oh-boy, had she fantasized. In fact, she should go ahead and name her vibrator Sergeant Rollins since he'd been the sole inspiration behind the tool's use for the past few months.

"Are you still there?"

Dillan's voice pulled her from her reverie. She realized she'd missed the elevator and had to re-push the button.

"Still here. Headed up. See you in sixty seconds." She hung up without signing off and then took three slow breaths to calm her racing heart before stepping into the elevator.

Her reaction to the idea of seeing Britt Rollins again was silly. He was just a man. She'd grown up in a house full of men. She worked in a field that was predominantly populated by men.

They're not all that.

Except…something told her the sergeant was different.

"Yo!" Dillan said as soon as the silver door slid open onto their floor. He had his tablet in hand. The screen shined into his face and highlighted the eager glint in his eye. "This is a good one. A real Harrison Ford-type deal."

She blinked, wondering what Han Solo had to do with the Black Knights and their new case.

When Dillan saw her confusion, he rolled his eyes. "As in *The Fugitive*."

"Oh." She nodded, reminding herself that Harrison Ford was famous for roles outside the *Star Wars* universe.

With a practiced ease, she made her way through the maze of cubicles to the corner cubby she shared with Dillan. The movies made it look like FBI agents had private offices and wide wooden desks. But the reality was that America was a big business and treated its federal police force like most corporations treated their employees. They were packed in like sardines to optimize the workspace and minimize the overhead.

Sinking into her rolling chair, she absently tossed her fanny pack into the side drawer of her plain, metal desk—she'd never understood the appeal of a purse—and looked expectantly at Dillan as he took his place at the opposite desk.

Most days, she wasn't hyped about the idea of staring at his too-handsome face for eight to ten hours straight. But today, his excitement was contagious. She found herself leaning toward him eagerly. "Okay. Give it to me. What are we dealing with?"

CHAPTER 2

Black Knights Inc., Goose Island

Remember that thing Britt said about finding a home at Black Knights Inc. and feeling like those who worked there were family?
He took it back.
They weren't family. Quite the contrary. He wanted to run upstairs, grab his trusty sidearm, and start shooting them all…in the legs—they needed maiming, not killing. Besides, if they were busy staunching blood and gritting their teeth against pain, they wouldn't have time to give him any more shit.
And boy howdy, nobody was better at dishing out shit than the Black Knights.
On the train ride back to their side of town, Britt had repeatedly threatened Hewitt with great bodily harm should Hew decide to out him and his current…um…*preoccupation* with one Agent Julia O'Toole. But no matter how precise and inventive Britt's threats had been, Hew hadn't agreed to keep quiet.
In fact, Hew hadn't agreed to anything.
He'd simply popped his AirPods into his ears, pulled a tattered paperback copy of Paulo Coelho's *The Alchemist* from his back pocket, and ignored Britt for the entirety of the ride.

Britt had considered snatching the book from Hew's hands and tossing it out the window. But he quite liked his nose the way it was—namely, *not broken*—and so he'd been forced to sit back and hope beyond hope Hew would have mercy.

He should have known better.

He was pretty sure *Hew* and *mercy* were listed as antonyms in the thesaurus.

The minute the two of them walked through BKI's front door, Hew had hooked a thumb over his shoulder toward Britt and announced, "You'll never guess what I found this sonofabitch up to!"

"Did you wake up and take an asshole pill this morning?" Britt had demanded, his hands curling into fists.

Hew had wiggled his eyebrows. "No need for supplements. I come by it naturally." And then Hew had filled everyone in on how he'd caught Britt, to use Hew's word, "mid-stalk."

Now, Britt found himself seated at the large island in the kitchen while everyone who'd been onsite during Hew's big announcement took turns asking him questions and relentlessly teasing him.

He wanted to crawl under the tall, metal bistro table in the corner or disappear into the brick walls. But there was nowhere to hide from his colleagues.

"You're stalking an FBI agent?" Ozzie, an original Knight and their current tech guru, stared at him wide-eyed. Britt couldn't tell if Ozzie was impressed or appalled. "Damn, bro. The balls on you would shame a rhino."

Okay, so he's impressed.

Too bad it wasn't the kind of admiration Britt wanted.

"I take exception to Hew describing it as *stalking*." His jaw was clenched so hard he marveled he could speak at all.

"And what name would you give to the action of a man following a woman around, unbeknownst to her, and watching her with a look in his eye that says he'd like to club her over the head caveman-style and drag her by her hair back to his lair?" Hew countered while happily breaking a freshly baked blueberry muffin in half and smearing each side with a generous portion of butter.

The old menthol cigarette factory was a wonderful mix of homey and industrial. Out in the shop, the smell of grease, fresh auto paint, and metal shavings permeated the air. But inside the kitchen, the scents were familiar and comforting. The earthy kick of too-strong coffee mixed with the sweeter aromas of warm pastries.

Eliza Meadows—soon to be Eliza Wakefield because she'd said yes when Fisher Wakefield had popped the question—could put together mission parameters, give them a dissertation-worthy lecture on global politics, and hobnob with D.C.'s glitterati without batting a lash. But it was a well-known fact her favorite pastime was puttering around the kitchen, cooking up tasty delights worthy of the blue ribbon at any county fair.

"Of all the times you could have chosen to pull your nose out of a book and string more than twelve words together, why'd you pick today?" Britt glared at Hew.

"Ah, ah, ah." Hew wagged a finger. "Nice try. But answering a question with a question is the oldest trick in the book." He thickened his accent. "And I ain't falling for it."

"I'm *observing* her," Britt declared with a sniff. Then he attempted to succor his sorrows by shoving a strawberry tart between his lips.

The taste was so divine his eyes tried to roll back in his head.

Unfortunately, despite the comfort of the pastry, his sorrows were still happily ensconced in their front-row seats. Mostly thanks to Boss, who, as his nickname suggested, had been the brains and brawn behind the birth of Black Knights Inc. Frank "Boss" Knight had handpicked the original twelve members, had taken over running the civilian side of things once the former president no longer needed the OG crew, and still helped Britt and his teammates out whenever the occasion arose. In short, he had been and ostensibly still was…the *boss*.

"Observing her implies you have some professional or scientific curiosity." Boss's low, guttural voice was made for radio. FYI, the man had a face made for radio, too. His features were as blunt as a closed fist. Considering the unnatural flatness across the bridge of his nose, Britt assumed many closed fists had made them that way. "So tell us, what is it about Agent O'Toole that you find professionally or scientifically curious?"

"Is it the way her bottom fills out those slacks she wears?" This from Sam Harwood, the former Marine Raider and current target of Britt's heated stare. "Or is it 'cause you like waxing your axe while fantasizing 'bout her putting her cuffs on you?"

Closing his eyes, Britt prayed to any god who would listen to take pity on him.

"Not to risk putting another frown line on your already crowded forehead," Eliza chimed in gently, "but if you *like* her, why haven't you asked her out? I know you aren't suffering from a lack of confidence. I've seen you pick up dozens of bar bunnies over the years. So why all the subterfuge now?"

Britt donned what he hoped was the facial equivalent of a chalkboard that'd been wiped clean. "Who says I like her?"

"Please." Sam snorted. "There's no putting the jam back in that jar. You wouldn't be skulking around after a woman you didn't like."

Britt considered telling Sam to go do something with himself that was anatomically impossible. Instead, he took the high road—*go me!*

"Fine. You all caught me. I was impressed by how she handled herself during the Senator McClean case. And if I hadn't happened to run into her again the morning I rode down south to look at some handlebars, then things would have ended there. But I *did* run into her again. She was off-duty, wearing street clothes, and hanging out at this park with her family. I found myself…*intrigued* by her."

Sam snorted. "*Intrigued.*" He made air quotes. "Said every stalker who ever lived."

"Fine." Britt tossed his hands in the air. "So I *like* her. She's pretty and smart. But she's also a *fed.*" He stressed the last word. "Give the woman an hour in this place, and she'll figure out we're a hell of a lot more than a bike-building outfit. So, since I can't ask her out, I've been doing the next best thing: sneaking a few glimpses of her when I get the chance. Is that so wrong?"

"There's nothing that says you can't date a federal agent," Eliza countered. "Hunter *married* one."

Hunter Jackson had been the first of the Knights version 2.0 to have fallen ass over teakettle into that crazy little thing called love. But there was one crucial difference between Hunter and Britt that Eliza wasn't taking into account.

"Correct." He nodded. "Hunter *married* her. As his wife, she is duty-bound to keep his secrets. But there's no guarantee that'd be the case with Julia once I've scratched this itch and sent her on her way."

Eliza frowned. "You act like *sending her on her way* is a foregone conclusion. Who's to say you won't take a page out of Hunter's book?"

The snort that burst from him shocked him with its force. "Me," he managed once he'd gotten himself under control. "*I* say. I know you're all"—he waved a hand to indicate the gathered group—"so annoyingly in love that you can't imagine anyone *not* wanting what you have. But marriage? Kids? Happily ever after?" He scoffed. "I'm sorry, but have you *met* me?"

Boss crossed his big arms over his even bigger chest. "That's what we all said." He dragged his coverall-wearing wife, Becky—who'd been blessedly silent up to that point—under his arm and planted a kiss atop her head. Since she was more than a foot shorter than he was, he had to bend down to do it. "I'd resigned myself to being a bachelor for life until this one came along."

Becky plucked a red Dum Dum lollipop out of her mouth and pointed it at Britt. "I never thought I wanted a ring on my finger or a bunch of ragamuffins running around my house. But then I met the big guy here"—she patted Boss's chest—"and everything changed. You'll start singing a different tune when you find the right one. And who knows? Maybe Agent O'Toole is the right one."

The mere thought had cold sweat breaking out on Britt's brow. "Nope." He shook his head. "Not me. Not ever."

Every face in the room morphed into a frown. But it was Sam who asked, "Why not?"

Before Britt could answer, Fisher Wakefield, former Delta Force officer and Britt's brother from another mother—aka: his best friend—walked into the kitchen while running a hand through his shower-damp hair. He came to a stop when he sensed the odd atmosphere. "Uh. What did I miss?"

"Britt's been stalking Agent O'Toole," Hew said around a mouthful of muffin.

Britt refrained from smacking his forehead into his palm. But the temptation was there.

An evil grin slowly spread over Fish's face. "Why, Britton Daniel Rollins. How absolutely scandalous of you."

Oh, god. Not the government name.

Britt braced himself for whatever scathing witticism was next poised to come out of Fish's mouth. Thankfully, he was spared the mortification when his phone jangled to life in his pocket.

One look at the screen told him it was Rafer Connelly at the front gate.

"Saved by the bell." Eliza smiled at him softly.

"Right." He nodded, but his expression was the epitome of sarcasm. So was his tone when he added, "Everything is coming up Britt!"

Eliza's smile turned sympathetic. Then she squealed when Fisher swept her off her feet to press a smacking kiss on her lips.

For years the two of them had bickered like they were getting paid for every insult. But ever since they'd admitted their animosity was really L.O.V.E, they'd been on each other like cold on ice cream.

It was annoying.

And adorable.

But mostly annoying.

"Put me down, you big oaf!" Eliza swatted Fish on the shoulder, but there was no real force behind it.

"Fine." Fisher lowered her slowly, letting her body drag against his so that by the time Eliza's feet hit the floor, her cheeks were flaming red. "You woke up on the bossy side of the bed this morning, huh?"

The smile she slanted him was pure seduction. "You love it."

Fish's return grin was that of a man who'd gotten everything he wanted out of life. "Yeah, I do. I really do."

"Ugh." Sam rolled his eyes. "Get a room."

Fish frowned at Sam. "Don't yuck our yum just because you're cranky that your girlfriend is out of town again."

Sam's girlfriend, a purple-haired computer whiz named Hannah, was employed by the Cyber Crimes Division of the DOD. She'd recently been working on cases that required her to travel. It was a situation that made Sam—who was otherwise a pretty amiable guy—decidedly grouchy.

Sam opened his mouth to answer, but Britt didn't stick around to hear it. Instead, he quickly made his way to the door and thumbed on his phone.

"What's up, Rafe?" Before Rafe could answer, Britt grimaced and added, "Sweet Jesus. Is there anything in your Spotify account that doesn't make me want to take a bath with a toaster?"

The Connelly brothers, the four huge, freckled native Chicagoans who took shifts manning the gate, were great at their jobs. They were never late. They never complained about the long hours or the boredom that was occasionally followed by bursts of excitement or gunfire. And they could tell jokes better than standup comedians.

But they had *shit* taste in music. Geralt was a fan of jazz. Manus preferred death metal. Toran had recently gotten into a musical genre called "folktronica." And Rafer? Well, Rafe blared nothing but yacht rock.

The dulcet tones of Rupert Holmes singing his one-hit wonder "Escape" drifted over the open connection.

Not that Britt couldn't appreciate some soft-sational seventies tunes. But he'd always thought "Escape"—otherwise known as "The Pina Colada Song"—was complete garbage.

I mean, they both set out to cheat on each other. And then, when they catch each other, they just laugh and act like their mutual deception is nothing?

Ignoring him, Rafer announced, "You've got company."

Britt hurried out to the shop, where a monitor was mounted on the wall beside the front door. The screen was tuned to the security feed at the front gate.

He squinted at the two figures on the feed. The first was a woman huddled in a light jacket. The second was a man leaning an arm casually into the window of the guard house.

But not just *any* man. Britt's *brother*.

Knox had gone missing soon after being released from his last stint in the pen.

On the one hand, Britt was relieved to see him alive and kicking. The last time they'd talked, Knox had been amped about some new venture, and Britt had assumed the next word he'd hear about his brother was when Knox was either back inside the big house or *dead*. On the other hand, he was filled with a deep sense of dread. Because as much as it pained him to admit it, Knox's sudden arrival could mean only one thing.

Trouble.

CHAPTER 3

Sabrina Greenlee wrapped her arms around herself to keep her heart from flying out of her chest.

She hoped, however, that anyone looking at her would simply think she was attempting to stop the cool north wind from tunneling under the hem of the jacket she'd stolen off the rack at that truck stop in Indiana.

Yes, stolen.

I'm a thief.

Discounting the M&M's she'd taken from a gas station when she was three—and that didn't count because she'd been too young to understand how commerce worked—she'd never swiped anything in her life. However, in the last twenty-four hours, she'd stolen more things than she could count.

Okay, that wasn't true. She'd kept count.

She wasn't sure why. If she'd been religious, she would've said it was so she could ask God for forgiveness for each and every transgression. If she'd been a kleptomaniac, she would've said it was so she could relive the thrill of the crimes. But since she was neither, she supposed she'd kept a mental tally because she told herself if she lived through this ordeal, she would go back and repay the people and places she'd wronged. Put some change back into her karma bank.

You know, get right with the world.

To the elderly gentleman who'd offered them a ride, she'd tell him exactly where they'd left his car. After Knox had kicked the man out at a crossroads, they'd proceeded north until the old sedan had run out of gas. Knox had coasted the vehicle off the country lane into a stand of trees. Chances were, it would remain hidden there unless someone happened upon it.

She could make whole the roadside cafe where she and Knox had dined and dashed—well, Knox had dined. She'd only dashed because she'd been too sick with terror and grief to keep anything down. Neither of them had had cash or credit cards on them. But even if she'd had her Visa, Knox would not have allowed her to use it.

No paper trail.

That was rule number one when going on the lam.

Ha! Her snort, even though it existed only in her head, was tinged with hysteria. *Look at me! Acting like I know the rules of being a fugitive.*

Scenes from *Thelma and Louise* ran through her head. Then she decided that wasn't a good comparison since Knox was a guy.

We're more like Bonnie and Clyde, she decided. Then she felt light-headed because Thelma, Louise, Bonnie, and Clyde all died.

Are there any *movies where two people on the run from the law both make it out alive?*

None sprung to mind, which made the sick sensation in the bottom of her stomach start swirling.

She forced her attention back to her list of injured parties. Recounting her sins was better than contemplating her potential demise.

There'd been the truck driver who'd taken them through Kentucky. Knox had stolen forty dollars from the guy's glovebox when they'd stopped for gas. There was the convenience store clerk she'd distracted with inane conversation so Knox could pocket two Snickers bars without getting caught. And last but not least, there was the truck stop that was missing one cheap, plastic rain jacket.

It'd been nearly eighty degrees the night they left Charleston.

Ha again! Left Charleston? It's more like we ran for our lives.

But she'd bet it was in the fifties here in Chicago. And the wind had a definite bite, a cold, sharp-fanged warning of what would come in the next few months.

She concentrated on that, on her *physical* discomfort, as they waited for Knox's brother to exit the large, three-story factory building that sat like an insolent, brick-faced king behind the tall iron gate. If she focused on how much her head hurt and how every subtle gust of wind tried to cut her to the bone, she could forget the horror and grief that turned a knife in her heart and slashed relentlessly at her gut.

My god, Cooper…

She didn't dare close her eyes. If she did, she knew what she'd see playing against the backs of her eyelids. Her brother's last moments, his last act—one of stupidity and heroism.

If she pictured that, she'd give in to her heaving stomach and throw up the partial Snickers she'd eaten because Knox had threatened to shove it down her throat if she didn't put it there herself.

Don't think about it. Don't think about it.

It had been her refrain since Charleston.

Don't think about the abuse you suffered at the hands of that man.

Don't think about the awful way your brother died.

Don't think about it. Don't think about it.

She stared *hard* at the factory building, so hard without blinking that by the time the front door opened, her eyeballs burned like her tears had turned to kerosene and someone had lit a match.

"Breathe." Knox pushed away from the guardhouse's window to throw an arm over her shoulders. "We made it. Britt will help us."

She swallowed past the lump in her throat and nodded, never taking her eyes off the handsome, fit fellow who strode toward them with purpose. She noted the scuffed biker boots, the black leather jacket, and the T-shirt beneath that sported an image of Wolverine and Deadpool with their arms thrown around each other. Printed below the image was one word: Besties.

In any other circumstance, she would've smiled. In *this* circumstance, she knew if she allowed her face the freedom to move, it would crumble, and then she'd be done for.

Don't think about it. Don't think about it.

Britt Rollins resembled Knox in many ways. The brothers had the same lean, muscular build, the same mop of wavy, messy hair, and the same eyes—icy blue, so light they were almost eerie. But that's where the similarities ended.

Knox had the hard look of a man who'd done serious time. Sunken cheeks. Perpetually pinched mouth. And Britt? Well, except for the mean-looking scar that zigzagged across his temple pseudo Harry Potter-style, Britt looked like the kind of guy she might let buy her a drink at a bar. He was handsome in an understated way that made a woman feel simultaneously intrigued and safe.

Of course, when he got close enough, she realized he was *far* from safe. His expression might be polite and easy, but the harsh flash of his eyes was neither. And when he slipped through the gate after it clanged open on its track, the shift of his muscles assured her there wasn't a hint of softness about him.

Except for maybe the curling of his lashes and the full, almost pouty curve of his lower lip.

She expected him to smile, hug Knox, and welcome them in. When he did none of that, when he simply tilted his head to the side and said lowly, "Hello, brother," the sour taste of fear filled her mouth.

Or, more accurately, *refilled* her mouth. She'd been terrified for the last two days. Ever since those three men burst into Cooper's house and dragged them into the back room kicking and screaming.

Well, to be clear Knox had been kicking. Cooper had been screaming. She'd simply twisted against the heavy hands that had grabbed her arms. She'd been too shocked to kick, too stunned to scream.

"Hey, little brother," Knox said now. "How ya been?"

"Livin' the dream." Britt's piercing blue gaze slid from Knox to Sabrina. He didn't try to hide the speculation and the calculation in his eyes, and she suddenly felt like an insect pinned to the corkboard of some kid's science fair project.

Had Knox been too quick to believe his brother would help them? Had they made the journey for nothing? And if they had, what next? Canada? Mexico?

Her mind jumped from one worst-case scenario to the next until the seconds slowed and became small eternities wherein she wanted to scream. Wanted to cry. Wanted to run in front of the next city bus because then she could stop being so scared, so horrifically sad, so—

"Who's this?" Britt inquired of his brother, but he was still eyeing Sabrina. It was clear he expected her to answer.

She swallowed and extended a hand. When he accepted it, he must have felt how much it shook because his eyes narrowed ever so slightly, and a look of unease tightened the skin across his face.

"Sabrina Greenlee," she whispered, wondering if she looked as bad as she felt. Because she *felt* like a colony of vampires had snacked on her, drained her of all but the last of her life force. "Nice to meet you. Knox has told me so much about you."

"Well, that makes one of us," Britt said, and something softened in his face as he watched her will herself to keep standing. Then his nostrils flared as he turned back to his brother. "So, you want to tell me what this sudden visit is about?"

"I do." Knox's arm once more went around her shoulders. His subtle, not-so-gentle squeeze told her to keep it together for a little longer. "Invite us in, and I will."

Britt hesitated. Not for long, but it was enough time for Sabrina to catch the subtle flex of his jaw.

He doesn't want us here, she admitted with a sinking sensation.

Then, she breathed a sigh of relief when, with a dip of his chin, Britt said, "Sure. Come on in."

He went to turn away, but Knox stopped him with, "Hold on. Don't I get a hug?"

When Britt swung back, he wore an expression Sabrina couldn't read. Seriously, the man epitomized the phrase *poker face*. Then he stepped forward and pulled Knox into a hug.

She moved aside to give the men room but didn't move so far away that she missed how Britt closed his eyes when he held his brother close. Nor did she miss the look of resignation on his face when he pulled away and turned for the gate.

She understood.

Resigned is how she would describe her relationship with her own brother. It's what happens to a person when they've been disappointed repeatedly. It's what happens when hope dwindles to disappointment and eventually melts into a sort of apathy.

How many times had she begged Cooper to straighten out his life? How many times had he promised he would only to call her in the middle of the night to tell her he'd been arrested?

She'd bet Britt had experienced the same.

Except...the difference between her and Britt Rollins was that Britt might still get a chance to see his brother make good. She never would.

Cooper was dead.

Dead.

No, not just dead. *Murdered.*

Don't think about it.

As she followed the brothers past the gate and into the factory grounds, she distracted herself from her thoughts by forcing her attention to her surroundings.

Off to the west sat a squat little cottage. She wondered if it'd been home to the factory foreman back when the place had been...well, whatever it had originally been. Off to the east was that imposing brick wall that surrounded the entirety of the grounds. It rose ten feet and was topped by military-grade razor wire. And directly in front of them was the massive metal door that acted as the factory building's front entry.

When Britt turned the handle, it made a strange clank and a hiss, and she wondered what activated the locking mechanism.

Then, all thoughts were pushed into the back of her mind because Britt led them inside, and she was instantly hit with sensory overload.

The space was cavernous, with soaring three-story ceilings and massive windows letting in the morning's light. The motorcycle shop spread out before her. Bikes in various stages of assembly sat atop narrow metal tables. There was a glass-walled cubby at the back where a woman in pink coveralls spray-painted a gas tank hanging from a hook in the ceiling. And a giant machine near the outer wall cut into a length of sheet metal.

In front of the workshop sat a double row of custom-made motorcycles that didn't look like anything she'd ever seen riding down the road. They were too fantastical. Too colorful. Too chromed out and complicated to be labeled anything but art.

When Knox told her his brother built custom motorcycles in Chicago, she'd expected to arrive in the City of Broad Shoulders to see a typical mechanic's shop. You know, the prefab building that'd been weathered by time. The rusty sign proclaiming the place's purpose. The no-frills parking lot filled with the vehicles of customers and mechanics alike.

She'd been more than a little surprised to see instead the grand, brick building protected by the guardhouse and surrounded by a brick wall that would've made the Qin Dynasty proud.

But she got it now.

Boy-howdy, did she.

The tools, machines, and motorcycles housed within the walls of Black Knights Inc. had to be worth more than most folks would see in ten lifetimes.

Twisting her head, she noted the metal staircase as it rose to an open area on the second floor. She could see a long conference table beyond the iron railing as well as some rather impressive-looking electronics. To her left was a narrow hallway. Motorcycle license plates covered its brick walls. All were rusty and aged and looked like they belonged in an antique shop.

The smell of grinding metal and high-gloss auto paint wafted from the direction of the workshop. But she would swear that beneath those scents she could detect something sweeter, like sugar and cream and hot, melting butter. It emanated from the direction of the hall, and she wondered if the passageway led to a kitchen.

Croissants, she realized. The smell reminded her of the croissants they baked at her favorite coffeehouse back home.

A sudden pang tore through her stomach. It wasn't hunger, though. It was homesickness.

Would she ever return to Charleston? To those flood-prone cobblestone streets and the quiet marshes packed with water primrose and alligator weed?

Would she ever return to her clients? To the people who depended on her to keep them trending on TikTok and Instagram so their products continued to fly off the shelves?

And yes, it was insane to be thinking about her job when she'd had a pistol jammed into her mouth, when her brother was dead, when she was running for her life from a group of men who'd made her their enemy simply because she'd been in the wrong place at the wrong time. But there was a part of her that hoped this whole thing could be cleared up and she could go back.

Was that wishful thinking?

As the hours wore on, she began to suspect so.

She began to suspect that night at Cooper's house was what Gen Z-ers called a "canon event." There was her life before, and there would be her life after.

If I even have *an after.*

"Love iiisss all around you!" Someone sang from the second floor, pulling her from her ever-spiraling thoughts.

The sights and smells inside the old brick building were overwhelming. But they were nothing compared to the noise.

If Sabrina had been asked to describe the sound of chaos, she would have detailed Black Knights Inc.'s auditory overwhelm.

"Love Song" by Tesla blared from speakers on the second floor. The music was accompanied by the rather lovely—but earsplittingly loud—voice of the faceless, nameless singer. A guy with a handheld grinder worked on a tailpipe, sending out sparks and shrieks of sound. An intermittent hiss came from the sprayer in the hands of the woman in the paint corner, a feral growl of what sounded like a blender came from somewhere down the hallway, and that blasted machine cutting sheet metal whined ceaselessly.

She was tempted to cover her ears but was interrupted when a giant man with a buzzcut and what seemed to be a bad attitude—if his expression was anything to go by—materialized in front of her. She blinked into his merciless face and decided he'd look right at home guarding the gates of hell.

"Yo, Ozzie!" The big man shouted in a voice that boomed like thunder. She flinched at its force while simultaneously marveling at its ability to be heard above the racket. "Cut the music! We have guests!"

In an instant, the wall of sound that was Tesla fell silent. A second later, the guy using the grinder switched off the tool and laid it atop the metal table. And a second after that, what Sabrina assumed was a blender stopped its ear-splitting buzz.

The woman in pink coveralls still used the paint sprayer. And the sheet metal machine still complained about its work. But those two noises were nothing compared to the deafening anarchy from before.

"Boss." Britt inclined his head toward Buzz Cut now that they could converse without screaming at the top of their lungs. "Let me introduce you to my brother, Knox, and his…" He trailed off as he looked expectantly at Sabrina.

Had he forgotten her name?

"I'm sorry." His expression again turned speculative. "I didn't ask what your relationship is with my brother. Are you his girlfriend or…" He let the sentence dangle, waiting for her to fill in the blank.

"I'm his…" She paused and considered. She'd been about to say *friend*. But she'd only known Knox for two days. He'd been Cooper's friend. Not hers. "We're *new* friends," she finally finished.

Surely after what they'd been through, they were more than mere acquaintances.

"Right." Britt's eyes narrowed slightly. "Boss, this is Sabrina Greenlee, Knox's new friend. And this is Frank Knight." He gestured to the giant. "But you can call him Boss. Everyone does."

"Everyone but my illustrious wife." The big man winked and hitched his chin toward the woman with the paint sprayer. "She refuses to give me the title since she wears the pants in the family." He offered his giant baseball mitt of a hand to Sabrina and Knox.

Sabrina murmured the appropriate pleasantries but only paid half attention to her words. As more people gathered around, she began to feel claustrophobic despite the grandeur of the space.

The man using the grinder on the tailpipe introduced himself as Sam, and she was immediately struck by his ocean-blue eyes and classically handsome profile. A tall, sandy-haired guy with a face that belonged on the silver screen shook her hand and told her his name was Fisher. He threw his arm around the shoulders of a dark-haired woman who looked far too sleek and elegant to work with rough and rowdy motorcycle mechanics. She inclined her perfect chin toward Sabrina while introducing herself as Eliza.

Sabrina's underfed and overwhelmed brain spun with all the new names and faces. Then, her gaze landed on the gentleman who stood slightly off to the side of the gathered group…and the world went still.

He was quite possibly the most visually pleasing man she'd ever clapped eyes on. And when his piercing gaze found hers, she would swear all the oxygen was sucked right out of the room.

He was fit. Like, *very* fit. The type of fit you'd expect to see on the cover of *Men's Health*. A wild cap of auburn hair sat atop his head, his green eyes reminded her of Saint Patrick's Day, and a well-trimmed beard covered a jawline that celebrities paid thousands of dollars to plastic surgeons to achieve.

"Name's Hewitt." He extended his hand, and she looked down to see long, knobby-knuckled fingers and an impossibly wide palm. "But everyone calls me Hew."

She swallowed and hesitated to accept his handshake. She wasn't sure why. She'd shaken hands with all the others.

Maybe it was because she felt overwhelmed by his sheer, masculine beauty. Or perhaps it was because she couldn't figure out if the harsh expression on his face was one of assessment or objection.

"Sabrina," she whispered.

Is that my voice?

"Nice to meet you, Sabrina," he said when she finally summoned the courage to take his hand.

She wasn't sure what she'd expected, maybe for his handshake to be as harsh as his expression. But the fingers he wrapped around hers were gentle.

She was about to return his acknowledgment when Britt held up a hand. "Shhh!" he said, his phone pinned to his ear. "All of you, hush. I can't hear what Rafer is saying."

Hew dropped her hand. Was it strange that she'd just met him, and yet she missed the warmth and grounding effect of his steady grip?

"Say that again, Rafe," Britt barked into his phone. Sabrina watched his eyebrows go from forming a deep V to lifting into high arches. "O'Toole is here? What's she want?" His expression went as hard as stone as his gaze landed on Knox. "I will kick your ass up between your shoulder blades; I swear to god," he snarled lowly as he held his cell phone to his chest to muffle the microphone.

"What?" Knox lifted his hands. "Who's O'Toole?"

"She's an FBI agent. And she's here wanting to talk to me about *you*."

"Fuck," Knox grumbled as his gaze darted to Sabrina.

She suddenly felt the strangest sensation. It was like she was leaving her body. The noise of the sheet metal machine sounded very far away. Her vision tightened into a tunnel. And the ground disappeared from beneath her feet until she was free-floating in space.

"Damnit, she's going down," Hew said in an accent that reminded her of *Good Will Hunting*.

Who's going down? she wondered dreamily a second before the world faded to black.

CHAPTER 4

"**A**gent O'Toole!"

The deep, resonant sound of Britt Rollins's voice made Julia smile. But she wiped her expression clean in the next instant. Despite her dreaming of finding an excuse to visit Goose Island to see him again, this wasn't a social call.

"Hello again, Sergeant Rollins!" She lifted her voice above the noise of a street sweeper as it chuffed and hissed on the road behind her. Then, she eagerly watched Britt make quick work of the expanse between BKI's front door and the high, wrought iron gate.

He wore faded jeans, a classic black biker jacket, and his signature Marvel T-shirt. His hair was longer than she remembered. It stuck up in wavy tufts and curled around his ears like a lover's fingers. He'd let his facial hair grow too. Previously he'd sported something slightly more than a five-o'clock shadow. Now, he had a well-trimmed beard that followed the lines of his angular jaw.

It all suited him. The added hair made him look less like the boy next door and more like the *man* next door.

Hubba, hubba.

She'd almost convinced herself that he wasn't *really* the sexiest thing on two legs. Convinced herself that his muscles didn't *really* coil under his clothes like knotted rope. Convinced herself that his long lashes didn't *really* cast sooty shadows across his cheeks.

But who was I trying to kid? All of that is true.

"I know it's cliché." She held out her hand for a shake after he'd stepped through the open gate. "But long time no see."

Something skittered through those crystalline eyes of his, but it was gone so quickly that she decided she imagined it. Then she forgot everything, including her name, when his fingers slid into her grip and a frisson of... *something* tripped up her spine.

"Rafer tells me you're here to talk about Knox." He inclined his head toward the big, redhead in the guardhouse. "What's my brother gone and done this time?"

"It's a long story." She watched him closely as she posed her next suggestion. "You guys got some of that motor oil you pass off as coffee inside?" She hitched her chin over his shoulder toward the factory. "I could use a kick. It's already been a long morning."

It wasn't a lie. Her cat Binks had startled her awake at four-thirty with his repeated—and rather dramatic—attempts to bring up a furball. The racket had disturbed Gunpowder, who'd squawked his disapproval before starting in on his rendition of Tenacious D's "Fuck Her Gently"—a holdover trick from his previous life as the office pet of a notorious weapons dealer. With the cat and the bird making noise, the two dogs had decided it was time to engage in a WWE-style smackdown ranging from the foot of her bed to the pillow she'd shoved over her head.

Needless to say, she'd given up on getting that last hour of sleep and had stumbled from under the covers to start her day. Now she felt that lost hour, and the only solution was caffeine.

Correction: more caffeine.

Of course, the *main* reason for her asking to go inside BKI was to get a look around. To take a peek into the faces of Britt's coworkers. To let her gut get a feel for whether or not the Black Knights—Britt Rollins included—were hiding something.

Namely, a fugitive by the name of Randal Knox Rollins.

Britt's gaze followed the hitch of her chin toward the imposing façade of the three-story structure. For a second, she thought he might decline to invite them in. And *that* had her FBI instincts perking up. Then he motioned for them to follow him across the grounds, and she figured his slight hesitation derived from his annoyance at being forced to talk about his ne'er-do-well brother.

She got the impression he'd lost more than a few hours of his life speaking to the authorities about Knox.

A cloud floated across the sun and had her glancing into the sky. On Goose Island, the towering skyscrapers of downtown didn't blot out the heavens. She had no trouble seeing the bright blue of the morning was quickly turning overcast.

Some years summer clung to the city with a dogged grip, refusing to let go until well into October. Other years it surrendered as easily as the Jedi gave up after Order 66. Just *poof.* Here one minute, gone the next.

"What?" she asked when Britt looked back at her with an expression she couldn't read.

That was the thing about him. Despite his jagged forehead scar, he had an affable face. The kind of face she'd assume would be transparent, every emotion there for the world to see. But the opposite was true. Most times, she couldn't get a bead on him.

"Just wondering how you've been, Agent O'Toole," he said in that Lowcountry drawl that had her dreaming of fried okra, sweet tea, and porch swings.

Before she could answer, Dillan piped up. "And what about me, Rollins? Haven't you been wondering how *I've* been?"

Britt chuckled. The deep, *sexy* sound swirled around in Julia's ear like a warm tongue.

"Sure, Agent Douglas." They'd made it to the front door. Britt pulled the metal slab wide. "How have you been?"

"Bored stiff," Dillan admitted, waving for Julia to precede him over the threshold. "O'Toole and I have been on what amounts to desk duty since the McClean case. But now here we are. Our first real case brings us back to Black Knights Inc. What are the odds?"

Britt didn't answer. He was too busy watching Julia as she brushed by him.

She would *swear* she could feel his body heat reaching for her. Swear she could sense an invisible force pulling her toward him, like the Death Star's tractor beam had pulled in the Millennium Falcon.

He felt it too, didn't he?

A quick glance showed his face was as enigmatic as ever.

Grr. Hiss. Boo.

The custom motorcycle shop was exactly as she remembered it: huge and loud and full of hand-built machines that made dollar signs dance in front of her eyes. Hair metal boomed from the speakers on the second floor. The smell of grease guns hung in the air. And Britt's coworkers were all hard at work with grinders, paint sprayers, and TIG welders that spat out sparks like mini Fourth of July fireworks.

"It's a crazy day!" Britt yelled above the chaos. "We have three custom orders that need to ship out by the end of the week and a half dozen production bikes that are on backorder! Why don't we take this into the kitchen!"

She nodded her consent. One, they needed a quiet place to talk about his brother. Two, surely the kitchen was where they kept the coffee.

Ever the vigilant fed, she took note of the half-bath they passed on their way down a hallway decorated with rusty motorcycle license plates.

No Knox Rollins in there.

Her eyes darted around the industrial—yet somehow still homey—kitchen as soon as they entered. There was a large center island, a commercial-sized refrigerator, and a gas oven that looked like it belonged in a chef's house. But…

No Knox Rollins here either.

There *was* a rather large coffee maker on the counter, though. It sent up a siren's song, and she wondered if Britt would think her rude if she helped herself.

"Agent O'Toole! Agent Douglas! What are you two doing here?" Looking as classy and put together as always, Eliza Meadows emerged from a pantry while wiping her hands on the cherry-red apron tied around her waist. "Has there been some new information about Senator McClean or—"

"No, no." Julia shook her head. "Nothing like that. We're here to talk to Sergeant Rollins."

"Britt?" Eliza glanced at the man in question. "Why?" Her gaze swung back to Julia. "What did he do?" Her tone turned matronly. So did her stance as she shoved her hands onto her hips and pinned Britt with a dour look. "What did you do?"

Britt threw up his hands. "Nothing! I swear! They're here about Knox."

"Oh." Eliza grimaced. "Right." She untied her apron and left it atop the counter. "I'll make myself scarce then."

"You don't have to do that," Britt told her, but she was already on the move.

Once she pulled even with him, she patted his shoulder in consolation, went up on tiptoe to hug him, and whispered something in his ear. Julia assumed it was words of comfort or encouragement.

"I'll be upstairs if you need me," she called over her shoulder once she reached the doorway. Then she disappeared through the opening, and Julia, Britt, and Dillan were left alone in the kitchen.

"Take a seat. Both of you." Britt waved to the barstools shoved beneath the lip of the island. After Julia snagged a seat, his gaze caught hers and held. "You wanted coffee, right?"

"If it wouldn't be too much trouble," she said nonchalantly, although the gleam in her eye when she darted a glance at the carafe probably gave away her desperation.

Well, that and the drool hanging off my bottom lip.

Britt poured the fragrant, steaming liquid into a mug and slid it her way. "You take it black if I recall."

She had the urge to preen and bat her lashes because he remembered how she took her coffee, proving how ridiculous her obsession with him was.

Note to self. Try fantasizing about someone else the next time you reach into the top drawer of your bedside table.

"Agent Douglas?" Britt held up a second mug, but Dillan waved him away.

"This one drinks enough for both of us." Dillan hooked a thumb in Julia's direction as she took her first swallow of the thick, rich brew. The smoky, carbony flavor melted over her tongue and tickled the part of her brain that was addicted to the lovely buzz of caffeine. "Besides, I try to stay away from all psychoactive substances. My body is my temple, after all."

Julia refrained from rolling her eyes.

But just barely.

Britt pointedly poured himself a cup of coffee while eyeing Dillan—she fell a little bit in love with him for that—and then hitched his chin toward the pie stand topped with fresh muffins and scones. "Help yourself." His accent made it sound more like *help yahself*. And all the times she'd imagined him shirtless and sweaty and telling her about the unspeakable things he planned to do to her naked body slid through her mind and liquified her bones from the marrow out.

It was a good thing she was sitting down.

Her stomach growled. But she wasn't sure if it was from lust or hunger. And she didn't dare reach for a muffin even though they looked delicious. She was afraid her hands were shaking.

Dillan didn't reach for a muffin either because…he was *Dillan*—the man avoided refined sugar, fearing it would reduce his six-pack to four. And she realized seconds had ticked by without anyone making a move or saying anything when Britt finally cleared his throat.

"So what's my brother done this time?"

Right. That's why she was here. To talk about his brother, the fugitive. Not to ogle the way his T-shirt clung to his biceps when he shrugged out of his leather jacket and tossed it over the metal chair pushed under the bistro table in the corner. Not to notice the bulge at the front of his jeans when he hooked his thumbs into his pockets. Not to get sucked into the whirlpools of his icy-blue eyes when he stood across the island from her and watched her face closely.

"When's the last time Knox called you?" she asked instead of answering his question.

He crossed his arms over his chest. She didn't notice how it made his shoulders bunch into round balls.

Okay, so I noticed. But only a little bit.

"The last phone call I had from Knox was a few months back. Right around the time y'all were investigating the shooting at the senator's house. Knox told me he'd gotten an early release. Said he was already on to something big."

"Mmm." She frowned into the steaming liquid in her mug as an excuse to drop his gaze. It was hard to think when she was looking directly at him. "And did you question him about what that *big* thing was?"

"Honestly?" Something in his voice—a roughness maybe?—had her glancing up. "I didn't want to know. I've learned it's better to stay out of Knox's business. Plausible deniability and all that."

She nodded and felt a pang of sympathy for his plight. She also wanted to sigh with relief that he wasn't caught up in his brother's mess. But both of those things were eclipsed by the realization that, unless things changed and Knox sought out Britt for help, she'd have no excuse to return to Black Knights Inc.

Damn, girl. You got it bad, that little voice whispered. To which she immediately replied, *No shit.*

"But something tells me you're not going to let me keep my head buried in the sand on this one," he continued. "Something tells me the time for plausible deniability has passed."

Dillan was the one to answer. "We can keep you in the dark if that's what you want. But then my next question would be, without knowing what your brother has done, would you be willing to call us the instant you hear from him? Or would familial loyalty stay your hand?"

Britt's Adam's apple bobbed up the length of his tan throat. Julia saw a flicker of indecision in his eyes.

"I reckon you're right." Britt sighed with resignation. "Unless I know what he's done, my first instinct will be to help him. So come on." He made a come-hither motion with his fingers. "Give it to me with both hands and two smoking barrels."

Julia took a deep breath before launching into the story Agents Keplar and Maddox had told her. She used softer language and employed far fewer attacks on Knox's character than the South Carolina agents had. And yet, despite her retelling the tale as gently as possible, the longer she spoke, the more still Britt got.

By the time she finished, he'd turned to stone. Not a single breath lifted his broad chest. Not a single heartbeat pulsed in the prominent veins running up the sides of his neck. And his jaw was cinched down so tight that she imagined it'd take a can of WD-40 to unhinge it.

Without her words echoing around the room, quiet filled the space. She became aware of the other noises in the kitchen. The ice maker in the refrigerator dropped a load into the bin with a muted rumble. The faucet at Britt's back leaked a single drop of water into a sudsy pot with a soft *plop*. And from somewhere close behind her, a familiar purr sounded.

She glanced over her shoulder to see Peanut—a ridiculous name for a cat the size of a small pony—sniffing at the crack beneath the pantry door.

Glad for the distraction, she headed for the rotund tom instead of continuing to watch Britt struggle not to bleed out from the bomb she'd just dropped on him.

"Hello again," she murmured, grabbing Peanut under his round belly and trying to stand.

She failed on her first attempt. She'd guess he weighed three times more than her own sweet, hairball-prone Binks. But she was successful on her second try and settled him comfortably in her lap once she retook her seat on the barstool.

He immediately went to work full-time at the biscuit factory. And when she gave him the requisite cheek massage, his motor turned over. His purr filled the room.

It was a comforting sound and gave her the courage to glance back at Britt, hoping he was closer to coming to terms with his new reality.

No such luck.

He looked as stony and as unreadable as ever.

She got it. Knox hadn't exactly been a model citizen. The car theft, identity fraud, and embezzlement had been more than enough to warrant the time he'd spent behind bars. But none of that compared to murder.

"I can't believe it." Britt finally spoke. The gruffness of his voice made her wish he hadn't because she could hear his pain in every word.

"I wish I were wrong," she murmured, wincing when Peanut's overzealous kneading breached the fabric on her suit pants and reached her skin. "But his handlers in Charleston sound certain of the facts."

"Fuck." He swiped an agitated hand through his dark hair, causing his cowlick to stick up. Then, he winced. "Sorry for the profanity."

"No need to apologize," she waved him off. "It's a fucking fuck of a situation, that's for fucking sure."

Just as she'd hoped, her attempt at levity had the tension in his shoulders softening.

"Born and raised Chicagoan here." She hooked a thumb back at herself. "The F-bomb is pretty much mandatory 'round these parts. I'd be far more scandalized if you'd said *shoot* or *darn*."

He chuckled, but there was no real humor in it.

And that was her cue.

As much as she'd love to sit there and drink in every subtle shift of his muscles, every minute expression that crossed his handsome face, every lovely word that drawled out of his mouth, they'd come to see if he'd heard from his brother. He hadn't. Thus, their mission was complete, and it was time to return to the office.

Peanut meowed his displeasure when she dumped him off her lap. She was so used to pet hair that she didn't bother wiping the gray fur off her slacks when she stood.

"Sorry to hit you with this kind of bad news and run," she said. "But Agent Douglas and I need to let our colleagues on the East Coast know what we found here." She made a face. "Or, rather, what we *didn't* find here."

She pulled her business card from her jacket pocket—yes, calling cards were still helpful in her line of work—and slid it across the island.

"That's my office phone. I've written my cell number on the back. Call me, night or day, if your brother checks in." She hesitated to say this next part but figured he needed to hear it. "If Knox turns himself in, chances are he'll walk away from this without any extra holes in his body. I can't guarantee he'll walk away at all if he doesn't. It would be an understatement to say his handlers sounded unhappy. Your brother's betrayal cost them millions of dollars in man-hours and set them back years in their efforts to bring down that cartel. I think they're itching to shoot first and ask questions later."

Britt took a deep breath and nodded. "Right. Thanks for the heads-up."

"No thanks necessary," she assured him, and since she couldn't think of anything more to say, she threw back the last of her coffee and turned to leave.

She'd made it to the door when Britt called out, "I guess when it comes to my brother, it's true what they say, huh?"

She swung around with a questioning frown.

"Once you start down the dark path, forever will it dominate your destiny."

She immediately recognized the quote from *The Empire Strikes Back*.

The first time they'd met, he'd said something to the effect of, *"Aren't you a little short for a fed?"* To which she'd immediately responded, *"I'm Luke Skywalker. I'm here to rescue you."* Confusion had ensued, and she'd had to explain that growing up with three older brothers who were all *Star Wars* fans meant she was steeped in quotes from the movies. And thus had begun their *Star Wars*-themed flirtations.

She'd replayed each and every one of them at least a hundred times in the months since last she'd seen him. And she was *beyond* delighted to discover he remembered their banter, too.

"Oh, I don't know," she countered as her blood sang happily through her veins. "As long as he lives, hope lives."

Her quote was a little more obscure. But he didn't disappoint. "*The Last Jedi?*"

"Right on the money," she told him and *damnit!* She *liked* him.

She *hadn't* built castles in the sky when it came to him. He *was* as witty and as wonderful as she remembered.

Screw it, she thought. *The timing is terrible, but it's now or never.*

Glancing at Dillan, who looked rather bored now that it seemed they *wouldn't* be hunting a fugitive, she whispered, "Mind giving me a minute alone with Sergeant Rollins?"

A line appeared between her partner's eyebrows, and she was reminded that he had just enough brain cells for basic motor function when it came to subtlety and innuendo.

"Why?" he asked.

The look on her face called him ten kinds of idiot. But her tone was sugary-sweet when she hissed, "Because I have something of a personal nature I'd like to discuss with him."

"A personal nature?" Dillan's frown deepened. "What could you possibly—" His eyebrows reached for his hair. "Oh. Right." He glanced at Britt, who stood on the other side of the kitchen island, watching them curiously.

She waited until Dillan disappeared down the hall before clearing her throat and taking a step back toward the center of the room. When she realized she was wringing her hands, she shoved them deep inside her jacket pockets.

Her palms were sweaty.

So was her upper lip.

The comforting feel of the cat making figure eights around her ankles was the only thing keeping her Jell-O knees from giving out completely.

How do men do this?

"Are you seeing anyone, Sergeant?" she blurted, horrified by how much her voice shook.

Britt's beard-covered chin jerked back. "What does me seeing someone have to do with my broth—"

"This isn't about Knox," she interjected.

He blinked when he realized what she was asking. "No." He shook his head, his voice suddenly quieter…*gentler*. "I'm not seeing anyone."

She felt equal parts relieved—*woot! He's not seeing anyone!*—and dismayed because now came the truly hard part. The part where she had to lay all her cards on the table and see if he was interested in playing a hand.

"I know this is bad timing. I mean, I came to inform you that your brother's done the worst thing possible and is in the biggest trouble of his life. And I get it if you tell me to fuck off. But if I've learned anything in my thirty-three years, it's that I'll never get what I want unless I ask for it. And if I don't ask this now, I don't know if I'll get a chance to ask it again. So… would you like to maybe meet me for a drink sometime? *After* this thing with your brother is settled, of course. I know that'll be weighing on your mind in the meantime."

Whew! She'd done it. She'd asked him out.

She waited for his response with bated breath. Then, she waited some more. And then she waited some *more*, and while she waited, she replayed her question in her head, wondering if she'd worded it correctly.

Yup.

She'd definitely asked him out. She'd preceded the invitation with a lot of words—she tended to ramble when she got nervous. And she could have left out the word *maybe* when she'd asked if he wanted to meet her for a drink. But even *with* the maybe thrown in there, there was no way anyone could have misconstrued her meaning.

As the silence stretched on, she began to wonder if it were possible to die from mortification. And, as usually happened when she felt backed into a corner, the Southsider in her took over. "Yo, Rollins. In case you missed it, that's the conversational baton I passed you."

His usually expressionless face suddenly looked…*pained?*

Oh, god. Okay. He's going to try to let me down easy.

"I think you're beautiful and brilliant and one of the most intriguing women I've had the pleasure of meeting," he said quietly.

Her heart burned like it had a hundred papercuts doused in rubbing alcohol. "Please." She held up her hand. "Don't damn me with faint praise."

His brow wrinkled. "That's not what I'm doing. I'm sorry if that's—"

She interrupted before he could finish. "And please don't apologize. *I* should be the one apologizing. Given the situation, my asking you out is wildly inappropriate. I see that now. You think you could chalk this whole catastrophe up to me getting too little sleep last night and just forget I ever said anything?"

"Never." He shook his head, humor flashing in his eyes. "The unmatched Agent Julia O'Toole asked me out. This is a Dear Diary entry."

"Ugh." She screwed her eyes shut. "I'm going to turn around now, walk out that door, and pretend this never happened."

She started to do exactly that. But before she'd taken two steps, his voice stopped her. "My reason for not jumping on the opportunity to meet you for drinks has nothing to do with my brother, bad timing, or the fact that you came here on business."

Her shoulders threatened to droop. She firmed them as she swung around so she could face him.

"I'm turning you down because I don't believe in happily-ever-afters, and I get the impression you do," he continued.

Well...she hadn't been expecting *that*. Blinking in confusion, she asked, "You don't believe in happily-ever-afters?"

He rounded the island to stand in front of her.

She wished he hadn't. Up close, she could smell his aftershave. It was exotic and spicy, like black orchid and cinnamon. She wanted to pull him down so she could bury her face in his neck and inhale. Just drag his scent deep into her lungs.

"I believe in them for other folks," he admitted. "Just not for myself."

Right, she thought with a silent snort. *I get it.*

"You don't believe in happily-ever-afters for yourself because you're a lone wolf, and there are too many fish in the sea to catch one and be done?"

She didn't care that she'd mixed her metaphors. It was becoming clear he was one of *those* types. The type that used phrases like *alpha male* and *boys will be boys*.

He blanched and ran a hand through his hair.

She wished he'd stop doing that. When he did, it made his cowlick stick up. And despite her having lost all interest in him as a potential bed partner, she still had to fight not to reach up and pat it down.

Would his hair feel soft or coarse? Cool or warm to the touch?

It doesn't matter! she firmly told herself. *He's an asshole. And we avoid assholes like the smelly shitbags they are.*

"God, no," he finally said with a hard shake of his head. "I'm not a total douche nozzle."

She crossed her arms and ankles—an unconsciously protective stance that meant Peanut lost the ability to jungle gym his way around her calves. He meowed his displeasure before wandering off.

Eyeing Britt consideringly, her expression told him that the jury was still out on the whole douche nozzle verdict.

"A happily-ever-after comes with risks I'm not willing to take," he explained, and something moved across his face. Some emotion she couldn't name.

"What sort of risks?" she couldn't help asking.

Yes, she should shut up. Yes, she should turn and leave. It didn't matter what his reasons were for rejecting her. He had. End of story.

Except…she *hated* question marks. Call it a byproduct of the job or call it natural curiosity.

"Let's just say the big L is out of the question for me."

She blinked. Then she shook her head. "So what? You don't date. Like, *ever*? Because it might turn into something more?"

She found that hard to believe. He was the sort of man who would need floaties to swim through all his female admirers.

"I date. I just don't date anyone who wants more than I can give."

"And what can you give?"

"Fun for now but not forever."

She laughed. "So what made you jump to the conclusion when I asked you out for a drink that I was in the market for forever?"

"Aren't you?" he countered.

"Answer the question, Sergeant Rollins." She cocked her hip so she'd have somewhere to shove her fisted hand.

"I like it when you use your FBI voice on me." The smile he gave her was fully weaponized. Like, seriously, it could lay waste to a woman's heart. And ovaries.

"You won't distract me," she said with a sniff, even though she was so distracted. "When I asked you for a drink, what made you think I was looking for forever?"

"Family history," he said simply.

It took great willpower not to call him a dirty name. "Are you being purposefully cryptic or has caffeine overload stolen my ability to think straight?"

He chuckled. And just like before, that sound went all through her. "I googled you, Julia."

She gulped because her given name sounded so very right in his mouth. "You *did?*"

"I *told* you I find you brilliant and beautiful and intriguing. Of course, I did a deep internet dive. Isn't that what folks do when they meet someone they like?"

"Oh, I don't know." She shrugged. "I usually just plug their name into the FBI database and see what pops up."

He chuckled again. And *damnit!* The low, throaty sound turned her brain to mush and threatened to have it leaking out of her ears.

"Not all of us have access to the FBI database," he countered.

"Color me curious. What did you find?"

"About you specifically?"

She nodded.

"Not much. You don't have an Instagram account. You're not out there tweeting away your day." A line appeared between his eyebrows. "Or whatever it's called now that the name isn't Twitter. So, I was left with the various news articles that mention you. Oh, and I perused your online high school yearbook." One corner of his mouth quirked. "You chose your senior quote to be, 'Any pizza is a personal pizza if you try hard enough'?"

She grimaced. "I fancied myself a comedienne. If you aren't tall, blond, and beautiful in high school, you have to find other ways to make the kids like you. Or else you're likely to find your locker rigged with mousetraps or filled with those little round papers that come out of a hole punch."

He canted his head. "But you're two out of three. You're blond *and* beautiful."

She glanced at the recalcitrant strand of hair that'd fallen from her bun to curl over her shoulder. "I'm *barely* blond. And I'm passably pretty now that my braces are off and now that I know I should have two eyebrows instead of one."

He grinned unabashedly. "I especially liked the photo of you in shop class wearing goggles and holding up the birdhouse. Did you mean for the roof to be lopsided or…" He let the sentence dangle.

"Look." Now, both her hands were planted on her hips. "Not *all* of us are mechanically inclined. I should get points for taking shop class at all since it was filled with football players whose IQs matched their shoe sizes."

This time he tossed his head back and laughed. The sound was so big and deep and full of fun that she found herself smiling in response.

When he sobered, she pinned him with a look. "So tell me, what was it about those news articles and my cringe-worthy high school yearbook that led you to believe I'm after the white dress, the diamond ring, and the house on the hill?"

"Nothing."

She thought he was going to elaborate. When he didn't, when he just stared down at her with humor and…was that *heat*…in his eyes, she sighed heavily. "And now we're back to me thinking you're either being purposefully obtuse or wondering if my caffeine consumption had finally addled my brains."

"Your family likes to take *a lot* of pictures and make *a lot* of posts," he explained. "So I know your mom and dad are happily married after forty-five years. And I know all three of your brothers put rings on their high school sweethearts' fingers and have the houses, the minivans, and the kids to show for it."

"Damn Facebook!" She shook a fist in the air. "It was the end of privacy."

Her mother and sisters-in-law loved to post the minutia of every family dinner and holiday celebration, which meant their lives—and Julia's life by association—were blasted all over the internet.

"You come from the land of backyard barbecues and nuclear families," he said with an easy shrug. "It stands to reason you dream of the same fate for yourself. Am I wrong?"

She didn't lie. But she didn't exactly give him the whole truth either. "I do dream of having all that. *Someday*. But you're pretty cocky to assume I was thinking about any of that with *you*. Who says I wasn't trying to jump your bones? A little slam, bam, thank you, man?"

"Miss Julia," he said in the way only Southern boys could. "This thing between us." He motioned back and forth between them. "Call it an affinity, call it chemistry, call it whatever you want. But the one thing you *can't* call it is casual."

So he *did* feel that thing between them. It wasn't just her.

She didn't know if she wanted to shoot a victorious fist in the air or break down and cry because he wouldn't let them explore it.

"If we were to start something," he continued, "it'd end in hurt. I don't want that for either of us."

She shook her head. "I wouldn't have taken you for a cynic."

"I prefer the term *pragmatist*."

"Says every cynic ever."

He simply shrugged, and disappointment replaced the butterflies that had fluttered in her stomach since she clapped eyes on him when he exited the front door.

"You know, my mom always says when someone tells you who they are, believe them." She held out her hand and tried not to shiver when his rough palm met hers. "So, thanks for telling me exactly who you are. I hope you have a nice life."

A muscle ticked in his jaw. "I hope the same for you, Julia."

God, *why* did it sound so good when he said her name? It was just her name. She'd heard it thousands of times out of hundreds of different mouths. But something about Britt's accent…

A subtle rustling had her glancing over her shoulder. Peanut was back to sniffing the crack under the pantry door.

"I think he's after a treat," she said, latching onto the perfect excuse to vamoose herself from the scene. They'd said everything that needed to be said hadn't they? Besides, the sooner she got to the car, the sooner she could get back to the office, and the sooner she could excuse herself to the restroom, where she could grab a few minutes of solitude to work through the disappointment that sat on her shoulders like a four-ton elephant. "I'll grab one for him on my way out if that's okay?"

She went to pull her hand from Britt's grip, but he held on tight. Frowning slightly, she glanced first at their clasped fingers—his hand looked so large compared to hers—and then into his whirlpool eyes.

"What?" she asked uncertainly.

"A kiss before you go?" His voice had gone so low she struggled to hear it. But there was no mistaking the gleam in his eye.

Her silly ovaries started celebrating with party horns and confetti cannons. Lucky for her, her head was still screwed on straight. "Why? So we can torture ourselves?"

"No." He tugged on her hand. She stumbled forward until her toes touched his. He was a head taller than her, so she had to crane back her neck to hold his gaze. "So we'll at least have this. This one little thing before we say goodbye forever. Something is better than nothing, don't you reckon?"

She should tell him *no*. She should jerk her hand from his. She should march right out of the building and never look back.

Instead, she nodded so quickly she thought she heard her brain clanging against the sides of her skull.

CHAPTER 5

Hewitt Birch had spent most of his life *avoiding* interpersonal drama. But a big ol' boatload had just fallen into his arms.
Literally.

The dark-eyed waif, who had hoarsely introduced herself as Sabrina Greenlee, had teetered toward him when she realized the FBI was on the scene. He'd caught her before she could hit the ground. And then, when it became clear the feds weren't content to speak with Britt at the gate and had every intention of walking through BKI's front door, he'd hoisted her up against his chest as chaos erupted around him.

Boss had yelled for everyone to return to their workstations and act like it was business as usual. Ozzie had switched on the music, and the shop had once again been sweatin' to the oldies—or the eighties, as it were. And Eliza had hissed, *"There's no time!"* when Hew suggested he hide Sabrina and Britt's brother upstairs in his bedroom.

Which is how he found himself sitting cross-legged on the pantry floor with Knox Rollins on his right and an unconscious woman in his lap.

Formerly unconscious, he corrected himself.

Sabrina came awake with a frightened gasp. Her foot kicked over the box of strawberry-flavored Pop-Tarts sitting beside a basket of russet potatoes.

"Shhhh." He pressed his hand over her mouth, frowning slightly when the feel of her warm breath against his palm had the hairs on the back of his neck lifting in a way he recognized.

It had only been three weeks since he'd taken someone home from Red Delilah's Biker Bar. And he'd gone far more than three weeks without nookie before. In fact, when he'd been a newbie Nightstalker flying missions across the Hindu Kush, he'd gone a full two years without the comfort of a woman.

So maybe it was all the amoré floating in the air at BKI that made him ultra-sensitive to the touch of a woman.

The original crew was so partnered up and content it was almost sickening. And one by one, he'd watched his active-duty friends succumb to flying sparks, skipping hearts, and weak knees. First, there'd been Hunter. Sam had quickly followed. And now Fisher—whom Hew had thought would remain a bachelor forever—was planning his wedding.

So, yeah. It was in the air. Which meant maybe he shouldn't be surprised he was reacting to the little flotsam perched lightly in his lap.

Although the bloodless look of her skin and the deep, sleep-deprived shadows smudging the undersides of her eyes assured him that the *last* thing she needed was some huge, hairy man having less-than-platonic thoughts about her.

"Mmm!" she mumbled against his hand, her fingers gripping his wrist. Her short nails sharply pinched into him, and if he'd had thinner skin, she would have drawn blood.

"Shhhh!" he whispered again, pressing his hand harder against her lips while squeezing her arms tight against her sides to stop her squirming. "Be quiet!"

To his relief, she settled against him. But fear clung to her like fog on a New England bay, making her muscles quiver and her chest heave with quick, shallow breaths. The absolute horror he saw in her eyes when she stared up at him gutted him.

"You're okay." He leaned down to whisper in her ear. "You're safe."

His lips barely brushed the delicate skin of her lobe. He noticed her hair smelled of car exhaust, sweat, and the unmistakable tang of terror. But beneath those scents was something sweeter…the lingering hint of her shampoo.

"You have to be quiet," he added. "The feds are right outside the door. Do you understand? Nod if you understand."

He pulled back slightly so he could see her face. Up close, he noticed the thickness of her long, dark lashes and the little mole beneath the arch of her left eyebrow.

When she nodded, he tentatively lifted his palm. But her lips left behind a ghostly imprint on his skin, a tingling sensation in the exact shape of her mouth. Instinctively, he curled his fingers around it. Then he loosened his hold on her so she could sit up. Unfortunately, the move had her ass brushing against his dick, and the over-eager sonofabitch twitched with interest.

He was about to give it a strict—although silent—talking to that started with *now's not the time* and ended with *seriously, bro, read the room!* But before he could begin, she shifted again, and there was no longer any need to criticize his pecker. The thing nearly turned inside out in an attempt to crawl inside his body and escape the pain of his balls being smashed like pancakes between the sharp point of her tailbone and the relentless surface of the polished concrete floor.

The urge to throw back his head and howl was intense. But he managed to bite the inside of his cheek, reduce his howl to a gruff-sounding grunt, and adjust his hips so his poor testicles pulled free and returned to their formerly round shape.

Wincing, she mouthed, "Sorry."

He nodded and tried to smile but figured his expression was more of a grimace. He was so focused on not throwing up that he didn't immediately notice she hadn't climbed off his lap. But he *definitely* noticed when she placed a slim hand on his shoulder to steady herself so she could look around.

He understood the confusion in her eyes. If he'd come awake to find himself inside a cramped pantry with stacked cans on one side and cases of Goose Island IPAs on the other, he'd be disoriented, too.

When she returned her attention to his face, one sleek brow lifted in question.

All he could do to answer her was shrug. And maybe get a little lost in the depths of her dark eyes.

The chorus to Van Morrison's "Brown Eyed Girl" drifted through his head.

She swallowed convulsively and shuddered when the muffled voices of those in the kitchen drifted through the closed door.

Hew couldn't make out what was being discussed. The old factory had been constructed with thick brick walls and insulated with horsehair. Sound didn't travel far. But he got the impression that whatever was being talked about outside had everything to do with Knox Rollins and little to do with Sabrina.

It was clear the poor woman was collateral damage in whatever trouble Knox Rollins had brought to their doorstep. She didn't have the hardened look of a criminal. Her body was too lithe; her hands were too soft. Her jeans were dirty, but they were designer. Her ballet flats were scuffed and scarred but were genuine leather. And the small hoops in her ears looked to be 18 karat gold.

Before she'd gone on the run, Sabrina had led a relatively comfortable life.

Of course, that certainty made him wonder how she'd gotten herself mixed up in Britt's brother's mess. What unfortunate set of circumstances had found her in the company of a convicted felon with the FBI hot on her heels?

All thoughts drained from his head like his skull was a rusty sieve when she leaned forward to press her cheek against his. Her skin was cool and soft. By contrast, her breath was hot and moist in his ear. "Water?"

He nodded. The move rubbed the coarse hairs of his beard against the delicate skin of her face, making him aware of himself in a way he'd never been before. There he was, this lumbering oaf, all huge and hairy and hard. And there she was, so frail and feminine and fragile.

It was like a delicate snowflake had fallen into a polar bear's lap.

Twisting slightly, he found a case of water shoved beneath the shelf to his left. A thin film of plastic held its bottles together. But he could silently slide one from the hole someone had torn into the side.

The cap came off with a twist of his wrist, and he gladly handed her the H_2O. Her lips were so dry that when she pulled them into a parody of a smile, her bottom lip split down the center. She winced and flicked out her tongue to lick at the tiny drop of blood beading in the breach.

Poor little lamb.

He wanted to run his hand along her spine but didn't dare. It was one thing to hold her in his lap. It was another thing entirely to touch her in ways she hadn't asked for.

He satisfied himself by leaning back on his hands and watching her long, pale throat work as she gulped down the water like she'd been walking through the desert for days. After she tipped the last drop into her mouth, she blew out a shaky breath and handed him the empty.

He was careful not to squeeze it, fearing it'd make that terrible crackling sound. Then he hitched his chin toward the case of water, silently asking if she'd like another.

She shook her head, making her hair swish across the plastic of her bright blue raincoat. Then she got distracted by the furry paw peeking beneath the door, batting at the air.

Hew sat up straight as his breath strangled in his chest. *Damnit, Peanut! You're gonna get us caught!*

Thankfully, in the next instant, the paw disappeared. And when he didn't hear the sound of approaching footsteps, he breathed a sigh of relief.

Sabrina stared at the door like the devil himself was on the other side. He took the opportunity to study her profile.

She had high cheekbones and a pointed chin. Her nose was straight, with only the slightest bump in the bridge. And her hair was thick. It fell down her back in soft waves. The color matched her rich, dark chocolate eyes.

It was her mouth that truly enchanted him though. It was wide and lush-lipped. Like Julia Roberts or Jessica Biel, it took up too much of her face. But he would bet his bottom dollar that meant she had the kind of smile that could brighten the darkest day and melt the ice off the coldest heart.

Will I ever get the chance to see it? he wondered absently.

She turned back and caught him staring and he wanted to kick his own ass for not being more discreet. Easily reading the appreciation, the *hunger*, in his eyes, she blanched an even paler shade of ivory and squirmed off his lap.

And who could blame her? he thought, helpless to assist her in her efforts. For one thing, she might scream if he put his hands on her. For another thing, he was afraid if he tried to help, he might hinder her ability to dismount without making noise.

It was a little awkward—and he suffered another ball-squish in the process—but eventually, she maneuvered off his lap and huddled on the floor beside Knox. She pulled her legs up to her chin and wrapped her arms tightly around her knees.

Way to go, jackass, he castigated himself, already missing the weight of her, the warmth of her.

When voices sounded outside, he watched her eyes grow as big as saucers. She shoved a hand over her mouth to hold in a scream. Then she buried her face into the tops of her knees.

What the hell happened to her to make her so scared? he wondered.

He took the thought a step further. *And whatever it was, will she recover from it? Or will it consume her like a living thing until there's nothing left but the rot?*

He'd seen it happen before. Seen decent kids turn terrible after suffering the abuse that seemed an inevitable part of the foster care system. Seen good fighting men go bad from dissociating so often from the horrors of bloodshed that they lost the last scrap of their humanity.

That which doesn't kill us makes us stronger.

Whoever said that was a damned idiot. Too often, what didn't kill a person only made them wish it had and—

His thoughts were interrupted when a loud *thud* sounded against the pantry door.

His heart, which had remained rock-steady the last time he'd flown BKI's old Blackhawk toward a moving warship only to execute a perfect pop-up breaking maneuver before hovering steady so the Black Knights could fast-rope down onto the bow, now thundered out of control.

He fully expected the feds to bust down the door. He was a little shocked when he heard a…*moan?*

What the hell is happening out there in the kitchen?

CHAPTER 6

Britt Rollins was kissing the bejeezus out of Agent Julia O'Toole in the middle of the kitchen.

Scratch that.

He was kissing the bejeezus out of Julia O'Toole up against the pantry door.

They hadn't started there, of course. They'd started behind the center island because it was there Julia had noticed Peanut. And it was there she'd suggested giving the cat a treat before leaving.

Talk about making your ding dong and your ping pongs shrink up into raisins!

Thanks to Eliza's quick whisper in his ear before she'd made like a banana and split, Britt knew the pantry was where his brother and the frail-looking brunette were hiding.

Needless to say, he'd needed to distract Julia from her exit strategy. The first idea that had come to mind was a kiss.

He wasn't *surprised* that's where his brain had gone. He'd wanted to kiss the smart, sassy fed since she made her first *Star Wars* joke, and he realized she was more than a baddie with a badge.

What he *was* surprised by was that she'd actually agreed. *More* than agreed. She'd gone up on tiptoe, grabbed him by the ears, and slammed her mouth over the top of his.

Now, *he* was the one distracted.

In the last fifteen seconds, Julia O'Toole had become his whole world. He didn't care about the cat. He didn't care about the people hiding in the pantry. He didn't even care that he was harboring a fugitive and, by association, forcing his friends and coworkers to do the same.

He only cared about the sweet, silky tongue Julia delved into his mouth. He only cared about tasting the delicious hint of coffee on her lips as she laved, sucked, and licked. He only cared about breathing in every warm, moist breath she shared with him.

They'd gone from zero to sixty in two seconds flat. From standing there staring at each other to her trying to climb him like a cat climbs a tree while he attempted to trace every inch of her body with his hungry, roving hands.

She had curves enough to make a man lose his damn mind. Her waist was narrow. Her hips were flared. And her ass? Oh, her ass was the eighth wonder of the world. Plump and plentiful enough to overflow his hands when he bent to fill them.

"God, yes," she breathed into his mouth as he lifted her onto her tiptoes to better align their bodies.

He'd never known anything like it.

Sure, he'd known desire. He'd known craving and longing and even red-hot *lust*. But this thing with Julia was different. It was cellular. Molecular. *Atomic.*

He wanted to *consume* her. Absorb her. Enmesh every particle of his body with every particle of hers until there was no way to separate them or tell one from the other.

It was terrifying. And yet…he couldn't stop.

Couldn't stop himself from tilting his head so he could have better access to her busy, *busy* lips. Couldn't stop his tongue from taking long, languid forays into her open, eager mouth. Couldn't stop himself from shoving her against the pantry door so he could press himself fully against her, feeling all her lovely, firm curves mold into his muscled, hard planes.

Her fingers moved from his hair to his face. From his chin to his chest. Her palms were a little rough—probably from target practice. But the rest of her? Sweet baby Jesus, the rest of her was ungodly soft.

She moaned, and the sound reverberated down to his throbbing balls. When she lifted a leg to hook a heel behind his knee, the highly sensitive flesh covering his cock ached so badly he wondered if it would continue to hold the turgid length of his erection or if it would split right down the middle.

In the furthest reaches of his mind, in the part that *wasn't* consumed by all that was Julia, he recalled a conversation he'd had with Boss over beers on the back patio. He'd been talking about life and love and Boss's incredible luck in approaching Becky about using her custom motorcycle shop as a cover for his newly formed covert defense firm.

"What are the odds y'all's business partnership would grow into a romantic one?" he'd mused.

"If you'd asked me ten years ago, I would've said the odds were pretty slim," Boss had replied. The fire burning in the pit had made flames dance in the older man's eyes. *"But I've grown more philosophical with time. Now, I believe in all that string theory stuff."*

"String theory?" Britt had frowned as he took a sip of beer. The tangy scent of hops had mixed with the smokey zest of the burning wood. *"As in particle physics?"*

"I leave that to Ozzie." Boss had chuckled. *"No. I'm talking 'bout the string theory of love. The idea that people are connected by unbreakable strings that transcend time, distance, and geography. The idea that what brings us together isn't choice but fate."*

Britt had laughed. *"Never would have pegged you for a Swiftie, Boss."*

"Huh?"

"A Taylor Swift fan."

Boss had blinked. *"Did I jump into a different timeline? How the hell did we go from talking 'bout string theory to Taylor Swift?"*

"Because she has that song. 'Invisible String.' The lyrics describe everything you're saying."

When Boss had only stared at him, he'd hummed a few bars.

"Right." Boss had nodded. *"I think I've heard Fish play that on his harmonica."* Then he'd shaken his head. *"The string theory has been around longer than Miss Swift's song. I can promise you that. I can also promise you that from the very beginning, it felt different with Becky. It was like I saw her, and a hidden part of me I never knew existed recognized itself in her."*

Is *that* why Britt had continued to stalk Julia despite his every intention to stop? Why he'd been uninterested in any other woman since the moment he'd clapped eyes on her? And why he'd been so quick and so sure in his decision to turn down her invitation for a drink? Because a hidden part of him recognized itself in her?

The answer to that question dissolved in his head when she speared her hands into his hair, her nails biting softly into his scalp. She moved her body against his in a rhythm as old as time, and yet somehow…because it was *her*…it still felt thrillingly new.

He was acutely aware of every point they touched. The warmth of her womanhood breached the layers of fabric separating them and bathed his erection in humid heat. The hard pebbles of her nipples brushed against his chest, a delicious addition to the friction she created with her hips. And the soft, searching, *hungry* feel of her lips against his had him sliding a hand to the back of her neck to pull her closer. Closer. Closer still.

It was magical. It was maddening. It was…

Too risky!

It took herculean strength to break free from the kiss when every cell in his body cried out in protest. But he managed it with only a low, gruff grunt.

After he put a few feet between them, he could do nothing but stand there with his hands on his hips. His head bowed in surrender. His chest rose and fell with his harsh breaths.

Oh-eleven-hundred, said the hands on his watch. *Get her the hell out of here before you do or say something you'll regret*, said his overheated brain. *Kiss her again*, screamed his excited body.

He glanced up and immediately regretted the decision.

Julia stood with her back against the pantry door, and she looked…

Like Aphrodite sprung to life. A sex goddess in the flesh.

His fingers had knocked her bun loose so that her thick hair hung over her shoulder in a silky rope. Her cheeks were flushed peony pink. Her dark lashes hung low over her half-lidded eyes. And her lips were plump and swollen from the pressure of his mouth.

"Holy shit." She blew out a ragged breath. "That was…"

"Yeah." He nodded when she didn't finish her thought. It didn't *need* to be finished. He wasn't sure it *could* be finished since he couldn't think of a single word in the English language to accurately describe what *that* was.

"I…uh…" She pushed away from the door. "I wasn't expecting to get so carried away."

He chuckled, but it sounded more like a grunt. Falling back on fun so she wouldn't guess how much he was reeling, he told her, "We Southern boys may be slow with our words, but we're fast with our seductions."

A mischievous grin played at the corners of her mouth. "Oh, it was *you* seducing *me*? I thought it was the other way around."

"Maybe," he admitted, his voice rough. "It was hard to tell who was doing what. You know, with all the tongues and the hands and the grinding."

"Amen." She nodded with a throaty chuckle. Then she looked down at the state of herself and set about straightening her clothes.

"I knew we'd be good together," she said without any hint of humility or embarrassment. "But sometimes I amaze even myself."

He recognized the line from *A New Hope* and followed it up with one of his own. "Great, kid. Don't get cocky."

She'd lifted her arms to re-pin her bun, but his response had her dropping her hands to stare at him. "I think I might really like you, Sergeant Rollins," she confessed with a wry twist of her lips.

His stomach took a free fall like he'd executed a HALO jump.

He should end the conversation now. He should herd her toward the door. He should wave her a fond farewell and hope he never laid eyes on her again.

Instead, he admitted, "I *know* I really like you, Agent O'Toole. And that's the problem."

"I like it better when you call me Julia."

He swallowed convulsively. "We should probably try to keep things professional given how easy it is for us to fall into the opposite."

"Spoilsport." She pretended to pout, and he had to look away from the temptation of her pursed lips. "You sure you don't want to meet me for that drink, Britt?" she cajoled, and holy crap, when she said his name like that, he wanted to throw back his head and howl. "Last chance."

"What just happened between us"—he waved a hand between them—"proves I was right when I said we're incapable of casual. So one drink would turn into ten drinks, which would turn into ten weeks and then ten months and—" He shook his head. "I can't do it. I don't *want* to do it."

For a handful of seconds, she simply stared at him, and he thought maybe she'd try to convince him.

He didn't know if he was relieved or disappointed when she hitched a shoulder and turned for the door. "Your loss, Sergeant," she called over her shoulder before stepping into the hallway.

He watched the swish of her hair across her back. Watched the sway of her hips and the unhesitating determination in her steps. Then, she was gone without a single backward glance.

My loss, indeed, he thought as he listened to her footsteps get swallowed up by the noise of the shop.

Shaking his head, he refused to name the hollow feeling that opened up inside him at her departure. Instead, he focused his thoughts on talking down his erection.

The idiotic thing had yet to receive the memo that it wasn't going to take a happy little trip to Poundtown. It was still hard enough to strain the denim of his fly and have him standing funny.

Not that he could blame it. Because…*Jesus, god, Julia is…*

Words failed him. *Sexy* was an understatement. *Hot as hell* came closer to capturing her allure, but it was still inadequate. And since he didn't have time to write the sonnet it would take to describe the wonder of her—and since his poetic skill topped out *there once was a girl from Nantucket*—he blew out a steadying breath, adjusted himself into a more comfortable position behind his fly, and opened the pantry door.

Knox and the woman he'd brought with him sat huddled against the back wall. Hew sat crisscross applesauce-style in front of them, which was a little like seeing a grizzly bear twisted into a pretzel.

Britt accurately read the question in his teammate's eyes and raised a hand. "It's a short story titled: I needed a distraction to stop her from coming in here in search of Peanut's cat treats, and the only thing I could think to do was kiss her."

Hew snorted as he shoved his substantial bulk to a stand. "Pretty long title for such a short story."

Britt waved him off and watched his brother offer a hand to Miss Greenlee.

Strange that Julia didn't mention Sabrina when she was accusing Knox of murdering his former cellmate, Britt thought, eyeing the woman in question.

She had a pretty face and the kind of mouth that promised heaven. But her current expression looked like hell.

Knox didn't look much better. Now that Britt had the opportunity to study his brother, he could see the stress that pinched Knox's eyes and hardened the muscles in his jaw. Frown lines deeply etched the sides of Knox's mouth, and there were gray glints in the stubble pebbling Knox's chin.

Knox caught Britt staring and twisted his lips. "Yo, Captain Side-Eyes. Go ahead and spit out whatever is causing you to look at me like that."

"The feds said you double-crossed your handlers and killed your former cellmate in cold blood." The words tasted like poison as they dripped from Britt's tongue.

He hadn't wanted to believe anything Julia had told him. He knew his brother wasn't exactly what anyone would call an upstanding citizen. But the thought of Knox *killing* someone stretched his credulity.

Knox had taken on a paper route when he was twelve so he'd have pocket money for cat food to feed the neighborhood strays. In sixth grade, Knox had befriended Tyler Jenkins, a kid with cerebral palsy, because none of the other punks had wanted to hang out with a little boy who scooted around in a motorized wheelchair. When their father died, Knox hadn't batted a lash at dropping out of college to come home and take care of Britt and—

"He didn't do it."

Britt blinked at the skinny brunette and watched as she vehemently shook her head.

"Knox didn't kill my brother," she swore in a voice that somehow sounded both watery and hoarse.

"Wait." He rubbed at his suddenly pounding temples. "Knox's former cellmate was your brother?"

She nodded. "His name was Cooper Greenlee. He took a bullet to the brain trying to save me and—"

Her voice cut off as a sob burst from the depths of her chest. Huge, glistening tears flooded down her cheeks. And before he knew what was happening, she wilted.

She just sort of *sunk* down onto her knees, buried her face in her hands, and let loose with a sound that epitomized heartbreak.

To Britt's astonishment, Hew fell to his knees beside her.

So, to recap, Knox and his former cellmate had partnered with the FBI to bring down a major narcotics trafficking organization. But according to the feds, Knox had double-crossed them, killed his cellmate, and gone on the run before he could turn state's evidence. And yet, according to the former cellmate's sister—whom the FBI didn't seem to know about—none of that was true. Only instead of Sabrina Greenlee walking through the feds' front door and clearing Knox's name, she'd let Knox drag her halfway across the country.

Britt was missing something. Or, more likely, he was missing a *lot*.

"We need to talk," he told his brother, a muscle twitching beside his right eye.

"No shit." Knox nodded.

CHAPTER 7

FBI Field Office, Lexington, South Carolina

Special Agent JD Maddox took another look through the crime scene photos.

He was used to seeing death. It was never pretty, but it was part of his job, and so...yeah, he'd learned to live with it. Although it was *particularly* obscene when that death came by way of a lead round traveling at over a thousand miles per hour.

Cooper Greenlee's sightless eyes stared out at him from the picture. The man had fallen against a wall. Or rather, he'd died sitting propped against the wall, his legs sticking out straight and his hands lying palm-up at his sides as if he'd been a ragdoll arranged on a shelf by a child.

The photo might've looked uninteresting, *mundane* even, if the contents of Greenlee's skull hadn't been painted across the wood paneling behind his head.

"I'm having a hard time believing Rollins would do this." He shook his head as he continued to examine the photos fanned out across his desktop.

"Is this your first day as an agent?" Keplar snorted his derision from his spot at the desk to JD's right. "You don't think a hardened criminal would take out another hardened criminal?"

Ryan Keplar had been JD's partner for the last six months. Ever since

JD had joined the most considerable joint task force the state of South Carolina had ever put together.

It hadn't been an *easy* partnership. Keplar was old school. A guy who believed the badge made him bulletproof. The kind of fed who preferred tough talk over tactical negotiations.

The first time JD met Keplar, the older man had crossed his arms and looked down his nose at JD like JD was a teenager offering him a shady-looking ID, and Keplar was the bouncer deciding whether to let him into the club.

Not much has changed since then, JD mused and stuffed the photos back into the file folder they'd been delivered in.

"They just seemed so close, you know?" He watched his partner closely. "More like friends than former cellmates. I can't picture Rollins pulling the trigger."

"Rollins and Greenlee were both felons," Keplar insisted. "Neither one of them got the title by being an upstanding individual. A nine-millimeter slug made chunky salsa out of Greenlee's gray matter, and now Knox Rollins is on the run. You do the math."

"But why?" JD shook his head. "Why murder his friend and partner?"

"Why else?" Keplar waved a dismissive hand. "He probably cut a deal with the cartel. Probably told them he wouldn't take the witness stand if they agreed to give him a big payout and a chance to make his way to a non-extradition country."

Keplar had been reviewing the CCTV footage he'd asked their counterparts in Chicago to provide. But he glanced away from his computer screen to pin JD with an irritated look. "Maybe they *both* cut the deal, but Rollins decided to kill Greenlee and keep all the cash for himself. Or hell, maybe Greenlee refused to go along with the plan, so Rollins removed Greenlee's piece from the board."

"You *really* believe that?" JD watched Keplar's eyes. "You *really* believe it was that simple?"

"Occam's razor, kid," Keplar said with an arrogant snort a second before his cell phone jangled to life. He snagged it out of his suit jacket on the second ring. "Special Agent Keplar." His south-Georgia drawl sounded soft and round to JD's Lowcountry ears.

JD couldn't hear whoever was on the other end of the call, but he surmised from Keplar's side of the conversation that it was the agents in the Windy City.

"Damn," Keplar continued. "Well, thanks for checking. And thanks for sending over the footage. I'll keep going through it. Just in case."

"I take it Rollins's brother hasn't seen hide nor hair of him?" JD said once Keplar thumbed off his phone and stuffed it back into his jacket pocket.

"Agent O'Toole gets the impression Knox and his brother aren't close. So maybe we were wrong to assume that's where Knox was headed."

"Then what the hell was he doing in Indiana?"

After discovering Greenlee's body, they'd spent nearly thirty-six hours trying to pick up Knox Rollins's trail. They'd about run out of ideas when a state trooper who'd seen their APB caught sight of Knox exiting a Flying J Travel Center. The trooper hadn't been able to follow Knox. He'd gotten distracted when the semi-truck trailer waiting in the diesel line had been T-boned by a sixteen-year-old in a souped-up Dodge Charger. But luckily, the trooper had been able to call in the sighting while simultaneously going to help with the wreck.

Knox had been long gone by the time JD and Keplar got their people to the travel center to check out the trooper's tip. But they'd pulled the security footage and confirmed Knox Rollins had, indeed, been there.

The camera angle had been bad. And Knox had only appeared on the screen for a few seconds. But there was no mistaking the man's eerily light eyes or the large cowlick that made the hair on his right temple stick up straight.

"Maybe he's trying for Canada?" Keplar mused now, going back to the footage. "That border is porous as hell, especially around the Great Lakes and…" He trailed off as he eagerly leaned toward his monitor. "Well, shit on my biscuit and tell me it's butter. Would you look at that?" He pointed a stubby, blunt-nailed finger at his screen.

JD scooted his rolling chair across the three feet separating their desks. Planting his duty shoes on the polished floor brought him to a sudden stop.

"Where's this from?" He squinted at the grainy, freeze-framed image of Knox Rollins outside a set of high, wrought iron gates.

"The CCTV camera mounted to the light pole across the street from Black Knights Inc."

JD glanced toward the bottom of the screen, where the pixilated time stamp glowed in bright white. "So Britt Rollins lied to our friends up there in Chi-Town." He sat back in his chair, vindicated he'd been right when he'd floated the idea that Knox was spotted in Indiana because he was running up to see his brother.

"Seems so." Keplar used his mouse to restart the video and frowned when another figure entered the frame. "But who the hell is that?"

JD leaned forward once again. The strong, chemical smell of Keplar's cheap aftershave tunneled up his nose. He breathed through his mouth as he looked at the second figure.

It was clear it was a woman. She had long dark hair and wore a shiny blue raincoat. But beyond that…nada. The footage was too blurry. Even still, he pointed at the image and asked Keplar, "Does she look familiar to you?"

Keplar barely spared her grainy photo a glance before declaring, "Never seen her before. Probably some transient Rollins picked up on the trip."

JD studied the face on the screen while shooting a side-long look at his partner. He was surprised Keplar wasn't more curious about this second player. "If I was on the lam for murder and double-crossing the government, the last thing I'd do is stop for nookie."

"When you've been on the job as long as I have, you learn not to apply logic or reason to felons and conmen. They don't think like we do."

JD let the subject die a quick death since it was clear Keplar had no stomach to pursue it further. "So, we're headed to Chicago, I take it? You want me to call Agents O'Toole and Douglas and let them know we're on our way?"

"Hold off on that." Keplar shook his head. "I don't want them jumping the gun and going back to that motorcycle shop. Knox Rollins is *our* Frankenstein's monster. I want to be the one to bring him in." Something moved in Keplar's eyes that made the hair on the back of JD's neck lift. "Or bring him down."

CHAPTER 8

Black Knights Inc.

Britt watched Eliza escort his brother and Sabrina Greenlee to the stairs leading to the third floor. She promised them private suites to rest and rinse off the dust from the road.

Knox murmured his thanks. Sabrina remained silent and gripped the handrail like a lifeline as she slowly climbed the stairs behind the other two.

Poor woman is dead on her feet, Britt thought and waited until they disappeared before glancing at the people gathered around the conference table. The faces staring back at him showed no malice or resentment that his sole living relative had brought a heaping helping of trouble to their doorstep.

Quite the contrary, all he saw was sympathy and understanding.

Somehow, that was worse.

He'd found a home amongst these good folks. They'd welcomed him with open arms and full hearts, and he'd have sooner stepped on his own dick than do anything to harm them. And yet… he harmed them by making them complicit in his bid to protect his brother.

He reached for his third—or was this his fourth?—cup of coffee and took a long sip of the bitter brew. He needed the extra time to gather his thoughts because the tale Sabrina and Knox had laid on them had a lot of moving parts.

On the one hand, Britt was ecstatic to learn his brother wasn't responsible for Cooper Greenlee's death. On the other hand, he hadn't the first clue how to help Knox clear his name since it'd been made clear that none of the government officials Knox had been working with could be trusted.

Setting his mug on the table with a muted *thump*, he made a sudden decision and announced firmly, "They can't stay here."

Ozzie ran a hand through his mad scientist hair. Boss spun his favorite K-BAR blade in a circle atop the table. And Becky pulled a Dum-Dum lollipop from the top pocket on her pink bib overalls, unwrapped the candy, and shoved the bright blue sphere into her mouth.

Everyone else remained still, silent, waiting for him to elaborate. He couldn't because his plan was amorphous and forming. He didn't want to talk out of his ass until he was sure what his ass wanted to say.

After a handful of seconds, Becky ventured, "You want to chuck them out on the street when every agent in the bureau will be gunning for them? And when you've been warned those same agents are itching to make your brother the fall guy for whatever went wrong on their case?"

Britt shook his head, feeling stuck between a rock and a hard place. Between the family he'd found and the family he'd been born to. "I can't drag y'all into this. I can't ask you to harbor a fugitive and risk your good names when I have no idea where to start in clearing his."

"He says there has to be someone on the inside," Ozzie ventured. "Someone working the case who gave him and his partner up to the cartel."

"Yeah, but who?" Britt grimaced. "Knox says they were planning to arrest the leaders of the narcotics trafficking organization on charges ranging from drug trafficking and illegal possession of firearms to wire fraud and money laundering. That means we're not just talking about the rat possibly being someone inside the FBI. It could be someone who works for the ATF or the IRS. That's a lot of alphabet-soup agencies to sift through to try to find one corrupt asshole." The coffee had soured in his stomach. He frowned when he added, "Where I'm from, we call that a classic case of too much shit and not enough shovels."

"Follow the money," Ozzie said. "And the online chatter. There's always at least *one* of those things."

"And how long will *that* take?" Britt questioned. He knew the answer was "too long" by the way Ozzie grimaced.

"So what's the alternative?" This was from Hew. His broad brow was creased in deep furrows.

"The only thing I can think to do is help them get out of the country. Maybe…" Britt shrugged as a plan began to solidify in his head. "I don't have a lot saved, but I've got enough to help them start a new life and—"

"I don't want a new life."

Britt saw Sabrina Greenlee standing at the base of the stairs. She'd removed her raincoat, which highlighted the dejected slump of her shoulders and the nervous way she twisted her hands together.

"I-I…" She swallowed and tried again. "I didn't mean to spy. I came down to get something to eat before jumping into the tub. The last thing y'all need right now is for me to faint again and drown in my own bathwater."

Eliza appeared on the step behind her. "I'll get you something so you don't have to go all the way down to the first floor. What do you want? A sandwich? Some yogurt? I made fresh blueberry muffins and strawberry scones this morning."

Sabrina moved aside to allow Eliza to pass. "You don't have to do that. You've all done so much already and—"

"Nonsense," Eliza cut her off with a wave of her hand. "We're happy to help."

Britt read the indecision on Sabrina's face. Eventually, exhaustion won out. "Your muffins and scones sound amazing," she told Eliza earnestly. "But I don't think I can keep much down, so maybe…maybe the yogurt?"

"You got it." Ever the consummate hostess, Eliza scurried toward the metal staircase that would take her to the first floor. Or…as much of a scurry as Eliza ever managed, which was more of an elegant quickening of her steps.

Sabrina's eyes and voice were hesitant when she returned her attention to the gathered group. "I don't want to start a new life." Her tone grew more confident. "I want to clear Knox's name. If I just *talk* to the FBI and tell them what I saw and know, then surely they'll stop hunting us. Surely they'll protect us while they find the culprit within their ranks."

The defiant tilt of her chin made Britt wonder if beneath the drained, malnourished stray resided a woman possessing more than her fair share of grit.

The abuse she'd suffered at the hands of the men who'd come for Cooper and Knox had only been intimated at in the tale Knox spun. But Britt was good at reading between the lines. She'd been brutalized. And when her brother had tried to save her from the worst of it, she'd watched him take a round to the brainpan.

That she was still on her feet and not catatonic in a corner somewhere spoke to her tenacity.

He softened his tone when he told her, "I wish I had as much faith in the wheels of justice as you do. But whoever outed Knox and your brother to the cartel is corrupt. This person didn't think twice about forfeiting the lives of two men. Your life won't be any different."

He watched her long, pale throat work over a swallow. She'd been through hell and he hated piling on. But there was nothing for it. She *had* to know what she was up against.

Hew was the one to drive the point home. "If you walk into the nearest FBI field office and share your account of what went down at your brother's house, there's a good chance the double-crosser will find a way to discount you. Or, the easiest thing they could do is share your location with the cartel and let the drug lords do the dirty work for them. No." Hew shook his head. "The only safe bet is to find the rat first and add your testimony to Knox's account of things later."

Britt watched what little blood remained in Sabrina's face drain away. "Th-that's what Knox said," she whispered, her chin trembling. "He said our best bet was to make it here with the hope that his brother—" she hitched her chin toward Britt—"could hide us or help us disappear. I just—" She twisted her hands so hard Britt worried she might snap off a finger. "I just didn't want to believe him that there's no way out of this."

To Britt's surprise, it wasn't tough-gals-stick-together Becky who jumped up to put a comforting arm around Sabrina's shoulders. It was Hew. The man looked huge next to the doe-eyed brunette.

"Come sit down before you fall down," he murmured, and Britt watched in astonishment as the big man gently steered her toward the conference table.

She retook the seat she'd abandoned earlier, sniffed back her tears, and nodded her thanks. "You're friends with that FBI woman, right?" She turned a beseeching gaze on Britt. "The one from the kitchen? She's not associated with the case Cooper and Knox were working. Couldn't you convince her to listen to us? To *help* us?"

Mention of Julia had visions of that kiss dancing in Britt's head.

Every pleasurable sensation he'd ever experienced had been instantly forgotten the minute her lips touched his, and he'd been lost. Lost in the feel of her busy hands. Lost in the all-consuming, hungry wetness of her mouth.

Kissing Julia had felt like touching the sun. Letting her walk out that door, knowing he'd deceived her, had hurt like heartbreak. And now he was being asked to drag her into this mess—the thought was as enticing as it was terrifying.

"Wait." Becky popped the sucker out of her mouth to point it at Britt. "So you're *friends* with Agent O'Toole now? I thought you were stalking her."

"I wasn't *stalking* her," he insisted for what felt like the one-millionth time. "I was just…"

He didn't finish the sentence because he couldn't finish the sentence since he was…you know…stalking her.

"What makes you think Britt and the FBI agent are friends?" Ozzie asked, his laptop open in front of him. His fingers flew across the keyboard, but Britt had learned Ozzie could give both ears to a conversation while simultaneously giving both hands to his computer.

"Because he kissed her," Hew declared, and that was enough to cause Ozzie's flying fingers to come to an abrupt landing.

Britt glowered at Hew. "I swear you're begging me to junk punch you today."

"You *kissed* her?" Becky's eyes were wide in emphasis.

"I was *distracting* her. Peanut"—the cat had been sitting at the end of the table, leg behind his head so he could thoroughly clean his balls, but he lifted his face away from his task when he heard his name—"almost outed their hiding spot." Britt gestured toward Hew and Sabrina. "It was the only thing I could think to do to keep O'Toole from opening the pantry in search of cat treats and—"

He held his palms out in front of him in a classic traffic cop "stop" hand signal. "You know what? It doesn't matter. What matters is Julia O'Toole *isn't* my friend. So she's not an asset we can rely on here."

CHAPTER 9

FBI Regional Headquarters, W Roosevelt Road

Julia powered off her computer monitor, straightened the files on the edge of her desk, and opened the side drawer to pull out her fanny pack.

"Yeah." Dillan pushed back in his chair and grumpily shoved down the shirtsleeves he'd rolled up his forearms. "Might as well call it a day since absolutely jack shit happened and since absolutely jack shit is likely to happen."

He'd been pouting like a child denied his favorite treat since they'd learned they wouldn't be joining the hunt for a fugitive. If petulance had a name, it would be Agent Dillan Douglas.

Not that she blamed him. The itch to get back in the field had gone from a minor inconvenience to a raging case of poison ivy. Her brain needed to *work*. So did her body.

Speaking of my body...

It had tingled for a good two hours after leaving Black Knights Inc. Everywhere Britt's broad hands had touched her, little bubbles of pleasure had fizzed and popped under her skin.

She was reminded of something her sister-in-law once said: You can't say *happiness* without *penis*.

It was true. For those few minutes with Britt's lovely hardness pressed against her, Julia had been blissfully happy.

Too bad that's all it'll ever be. A few stolen moments. A few stolen kisses.

Now, she wondered if she was forever ruined for others. She'd been so distracted by the pleasure he pressed on her that a nuclear bomb could have detonated in the middle of the city, and she wouldn't have noticed until the blast melted the flesh from her bones.

And what a way to go, a little voice hummed. *In the arms of Sergeant Britt Rollins.*

She barely refrained from rolling her eyes at how pathetic that sounded. How pathetic *she* sounded. Then, she got distracted from her inner dialogue when someone mentioned her name.

Glancing toward the elevator bank, she saw two men talking to Agent Stuart Brown.

Stu was a terrible flirt. Julia had turned down his invitation for drinks half a dozen times. And if he'd been even the slightest bit miffed by her refusals, she might have reported him to HR. Fortunately, after each rejection, he'd only shrugged, grinned, and gone on his way.

Now, he pointed a finger her way, and she watched the two strangers turn in her direction.

The younger man had thick, sandy-colored hair, freckled skin, and a gym-bro build. When his eyes met hers, his expression was politely interested.

The older man was the polar opposite. His black hair was thinning on top. He was ruddy-cheeked, with a physique that said he enjoyed refined sugar and complex carbohydrates. And his expression was as dark and as fierce as hell's midnight.

Dillan came to stand in front of her. She wasn't sure if he was being protective—which was laughable—or if he was trying to give the impression *he* held the higher rank—which was annoying but not unusual.

"Move!" She tapped the back of his knee with her toe. "You're blocking my view."

"What are you talking about?" His Superman profile showed the smirk he wore. "I *am* the view."

She rolled her eyes. "What must it be like to have the audacity of a mediocre, middle-aged white man, I wonder?"

His wide jaw thrust out in pique. "Who you callin' middle-aged? I just turned thirty-eight!"

"*That's* what offended you? Not the mediocre part?" She shook her head. "You, sir, have lowered the bar of humility so far it's in hell."

"Hate the game, not the player," he returned with a toothy grin.

"The nineties called. They want their hackneyed cliché back."

She could see his mind whirring, searching for a sufficiently sarcastic comeback. When he couldn't come up with anything, he swung back to watch the new arrivals who snake their way through the sea of cubicles. "You know these guys?"

"Never seen them before," she assured him.

But she knew their type.

She *was* their type.

It was more than the JoS. A. Bank suits, the lug-soled duty shoes, and the poorly concealed shoulder holsters. It was the look in their eyes. The way they held their jaws. That certain strut that said they expected to be afforded an appropriate level of deference and respect once they reached their destination.

We really are an arrogant lot, she thought absently and then pushed to a stand next to Dillan to greet the arriving agents.

"Agents O'Toole and Douglas?" The older man asked, although his expression said it wasn't really a question—just a courtesy.

"Who's asking?" Dillan's tone was imperious.

The urge to roll her eyes again was intense. Growing up with brothers, she was no longer surprised that every interaction between men somehow turned into a dick-measuring contest.

"I'm Special Agent JD Maddox." The younger of the two strangers thrust out his hand. "This is my partner, Special Agent Ryan Keplar."

"Nice place y'all have here," Keplar said as he glanced around the land of whiteboards, file cabinets, and coffee mugs. "Ours down in South Carolina doesn't hold a candle. The toilets back up when it floods, and we don't have these pretty floor-to-ceiling windows."

His words sounded complimentary. But Julia didn't miss the condescension in his tone.

Keplar was the kind of guy who thought ear protection at the shooting range made agents soft. The kind of guy who still used investigative techniques based on stereotypes. The kind of guy who carried a revolver instead of an automatic because he believed revolvers were more reliable—

cocky enough to think he only needed six rounds to hit his target.

She tried not to make snap judgments about people—although being able to size someone up in under thirty seconds was one of the reasons she'd been promoted to lead agent—but she couldn't help deciding then and there that she didn't much care for Special Agent Ryan Keplar.

In contrast, Agent Maddox seemed genuinely cordial when he brushed off his partner's words by chuckling. "We might have floor-to-ceiling windows if we had a view like this." He pointed to the skyline, which was particularly powerful-looking because it was silhouetted by the setting sun.

Even without having been given their names, she would've recognized both men from their voices alone. Maddox had a smooth tenor, and Keplar had an inflection that said he might live and work in Charleston now, but he'd been born and raised in a state much farther south.

Alabama maybe? Mississippi?

After shaking hands with both men, she turned to find Dillan looking happy enough to levitate. She frowned at her partner. "What's with your face?"

He rubbed his hands together. "We might get to join the hunt for a fugitive after all. I assume that's what's brought you guys here despite the two of us"—he wagged a thumb back and forth between himself and Julia—"coming up empty-handed this morning. You're convinced Knox Rollins is in town?"

"We *know* Knox Rollins is in town," Keplar declared. "We saw him plain as day on that footage you sent us."

Julia's stomach hollowed out at the news. "Knox showed up after we left this morning?"

She hated that Britt hadn't called them like he said he would. Hated it more that she cared at all because she *shouldn't*. Sergeant Britt Rollins was nothing to her.

Nothing but a delicious fantasy that'll never come true.

"Nope." Keplar shook his head. The overhead lights glinted off the sheen of his bald spots. "Arrived at Black Knights Inc. about five minutes before y'all did." He inclined his chin toward Julia and Dillan. "He was inside when you were questioning his brother."

Three things happened then.

Julia felt the blood drain from her head. Her entire body flashed hot and cold. And her vision turned black around the edges—a sure sign her anger was getting the best of her.

Britt Rollins had lied right to her face—which would not have been unforgivable in and of itself. When confronted by an authority figure, it was human nature to conceal the worst of oneself or put forth the best of oneself. She was used to people stretching the truth when she questioned them.

But what she found unforgivable—and what had her teeth grinding so hard she could hear her enamel complaining—was that he'd *then* gone and *kissed* her. Kissed her like she'd never been kissed before and like she worried she'd never be kissed again. And for what?

To add insult to injury?

To prove to her just how much she'd let her lust for him override her ability to identify bullshit when she smelled it?

To distract her from the fact that his brother was hiding somewhere under his roof?

The rat bastard!

CHAPTER 10

Black Knights Inc.

B*ritt loaded Haint's saddlebags and checked his watch for the third time in as many minutes.*

What the hell is taking so long?

It was a long ride up to Traverse City, Michigan. It would be even longer because they were journeying on the backroads in the dark. And every minute they remained at BKI was one more minute that he made his friends and teammates complicit in his endeavors.

He wanted to be hell and gone like…*yesterday*. But they'd decided to wait until after dark to make their move. There were fewer cars on the roads after dark, which meant fewer chances for accidents that would require the cops to arrive on the scene. It also meant fewer folks awake to make note of two whimsical motorcycles riding down the road.

In his line of work, darkness was always preferential to daylight. And when it came to spiriting an ex-con across state lines and up the entire east coast of Michigan, darkness wasn't just preferred; it was required.

The hours he'd spent waiting for the sun to set had been filled with brainstorming sessions with his team. It had been decided that their best course of action was to get Knox and Sabrina out of Dodge, squirrel them away somewhere safe and secure and far from the prying eyes of the feds.

Hunter had offered the use of his off-grid cabin outside Traverse City, Michigan. It had all the amenities of home while remaining completely untraceable. Knox and Sabrina should be comfortable there while Ozzie did what Ozzie did best: use his wunderkind hacking skills to pinpoint the true traitor.

After Ozzie *had* found the guy—or gal, Britt wasn't sexist—*then* Knox and Julia could take their proof to the folks in the bureau. That, along with Sabrina Greenlee's testimony, should be enough to clear Knox's name.

Easy peasy lemon squeezy.

Except, Britt couldn't shake a growing sense of foreboding that somehow, in some way, this whole thing was going to go tits up.

His track record as a soldier was top-tier. He'd led his Ranger unit on dozens of successful missions without losing a man. And he was proud to say the same was true since he'd become a Black Knight. But his track record as a civilian? Particularly once his family was involved?

That was an entirely different story. And it was *those* odds that made him feel like someone had tied his knickers in a knot.

He paced the length of the shop twice and only stopped because Eliza suddenly appeared in his path.

"What's with you?" She canted her head and frowned at him.

"What do you mean?" He could feel his eyebrows pull toward the center of his nose.

"You mainline adrenaline like it's ice water running through your veins. Mr. Cool, Calm, and Collected no matter what sort of shit is hitting the fan. But look at you now. Someone might think you have ants in your pants."

The truth was his lazy, devil-may-care coolness only applied to situations where he felt in complete control. Where he had a plan and parameters and every procedure memorized backwards and forwards. And this? This wasn't a base jump off a cliff that he'd studied six ways from Sunday or a mission he'd poured over for hours so he knew all the ins and outs. There were a lot of what-ifs and unknowns here.

Too many what-ifs and unknowns. He shifted uncomfortably.

Instead of answering her question, he posed one of his own. "What's the holdup? Why aren't we on the road already?"

"Your brother is brushing his teeth, and Sabrina is getting dressed. My feet are bigger than hers, so I made her double up on socks to fit my boots. As long as she doesn't have to do any running, I think she'll be fine."

"If she's running from something, that means we've got much bigger problems than boots that are too big."

She made a face and then handed over a small bag. "I put a few changes of clothes in here for her. Nothing fancy. Jeans, socks, and a couple extra flannel shirts."

Britt shot her a side-long glance as he added the small duffel to his saddlebags. "When do *you* ever wear flannel?"

She sniffed in feigned offense. "I can do rustic."

He glanced over the expensive tailoring of her shirt and the intricate weave on the material of her slacks. His expression called bullshit, even if he was smart enough to keep his trap shut.

"Fine." She crossed her arms. "The flannels were a gift from Becky two Christmases ago. I've never taken them out of the package." She scrunched up her elegant nose. "I think she envisioned I'd wear them on the nights we sit around the firepit. But why would anyone choose a scratchy flannel shirt when there are Merino wool sweaters to be had?"

Britt took a peek down at the flannel shirt he'd slipped over his tee, then looked back up at her and grinned. "Peasants, am I right?"

"Pfft." She flapped a hand, and he took that as his cue to secure the buckle on his saddlebag.

Stepping back, he admired his ride.

Each Black Knight had their own custom Harley. It was one of the perks of working for BKI. They'd consulted with Ozzie and Becky on the design for each bike. And then they'd gotten a crash course in mechanics by building their own pieces of rolling, roaring, road-eating art.

Haint was named after the paint color used on porch ceilings down South. The Gullah—a subgroup of African Americans who lived in the coastal regions of Florida, Georgia, South Carolina, and North Carolina—believed haints, or ghosts, couldn't cross water. So they painted their porch ceilings a pale, oceany blue-green to repel any spirits who approached their homes to haunt them.

The tradition had spread past the Gullah community and had been adopted by just about every self-respecting Southerner. It was one of the quaint, everyday things he missed about his hometown.

Well, that and okra soup, he thought with a longing sigh.

He could fry up green tomatoes with the best of them, brew up a mean pitcher of sweet sun tea, and devil crabs like nobody's business. But he had *not* made a decent pot of okra soup since moving to Chicago.

He blamed it on being unable to find fresh okra and dealing with the frozen stuff.

Great. And now I'm hungry for fried green tomatoes.

He ignored his grumbling stomach and straddled Haint's leather seat—which Becky had dyed a deep, rich, moccasin brown. After unscrewing the gas cap, he swayed the motorcycle to and fro. This allowed him to see the fuel sloshing in the large tank. Once he was assured it was topped off, he replaced the cap.

His gas gauge had never let him down. But he'd learned his lesson about *not* relying on the reader and instead always putting eyes on his fuel level because the one time he *hadn't* checked the tank on his dune buggy, he'd been forced to walk fifteen miles through the Agafay Desert back to Marrakech.

Not only had he been dirty and dehydrated by the time he'd reached civilization, but he'd also been sunburned all to hell and had nearly stepped on *two* separate desert-horned vipers.

He checked the fuel on the production bike Knox would ride. Checked the oil too. And then he double-checked the route he'd marked on his encrypted phone—the one he usually used while on a mission.

After that, there was nothing left but to get to it.

Time to put out the fire and call in the dogs.

"Mind hanging onto this for me until I get back?" he asked Eliza.

"It would be my pleasure." She accepted his personal cell and shoved it into the hip pocket on her slacks.

If anyone—namely the folks after Knox—tried to track Britt via his cell phone, they'd find themselves at Black Knights Inc. and be faced with his coworkers who, conveniently, wouldn't have the first clue where he'd scampered off to.

"You're a saint," he told her by way of thanks. "Has anyone ever told you that?"

Her grin was positively devilish. "Certainly not Fisher."

He held up a hand. "Please stop. It's like when your parents talk about having sex."

"Except you're three years older than I am, so comparing me to your mom is absurd."

"Doesn't matter. You and Fish are family. So…" He shivered. "Same difference."

She chuckled and shook her head. "Speaking of sex and people who are a far cry from saints, how was that kiss you shared with Agent O'Toole in the kitchen?"

So good it made my jeans feel two sizes too small, he thought as images of Julia with her hair tumbled down over her shoulder and her cheeks flushed with passion screamed through his brain.

Aloud, he only admitted, "Better than it had any right to be, seeing as how we were two feet away from where my ex-con brother was sitting on the pantry floor."

"Yeah." She nodded. "It was like being inside a welding factory the instant you two stepped into the kitchen together."

"I'm not following." He frowned.

"Sparks, Britt," she explained. "Tons of sparks. I was tempted to shield my eyes."

"Yeah, and that's the kind of fire I got no business playing around with," he declared staunchly.

Eliza narrowed her eyes. "That's an odd sentiment coming from a man who's made risk-taking his entire personality."

"There are risks, and then there are *risks*," he countered. To distract her—and himself—he frowned at the empty staircase. "I'll go get Knox. You mind checking on Sabrina? Make sure she hasn't passed out again?"

"Give her a break." Hew appeared at the top of the stairs. "She's been on the run for two days." He tromped down the metal treads, his biker boots booming like thunder. "You can be patient for five more minutes and let her catch her breath before you ask her to go on the run again."

Britt jerked back his chin when Hew headed toward his own ride. The former Nightstalker wore his riding jacket and had his overnight go-bag slung over one shoulder.

"Where are you off to?" Britt demanded.

"I'm going with you." Hew's response brooked no argument.

Britt argued nonetheless. "Bullshit. It's bad enough Hunter is letting us use his cabin and Ozzie is sticking his neck out by hacking into the lives of the folks on the joint task force. I don't want you—"

"See, that's where you got things all wrong," Hew interrupted as he opened the tour pack on the back of Freedom, the gray-blue chopper Britt had recently helped him refit with a big, twin exhaust.

Britt frowned in confusion. "Did I miss something? Did Hunter rescind his invitation? Is Ozzie *not* going to—"

"No," Hew cut in again. "You're wrong if you think I give a fiddler's fuck what you want."

Britt's growing apprehension had the hairs on his arms lifting like little semaphore flags. "This entire situation is a five-star screwup if ever there was one. There's no guarantee the feds won't find us." He was desperate to mitigate the fallout from the bomb Knox had detonated by coming to Chicago. "And you don't need to be there if they do. If anyone has to go to jail for helping my brother, it should be me."

Hew crossed his big arms over his even bigger chest. "Two things," he said in that Mainer accent that sounded curt and cutting. "One, martyrdom isn't a good color on you. That's just a fact."

"Yeah," Britt muttered, "if you've suddenly changed the definition of *fact* into *shit you just made up*."

"And two," Hew continued, "I'm a big boy. I can make my own decisions. I'm coming with you."

"Damnit." Britt ran a hand through his hair. "What happens if push comes to shove and I'm forced to stand my ground to protect my brother?"

"I know my specialty might be piloting war machines through the sky, but I can outrun, outgun, and outmaneuver with the best of you."

"I *know* you can. But have you considered that that outrunning, outgunning, and outmaneuvering you're so good at will involve the feds? As in the Federal Bureau of Investigations?"

"You mean the same Federal Bureau of Investigations with a rat in their house? The same Federal Bureau of Investigations itching to put your brother in the ground for something he didn't do? You expect me to stand by and watch an innocent man go down just because he's not *my* brother?"

Britt tried one last time to change Hew's mind. He made sure his expression was as earnest as his tone. "I can't have you on my conscience if things go pear-shaped. This is *my* mess to clean up, and I—"

Hew interrupted with, "Your mess, my mess. None of that matters. We might not share blood, but we share a common goal: to keep everyone who works here alive until Madam President leaves office and we're no longer in her service. If this situation with your brother *does* go pear-shaped, you'll have a better chance of keeping your head on your shoulders with me by your side. Besides..." Hew grinned. "I've been itching to see this cabin Hunter has kept so secret. He says he has a first edition of *A Wrinkle in Time*."

"Ahhh." Britt nodded. "So the truth comes out. This is about a book. I should've known."

"What?" Hew blinked innocently. "Can I help it if I'm motivated by loyalty *and* literature?"

Britt tried and failed to come up with another argument that would sway Hew's decision. The truth was, despite not wanting to involve his teammates more than he absolutely had to, he was glad for the company. Glad he'd have another set of eyes and ears on-site...just in case.

"I don't know whether to kiss you or tell you to go fuck your own face," he finally told Hew, shaking his head in defeat.

"Spoken like a true prodigy." That one corner of Hew's mouth quirked. "I'll take a pass on the kiss. And the other? I don't bend that way. Believe me, I wish I could. Because what's one more sin in a life already filled with transgressions?"

Britt guffawed while Eliza gasped. Her expression was scandalized. "I swear I'd love to shove all your heads in soup pots and kick them around the kitchen."

"Are you including Fisher in that fantasy?" Britt asked her with a teasing wink.

She lifted her chin. "My darling fiancé quotes poetry. He doesn't openly opine the sad fact that he can't suck his own dick."

Now, Britt was laughing in earnest. "Did you just say *dick*?"

She rolled her eyes. "Just because I don't curse six times in each sentence like the rest of you doesn't mean I don't know what the words mean. And just so you know—"

She was cut off when Knox and Sabrina appeared at the top of the stairs.

Knox looked better after having showered and stolen a few hours of sleep. He'd borrowed a pair of Britt's jeans and wore the faded, scuffed leather jacket Hunter had left behind when he moved out of the old factory building into a condo with his wife in the Streeterville neighborhood.

Sabrina, on the other hand, still looked awful. The woman wore her fear like a fashion statement. Britt would swear he could see a heavy cloud of sorrow hanging above her head.

He clocked the dark, freshly-pressed jeans she'd borrowed from Eliza. And sure as shit. The flannel shirt she wore still had the creases in the arms from where it'd been folded up at the factory.

Sabrina had pulled her dark hair back into a sleek ponytail, and her huge, doe eyes were still shadowed and bruised-looking. But the expression in them was nothing shy of…Britt decided the word was *hopeful*…when she saw Hew latching the fasteners on the back of his tour pack.

"Are you coming with us?" Her voice was so soft he could barely hear her above the sound of Knox stomping down the stairs.

Hew didn't speak. He nodded his head once as he watched Sabrina Greenlee descend the stairs.

Britt regarded his teammate's expression with a raised eyebrow.

Hewitt Birch had exactly three emotional settings: boredom, casual sarcasm, and extreme hypervigilance.

The first two Britt was used to seeing. Hew made his boredom known by keeping his face buried in a book. The casual sarcasm was something the big ape whipped out and used against his teammates when they least expected it. But the extreme hypervigilance? Well, Hew usually saved *that* for when he was behind the controls of their Black Hawk helicopter.

And also, apparently, when he's got eyes on Sabrina Greenlee.

"You're riding with me." He made a come-on gesture at Sabrina when she stepped off the last tread.

Britt blinked his surprise. Eliza and Sabrina both did the same. It was only Knox who frowned and shook his head. "I've been looking after her for the last three days. I should keep on keeping on if you don't mind. That's what Cooper would want."

"You're still suffering an adrenaline crash," Hew explained casually as he swung his leg over Freedom's black leather seat. "And this is going to be one long-ass ride. It'll be a lot harder and a lot more exhausting if you're having to balance a passenger. Besides, the bike we got you on only has a camelback seat. No backrest for the second rider. I got a king and queen seat on my ride." He hooked a thumb over his shoulder to indicate his seat setup. "She'll be a lot more comfortable with me. Unless…" He lowered his chin and aimed his next words at Sabrina. "You're not okay with that idea?"

"I-I..." She twisted her fingers. "I want to do whatever's best for everyone."

"Good." Hew bobbed his head decisively and patted the cushion behind him. "Mount up."

"You need help with your ride?" Britt asked his brother when Sabrina shrugged into the heavy leather jacket Eliza had scrounged up from somewhere and then scurried over to Hew to do as he commanded.

"You were still in diapers when I was riding that two-stroke pocket bike Dad bought me." Knox clapped a hand on Britt's shoulder. "I reckon I can handle the luxury units y'all build here. It'll be all soft and comfy, like driving a Lincoln."

Britt stared into his brother's eyes. It was like looking in the mirror at himself. Only it reflected an image fifteen years in the future.

Knox might've only had four years on Britt. But prison was brutal on a man. It had aged Knox prematurely, blotching his skin, furrowing his brow, and dimming the light in his eyes.

The *guilt* of that ate at Britt. But maybe, just maybe, this was his redemption arc. Maybe if he kept his brother safe until Ozzie could find a way to clear Knox's name, then he could finally pay Knox back for the sacrifice Knox had made for him all those years ago.

"I didn't say it earlier, but—" He had to stop and clear his throat. "But it's good to see you, man. I've missed you."

Knox's eyes looked suddenly overly bright. "Just wish I was here under better circumstances."

There was a burn behind Britt's eyes when he nodded. "Me too, brother. Me too."

"I was trying to play it straight this time." There was no mistaking the note of anguish in Knox's voice. "I swear, I was, Britt."

Knox rarely called Britt by his name, preferring to use *brother* or *bro*. This meant that when Knox *did* use his name, it felt particularly poignant, as if the divide between big brother and little brother disappeared, and they were simply two men who'd known each other their whole lives and who had loved each other just as long.

"I know you were." Britt swallowed loudly. Then he figured he better inject some levity into the conversation before they melted into twin puddles on the floor. "As for the circumstances, aren't the bad ones what usually bring us together?"

Knox grunted. "Seeing as how the last time you came to see me was the day I was sentenced to that stint in Kershaw, and the last time I went to see you was when I got compassionate leave to visit you in the hospital after that bullet nearly took you out, then yeah. I reckon you're right. We might never cross paths if it weren't for bad circumstances."

Knox nudged him with his elbow. "Speaking of that bullet, are you ready to tell me how you got it? Because even outta your head on pain meds, you refused to give me the story."

Britt smiled and shook his head. "Classified information doesn't suddenly become *unclassified* just because I waved farewell to my Ranger unit."

"Speaking of…" Knox lowered his voice and glanced around. "I came here hoping you could help me hide. Or maybe help me get out of the country. I never expected you and your friends to help me find whoever double-crossed me. I never thought you'd even know *how*." He shot Britt a side-long glance. "Is there something you haven't told me about what it is y'all do here?"

Britt couldn't lie to his brother. But neither could he tell Knox the whole truth.

"We don't have a lot of money here at Black Knights Inc., but what we do have are a very particular set of skills. Skills we've acquired over very long military careers. Skills that make us a nightmare for people like your rat," he said, having bastardized the famous speech in *Taken*.

"Okay, Liam Neeson. Keep your secrets." Knox chuckled, and Britt had forgotten how much he enjoyed that sound. It had been too long since he'd heard his brother's laugh. Then, another noise cleaved through the quiet of the shop. And that one wasn't nearly as sweet.

The hairs on Britt's scalp lifted so fast and so high it was a wonder they didn't all jettison clean off his head.

"What's that?" Knox asked as the *eee-ooo-eee-ooo-eee* filled up the space.

Sam and Ozzie appeared at the railing on the second floor, staring down at them in alarm. Fisher ran in from the kitchen, his hair looking as wild as Ozzie's. And Eliza scurried over to the security monitor by the front door.

"That, my dear brother," Britt grumbled as he threw on his jacket, "is the dulcet tones of the shit hitting the fan."

"The feds are at the front gate!" Eliza yelled. "Six vehicles and a bunch of men in tactical gear! Get out of here!"

Britt didn't need to be told twice.

Freedom roared to full-throated life, and two seconds later, the production bike Becky had loaned Knox did the same. Britt had already rolled aside the large Craftsman toolbox that concealed the button that activated the hidden door to the Batcave. So, all that was left to do was push it.

"Yo, Fish!" he yelled as he straddled Haint and reached for his helmet. "Open sesame, will you?"

"On it!" Fish's long legs carried him to the brick wall and the button in half a dozen strides.

Britt didn't need to look to know Fish had smashed the button or that the bricks on the wall had separated to reveal the yawning black maw that was BKI's secret exit. He could see the truth in Knox's wide eyes and Sabrina's slack jaw.

"Who the hell are you people?" Sabrina squeaked as Britt tightened the strap under his chin and thumbed on his pride and joy's engine.

"The folks who are trying to save your ass," he yelled above the noise of the alarm and the motorcycles' engines. Then he walked Haint to the lip of the tunnel and was slapped in the face with the smell of wet concrete and freshwater fish.

"Agent O'Toole is talking to Manus at the front gate!" Eliza called. "She's showing him papers! I think they're warrants!"

Britt caught Eliza's stare and mouthed, *I'm sorry.*

She shook her head, gave him a wink, and then made a shooing motion with her hand.

"*Go,*" Fish said from beside Britt. The man's hand was poised to press the button and close up the wall the instant the three bikes were in the tunnel. "Don't worry about us. We got this."

Britt hated, absolutely *hated* leaving his friends in the lurch. But the best thing he could do was get his brother far, far away from them and the agents poised to bust into the place.

"Thank you. I owe you." He nodded at Fish before nosing Haint's fat front tire over the lip of the chasm.

Julia O'Toole was at the gate with warrants, proof she knew about his brother. And proof she knew he'd played her earlier.

Knowing what she must think of him had bile burning in the back of his throat.

But he shouldn't care, right? He'd already written her off, told her in no uncertain terms there would never be anything between them. It shouldn't matter *what* she thought of him.

And yet, as he twisted the throttle and started down the steep incline, he couldn't escape one simple truth. He *did* care.

More than cared. It felt like there was something vast and heavy pressing down on him. And as someone who took pride in being self-aware, he didn't shy away from labeling what that something was.

I will spend every day missing a woman who was never mine to begin with.

CHAPTER 11

Julia sat on the barstool she'd occupied hours earlier and refused to think of the kiss she'd shared with Sergeant Britt Rollins just three feet away.

Correction: the missing *Sergeant Britt Rollins.*

Every person lined up across the kitchen island had suddenly developed a severe case of ignorance. Or amnesia. None of them knew where Britt had gone. None of them knew his brother had visited BKI. None of them had seen the woman Knox Rollins brought with him.

In fact, none of them seemed to know much of anything besides their names, their occupations, and what they'd had for dinner.

Frank Knight, owner of Black Knights Inc., beef stroganoff.

Eliza Meadows, office manager at Black Knights Inc., Cobb salad with honey mustard dressing.

Sam Harwood, mechanic at Black Knights Inc., leftover pizza from Pizano's and two Goose Island IPAs.

So forth and so on, including Becky Knight, Fisher Wakefield, Ozzie Sykes, and Graham Coleburn.

It was like the civilian version of the name, rank, and service numbers soldiers were taught to repeat when the enemy captured them.

Not that I'm surprised, she thought irritably. *Since more than half of these assholes used to* be *military.*

Okay, maybe it was unfair to paint the Black Knights in broad strokes with the asshole brush. Especially since, previously, they'd been nothing but respectful. *Helpful* even.

Of course, their earlier aid was probably why their sudden uncooperativeness rankled so much. She didn't like one-eighties from people she thought she could…maybe not *trust*. She didn't know the Black Knights well enough to trust them. But she'd credited them with good intentions, presumed their candidness, and thought they'd come to regard her well enough to…

Answer my damn questions when I ask them!

But they'd been a united front of ignorance since she posed her first inquiry. Even when she'd called Britt's number—which she'd found thanks to the tech guys back in the office—and the cell phone in Eliza's pocket had jangled to life, all Eliza had done was frown at the phone and say, *"How odd. How did Britt's phone get in there?"*

How indeed? Julia had thought angrily.

Seriously, if she'd been a teapot, steam would've poured from her ears while a piercing whistle sounded through her nose.

"So you have no idea where Britt Rollins might be." She sucked on her teeth as she stared daggers at the gathered group across from her. "What about Hewitt Birch? I can't help noticing he's missing, too."

It was Eliza who answered with a shrug. "Everyone who lives and works here is free to come and go as they please. No one is keeping tabs on anyone."

"And if I were to have my tech guys find Mr. Birch's cell phone number and I called it, would it also ring in one of your pockets?"

Eliza blinked innocently. "I suppose you won't know until you try."

Homicide. Julia suddenly understood the urge to commit it.

"We've checked every closet, every corner, and under every bed," Agent Maddox said as he swept into the room. His mussed hair and crooked tie were visual reminders of the exhaustive search they'd done inside the three-story factory building over the span of the last two hours. They'd also turned the little foreman's cottage out front upside down and inside out with the same amount of luck, which was *none*. "No sign of Knox Rollins or his brother. But we've confiscated a shit-ton of weapons."

Maddox came to stand behind Julia's chair. She could smell his cologne.

It wasn't as exotic and spicy as Britt's, but it was still quite lovely in an understated way that didn't excite her ovaries the least little bit.

Stop thinking about Britt Rollins's cologne, you horny idiots! she silently cursed said ovaries. And then, for good measure, she added some good advice for herself. *And you! Start thinking about what you can use against these people to make them talk!*

Even if she hadn't had video evidence proving Knox Rollins and the mystery woman had entered the building, Julia would've known the BKI employees were lying to her. Now that she wasn't distracted by Britt's disruptive sex appeal, she could smell the deceit in the air. It hung over the group like a caustic cloud, tickling her instincts and grating on her last nerve.

A *thump* sounded overhead, causing Frank "Boss" Knight's jaw to harden. The noise from above announced loud and clear that her colleagues weren't exactly being *careful* in their search of the premises. Julia had felt bad about that in the beginning.

Now, when Boss pinned her with a jaundiced look that said without words, *"Aren't you going to do something about that?"* all she did was shrug.

If he wasn't going to be helpful, neither was she.

Tit for tat. Turnabout is fair play. What's good for the goose is good for the gander, etcetera.

He uncrossed his massive arms and pushed away from where he'd been leaning against the counter.

Frank "Boss" Knight was what she'd call a *serious character*—you know, if she was prone to understatement. She didn't suspect it would be a pleasant experience to be on the receiving end of his ire, and she braced herself accordingly.

But before he could say anything, his wife—who had arrived on the scene thirty minutes after Julia waved her warrant under the noses of the onsite employees—placed a restraining hand on his arm.

He obligingly stepped back to re-lean against the countertop. Becky patted his shoulder, offering him a soft smile, and it was sort of like watching a kitten comfort a silverback gorilla.

"What do a bunch of motorcycle mechanics need with so many weapons?" Maddox asked, glancing between Julia and the line of BKI employees.

"As I'm sure your colleague has told you," Boss rumbled, sounding like he ate gravel for breakfast, lunch, and dinner, "we're all former military. Once you get used to wearing a sidearm, you feel naked without one." The man's steely gaze landed on the shoulder holster visible beneath Maddox's jacket. "You understand, right?"

Before Maddox could answer, Becky piped up. "Every weapon in this place was legally purchased and is permitted. You have no right to confiscate them."

Her cheeks were flushed bright red. But Julia got the impression her heightened color wasn't a result of fear or nervousness. It was a result of her barely controlled rage.

Becky Knight was the embodiment of Shakespeare's line: *though she be but little she is fierce.*

"And last I heard," Eliza added, looking as cool and unbothered as ever, "this is still the U.S. of A. We still have Second Amendment rights."

Julia flipped her laptop around so the gathered group could see the closeup of Britt holding BKI's front door wide to admit his brother and the woman Julia had dubbed Jane Doe Raincoat. The image was grainy. The CCTV camera it'd been taken from wasn't high quality, but even still, there was no mistaking one of the two individuals with Britt.

Knox Rollins was the spitting image of his younger brother.

Or, at least, he *had* been at one time.

"You expect me to believe Sergeant Rollins somehow secreted his brother and this woman into the building"—she lifted a dubious eyebrow—"and then somehow secreted them back out again without any of you seeing them or knowing anything about it?"

Heads bobbed in unison, and the frustration simmering inside Julia since hour one of the search suddenly increased to a boil. Little beads of sweat popped out on her upper lip.

"Bullshit," she hissed and watched one of Eliza's sleek black eyebrows flick up her forehead. The others' expressions remained infuriatingly passive. "I'm not Willy Wonka. Sugar-coating things isn't my style. So, believe me when I say that if one of you doesn't start giving me answers, I'm hauling all of you in tonight."

"On what charges?" Boss's bored tone was belied by the muscle on the side of his wide jaw ticking fast enough to beat the band.

"Aiding and abetting, harboring a fugitive, obstructing justice, you name it."

"You can't prove any of that." This from Becky.

"I don't have to prove it to pull you in for questioning."

"You think our answers will change because you've cuffed us and stuffed us?" Boss chuckled, but there was no humor in it. "Lady, you got no idea who you're dealing with if you think a little time behind bars will make any of us give you information we don't have."

"Oh, I know you guys are tough." Julia frowned. "Bunch of former flag wavers turned grease monkeys. You're as tough as they come. But in my line of work, when something looks fishy and smells fishy, it's a goddamn whale." She blinked when she realized her mistake but covered it up by jabbing her finger into the soapstone countertop. "And yes, I know a whale isn't technically a fish, but you get my point. This whole thing stinks to high heavens. Every single one of you knows a lot more than you're letting on and I—"

The diamond-hard looks in the eyes staring back at her stopped her in her tracks. Tough talk wasn't going to work on these people. They *lived* on tough talk, and hers only made them more obstinate.

She'd let her emotions get the better of her. Let her memories of Britt as he stood over her, emanating danger and sex appeal in a testosterone-laden cloud override her instincts as an agent.

Damnit, Jules! Forget Britt Rollins and pull your shit together. You're better than this.

Blowing out a deep breath, she sat up straighter and changed tactics.

"Look, I understand why you want to protect Sergeant Rollins. I've been around you all enough to know you consider yourselves more than colleagues or coworkers. You're family. I *get* that. I have a big, tight-knit family, too. And I'd do anything to keep them safe. But Knox Rollins and whoever this woman is"—she tapped the top of the laptop screen—"*they* aren't your family. So help me find them, and I promise I'll do everything I can to see that Britt comes out of this unscathed."

"There are outbuildings out back," one of the tactical guys said while glancing through the windowpanes in the back door.

"There are?" Julia forgot her line of bargaining and blinked in surprise. When she thought back to the handful of times she'd visited the old menthol cigarette factory, she realized she'd never gotten a look at the *back* of the property. She'd assumed the factory building abutted the river.

"Yes, ma'am. Three of them."

She hopped from the stool and headed in the tactical guy's direction, anticipation making her blood fizz.

She'd managed five steps before Eliza shook her head. "Your warrants don't cover our outbuildings." She had the warrants Julia had secured from the judge in one hand and waved them like a fan in front of her face. "They cover the old foreman's cottage and the factory. That's it. You step one foot inside any other structures on this property, and you violate the Fourth Amendment's exclusionary rule."

Julia felt her nostrils flare. "Did I miss the part where you went to law school?"

"I have a BA in political science, a master's degree in economics, and a doctorate in public policy. That kind of makes me a lawyer by extension."

Stomping to the back door, Julia peeked through the panes to find an expansive patio. Flagstones extended from the factory building out thirty yards to the brick fence topped by razor wire. There was a large firepit surrounded by comfortable-looking Adirondack chairs. There was a built-in kitchen area complete with a grill, smoker, and what appeared to be a dorm fridge. But most glaringly, three outbuildings stood in a row like good little soldiers.

Two of the buildings weren't much bigger than storage sheds. The third was more the size of a small barn.

"All it'll take is one phone call and I can get the judge who issued that warrant"—she nodded to the pages in Eliza's hand—"to extend the search to those outbuildings."

"Fine." Boss shrugged shoulders as big as bowling balls. "Get on it then. Make the call. Time's a wastin'."

"Go outside and watch over the structures," Julia instructed the guy in the SWAT gear. With his body armor, helmet, and eye protection on, it was impossible to tell him apart from the other tactical team members. She only knew who he was because he wore a Velcro name patch over his right pectoral muscle. "Thank you, Agent De La Cruz," she added when he opened the door to do as instructed.

She was in the process of pulling her phone from her pocket to make that call to the judge when Agent Keplar ran into the kitchen. His bald patches were especially shiny since he'd been the first in and out of every room. She wouldn't have thought him the type of agent to have the energy of that pink bunny from those old battery commercials, but he'd surprised her with his vigor.

"Where?" he barked into his phone. His slightly manic-sounding tone had her putting her own phone away. "Okay. Keep eyes on them if you can and keep relaying their location. We're on our way." He shoved his cell phone into his coat and turned to his partner. "We're outta here. Three motorcycles were spotted stopping for gas outside of New Buffalo. The officer who reported them saw our BOLO and is in pursuit with orders not to engage until we catch up."

"Roger that!" Maddox said, hot on the heels of Keplar when the older man turned and raced for the door.

"We're coming with you!" Gesturing to Dillan, Julia charged after the two South Carolina agents.

Something about Keplar's demeanor made her think the rate of gunfire would exceed the rate of discussion at a pace of about a thousand to one if he was allowed to catch up with Britt and his brother on his own. And even though she was furious at Britt for lying to her, even though she wanted to string him up by his balls for using his masculine wiles to distract her from her job, she certainly didn't want him *dead*.

"Take your goon squad with you!" Boss's deep voice boomed at her back before she could make it into the hallway.

She stopped long enough to motion for Agent De La Cruz, who stood in the open doorway, to follow. He no longer needed to guard the outbuildings, and she no longer needed to call in an extension on the warrant.

The Rollins brothers, their mysterious companion, and probably Hewitt Birch had abandoned the premises hours earlier. And by the sound of it, they were headed north.

Canada, maybe?

Adrenaline fired through her blood, allowing her to keep pace with her partner despite his legs being a good eight inches longer than hers. They raced after the visiting agents who'd already thrown open the front door.

The clatter of duty shoes and tactical boots was loud against the blacktop as the team hoofed it toward the tall wrought iron gate. The puddles left behind by the earlier rain reflected a starless sky. And one thought above all else echoed through her head in time with her own footfalls.

I get to see Britt again! I get to see Britt again!

She told herself she wanted to ensure he walked away from this mess in one piece. She told herself she wanted the opportunity to confront him and explain to his face that he'd been a world-class *ass* for kissing her when his intentions were far from pure. She told herself she wanted to prove to him that she was more than a walking sack of hormones, that she was a *good* agent who could *get her man* even when that man was someone she might have once wanted to get to know on a more personal level.

And while all of that was true…the *main* reason she was itching to see him again was to prove to *herself* that, now that she knew the truth about him, she could resist his…erm…particular charms.

Fool me once, shame on you. Fool me twice, shame on me!

CHAPTER 12

Huron-Manistee National Forest, Michigan

Britt cursed when his back tire slipped into a pothole on the unnamed—and barely paved—county road. The crevice was deep enough to cause Haint's fat back tire to fishtail for three full seconds before he could wrestle the bike back into the center of the crumbling asphalt.

As always, the near miss had the familiar burn of adrenaline sizzling through his veins. Usually, he considered that a welcome sensation.

Not tonight.

Tonight, there were *other* asses on the line besides his.

He spared a glance over his shoulder to make sure Hew and his brother didn't suffer a worse fate. The headlights on the bikes behind him were bright enough to blind. But he was relieved when neither suddenly bounced up and down nor veered off the side of the road into the dense trees looming over them.

The countryside was unfathomably dark. It was one of those grim, stygian nights that made men wonder if things like Bigfoot, Mothman, or the Chupacabra might actually exist.

Spec-ops soldiers loved a new moon. Dark deeds were best done in the heart of the deepest nights. But there had been lore inside his Ranger unit about the *black* moon, the second new moon in a single calendar month.

Despite its portentous-sounding name, his men had been convinced a black moon was a good omen.

Now, just to be clear, Britt wasn't superstitious by nature. But he did appreciate the power of *belief*.

He knew the guys under his command would operate as if fate was on their side if they trusted it was so. And just that little bit of extra courage, that additional dose of tenacity, could help them win the day.

He'd planned missions during black moons every chance he got.

There's a black moon rising tonight, he thought now, having made the connection that morning when he'd idly checked his weather app while sipping his coffee.

Unfortunately, something told him that, despite the moon's good omen, fate wasn't on his side. He blamed his doom and gloom on the call he'd received from Boss hours earlier.

"There's a BOLO out on you. Some local five-oh caught sight of you at your last refueling stop. He's on your tail now. Lose him," Boss had advised, pulling out his Navy SEAL commander voice. *"And then make sure you aren't seen again."*

Britt had done his best to do precisely as instructed.

It'd taken some tactical riding and half a dozen turns down tiny roads to shake the cop. And even after he'd assured himself they'd lost their tracker, he hadn't let up. He'd pushed himself and the other riders harder, choosing an even *more* obscure route north than the one he'd planned earlier.

It had been a grueling trip. Every muscle in his body ached from the effort of maneuvering Haint along the rough country roads.

Almost there, he assured himself. *Almost to Hunter's cabin.*

Hunter was a stickler about keeping the place to himself, so this was the first time Britt had been invited to visit. He'd heard enough about it, though, to know it wasn't hooked up to the electrical grid. There was no phone line. No gas line. No city water line. Hell, Hunter hadn't even bought the place in his own name. He'd purchased it through a shell company owned by an LLC, so no one could ever track him there.

Every cell in Britt's body focused on the miles that lay between him and promised salvation. Then his blood froze, and the air strangled in his lungs because…eyes.

Yellow, glowing eyes that reflected the beam of his headlight. They were close. Too close!

Damnit!

He smashed the levers on his grips with everything he had, and the big bike responded instantly. Haint's tires gripped the pavement with an earsplitting screech of friction.

Britt managed to control the bike's momentum for a couple of seconds. Then it became too much. Haint's rear tire lost traction, swinging around until Britt and the monster motorcycle skidded perpendicular down the road.

"Damnit!" This time, he cursed aloud as he slammed his boot into the pavement and strained to keep Haint from falling sideways and skipping across the top of the roadway like a rock skipping across water.

The friction heated the sole of his boot. His thigh muscles burned from the immense effort it took to fight with physics.

One second stretched into two. Two became three. And just when he thought he might slam into the group of deer standing in the middle of the road, Haint rocked to an awkward stop.

Dust from the slide slipped beneath Britt's helmet to fill his mouth. The smell of burned rubber and melted asphalt tunneled up his nose. He wasted no time flipping up his visor and staring hard at the animals that had nearly caused his demise.

Haint's headlight shined into the trees on the side of the road. But the headlights on the two bikes motoring up behind him spotlighted the group of does and the fawns they'd birthed back in the spring.

He counted twelve deer in all, but it was the lead doe whose gaze locked with his. Her huge, dark eyes were unblinking as she chuffed and pawed the pavement.

"Right." He nodded at the rebuke. "I was speeding. My bad."

She bobbed her head as if accepting his apology and then leaped across the lane in one graceful bounce. Her crew was tight on her heels…er… hooves, prancing after her in graceful bounds.

"Y'okay?" Knox asked him after he and Hew had growled to a stop behind Britt and cut their engines.

Britt thumbed off Haint's motor and the forest around them seemed to breathe in the sudden silence. "Yeah. I'm okay. But I think I might've shit out my own heart."

"Pretty fancy riding." Hew whistled his appreciation. "Thought you were gonna lay her down for sure."

"Becky will kill me if I wreck this paint job. She mixed about a dozen colors before she got it right." He patted his tank with its signature color and hand-enameled artwork.

Pulling in a long breath, he blew it out again just as slowly. Then, he repeated the process twice more.

As a spec-ops soldier, he'd learned how helpful breath work could be. From box breathing to resonance breathing, there was science to back up the anecdotal evidence that regulating oxygen intake activated the parasympathetic nervous system and helped to de-escalate and de-stress the body.

It was how he could mountain bike down a seventy-degree incline or go sandboarding in some of the most hostile environments on the planet without breaking a sweat.

Once the rush of blood no longer sounded in his ears, he could hear the distant rumble of thunder. He opened his mouth to tell the others they needed to get back at it to outpace the coming storm. Then he realized it *wasn't* thunder and immediately cut his headlight.

"Direction?" Hew pivoted his head as he tried to locate the source of the sound. He, too, killed his bike's lights.

"Southwest, I think." Britt yanked off his helmet to get a better bead on the familiar noise. "Yeah." He nodded once. "Definitely southwest. Flying low and slow. Hey, Knox?" he called to his brother. "You need to go dark."

Knox switched off the headlight on his production bike, and they were instantly plunged into full-on blackness. The darkness was so complete Britt couldn't see his hand in front of his face, much less the faces of those with him.

With the light no longer disturbing the peace of the countryside, the night animals resumed their chorus. Small, furry animals rustled the pine needles on the forest floor. A screech owl let loose with an eerie, even-pitched trill. But above it all was the muted *womp-womp-womp* of blades cutting through the dense air.

"Definitely low and slow," Hew's hushed voice came to Britt through the darkness. "It's a single engine, not a double. So we're probably talking a Bell 407 or maybe a 412."

"Load?" Britt asked.

Hew didn't need him to elaborate. They'd worked together long enough in unfriendly environments to develop a shorthand. "I'd say anywhere between six and ten agents, plus the pilot and copilot."

"Fuck."

"Wh-what's happening?" Sabrina's voice was high with alarm.

"A chopper is hunting us," Hew answered. "Filled with FBI agents, no doubt."

Britt's eyes sightlessly darted back and forth as he calculated their odds and decided they were scantily low on options. Thankfully, being low on options wasn't always a bad thing. Being low on options meant he didn't have to waste time deciding what to do next.

Unhooking the carrying case on his belt, he told Hew, "Here. Take the encrypted phone. The GPS is programmed for Hunter's cabin. You'll be there in under an hour if you keep up the pace we had going."

"Wait. What?" Knox demanded, and Britt heard the *snick* his brother's helmet made when he slammed up his visor. "What's happening?"

"I'm going to draw the feds away," Britt explained, quickly slipping on his helmet and resecuring the chin strap. "Y'all are going to stay here until it's safe to move, and then you'll head on to the cabin. Hew? You got a flashlight on you?" He toed out his kickstand and hopped off Haint.

"Copy that," Hew said, and Britt could hear his teammate climbing off his ride and unhooking the clasps on his tour pack. Ten seconds later, Hew shoved a heavy Maglite into his hand.

"Thanks," Britt muttered as he quickly pulled his own flashlight out of his left saddlebag along with a roll of duct tape.

Men who relied on their gear to keep them alive knew nothing was better than good old duct tape for quick fixes.

He taped Hew's Maglite to his rear fender with the bulb end facing the front of the bike. Then he secured his flashlight to his left wrist.

"How far back was that side road?" he asked Hew, his eyes adjusting to the darkness enough to show his companions as gray shadows moving against the black shadows of the forest.

"A mile?" Hew speculated. "Maybe a little more."

"I'll try to keep them occupied for as long as possible. When you think it's safe to move, do it. And don't look back." He stared hard at Hew's massive, gray hulk. "I'm depending on you, man."

"*Now* who's glad I came along, huh?"

"Yeah, yeah." Britt straddled Haint and maneuvered the bike until it was alongside the other two motorcycles, facing the direction from which they'd come. "I owe you one."

"One?"

"Fine. Half a dozen."

"That's better." Hew sounded pleased with the prospect.

"Okay." Britt took one more deep breath. "Everyone has their marching orders. Let's do this."

He went to snap on Hew's Maglite, but Knox stopped him with a hand on his arm. "This isn't your fight, Britt." Again with his given name. A lump formed in Britt's throat. "Maybe we should just—"

"If the feds catch you or Sabrina, there's no guarantee you'll survive the encounter," Britt interrupted. "Me? I've got a better chance."

"Because of the whole special operations soldier thing?"

"Something like that," Britt admitted evasively, not mentioning that he had friends in high places if worse came to worst.

Madam President had made it clear she would disavow all knowledge of Black Knights Inc. if the truth about the group ever came to light. But that didn't mean the leader of the free world wouldn't step up to help the Knights through back channels and by using surrogate actors when they asked her to.

If Britt managed to get himself caught and held by the bureau, everyone back at Black Knights Inc. would make it their mission not to let the president rest until she found a way to set him free again.

"I fucking hate this," Knox said.

Britt couldn't see his brother's expression. But he could hear Knox's misgivings vibrating through his voice.

"This is our best chance to get you to safety and clear your name." Britt covered his brother's fingers with his gloved hand. "Trust me. I got this."

Knox's words were hoarse with emotion when he whispered, "Thank you, brother."

And there's that damn lump back in my throat again.

Britt squeezed his brother's fingers one more time. Then, he swung around to tell Hew, "If I don't end up in cuffs, I'll meet y'all at the cabin once I know it's safe."

"You can get there without the GPS?"

"Studied the route so many times I could find it with my eyes closed."

"That's the Britt I know and love."

"W-were you a Boy Scout or something," Sabrina asked quietly.

"Nope." Britt shook his helmeted head. "But I've always taken their mantra about being prepared to heart."

Hew snorted. "Britt's reckless as hell with his own life, but he's the most dependable man on the planet when it comes to looking after everyone else."

"Aw, shucks, Hew. You lookin' to take me up on that kiss now?"

"Fuck off."

"Right back atcha."

"Copy that," Hew said, and Britt smiled as he clicked on Hew's Maglite, thumbed on the flashlight taped to his wrist, and cranked over Haint's engine.

He hoped the flashlights would give the illusion of three headlights. The trees were dense, so he felt confident the deception would work unless the feds used infrared.

Flipping down his visor, he twisted his wrist and was off in a flash of spinning tires and dust-covered chrome.

Haint cut through the humid air as easily as a hot knife through butter, hungrily eating up the crumbling asphalt. Britt kept one eye on the road in case of potholes while the other was trained on the side of the road and the turnoff he'd spied moments before he'd nearly plowed into the herd of deer.

There.

He caught sight of the speed limit sign next to the detour and grimaced. Now that he really looked at it, he could see the road was a little more than a double-wide track topped with gravel. Weeds and saplings grew up along the sides. And there were spots where rain runoff had washed out the center of the route.

Beggars can't be choosers, he thought as he planted a boot, swung Haint's backend around, and quickly turned onto the narrow track.

The smell of vegetation and decaying plant matter was strong enough to slip under his visor and fill his nose as he pushed Haint as fast as he dared over the uneven ground. The canopy was lower than it had been on the larger road. It brushed the top of his helmet in spots and made it impossible to see more than a dozen feet in front of him.

He cleared a mile in less than three minutes. A second and third mile slipped by easily. By the time he watched the fourth mile tick over on his odometer, he could hear the *womp-womp-womp* of the helicopter blades racing to meet him.

Follow the pretty lights through the trees! he thought as he narrowly avoided a large rock that had rolled into the middle of the road.

Haint's engine growled with impatience at the speed. He didn't dare push the motorcycle much over thirty mph, or the gravel would take him out.

He couldn't have that. Not yet. He needed to put more miles between himself and where Hew and his brother sat hidden in the dark.

Just a little bit farther, he thought as his tires bounced over a particularly uneven section of road. It was like someone had carved ski moguls into the track. By the time they smoothed out, he was surprised all his teeth hadn't rattled out of his head.

Another mile rolled over on his odometer. Then another and another.

He realized he was smiling triumphantly when dust from the road made his teeth feel gritty.

Go, Hew! He willed his silent thoughts through the night. *Now's your chance!*

He didn't need to glance overhead to know the FBI had located him. The *womp-womp-womp* of the rotor blades was loud enough to drown out Haint's engine noise. The trees in front of him swayed in the downdraft. And a spotlight swung back and forth, occasionally piercing the canopy to light up the roadway like the midday sun.

And then it happened. He should've known it would. He was deep in the forest on a road mankind rarely used.

"Fucking hell!" He slammed on his brakes and clenched his teeth when an entire section of the track disappeared in front of him. A recent storm had washed it away, leaving nothing but a three-foot drop into loamy soil behind.

Haint slipped into a skid and the gravel made it impossible for Britt to keep the bike on the road. The most he could hope for was a controlled crash.

His biker boot dragged across the rocky surface as man and motorcycle skated off the roadside and down the steep embankment. Then, there was no keeping his feet under him or keeping the bike up.

He kicked away from the falling motorcycle so it didn't come down on his leg. Then he barrel rolled down the hillside, keeping pace with his motorcycle as it crashed onto its side and skidded to a sudden stop a hair's breadth from the trunk of a thick pine tree.

He banged into the rear wheel and came to rest on his back, staring sightlessly up at the canopy as pine needles fell from the sky like spiky, green snowflakes.

Thump-thump-thump went his heart.

Tick-tick-tick went Haint's cooling engine.

Womp-womp-womp went the chopper's rotor as the big bird executed a quick one-eighty.

He'd have liked to lay there and catch his breath. But there was no time.

Working on instinct as much as anything else, he quickly flicked off the flashlights and Haint's headlight. He was immediately plunged into a world of darkness, and despite feeling every second ticking by like it was a physical force, he had to take a moment to let his eyes adjust.

He'd been taught that staring into the blackness wouldn't magically enlarge his pupils. The trick was to move his eyes and focus, really *focus* on attempting to see the landscape around him.

It took longer than he would've liked. But eventually, the stygian blackness lightened into deep shades of blue and gray. It wasn't enough to *see* by. But it was enough to allow him to get his bearings.

First things first, he thought. *Get as far away from the scene of the crash as possible.*

He had to zigzag around trees, crash through the underbrush, and avoid taking low limbs to the eyes. He figured he'd run another quarter mile when, suddenly, he could hear the chopper hovering somewhere behind him. The feds had probably spotlighted Haint's chrome and were fast-roping in.

Fast-roping involved attaching a thick, braided rope to a mount on the side of a helicopter. Tactical teams could then slide down the rope without using a harness or a descender—it was all about individual strength and the personal perseverance required to hang on tight enough to keep from hitting the ground at a speed fast enough to shatter a leg but yet loose enough to allow for a quick drop-in before the guy on the rope above came down on your head.

It was a risky maneuver, especially when trees obstructed the drop zone and a guy was loaded down with eighty pounds of combat equipment. But Britt figured the feds weren't nearly as geared up as he and the Knights usually were. This meant they'd not only be able to make the insertion easy-peasy, but they'd all be quick on their feet in pursuit.

He turned on the afterburners.

He was in superb condition. He had to be—it was in his job description. But the effort it took not to plow into obstacles because he was running near-blind had his heart banging against the cage of his ribs and his lungs working like bellows.

The chopper gained altitude—the rhythmic chuff of the blades wasn't as loud as it'd been only minutes before. And just as he'd feared, he could now hear the crunch of heavy boots in the forest behind him.

Three pursuers, he decided. *Maybe four.*

He wasn't sure how much time passed. When evading an enemy, the ticking clock seemed to speed up and slow down simultaneously. So it could have been mere seconds or many minutes later when he burst out of the forest into a clearing.

The lack of underbrush and trees was disorienting, but what was most shocking was that he could see. Like, actually *see*.

A hundred yards away, a small farmhouse with peeling white paint and a wraparound porch stood. The porch light was on. Because it was a black moon and because the overhead clouds blotted out the twinkle of starlight, the little yellow glow from the single fixture beside the front door was enough to light up the entire property.

A rusting but well-loved John Deere tractor crouched in the field in front of him. A shiny tricycle lay on its side beside an overgrown flowerbed. But the driveway was empty. And the fact that not a single light inside flipped on despite the roar of the helicopter circling overhead indicated to Britt that no one was home.

For a brief moment, he thought about taking refuge inside. But that's what the feds would expect him to do.

SERE training, don't let me down! he thought as he turned a quick three-sixty to assess all his options.

SERE stood for survival, evasion, resistance, and escape. He needed the evasion portion to throw his pursuers off his trail.

Reluctantly, he faced the forest again. It was human nature not to seek the darkness once you'd found the light. But heading back into the dense trees was his best bet.

He didn't retrace his steps. If the feds were any good, they were following the path he'd left behind. But he still headed back in the same *general* direction until he came upon a length of muddy ground.

Stepping into it, he picked up the pace even as the thick mud clung to the soles of his boots, trying to slow him down. The wet, sucking sound his steps made kept time with the loud *thump* of his heart. And he trained his near-blind eyes on the three feet in front of him at all times lest he plow into a tree or run into another wild animal.

He wasn't sure how far he'd gone when the shallow depression leveled out and the ground beneath him turned dry and crunchy with the usual detritus found on a forest floor.

Slipping his helmet off his head, he felt the cool fingers of the night air tunnel into his sweaty hair. The helicopter was farther off, somewhere to his right. But behind him, in the direction of the overgrown track, were the sounds of the feds. Their radios scratched and squawked as they relayed information to their superiors and each other.

They were close. Following the muddy footprints he'd left behind like Hansel and Gretel followed the trail of breadcrumbs.

Perfect.

He hated to do it. But the final breadcrumb would be his helmet. The helmet Becky had painted to match Haint's tank. The helmet he'd personally retrofitted with an internal sun visor and pin-lock anti-fog main visor.

Sometimes subterfuge demanded sacrifice.

He heaved the helmet as far as he could and listened to it crash into the undergrowth. Then he broke off a low-hanging pine branch, hooked the wooden end into his back belt loop so that the smaller, thickly needled branches fanned out against the ground behind him, and cut a ninety-degree path away from the one he'd been running and away from the direction he'd tossed his helmet.

The pine branch effectively brushed away his footprints. And when he figured he'd gone far enough to avoid the agents following his trail, he turned back toward the farmhouse.

He was in the clearing in less than five minutes. Emerging from the trees at the back of the property, he noticed a small, dilapidated barn with rakes, shovels, and hoes leaning against its side. But, most importantly, inside the open door, he saw the outline of an old truck.

From that distance, he couldn't make out what kind of shape it was in. Couldn't tell if it looked like it was drivable or not.

There's only one way to find out, he thought.

He stepped toward the structure but quickly darted back into the shadow of the trees when he heard the approaching helicopter. Fifteen seconds later, the bird appeared in the sky overhead, hovered for a moment, and then started to descend.

Shit.

With his *escape* route effectively cut off, he was stuck back in the evasion phase of his SERE training.

He looked around for a hiding spot and spied a large, fallen tree. It's been toppled some time back. And its death had heralded new life. Fungus and moss grew over its decaying carcass. Soon, nothing would be left of it but the countless lives it'd nurtured and sustained. In the meantime, though, it afforded him the perfect camouflage.

He wasted no time shimmying himself into the hollowed-out trunk. Dirt and debris fell into his face and hair—probably a few bugs, too—but he didn't bother brushing any of it off.

He'd hidden in worse environments. The crocodile-infested waters in the Nile Basin came to mind. So did the rural areas outside of Aleppo, Syria, where he'd been eaten alive by sandflies.

Carefully pulling over his hiding spot the bushes that had grown up around the fallen tree, he reckoned he was as concealed as he could make himself. Then, peering through the foliage, he watched as the helicopter's landing skids touched down in the open field.

The trees around the clearing bent and swayed in the wash from the rotors. And when the pilot cut the engine, the bird's loud roar became a dull *swish-swish* as the slowing blades lazily cut through the air.

Two men in suits hopped out of the aircraft, crouching low as they trotted into the open field. Then came Agent Dillan Douglas. He was followed closely by Agent O'Toole.

Julia.

Britt's heart ratcheted up a notch because…she looked absolutely beautiful. And *fierce*.

Her hair had come loose from its bun. It blew wildly around her heart-shaped face while her suit jacket flapped, revealing her shoulder holster and duty weapon.

What is it about a woman packing heat? he wondered, feeling a measure of chagrin when his body responded to the mere sight of her.

Okay, maybe it wasn't so much about a woman packing heat as it was *Julia* packing heat. Everything that woman did was sexy.

Including, he thought, *running me down like a rabid dog.*

CHAPTER 13

Majestic Ridge Road, Traverse City

Sabrina understood why sleep deprivation was used as a torture tactic. She was so tired she hurt. Physically *ached*. Her bones cried. Her muscles screamed. And her eyes were so gritty she would not have put up a fight if someone tried to pluck them from her head and toss them on the ground.

Sleep. Darkness. Oblivion.

Nothing had ever sounded sweeter.

She longed for it the way she'd once longed for her parents to actually act…well…*parental*. If her mother and father had chosen their children over booze and pot and partying, maybe Cooper would not have fallen into a life of crime. And if he hadn't fallen into a life a crime, he would not have partnered with Knox and the FBI on the sting. And if he'd never partnered with Knox and the FBI, he'd still be alive.

Still be teasing me about my abysmal taste in men. Still be randomly glitter-bombing my mailbox. Still be the first person I call when I've done something right and the last person who'd judge me when I've done something wrong.

Oh, Cooper…

Somewhere along the ride up Michigan's coast, the shock of his loss had been replaced by a pain that was unlike anything she'd ever felt. It wasn't simply an anguish in her mind; it was an agony that lived in her body. A deep, dull ache that radiated from her soul and mixed with her exhaustion until her limbs were leaden.

She'd spent the first couple hours of the trip carefully avoiding touching the big, brawny man named Hew. She'd already imposed upon his personal space enough.

She should've scrambled off his lap the instant her eyes opened in that pantry. But he'd been so warm, so strong—and his arms had been so comforting. Like a cat seeking the sweet warmth of a sunny patch, her instinct had been to remain exactly where she was.

She hadn't realized she was taking advantage of the situation until she'd turned and caught him staring at her with a strange look on his face.

Not wanting to *further* trespass upon his person, she'd hung on to the edge of her seat instead of him anytime they'd taken a corner or bounced over a bump. It wasn't until they'd been forced to shake the police cruiser that she'd reluctantly snaked her hands around his waist.

But now? Oh, now she didn't have the physical strength to worry about his personal space. Nor did she have the mental energy to care whether or not she was taking advantage of the situation.

He was the only thing keeping her on the back of the bike.

Her helmeted head rested between his mile-wide shoulders. She'd shoved her hands deep into the pockets of his thick leather jacket. And he supported all of her dead, drained, absolutely debilitated weight against his broad back.

She'd begun to give up hope they'd ever reach the cabin. Somehow, they'd slipped into an alternate reality where there was nothing but endless twists and turns on a road that reached to infinity.

The gravel beneath the rumbling bike's tires crunched softly as Hew executed yet *another* turn. This one put them on a narrow country lane. Pine trees, tall and solemn, rose like sentinels on either side, and the absolute darkness of the night swallowed the world beyond the reach of the motorcycles' headlights.

She lifted her chin slightly to get a better look at her new surroundings… and immediately wished she hadn't.

Shadows darted between the trees' pale trunks, fleeting and formless. Off to her left, she would swear she saw the glow of eyes—some night animal tracking their progress through its domain. Off to her right, a tree branch fell onto the forest floor, the bed of needles absorbing the landing and oddly muffling the sound.

Trees. Trees. Nothing but unlimited, eternal trees.

But then...

The forest gave way to a clearing. And in the center of that clearing, caught in the sharp beams of the headlights, sat a cabin.

It huddled low and furtive in the night. Its siding had grayed with weather and age, and its roof was overrun by thick, cloying moss. Not a single flicker of light showed in the dark windows that stared back at her like a pair of soulless eyes.

The air seemed to grow colder as they approached, as if the cabin exhaled a chill breath that crept across the little clearing and tunneled down the neck of her borrowed coat to nip with sharp teeth at the skin of her chest.

The front door was painted bloodred and reminded her of a closed mouth. She couldn't shake the sensation that it offered no welcome, only a malignant invitation to step inside, to become part of the darkness that clung to it like a second skin.

Either she shuddered or gasped or Hew simply sensed her horror because he slipped his big, gloved hand into his pocket to squeeze her fingers.

Good god, Sabrina. Stop letting your imagination play tricks on you, she silently chastised herself.

This wasn't a Stephen King novel. The things she should fear weren't a haunted car or an alien clown. They were *real*.

Her brother was dead. An entire cartel was after her. So was the FBI. And if she was to believe Knox and all the folks back at the motorcycle shop, that last thing was the most dangerous.

Hew cut the engine and toed out the kickstand. His helmet was unbuckled and off his head in one smooth motion. For the first time, she noticed the crescent-shaped scar on his temple—the smooth line was a silvery-white reminder of some long-ago injury.

When Knox walked his motorcycle up beside them and cut the engine, silence descended like a shroud. Not a cricket chirped. Not a night bird cheeped. Not a breath of wind rustled the needles on the trees' limbs.

Hew cocked his head like a predator scenting prey, and Sabrina felt her stomach hollow out as visions of Pennywise and Cujo danced in her head.

"Sabrina." The way he said her name, so clear and concise in the secret silence of the forest, made her jump. "You want to go ahead and hop off?"

It wasn't a question—even though it'd been posed as one. It was a command. And it was offered up in such an easy, off-handed way that she knew he was used to giving orders and equally used to having them obeyed.

What's his story? she wondered absently. *What was his life like before going to work for Black Knights Inc.?*

Everything about him screamed authority and self-assurance. Not *arrogance*. Just a soul-deep certainty that he could take all comers.

There was comfort in that, she supposed. Comfort in going on the lam with a man who'd been tested repeatedly and who'd come out the winner.

Maybe *that* was why she hadn't scrambled off his lap in the pantry. Maybe some part of her subconscious had registered the safety he provided. The security he offered.

Her mind mutinied at the thought of getting off the bike. But she dug down deep and managed to swing her leg over the back of the machine.

It was wild to think she'd spent hours doing little more than sitting in one place, and yet it felt like she'd run a marathon. Muscles she wasn't even aware she had ached, and her bones felt simultaneously heavy and hollow. When she pulled off her helmet, the whole world tilted.

"Whoa there." Hew grabbed her hand to steady her. She could feel the warmth of his skin even through the leather of his gloves. "Easy now. Give yourself a little time to adjust. You're like a sailor with sea legs. Sitting on the back of a motorcycle for hours on end puts a lot more strain on a body than you'd think."

"Thank you," she said absently as Knox cut off his headlight, halving the illumination around the little clearing and bathing the cabin in deeper shadows. "This place is…spooky," she whispered. Her breath formed little clouds that glowed like pixie dust in the lone beam of Hew's lone headlight.

"It's 'cause it's deserted and dark," he reassured her. "Once I get the generator going, you'll feel better. This is a safe place."

She wasn't so sure about that, but she didn't say as much as she watched him dismount in a practiced move that was all easy motion and bunching muscles.

He skirted around her, heading toward the backyard, and the beam of his headlight cast his shadow against the cabin.

He was a big man.

His shadow was even bigger.

Something about the way it moved over the gray siding and green moss roof sent that creepy, crawly sensation skittering along the back of her neck.

She shuddered when Knox wrapped a hand around her elbow. He gave it a reassuring squeeze. "He's right, you know. Britt wouldn't have brought us here unless it was safe."

His tone was…somber-sounding. Almost beaten. A quick glance at his face had her turning to stare at him more fully.

Knox Rollins had seemed so confident, so sure of himself throughout the entire ordeal that it'd been easy for her to be sure of him, too. Now he looked as awful as she felt. Broken and unspeakably weary.

"I'm sorry about your brother," she whispered. "I know you're worried about him."

"Thanks." He nodded. "I just wish I'd been able to—"

The low rumble of an engine interrupted him midsentence. And, just like that, the shadows disappeared.

The porch light beside the front door lit up, highlighting the window boxes attached to the windows. Someone had planted mums in them, and the red, yellow, and orange blossoms looked cheery and inviting. The graying siding no longer appeared aged and decrepit. It looked weathered and rustic. And the moss on the roof no longer seemed wild and unkempt. Now, it looked more like the roof of a little hobbit house, bucolic and cozy.

Inside, a lamp burned on a table. In the golden glow, she could see a comfy couch, a grouping of black-and-white photographs, and an overstuffed chair whose well-loved cushions promised peace and comfort.

She was no longer living inside a Stephen King novel. This place was something out of a children's book, cheerful and colorful and welcoming.

Hew came around from the back of the house and made a sweeping gesture toward the front door. "Your home away from home."

She was already on her way to the door—and the armchair inside that looked big enough to curl up on—but Knox's next words stopped her in her tracks.

"You think Britt's okay?" She could hear the anxiety in his voice, the *guilt*.

"Britt's the most resourceful sonofabitch I've ever met," Hew assured him as he marched back to his bike to thumb off the headlight. His accent turned the word *resourceful* into *re-sauce-ful*. "If anyone can outsmart the FBI, it's Rollins."

She watched Hew pull a bag from the compartment on the back of his bike. He'd unzipped his jacket. So when he slung the bag over his shoulder, it made one side of the leather material swing wide. Her eyes rounded when she saw the nylon shoulder holster and the matte-black butt of the weapon inside it.

It wasn't that she was shocked to find him armed. This was America—the wild, wild west of developed nations. A quarter of the population packed heat in one way or another. But Hew's setup was one more piece of a puzzle beginning to take shape in her mind.

No one at Black Knights Inc. had batted a lash at Knox's story. The handsome, wild-haired man named Ozzie had seemed sure he could find the villain who'd outed Knox and her brother to the cartel, given enough time. There was that strange, terrifying tunnel that appeared behind a secret brick wall in the motorcycle shop—a tunnel dug down *under* the frickin' Chicago River. And there was the way both Britt and Hew moved, with an economy of motion she'd only seen in stuntmen and soldiers.

All of that combined to tell her there was more to the men and women who worked at Black Knights Inc. than met the eye.

If it walks like a duck and talks like a duck, survey says it's a duck.

But for the life of her, she couldn't fathom what kind of duck she was dealing with.

Pinning Hew with a searching look, she asked, "Who *are* you people? The Black Knights, I mean," she clarified a bit breathlessly. "You're more than just motorcycle mechanics, aren't you?"

"If I answered that, I'd have to kill you."

It was said as a joke. But the hint of steel in his voice matched the hint of steel in his eyes.

When she shivered, it wasn't because the night was growing colder by the minute.

CHAPTER 14

Huron-Manistee National Forest

"No luck on the other two motorcycles," Agent Keplar grumbled, and Julia could sense the violence in him.

It'd become clear over the preceding hours that of the two feds from South Carolina, it was Ryan Keplar who was most determined to find Knox Rollins. A quick aside with Agent Maddox had revealed why.

Knox had been Keplar's asset. It'd been Keplar who'd first recruited Cooper Greenlee and Knox Rollins to be the FBI's moles inside the narcotics trafficking operation. This meant Keplar took Knox's betrayal and the subsequent implosion of their joint operation with the ATF and IRS personally.

Not that a scream of frustration didn't threaten in Julia's own throat. But her fury had nothing to do with Knox Rollins—she didn't know the man from Adam. It was leveled solely on Black Knights Inc. And, more specifically, Sergeant Britt Rollins.

"But they did find this." Keplar slapped a heavy Maglite flashlight into her hand. "It was taped to the motorcycle's fender." He hooked a thumb over his shoulder to indicate the line of pines standing guard around the farmhouse and its fields.

She could see the beams from the tactical team's flashlights bouncing around the thick tree trunks as they continued searching for the rider of the lone motorcycle. But it'd already been an hour since she'd watched them fast-rope out of the helicopter. And so far...nada.

Every trail of footprints they'd found in the woods had petered out. Every tree with limbs low enough to climb had been spotlighted and searched. And every streambed and washed-out crevice within a one-mile radius had been scoured inch by inch.

The rider was gone.

Either he'd managed to run beyond their search parameters, or he was hiding somewhere they couldn't find him without the help of thermal imaging. And the infrared drone they'd brought with them for that express purpose had given up the ghost on its maiden flight.

It was currently in pieces on the ground beside the helicopter as the agent certified to fly the sucker used a headlamp to do repairs.

Initially, Julia had been sure the tactical team would locate whoever had manned the wrecked motorcycle. After all, they were four highly trained agents who'd been schooled to find even the savviest of escapees. And besides, how far could one man get on his own?

But as the minutes dragged on—and from listening to the frustrated chatter over the radio—it had become increasingly apparent that the searchers had given up on their current tact and were preparing to expand their search.

Good luck, she thought despondently, knowing that the more time passed, the *less* likely they'd find their mark. Either the rider was putting more distance between them. Or he was holed up in a spot so covert and concealed that it would take a bloodhound to locate it.

"Taped to the fender you say?" She frowned down at the flashlight in her hand. "But why would—" She didn't finish her own question because the answer suddenly came to her. "The three headlights we were chasing." She closed her eyes and pictured the faint beams she'd seen over the side of the chopper as they'd hovered above the thick copse of trees. "It wasn't three headlights at all, was it?"

"Doesn't appear so." Keplar shook his head, a muscle beneath his right eye twitching. Even in the muted yellow glow of the farmhouse's porchlight, she could see his color was heightened. And despite the crisp nip in the air, sweat beaded his brow.

"That means whomever the rider is, he split off from the other motorcyclists after they lost that New Buffalo police officer." The next words tasted sour in her mouth. "And that means it's got to be Britt Rollins, right? He used himself as a distraction so his brother and the mystery woman could go on to parts unknown."

"Or, if you were right about Hewitt Birch being part of the group, maybe he was the one doing the distracting," Dillan supplied from his spot on the bottom step of the porch.

"Maybe," she allowed, although something told her if anyone was going to sacrifice themselves, it would be Britt.

She narrowed her eyes as she surveyed the dark fields beyond the farmhouse, imagining she could feel where he was if she concentrated hard enough. They had that connection, after all.

Agent Maddox climbed the steps to join Julia and Keplar on the porch. His sandy hair was wild and begging for a good brushing. Then again, so was hers. Helicopter rides weren't meant to maintain careful coiffures. "We ran the wrecked motorcycle's plates. They came back as belonging to Black Knights Inc., not Rollins or Birch in particular. We can't confidently say who was riding the bike. But whoever it was, they were the carrot. And we chased them down like a bunch of braying jackasses."

"And the CCTV footage we pulled?" she queried Dillan. Her question had him standing from his seat on the bottom step and dusting off his trousers.

"Nothing." He shook his head. "The techs back at headquarters checked the video recordings from the time you and I arrived at the factory building this morning to when we went back with warrants to search the place this evening. There's no footage of the Rollins brothers, Birch, or the mystery woman leaving. Not unless they were riding in the trunk of Becky Knight's car when she left for the evening."

"I guess it's possible they escaped in the trunk and hopped on the motorcycles elsewhere," Julia mused, her mind racing with possibilities.

"Yeah. But they'd have been stacked in like sardines." Dillan made a face. "Mrs. Knight drives a restored 1968 Porsche 911. That model isn't known for its cavernous trunk space. I can't imagine it would fit three grown adults."

Julia narrowed her eyes as more and more puzzle pieces *didn't* fall into place.

There's something very wrong about all of this, she thought.

She had a nagging sense of *something*. She couldn't put her finger on it, but it was there, itching, scratching at her brain like sand in her sheets.

"So what's our next move?" She posed the question to Maddox and Keplar. She and Dillan might've been the ones to facilitate the search, but it was the South Carolina agents' operation. It was *their* fugitive on the run.

"We head north." Keplar ran a hand back over his thinning hair. "We've already alerted the border authorities on both sides to be on the lookout for Knox Rollins. But he could cross into Canadian waters via Lake Huron if he steals a boat. Or if he stays on land until he makes it to Michigan's upper peninsula, he could do the same thing on Lake Superior. We need to get more birds in the sky." His disgust was palpable when he glanced over at the agent working on the drone. "And definitely more drones. Preferably ones that *work*."

"Should I call in the tactical team?" Maddox lifted a hand to the earpiece he wore.

"Leave two of them here to continue the hunt for whoever was riding that wrecked bike," Keplar declared. "If we catch them, we might be able to squeeze them into giving up the others' location or destination."

"I'd like to stay behind, too." The words were out of Julia's mouth before she'd even decided to speak them.

Maddox cocked his head, eyeing her curiously. "Why?"

"Because I'm a pretty good interrogator if I say so myself. Plus, I laid some friendly groundwork with the people at BKI when Agent Douglas and I worked the Senator McClean case. If the tactical guys catch Rollins or Birch, they'll probably open up to me before they open up to anyone."

"Your friendly groundwork didn't win you any favors when you went to the motorcycle shop this morning," Keplar said, his beady black eyes watching her closely. "Nor did it seem to sway the folks at Black Knights Inc. this evening."

Professionalism dictated she smile, say something appropriately deescalating, and then switch the subject. But she had three older brothers and an old-fashioned father who had taught her that backing down from an insult was tantamount to accepting defeat in an argument.

Her voice was so sugary-sweet that her teeth ached when she said, "That was me asking questions *nicely*. You haven't seen me when I decide to get nasty."

Plus, she thought, *if it was Britt riding that wrecked bike, I want to take the first stab at him. I want to look him in the eye and tell him he's the lowest of lowdown dirty dogs for using my attraction for him against me.*

"She's not lying," Dillan declared with a staunch dip of his chin. "When she sets her mind to it, she can make a priest forget the sanctity of the confessional."

Her jaw was slack as she gazed at her partner.

"What?" Dillan lifted his hands. "I may not like being bossed around by a pipsqueak I could punt over the fence, but that doesn't mean I don't appreciate your professional prowess."

A small smile tugged at the corner of her mouth. "That might be the nicest thing you've ever said to me. Extra points for the alliteration."

"Degree from Cornell, remember?" His arrogant grin widened over the name of his Ivy League university.

Her smile melted away as she rolled her eyes. "How could I forget when you never miss an opportunity to remind me?"

"Suit yourself and stay," Keplar tossed over his shoulder. He was already trotting down the weathered porch steps. "We'll let the tactical guys staying behind know you'll be here with them."

Agent Maddox turned from watching his partner jog toward the waiting chopper and offered her an abashed grin. "He's not that bad once you get to know him." When she lifted an eyebrow in disbelief, he relented. "Okay, fine. So he is that bad. Sorry." He shrugged and then took off after Keplar.

"You want me to stay with you?" The single glowing bulb beside the front door spotlighted Dillan's longing gaze as he watched the two South Carolina agents hop into the waiting helicopter and helpfully accept the drone pieces the operator handed them. Two of the four tactical guys emerged from the woods and crossed the cleared field as the pilot switched on the chopper's engine. The remaining two searchers began a methodical route around the perimeter of the farmhouse, the beams from their one-thousand-lumen flashlights lighting up limbs like it was high noon on a sunny day.

She had to raise her voice above the noise of the chopper as she nudged Dillan with her elbow. "Nah. You go on. I know you're itching to have your Harrison Ford moment."

His smile reminded her of a kid who'd just been given money for the ice cream truck.

"For the record, it's a Tommy Lee Jones moment I'm after. He was the federal agent who was after Ford. And thanks for understanding. If it wouldn't hurt my back to bend down so far, and if I weren't scared you'd punch me in the face, I'd kiss you right now."

"I might go ahead and punch you in the face just for making another short joke." She gathered her hair in her hand to stop it from whipping around her face.

"That's my cue!" Dillan lifted a finger. He didn't bother taking the stairs. He hopped off the porch and hit the ground running.

She shook her head at the skip in his step. Then she shielded her eyes from the frenzy of blowing dirt when the big, black bird hopped into the sky in a wash of hurricane-force winds.

Once the helicopter gained enough altitude, she stepped onto the top step and watched the chopper get swallowed up in the blackness of the night sky. After a while, the engine noise was little more than a distant purr, and all she could see of the aircraft was the rhythmic flash of the white navigation light on its tail.

She alighted onto the second step, intent on rechecking the area between the fields and the house even though she'd already checked it *twice*. But before she hit the third step, the hairs on the back of her neck lifted.

Not to put too fine a point on it, but now that she was alone—the tactical guys had moved their search around to the left side of the house—and now that the hulking helicopter and its promise of a quick escape had been removed, she had to admit the empty farmhouse in the middle of nowhere with its creaky boards and crumbling paint was spooky as hell.

It wasn't like it was *abandoned*. The recently swept porch, cheery welcome mat, and kid's toys littering the front yard said whoever owned the property had no intention of being gone for long. But without the living energy of people and animals, the place *felt* abandoned.

Abandoned and malevolent and somehow…sentient.

How many movies started as thrillers, with some flinty-eyed FBI agent on the hunt for a known criminal, only for the plot to suddenly devolve into a horror story where said agent was chased through the woods by something that was only supposed to exist in fairy tales to frighten children?

She wrapped her arms around herself. Not so much for the warmth but to hold herself together against the rising tide of unease.

A gust of wind whipped up the leaves collected in the overgrown flowerbed. It brought with it the smell of decaying plant matter and…was that death? Had some animal met its end nearby, and now its carcass sat rotting in the bushes?

The trees seemed to shiver, their branches clawing at the sky as if they, too, sensed something foul and menacing lurking just out of sight.

"Screw this," she muttered as she hopped back onto the porch and raced around two corners until she'd made it to the back of the house.

She spied the two beams from the tactical team as they continued their sweep. But getting visual confirmation she wasn't entirely alone didn't bring as much comfort as she thought it would.

There was a strange weight in the air. It was there at the edge of her awareness, waiting, *watching*. An electrical tension that made her skin prickle as if the night itself held its breath.

Get it together, Jules. Sheesh.

She squared her shoulders. Blew out a steadying breath. And then it happened.

A shadow moved.

Or…at least she *thought* it did. It was much darker at the back of the house without the porch light cutting through the relentless blackness of the night.

She stared hard, her desperate eyes scanning the area between the house and where the trees loomed out of the ground like silent sentinels that guarded secrets only the night knew.

There it was again.

Movement.

She was sure of it.

Wasting no time slinking farther into the safety of the shadows clinging to the old wooden porch, she pressed her back against the rough siding. Her hand automatically sought the butt of her duty weapon, her fingers curling around the cold metal as her pulse thundered in her ears.

Man or animal? she wondered and opened her mouth to call out to the two tactical guys. But indecision stilled her voice.

What if it *was* just an animal? A deer or a bobcat or maybe even a skunk? How foolish would she feel pulling the agents off their hunt to help her shoo away a harmless woodland creature?

Slipping into a crouch on the porch, she made herself as small as possible as her eyes strained to make sense of the movement across the field.

It was impossible to tell what it was. The darkness was too vast, too intense. But whatever it was, it was approaching. And quickly too. It pushed through the tall grass with silent, relentless resolve.

An owl screeched somewhere nearby. A rustle sounded in the weeds just off the back porch.

Predator and prey.

Which category did the approaching shadow fall into? And what was *she* by contrast?

The questions buzzed like angry wasps, each one stinging her with dread as the seconds ticked by and the unknown *thing* crept closer.

Then it happened. The black shadow took shape, sharpening from an amorphous blob into the silhouette of a man.

Some lonely, reclusive hermit who'd watched all the action and who'd waited to step into the clearing until he saw her standing by herself?

What did he want? To bash her over the head and drag her to his cabin deep in the woods where he'd hold her captive and force her to bear his squealing, grubby babies?

She'd have blamed her racing mind on having watched one too many horror movies. But she was an FBI agent. She'd seen how fact was oftentimes stranger—and more terrifying—than fiction.

With slow, practiced motions, she thumbed off the safety snap on her shoulder holster, wincing when the *snick* sounded obscenely loud inside the silence shrouding the porch. Then, inch by inch, she pulled her weapon from the leather.

The man was close now. Maybe fifty yards away.

His posture, partially hunched over, head on a pivot as he surveyed his surroundings, told her he wanted to gain ground without being seen.

Tension knotted her intestines until she felt nauseous. When the man turned and made for the small, dilapidated barn, recognition dawned like a slow sunrise. Her fears were instantly dispelled, and her jaw was instantly hard.

She'd know those broad shoulders and that flyaway hair anywhere. She'd seen them a million times in her dreams.

Sergeant Britt Rollins.

Gotcha!

CHAPTER 15

Britt's first indication that he wasn't alone inside the small barn was the hairs on the back of his neck lifting in warning.

And in that moment, it was less about training and more about instinct—ancestral knowledge lodged deep in the very nuclei of his cells told him to get ready to act.

His eyesight sharpened in the stygian gloom. His nose twitched with the smells of rusting metal and molding hay. His ears heard every sound as if blasted through a megaphone—the creak of the wood on the siding as a breeze blew by, the squeak of a field mouse in the back corner, and his breathing going slow and steady.

Before he'd begun his furtive trip across the field, he'd unzipped his jacket to give himself easy access to the sidearm strapped tight against his rib cage. But he didn't have time to slip it from his holster before the air shifted around him. Before he felt the cold steel kiss of a gun barrel on the back of his head.

If there had been a mirror in front of him, it would've reflected the quick upward twitch of his lips.

Rookie mistake, he thought as his training took over.

In one lightning-quick move, he spun. His hands made contact with the weapon, twisting so it snapped around at one-hundred-and-eighty degrees. If his assailant had had his finger on the trigger, it would've easily hyper-extended the digit and then just as easily snapped it in two.

He realized two things as he gained control of the pistol and pointed it between the eyes of the guy who'd tried to sneak up on him. The first was that his attacker hadn't had their finger on the trigger. There was no added resistance as the weapon changed hands, no bark of pain as bones broke. The second was that his would-be assailant wasn't a man but a woman.

Not just any woman.

The woman.

Even in the darkness, there was no mistaking her diminutive stature or the way two locks of hair had escaped her messy, windblown bun to hang next to her cheeks and softly frame her face. The whites of her eyes stood out in the gloom. And the defiant tilt of her chin had him fighting a responding smile.

He may have caught her off guard but hadn't bested her. She wasn't beaten. Quite the contrary, her stiff posture and glittering gaze challenged him to do his worst.

He lowered the pistol…er…*her* pistol, pointing the deadly end at the ground. Her eyes followed the movement, and he thought he detected the muscles in her jaws twitching a second before she lifted her chin, her gaze slicing through the dark to clash with his.

And there it is, he thought. *That undeniable…something.*

He could feel it stretching between them. *Pulling* at them.

She wore her rage as easily and clearly as he'd once worn a military uniform, and he imagined he could see the waves of challenge rolling out of her.

In contrast, he adopted a casual tone. "Fancy seeing you here, Agent O'Toole."

He had assumed she'd hopped on the chopper with the others. He hadn't *seen* her do it because he'd ducked deep inside the log when two searchers shined their flashlights all over his hidey-hole. Now, he chastised himself for not waiting to ensure no one other than the two tactical team guys had stayed behind.

"I thought you'd be on that helicopter with the others. Reckoned the bloodhound in you wouldn't let you give up the chase for the bad guys."

He wasn't sure what he'd expected her to say in response, but it certainly wasn't, "You *kissed* me, you motherfucker."

Ah, yes. The deepest depths of my betrayal.

He understood. It would have been one thing if he'd simply lied to her. But it was something else entirely to have used her desire against her.

To his chagrin, her mere *mention* of that kiss had his blood warming and running south of the border. But, for the time being, he ignored the little head in his pants to fully utilize the big one hanging off the end of his neck.

The way he saw it, he had two options. He could beg for forgiveness. Which would likely prove futile even though he actually *was* sorry he'd taken advantage of her. Or he could play the role she'd already assigned him. That of an unscrupulous asshole.

He went with option number two.

"I did kiss you," he admitted with a blasé shrug. "And if I were more of a gentleman, I might apologize for that. But since we both enjoyed ourselves immensely—"

When she opened her mouth to argue, he shook his head. "Don't do yourself the disservice of claiming otherwise." He stepped forward, invading her space. He wasn't surprised she didn't take a step back. Instead, she tilted her piquant little chin and shot daggers at him through her narrowed eyes.

God, she's glorious, he admitted as her subtle perfume invaded his nostrils and had his jaw hardening along with...other parts of his body.

"Because I remember how hungry you were," he continued relentlessly, his gaze dropping to her generous mouth. "How...*hot* you were." He intentionally added the pause and the emphasis.

They both knew he wasn't talking in generalities. One very specific part of her had been flaming hot...and sopping wet.

His words made her nostrils flare. Made her jaw set at a sharp angle. If rage had a physical form, it would be Julia O'Toole.

Fine. Good. She can hate me, he told himself. If she hated him, she'd stop him from pulling her into his arms and attempting a repeat of what they'd shared in the kitchen.

It was taking everything he had not to give it a try.

"If I were fifty pounds heavier, I'd kick your ass up between your shoulder blades and then rip off your dick and make you eat it," she snarled, her chest rising and falling in angry huffs that drew his eyes to the delicate hollow at the base of her throat.

He wanted to press his lips there. Taste the warmth of her skin until the flavor was imprinted on his brain. Drag his tongue over the little divot to hear her gasp and whisper his name.

"You're welcome to try, sugar pants."

Her right eye twitched. "Did you just call me sugar pants?"

"It was my second choice."

Her chin jerked back. "What was your first choice?"

"Sexiest woman on the planet."

She snorted. "Flattery will get you nowhere. I'm onto you. This thing…" She waved a hand between them. "It's smoke and mirrors. Just an act that I was dumb enough to fall for."

"Bullshit," he spat, offended she'd discount what was so clearly obvious between them.

"Excuse me?"

"You're a smart woman. You know better than to peddle bullshit." He took that last step, stopping when the tips of his biker boots kissed the toes of her duty shoes. "This thing?" He touched his chest before placing his palm flat over *her* chest. He wasn't a mammoth like Graham or Hew. But his hand looked huge against her small frame. His fingers rested on one side of her slim throat while his thumb rested on the other. He could feel the brutal hammer of her pulse. Feel the delicate warmth of her skin that beckoned… no, it absolutely *begged* to be explored. "Ain't no way to fake it. Everything else may be a lie. But *this*?" He ducked his chin so they were on eye level. So she could see the absolute truth glittering in his gaze. "This is real."

The light of battle shining in her eyes melted into longing. Her mouth fell open slightly, giving him a ball-tightening glimpse of her delectable pink tongue.

For a split second, he thought she might go up on tiptoe and kiss him. Might give in to that…*something* that seemed to be constantly pulling them together like opposite ends of a magnet.

He didn't know if he was disappointed or relieved when she turned away instead.

The hand he'd placed on her chest fell to his side, and he shoved it into his jacket pocket. Her body heat had branded his palm, and the softness of her skin lingered on the calluses of his fingertips. He wanted to hold onto both sensations. Protect them. *Savor* them.

Why does this woman have such a hold on me? he marveled.

It wasn't because she was beautiful. He'd known plenty of beautiful women. It wasn't because she was brilliant—although he'd always been attracted to brains. And it wasn't even because she was frisky and funny and fabulously sexy.

It was because he couldn't have her and because, for the first time in his life, he wished things were different. Wished *he* were different.

When she moved toward the door, alarm bells rang in his head and drowned out his shouting thoughts. He didn't know where the remaining tactical team members were, but he sure as shit couldn't have her alerting them to his presence.

"Don't take another step," he warned, his fingers curling tightly around the grip of her gun.

It was a large weapon for such a small woman. But he wasn't surprised. Julia was one of the most capable individuals he'd ever met. The kind of woman who'd grown up in a man's world and, through grit and determination, had clawed her way to the top.

Of course she'd carry a pistol that'd put a grown man flat on his ass with one shot.

Slowly, ever so slowly, she turned her head until she was staring at him over her shoulder. Even in the darkness, he could see how her eyes tracked down to the weapon in his hand.

He hadn't raised it, but the threat was there nonetheless.

"Or what?" she challenged. "You'll shoot me?"

"Never." The word was out of his mouth before he could stop it. He saw surprise briefly flash in her eyes before she shuttered her expression. "But I can't say the same thing for the men still out there searching for me. If it comes down to them or me, I won't hesitate."

He didn't include that he'd go for shots that *maimed* rather than killed. Admitting as much would lessen the strength of his threat.

Turning toward him fully, he watched as she tucked all her anger and betrayal into the corner of her heart. Her clenched fingers unfurled, and the righteous light of fury dimmed in her eyes, leaving only cool calculation.

Gone was the hotheaded, red-blooded woman.

In her place stood the calm, collected federal agent.

"Where is your brother?" The question was so direct that he was momentarily taken aback.

Before the idea fully formed—and certainly before he'd thought through all the repercussions—he blurted, "Come with me, and I'll show you."

"Wh-what?" she blinked.

"I'll take you to my brother," he reiterated.

Her eyebrows pinched together over her nose, emphasizing her disbelief and making him think how damned adorable she looked when she was in FBI agent mode. Then again, she looked damned adorable in family picnic day mode and wrestling with her dogs on the front lawn mode and clipping her cat's nails mode and…well…*any* mode, really. Because she *was* damned adorable. From the tips of her delicate toes to the top of her old-money blond head, she was the most delightful creature he'd ever crossed paths with and—

His thoughts had spiraled wildly, but her question had him crash-landing back into the conversation. "Why would you do that after everything you've done to keep him away from me?"

"I wasn't trying to keep him away from *you*. It's the organization you represent. There's more going on here than you realize. My brother is innocent." He frowned when it dawned on him that wasn't entirely true. And he was done misleading Julia. "Well…" He offered her a weary shrug. "As innocent as an ex-con can ever be. And I can prove it to you."

He saw the light of curiosity spark in her eyes. But her face remained expressionless. "If that's true, he would've gone to his handlers the moment Cooper Greenlee died. Instead, he ran halfway across the country. Innocent men don't run."

"They do when they can't trust their handlers," he countered easily. "They do when someone inside the joint task force gives them up and reveals their covers to the cartel."

The emotionless mask she'd donned slipped. "Who?" she demanded. "Who outed them?"

Taking a deep breath—*there's no going back now, Rollins*—he let her weapon dangle from his finger by the trigger guard. Holding it out to her as a peace offering, he said enticingly, "That's what I'm hoping you'll help me figure out."

She took a hesitant step forward. She eyed him like a mouse watching a snake when she lifted a hand toward the weapon he offered.

"Take it," he said softly. "It's yours."

In a flash, she snatched the weapon and spun it around so that the deadly hollow eye aimed center mass. She was smarter than she'd been before. This time, she kept more than an arm's length of distance between them.

"Why should I believe anything you say?" Her nostrils flared. "You had no problem lying to me this morning."

He watched her closely for the span of a dozen heartbeats. Noted the lovely way her breasts stretched tight the top button on her blouse. And decided he would give it to her straight and risk pissing her off further because he needed her to know. Needed her to realize this one fundamental truth.

"Now's probably not the time to split hairs." He shrugged. "But I never lied to you."

"The hell you didn't." Her grip on the pistol was rock steady.

"You asked me when Knox called me the last time," he explained, keeping his tone even. "I told you the truth when I said it'd been months since I talked to him on the phone."

"You're playing the semantics game with me?" Her jaw sawed back and forth. "Seriously?"

"I'm hoping to make you understand that, yes, I may have taken advantage of your wording and answered in a way that, while truthful, was also misleading. But, Julia..." Her lips parted oh-so-delicately when he said her name. "I never *lied* to you. I *will* never lie to you. That's a promise."

Her mouth snapped shut as she narrowed her eyes.

"It's the truth," he said simply. "But regardless of whether or not you believe me, the way I see it, you have two choices. You can arrest me, hold me, and miss out on the chance to figure out the truth about my brother. Or you can trust me, come with me, and help me blow this entire case wide open."

He reached for the sidearm concealed beneath his jacket to sweeten the deal.

"I *will* shoot you," she warned, instinctively putting more distance between them.

He lifted his hands, palm out. "You certainly weren't of a mind to do that when you pressed that there bang stick against the back of my head." He hitched his chin toward the gun in her hand. When she frowned, he clarified. "Your finger wasn't even on the trigger. If it *had* been, your lovely little digit would be pointing ninety degrees in the wrong direction."

Why did he feel so smug about that? About knowing she *hadn't* wanted to kill him?

"Yeah, well." She snorted. "I learned my lesson. I won't make the same mistake twice."

"If you humor me, I'm about to give you a second weapon that you can use to end me," he assured her. "You know, if you decide you're of a mind to."

The creak of the barn's siding sounded particularly loud as she watched him, debating. Then, she nodded. "Pull your jacket wide so I can see your every move."

It was too dark for her to see his *every* move. But he refrained from pointing that out. Instead, he used one hand to pull the flap of his jacket wide, revealing his shoulder holster and the Berretta M9 it held.

Using only his thumb and forefinger, he carefully unsnapped the safety strap and slowly pulled out the sidearm that had seen him through the Black Knights's hairiest missions.

This is my gun. There are many like it. But this one is mine.

The rifleman's creed shouted through his head—that iconic little ditty made famous by the Marines. It went against the grain, every soldier's instinct, to give up his weapon. But the situation called for a sacrifice. And for Julia's sake, he was happy to make it.

Holding the butt of the gun gingerly between two fingers, he offered it to her.

Her gaze flicked from his pistol to his face. He *hated* the distrust he saw in her eyes. Hated that he'd given her any reason to think he'd double-cross her. And he wasn't surprised when she snatched the weapon from his grip only to point it straight at his chest.

Now he had *two* pistols aimed center mass.

Lucky me.

"It has an ambidextrous external safety lever," he explained calmly. "So you can disengage it from either side."

"I *am* a trained agent," she snarled. "I know how to use a handgun."

"Okay." Once again, he lifted his hands, palms out. "It's just that I noticed you carry a Glock 19, which has the double trigger safety instead of the external lever, so—"

"I might shoot you just for being a condescending asshole."

His lips twitched, but he wisely shut his mouth.

For a couple of seconds, they simply stood there, staring at each other through the darkness. He watched her seesaw with indecision, and she watched him for any false move.

He didn't make any.

When her shoulders finally relaxed, he figured it was time to put the cherry on top of the sundae. "It'll be one hell of a feather in your cap if you're the one to uncover the rat inside that joint operation. And since you're in the business of putting bad guys behind bars, think how good it'll feel to pull a reverse Uno card and keep an innocent man *outside* of them."

He breathed a secret sigh of relief when she finally lowered both weapons. "You're lucky my natural curiosity always gets the best of me."

Warmth spread through his chest. He offered her a wide grin. "In my experience, there's no such thing as luck."

She didn't disappoint. She immediately picked up on the quote from *A New Hope*. But she didn't come back with a quote of her own. Instead, she said, "Okay, Obi-Wan. So you've got me where you want me. Now what?"

"Now we ride out of here so I can introduce you to my brother." He looked expectantly at the rusting truck.

Her gaze followed his. Skepticism colored her face. "There's no way that thing's engine works. I'll be surprised if it even *has* an engine."

He hadn't been sure either. But he'd ducked his head under the front bumper to get a look at the truck's condition in the seconds before she'd pushed her pistol into the back of his head. To his delight, instead of seeing rusting metal and frayed wires, he'd spied a recently replaced crankshaft and a brand-spanking-new battery.

He gently patted the hood. "Don't be so sure. The Millennium Falcon wasn't much to look at. But she made the Kessel Run in less than twelve parsecs."

Annoyed by his continued effort to make her smile, she shot him a dirty look.

Hey, that was better than shooting him in the chest. He'd take it.

After opening the passenger door—and wincing slightly when the rusty hinges groaned—he motioned for her to climb inside. She hesitated, just for a moment. Then she holstered her weapon, slipped his pistol into the pocket of her suit jacket, and slid easily onto the threadbare bench seat.

Had it not threatened to draw the tactical guys' attention, he would have whooped in victory. Instead, he quickly skirted the hood, climbed into the driver's side, and pulled down the visor.

No keys.

He next tried the glove box, the ashtray, and the top of the dash and came up empty-handed each time.

"Guess we're doing this the old-fashioned way," he muttered as he popped off the plastic casing around the steering column.

Thumbing on the flashlight still taped around his forearm, he shone the beam onto the exposed wires before slipping his multitool from his pocket. When he flicked open the knife, Julia edged closer to the door, her hand automatically going for the weapon she'd stowed in her holster.

"Easy," he told her, doing his best to concentrate on the scents of aged metal and spilled oil so he *wouldn't* get distracted by the faint smell of her perfume. "I'll give you my multitool after I finish."

She didn't say anything, but he heard the breath she released. He took that as his cue to proceed.

After finding the correct wires, he quickly stripped their insulation. True to his word, as soon as he was finished, he folded the knife back into the casing and handed it over.

A part of him thought she might wave him off. After all, what was a multitool against two pistols? But she didn't hesitate to snatch the gadget from his hand and slip it into her jacket pocket.

He bit the inside of his cheek to keep from grinning. Then he sobered and said, "And now it's time for some quid pro quo."

Her expression hardened. "I should've known this deal was too good to be true."

He refrained from thinking too long about how easy it would be to slide across that bench seat, take her in his arms, and prove she'd been a fool when she'd so easily dismissed the electric connection that sparked between them.

"You need to toss your phone." When she balked at the idea, he pressed on. "I can't have your colleagues tracking you before I show you my proof."

Her jaw sawed back and forth in indecision.

He made one last promise. "If you want me to drive you to the nearest phone after you've talked to Knox, I will. You can call in the cavalry to come get you. And I'm hoping, by that point, you'll be willing to keep our location a secret until we can clear Knox's name. But that'll be up to you." He offered her his most charming grin. "See? I'm willing to take a chance on you. How about you take a chance on me too?"

Her voice was rough when she said, "You're asking me to give up my one tether to the outside world while I let you take me to god knows where."

"You're the one with all the weapons," he countered.

She searched his eyes. She must've found something to convince her he was telling her the truth because she blew out a windy breath and slipped her phone from her fanny pack. She used the old-fashioned lever to roll down the window, then slid her cell phone through the breach. He heard it hit the dry dirt floor of the barn with a soft *thud*.

"Not that we're likely to be going anywhere," she said after she rolled up the window. "This bucket of bolts—"

Her sentence died in her throat when he sparked two wires together and the truck's engine turned over with a well-tuned purr.

"Gotta love country boys." He patted the dashboard affectionately. "Their equipment might look like shit on a shingle, but it usually runs like a racehorse."

She glanced at the exposed steering column and the dangling wires now illuminated by the light from the dash. "The Army Rangers teach you how to do that?"

He winced and admitted, "When your older brother gets his criminal start by boosting cars, you pick up a thing or two."

And then, before the remaining tactical team members could give chase, he slammed his foot on the gas and burst from the barn. The truck's nubby tires skipped across the gravel of the drive, forcing Julia to cling to the oh-shit bar bolted onto her door.

He glanced into the rearview mirror and saw the two remaining tactical team members racing across the field in their direction. Their flashlights blazed through the night to meet the red glare of his taillights.

Fortunately, they were too far away to take shots. And it wasn't long before the dust kicked up from the tires swallowed their images.

When he flew out of the driveway and onto the lane on two wheels, Julia screeched, "Where did you learn to drive?"

The laugh that burst from him was genuine. Despite how shitty his situation was, despite the danger to himself and his brother and the Black Knights, he had Julia O'Toole in the truck, and he couldn't remember the last time he'd been so happy.

"You're one to talk, Miss Hasn't Met a Curb She Doesn't Like."

"How would you know that?"

Shit.

He'd given himself away. Had broadcast the fact he'd been stalking her.

Thinking quickly, he turned the question back to her. "Am I wrong? Are you actually Dale Earnhardt in a dress?"

He breathed a sigh of relief when his distraction worked. "I *rarely* wear a dress. And isn't Earnhardt widely recognized as a world-class asshole? I think I'm offended."

He slid her a sly glance as he hung a right onto a county road. "That's too bad. I bet you look amazing in a dress."

She scowled at him. "Do us both a favor and keep your eyes on the road, Sergeant."

"Yes, ma'am."

He was grinning ear to ear.

CHAPTER 16

County Road 628, Traverse City

You're a damned idiot, Jules.

The refrain had circled in Julia's mind for the last hour. As the minutes stretched on, and as they'd taken so many turns down backwoods roads that she was completely turned around, it'd dawned on her that she was, in effect, putting her faith in a complete stranger.

Yes, she'd read Britt's file—what little of it was left. Yes, she'd spent months fantasizing about jumping on him like a bouncy house. Yes, she'd spoken to him several times, had flirted with him on half a dozen occasions, and had kissed him once. But what did she *really* know about him?

Jack shit, that's what.

Now here she was, driving through the middle of nowhere without any way to call for backup all because…what? Because he'd *asked* her to? Because he'd appealed to her natural nosiness? Because he was a baddie with a body?

You're a damned idiot, Jules.

If she'd been an actress in a movie, and had she also been in the audience *watching* that movie, she'd have thrown popcorn at the onscreen actress version of herself because *who goes with a perfect stranger into the middle of the freakin' Michigan wilderness with no way to get help?*

Casually, she slipped her hands into her jacket pockets. The fingers of her left hand curled around his multitool, and the fingers of her right hand curved around the butt of his Berretta.

When she chanced a glance over at him, she wasn't surprised to find his expression as alert and as focused as a hawk. Despite the casually expert way he guided the old farm truck along the rutted roads, he had a way of sitting perfectly still that was unnerving.

Special forces? Spies? Mercenaries? Those jobs attracted a certain kind of man. The duplicitous kind. The devilish kind. The *dangerous* kind. And just because he was currently being paid to turn a wrench, that didn't mean he'd forgotten all the diabolical things he'd been taught while being paid to play the heavy for Uncle Sam.

Fear fisted around her stomach as doubt continued to squeeze her heart.

"H-how much farther?" she asked, not caring for the hitch in her words.

"Not much." His deep voice filled the cab's interior. And when his icy-blue eyes cut toward her, a shudder of awareness tripped down her spine.

But was that awareness a result of the danger he posed? Or was it because he was so manfully enticing that, back when he was wearing the Army's uniform, he probably just melted his enemies' bullets before they could hit him?

"What's up?" He frowned, making the jagged scar across his temple pucker. "The look on your face says you think I'm taking you out into the woods to eat you whole."

She shuddered slightly, her finger curling around the trigger of his gun. "Are you?"

Talk about silence. That's what met her question. But it wasn't *just* silence. It was bigger than silence. It was like a yawning black hole of complete conversational void.

She instinctively thumbed off the safety on his Berretta.

Then he flashed her a grin. But not just any grin. It was the kind of grin that said he'd left behind a trail of vanquished foes and satisfied women. The kind of grin that romance novelists wrote about in steamy sex scenes. The kind of grin that had her nipples instantly tightening and her stomach feeling like it did that time they took a family vacation to Six Flags Great America and she rode the American Eagle roller coaster.

"Would you *like* me to eat you whole?" His voice had gone soft and low, and she would *swear* something inside her was pulling her toward him, *tugging* her in his direction.

He was right. Their connection wasn't a lie. It was real, tangible. But she refused to give into it, to let it muddle her mind. She needed all her wits about her.

Thumbing the safety back on his weapon, she pulled her hands from her pockets and crossed her arms. "I feel like we discussed this just this morning." She adopted a prim tone. "Did we or did we not decide there's no use in exploring this"—she made a gesture between them—"because *I* am on the hunt for a Mr. Right, and *you* are on the hunt for a Mrs. Right Now?"

"I'm not sure we put it in those specific terms. But, yeah. That was the gist of it."

"Good." She nodded. "Great. Glad we came away from that lovely little conversation with the same interpretation."

He said nothing to that. However, the glow of the dashboard lights showed a muscle ticking in his jaw.

For long minutes, they drove in silence. Then he turned off the narrow country road onto an even narrower country lane, and she sat up straighter as limbs from the trees on either side of the track scraped against the windows.

Her disquiet was back. Searching for something to say, some *distraction*, she blurted, "So what's the deal with Black Knights Inc.?"

The look he shot her was sharp but shuttered. "What do you mean?"

"I mean, it's owned by a former Navy SEAL and staffed by men who worked in every special operations outfit this country has ever put together. All your records are redacted out the wazoo. Most of you walk around armed to the teeth. And your computer setup on the second floor would give NORAD a run for their money."

"Boss is a big believer in giving former fighting men a chance to reintegrate into civilian life by offering them a place to work amongst like-minded folks, guys who've seen the worst that humanity has to offer and *get it*." He paused in consideration. "It's a strange thing to be dodging bullets one day and then be dropped back home and expected to pay rent the next."

She listened for lies and detected none. "And what about that computer setup?"

He slid her a considering look. "Becky and Ozzie are our top designers. They use all sorts of specialized software to draw models for the bikes long before we ever turn a wrench or fire up a blow torch."

She opened her mouth to press him further because she *knew* there was more. But he beat her to the punch.

"Plus, Ozzie is a white hat hacker," he confessed with a chagrined twist of his lips. "The best I've ever seen. He can break into any system and blow past any firewall."

She blinked her surprise. "You realize you just confessed a federal crime to a federal agent."

"Told you I'd never lie to you," he countered, and the tension that had momentarily tightened her shoulders drained away.

She might be the world's biggest fool—when it came to Sergeant Rollins, she probably was—but she believed him.

"You said he's a white hat hacker." She squinted at what appeared to be a break in the trees ahead. "Which means he only hacks to hurt the bad guys. Is this a job for him or simply a hobby?"

Britt huffed a laugh. "With Ozzie, the line is pretty blurred."

She opened her mouth to question him further but snapped it closed when the trees parted and the truck's headlights shone across the front face of a cozy cottage—red door, festive window boxes, climbing ivy that was turning colors for the seasons. Golden light glimmered through the front windows. A curl of smoke drifted from the stone chimney. And rain barrels sat at the corners, ostensibly to catch the runoff from the moss-covered roof.

It looked like one of those destination Airbnbs. The kind of place that appealed to couples who wanted the seclusion and the ambiance of the deep woods without having to pitch a tent.

"We're here," he announced, doing something under the steering column that had the old farm truck's engine cutting off. "And none too soon. We were down to an eighth of a tank."

She didn't bother answering. She was too busy gaping out the windscreen and trying to come to terms with the quaint little setting.

She wasn't sure what she expected when Britt offered to take her to meet his brother. Maybe something along the lines of a dilapidated warehouse on the waterfront or some smoky room in the back of an illegal gambling hall. But this was…charming. *Cozy* even. Definitely not what she'd call a clandestine destination for a federal fugitive and accused murderer.

Her hands automatically returned to the weapons in her pockets when the front door swung wide. But it was only Hewitt Birch who stood in the bright glow of the headlights.

"It's me," Britt called after he opened the driver's side door. The hinges made an unholy complaint at the movement. "And I brought company."

She figured that was her signal to exit the vehicle.

She pushed out of the truck just as the timer on the headlights shut off. Now, the little cottage was lit only from within. She tensed when Knox Rollins took up a position next to Hew. Of course, tension was replaced by a sharp sense of interest when the mystery woman she'd seen on the CCTV footage joined the duo on the little porch.

"Agent O'Toole," Britt said as he gestured to her and then toward the gathered group. "You know Hew. But let me introduce you to my brother, Knox, and his lovely traveling companion, Sabrina Greenlee."

Recognition sparked at the name. "Greenlee?" She arched a brow at Britt.

"As in Cooper Greenlee's sister," he confirmed her suspicion.

"Okay." She dragged in a deep breath. "You have my attention, Sergeant Rollins."

CHAPTER 17

Old Mackinac Point Lighthouse, Mackinaw City

JD Maddox watched his portly partner pace the length of the waterfront lawn next to the old lighthouse and waited for him to finish his phone call.

They'd been on their way to rendezvous with U.S. and Canadian authorities in Sault Ste. Marie when the tactical team members they'd left behind at the old farmhouse contacted them with the news that Agent O'Toole and the ancient, rusting farm truck that had been parked inside the decrepit old barn had gone missing.

The tactical guys hadn't been able to say if she'd been the one to steal the truck or if someone had kidnapped her—maybe the missing motorcyclist?—because they'd been too far away to determine how many passengers the vehicle held. But since they'd found her phone on the ground in the barn, everyone was leaning toward option number two.

Britt Rollins, or Hewitt Birch, or whoever had been riding that misty-blue motorcycle, had snatched O'Toole. And despite Keplar cursing a blue streak and hesitating for a moment as he had tried to decide what was more important, continuing to the meeting in the upper peninsula or coordinating the search for their missing associate, he'd finally ordered the helicopter's pilot to land the bird in the nearest clear spot.

For the last hour, JD, Keplar, and Agent Douglas had been on the horn to every local law enforcement outfit from Ludington to Marquette to be on the lookout for the truck. They'd demanded local sheriff's offices call their deputies out of bed and get them on the backroads to hunt for the missing agent. And they'd tasked the bureau's field offices in both Chicago and Detroit to send every helicopter and drone they had to the western border of Michigan.

It'd been quite the undertaking. But now it seemed the appropriate steps had been taken and they could finally, *finally* get back to hunting their fugitive.

JD glanced at his watch and noted the time. He'd officially been awake for thirty-six hours. The caffeine in his system no longer held the exhaustion at bay. Instead, it made him jumpy and paranoid.

This entire situation was getting out of hand. Or…rather…it'd *been* out of hand since Knox Rollins had decided to lead them on a merry chase across half the country. And as the hours ticked by, and as more and more people got involved, JD couldn't shake the growing sense of alarm that started in the pit of his stomach and radiated outward until his limbs felt twitchy and his hands felt shaky.

If only Knox had—

"That's the last of it," Keplar declared, interrupting JD's disquieting thoughts. The older agent lumbered back to where JD and the others stood beside the silent, black helicopter.

The lighthouse rising above their heads had been deactivated decades earlier. The only glow to illuminate the frustration on Keplar's face came from the landscape lighting strategically placed around the well-manicured grounds.

"What's the plan?" JD prompted, shivering in the cool breeze blowing in off the lake. Having grown up near the ocean, he was always taken aback by the icy smell of the Great Lakes. Where were the scents of fish, salt, and seaweed? It seemed strange that a body of water so large could smell so… sterilized. "Do we continue up to Sault Ste. Marie now?"

"No way." Agent Douglas shook his head. "I mean, I get you guys want to catch this murderous motherfucker, but that gets back-burnered until we find my partner."

Damnit. JD worked hard to keep the irritation from his face. *We wouldn't be in this situation of having our priorities divided if you'd stayed with your partner instead of following us like an over-eager puppy.*

Aloud, he simply said, "I thought you had the utmost faith that Agent O'Toole could handle herself?"

The look Agent Douglas shot him would've had a thinner-skinned man bristling. JD only lifted a challenging eyebrow.

Knox Rollins couldn't be allowed to escape the country. He was too valuable, too…*knowledgeable.* JD's superiors needed Knox found and dealt with accordingly so that—

"Agent Douglas is right," Keplar said to JD's astonishment, stopping his swirling thoughts in their tracks. "No man left behind."

"That's a military credo," JD argued, studying his partner closely. Never in a million years would he have pegged Keplar as a bleeding heart, feds-before-felons type of agent. In fact, he'd always thought his partner was more of an every-man-for-himself kind of cop. The sort of guy who didn't worry about the collateral damage along the way as long as he got the bad guy in the end. In fact, JD had been *banking* on precisely that. "Last I checked, we're not military," he finished with a twist of his lips.

"Doesn't matter." Keplar waved a hand. "We're still all brothers in arms. We have to prioritize finding Agent O'Toole."

A niggle of worry wormed its way through JD's chest. It turned into a snake of alarm when Keplar continued. "You stay here with Agent Douglas and continue to organize the search. I'll take the chopper to the upper peninsula and meet with the border authorities. No reason we can't kill two birds."

The snake of alarm turned into a leviathan of concern. "How about you let *me* go instead? Your relationship with Rollins means you're too close to this."

The clouds that had followed them throughout the day finally parted. Without the moon to dampen their glow, the stars shone against the black blanket of the sky. Their silver light reflected in the lake's glassy surface and showed Keplar's color going from ruddy to fire-engine red.

"Knox is *my* asset. I'll bring him in," the older man snarled, his lips pulling back to reveal his square, squat teeth.

Desperation had JD offering, "Agent Douglas can stay and head up the search for his partner. You and I can—"

"Last I checked," Keplar interrupted, "I'm still the lead agent. I call the shots."

JD opened his mouth to continue to argue, but Keplar turned to the remaining tactical team members. "Load up." He circled a finger in the air. "We're headed north."

JD had no choice but to step back as everyone climbed into the chopper—everyone but him and Agent Douglas.

When the pilot punched the ignition and the blades began to spin, he reluctantly followed the Chicago agent toward the steps leading to the lighthouse's front door. Two minutes later, he watched the helicopter leap into the sky and chart a course out over the water.

Goosebumps rose over his arms and the back of his neck. They had nothing to do with the rotor wash or the chill in the air and everything to do with the thought of Keplar finding Knox without JD there to make sure things didn't go awry. To make sure Knox didn't—

"Fuck," he cursed, cutting off his own thoughts this time.

Douglas lifted a questioning eyebrow, but JD simply waved him off.

CHAPTER 18

Hunter Jackson's cabin

Britt had closely watched Julia's face for clues to her thoughts while his brother and Sabrina repeated the tale they'd already told the Black Knights of the evening Cooper Greenlee died.

He'd seen suspicion morph into curiosity when Knox explained how the cartel had sent three of their hitmen to clip Knox and Cooper. He'd witnessed curiosity slide into horror when Sabrina recounted a bit of what happened to her and how her brother had died trying to stop her from suffering a worse fate.

Now, the only sounds to interrupt the quiet inside the little cabin were the pop of a log in the fireplace at his back—he'd grabbed a seat on the stone hearth—and the sticky noise Julia's throat made when she took a hasty sip from the mug of hot chocolate she grabbed off of the coffee table in front of her.

"I am so sorry for your loss, Miss Greenlee," she said quietly to the wan-looking woman seated on the opposite end of the well-worn sofa from her. "And for what you suffered at the hands of that man. I—" She stopped when her voice cracked. Her expression was similar to Britt's when a fellow soldier recounted the horrors of war. It was the face of someone who *knew*.

He wondered if she'd personally suffered—the statistics said one in five women in the U.S. had experienced attempted or completed rape—or if she'd simply brushed up against the noxious subject one too many times in her line of work.

He hoped it was the second. Because if it was the first, and if he ever found out who the sonofabitch was, he wasn't sure he'd be able to stop himself from making the asshole eat the bangy end of his sidearm.

"I'm just so terribly sorry," Julia finally finished, her voice thick with sincerity.

Water welled in Sabrina's eyes, but she dashed her tears away with the back of her hand. "Just help us find whoever set up my brother and Knox. Help us put the bastard behind bars."

Julia gave a determined dip of her chin. "I don't care for plenty of things. Orange marmalade, the month of March, and going to the dentist to name a few. But there's one thing I absolutely hate. And that's a traitor." Her jaw hardened. "I won't stop until the person behind this is held accountable."

Britt smiled as he crossed his arms over his chest. Like whiskey in a teacup, Julia O'Toole was as pretty as a picture on the outside but tough and take-no-prisoners on the inside.

"How did Keplar approach you?" Julia turned to Knox. "To be his asset, I mean. How did he convince you to gather evidence against the cartel?"

Knox sat in the overstuffed armchair in the corner. Julia's question had him running knobby-knuckled fingers through his hair. The gesture made the cowlick they'd both inherited from their father stand up straight.

"The cartel's main lieutenant, the second highest-ranking member of the gang, was in the cell next to us. Cooper and I were chummy with the guy." He glanced around the room and grimaced at the idea of admitting he'd happily rubbed elbows with a man who'd undoubtedly left a trail of death and destruction in his wake. "You get to know your neighbors in prison," he said by way of explanation, his tone apologetic. "And having them as friends rather than enemies is preferred."

"No one here will judge you for what you had to do to stay alive in prison," Britt assured him quietly.

Knox met his eyes. Britt made sure the truth of his heart was reflected in his unwavering gaze.

He was sad about Knox's path and choices. He felt guilty for being the reason Knox had taken that path and made those choices. But he had never, not once, been mad at Knox. And he had never, not once, judged his brother.

There but for the grace of God go I…

It was something their father had liked to say.

Britt remembered well the time he and his father walked through White Point Garden when he'd been…what? Five? Maybe six years old? They'd stumbled across a man abandoned by all that was good and true. The poor soul had been crumbled at the foot of an old Civil War-era canon, his body slack, his face angled downward and obscured beneath a scraggly beard.

Britt recalled the sallowness of the man's skin. Recalled the way the man's clothes, stiff and tattered, had clung to his thin frame with a reluctant grip.

He hadn't known what it was at the time; he'd been too young. But as an adult, he knew that what he'd smelled that day was the acrid scent of liquor, so much booze it'd stung his nostrils. And yet even that had been overpowered by the tang of unwashed flesh, stale urine, and disease.

When he closed his eyes, he could still see the man's hands, so weathered and creased. They had been on the ground, palms upturned in a gesture that had seemed to ask for nothing and that had expected even less.

"*Ew.*" He'd tugged on his father's hand and pointed. "*He's yucky, Daddy.*"

"*No, son,*" his father had countered. "*There but for the grace of God go I.*"

When Britt had asked his father to explain, his dad had squatted until they were at eye level. Then his father had told Britt that sometimes terrible things happened to good people, and sometimes when those terrible things happened to good people, those good people had no one to help them.

"*When your mother died, I wanted to crawl into a bottle of alcohol and never come out,*" his father had said. "*But I had you to take care of. I had your brother. And when I was drowning my sorrows with poison, I had friends who picked me up and dried me out and took me to meetings that made me see what I had to live for.*"

His father had gestured toward the man slumped against the cannon. "*Don't ever judge people who are struggling and suffering, son. Those people were children once, too. They were someone's sons or daughters. They are still the sons and daughters of society, and it's only through the luck of the draw that we all aren't here sprawled against the foot of a monument. Don't judge people because you have no idea what battles they've faced, what private losses they've suffered, what unseen enemies they've fought. Don't judge this man because you* have no idea what has brought him to this place of silence and cold metal, a place no one would ever want to call home."

And then Britt had gone with his father to the closest convenience store, where they had purchased a sandwich, a bag of chips, and a cold Coke. And he had looked upon that man with no judgment when they delivered the meal. Instead, he'd only looked with a sense of sadness that had weighed more heavily upon his young chest than the lead cannon balls stacked next to the monument.

Somehow, he must have conveyed all this with a look because Knox's shoulders relaxed. The shadow that had fallen across his brother's face vanished.

"Keplar promised us an early release and witness protection after the job was done, a sweet setup in some far-flung locale with babes in bikinis and all the umbrella drinks we could stomach. All we had to do was secure a spot inside the lieutenant's organization and then gather the evidence Keplar needed to bring the whole kit and caboodle down. So Cooper and I got even chummier with Ricky—that's the lieutenant's name," Knox clarified. "We convinced him we would be assets to the cartel if he'd put in a word of recommendation. And the rest, as they say, is history."

Julia nodded. "I think I'm almost up to speed. But there's one more thing I need to understand."

"Shoot," Knox said amiably, but Britt could see the exhaustion in his brother's face. The long days, the death of his partner, and all the running and hiding were catching up with him. Knox needed sleep. They *all* needed sleep. But first…Agent Julia O'Toole needed answers.

"How did the two of you get away?" She tilted her head between Knox and Sabrina. "You said three men burst into Mr. Greenlee's house, bragging about how you and Cooper had been outed by someone inside the joint operation. And when they found Sabrina there visiting, they decided to put off executing the two of you so they could…" She swallowed convulsively. "Do what they did. So how did you get away?"

Knox and Sabrina exchanged a look.

It was another look Britt knew well. The look shared between two people who'd survived terrible trauma together. That look said, *We know. We stand as witness. And now we must testify.*

Britt curled his fingers around the stone lip of the hearth, readying himself to hear the part of the story Knox and Sabrina had glossed over during the original telling. The Black Knights had been so focused on the next steps that no one had thought to ask about the initial step that had saved Knox and Sabrina's lives.

"They'd herded us all into the back room," Knox recounted, a muscle ticking in his jaw. "Fat Eddy Torres had Sabrina down on the bed while Arturo Garcia—everyone calls him The Rat—and Jonny Fuentes kept Cooper and me to our knees. They put guns to our heads and made us—" He stopped and swallowed, shooting a guilty glance toward Sabrina. "They made us watch while Fat Eddy tortured Sabrina."

Britt gritted his teeth.

That *any* man could hurt a woman, someone smaller and weaker than himself, wasn't something he would ever understand. Just like he'd never understand those heartless sonsofbitches who abandoned puppies on the roadside or who drowned kittens.

The one thing he *did* understand, beyond a shadow of a doubt, was that the world was full of evil men. And as much as it pained him, the fragile-looking woman on the end of the sofa had the terrible luck of running into a particularly bad one.

Although…she doesn't look very fragile now.

Sabrina's jaw was as hard as a rock. Her eyes were flinty as she stared unseeingly at the black-and-white photographs hanging on the far wall.

Something told him if she ever got the chance to put a lead round in Fat Eddy's brainpan, she wouldn't hesitate to pull the trigger.

Disgust laced Knox's every word as he continued. "Jonny made the mistake of getting down on Cooper's level to whisper in Cooper's ear and taunt him about what Fat Eddy was doing to his sister. That's when Cooper struck. He head-butted Jonny square in the nose."

"I can still hear the crunch of the cartilage," Sabrina said quietly. "I didn't know it sounded like that when someone's nose broke."

"Cooper more than broke Jonny's nose." Knox's voice was filled with satisfaction. "He knocked the sonofabitch out cold, and then he lunged for Fat Eddy. Since Fat Eddy's pants were down around his knees, the two of them went down in a heap on the floor, kicking and snarling and biting. Cooper was a wild man. Absolutely *feral*. You should've heard Fat Eddy squeal like a pig when Cooper bit off a piece of his ear."

"Like that old Johnny Cash song," Hew mused from his seat on the barstool at the counter outside the compact kitchen. The first edition copy of *A Wrinkle in Time* dangled between his fingers, but Britt had yet to see him crack the cover.

"Huh?" Knox blinked in confusion.

"Never mind." Hew made a rolling motion with his hand. "Proceed."

"So anyway, I used The Rat's distraction to make a play for his weapon. We were fighting over it, doing a bit of kicking and snarling ourselves, when I heard the gunshot." Knox winced. His Adam's apple made a jerky journey up the length of his throat and back down again.

"I managed to get The Rat's gun away from him. But when I turned around, I saw…" Knox lost it then. His voice broke. His eyes filled with tears. And he looked away from the group, toward the front door, as he battled his grief.

Britt understood in that moment that Cooper Greenlee had meant more to Knox than a simple prison cell bunkmate or undercover partner. The men had formed a true friendship. They'd shared true affection.

His gaze tracked over to the black-and-white photographs hung on the wall. There were three in all. One showed a much younger Hunter Jackson with his arm thrown around a stony-faced drill sergeant. Another showed a beautiful dark-eyed woman whom Hunter said had been like a mother figure to his unit when they'd been stationed in Afghanistan. And the third? Well, the third was a photo of the Black Knights.

In short, the pictures showed Hunter's family.

And that's what the Knights had become to Britt, too. Brothers in arms, for sure. But so much more. And the thought of losing even one of them made the hot chocolate in his stomach turn to acid. So he *got* Knox's grief. Understood it on a cellular level.

"During the struggle, Fat Eddy grabbed his weapon off the nightstand," Knox continued wetly. "He only managed one shot. But one shot was all it took. I think Cooper was dead before he knew what hit him."

"I *hope* he was," Sabrina whispered hoarsely, twisting her fingers together. "I hope he didn't even feel it."

"I should've…" Knox cut himself off so he could shake his head. When he glanced at Sabrina, there was no disguising the guilt in his eyes. "I should've done more. I should've…fought harder. Faster. Maybe I could have—"

"What happened to Cooper wasn't your fault," Sabrina assured him.

"He was my best friend," Knox argued. "We had each other's backs in prison. And when Keplar approached us to do the cartel job, we promised we'd have each other's back through that, too. But I failed him. When push came to shove, I couldn't have his back."

"But you did." Sabrina's chin firmed. "Because you did what he couldn't do. You got me out of there. You saved me. You're *still* saving me."

"I didn't save him, though."

Britt felt like he'd taken a hand grenade to the chest, his heart blown wide open, as he watched a single tear trek down Knox's leathery-looking cheek.

After dashing the drop away, Knox wrapped his fingers around the arms of the chair, and Britt took note of the scars on his brother's knuckles. A few of them were old, faded to little more than silvery-white lines. But some of them were new. Still pink and puckered.

Leftovers from his most recent stint, no doubt.

Julia cleared her throat. "So you were able to get The Rat's gun," she said quietly, pulling them all back into the conversation. "Fat Eddy shot Cooper. And what else? You said Fat Eddy only managed to get off one shot. Why was that? Why didn't it turn into a Wild West shootout?"

Sabrina was the one to answer. "Because he was outnumbered two to one by then. Because when my brother and that fat, smelly pig were wrestling, I scrambled off the bed and grabbed the gun from the unconscious man."

"Jonny dropped his weapon when Cooper headbutted him," Knox supplied helpfully.

"I turned and aimed it at Fat Eddy the instant I had it in my hands." Sabrina's shoulders began to shake, and Julia scooted down the couch to grab the woman's hand.

"Fat Eddy is a lot of things, but he's not an idiot," Knox interjected quietly. "He knew if he started spraying bullets, we'd return fire, and the odds were in our favor. So I held my gun on The Rat. Sabrina held her gun on Fat Eddy. And we backed ourselves right on out of that house."

"I should've shot him," Sabrina said now. "I was scared and in shock because—" Her voice broke, but her expression hardened. "I should've shot him," she repeated with a growl of disgust.

"You did the right thing by getting out of there," Hew assured her.

Whatever anger and anguish showed in Sabrina's expression was magnified in Hew's. Britt wondered if his irascible teammate might feel more for the brown-eyed waif than simple pity.

"He's right," Julia agreed. "And once we take down whoever set up Knox and your brother, I promise I'll help you make Fat Eddy pay."

A dozen heartbeats of silence followed that pronouncement. Then, Knox nodded. "I can see why Britt likes you. You're tough as old shoe leather. He always *did* go for the scrappy ones."

Britt shifted uncomfortably when Julia shot him a curious glance. He relaxed when she quickly turned her attention to his brother. "Do you think it was Keplar? He's been champing at the bit to find you. I'd say he's been almost zealous in his hunt. You think it was him who double-crossed you?"

Another log popped and fizzed. The smokey, woodsy scent mixed with the subtle tang of furniture polish. They were homey smells. *Comforting* even. On a different night, Britt might have appreciated them.

Tonight, they only registered in the far corner of his mind. Because his entire attention, every fiber of his being, was focused on Julia. On the little dent in the middle of her lower lip. On the way her light brown eyes melted to gold around her pupils. On the razor-sharp intelligence she displayed with every word out of her mouth.

He'd been plagued by uncertainty on the drive from the old farmhouse to Hunter's secret cabin, wondering if he'd made the right call by bringing her along or if his obsession with her had pushed him to make the dumbest decision of his life. Now, he felt the satisfying tug of vindication.

Julia O'Toole was everything he'd imagined her to be. And *more*.

"If you'd asked me that question three days ago, I'd have said there was no way. Keplar is rough around the edges, but he's no turncoat. His entire identity is tied up in being an FBI agent. He'd never risk his badge to make a quick buck from the cartel. But now?" Knox shrugged. "I don't know. Maybe. Anything is possible, I reckon."

Julia sighed and turned back toward Britt. He braced himself for the impact of her eyes.

He'd been unmoved by the glare of his drill sergeant in basic training, had barely batted a lash when he'd faced down the hateful gaze of an enemy combatant who'd managed to get the drop on him during a night operation in Kandahar, and, unlike some of the Knights, Boss's snarling scrutiny barely fazed him. But it took effort not to instinctively look away from Julia's intense focus, from that unwavering directness when her eyes met his.

"So I'm guessing you plan to have Ozzie hack into the professional and personal accounts of everyone who knew about Cooper and Knox's covers"—she inclined her head toward his brother—"and hope Ozzie can pinpoint which one of them is in league with the cartel?"

"Got it in one." He nodded and then blinked at Hew because Hew made the mother of all rude noises. If looks could kill, Hew's expression would have Britt six feet under and pushing up daisies. "What?" he demanded. "What's wrong with your face?"

"What's right with yours?" Hew countered sarcastically. "You told her about Ozzie? You realize she's a frickin' fed, yeah?"

Right. Shit.

He'd forgotten to warn Hew that he'd had to come clean about their onsite computer whiz.

"There are times when the only choices left to a man are bad ones," he confessed with a shrug.

"And what the fuck is *that* supposed to mean?"

Britt opened his mouth to answer, but Julia did it for him. "I'm not stupid, Chief Birch. I know the difference between a desktop PC and the serious setup you guys have there at Black Knights Inc. When I questioned Sergeant Rollins about it, he told me the truth about your coworker's side job."

Hew blinked in surprise. Britt figured that surprise had less to do with her knowledge of computing hardware and more to do with her having called him by his rank.

"And here's hoping you don't use that against us once this mess is over." The stare Hew pinned on Julia offered no quarter.

She didn't need any. She lifted her chin and challenged, "Your words form a statement, but your face forms a question."

Abso-fucking-lutely glorious, Britt thought proudly.

"My question is, will you use what you know about Ozzie against us once this is all over?"

Julia shook her head. "This might come as a shock to you, Chief Birch, but most agents don't get their jollies by going after every Tom, Dick, or Harry who toes over the line of legality. If I wanted to go after people who jaywalk or text while driving or floor it when they see a yellow light, I'd have to start with my own family."

Or yourself, Britt added silently. He'd witnessed her doing all three.

When Hew remained unconvinced, Julia glanced up at the overhead light as if it might hold the answer to how she could persuade Hew she was telling the truth. Eventually, she lowered her chin and said, "Britt says Ozzie is a white hat hacker. Which in my book falls under the heading: the ends justify the means."

Pride swelled in Britt's chest until there was no way to contain the grin that split his face.

"I don't know why you're looking so happy," Hew grumbled at him. "You just added another wrinkle to the fabric of this mess. Not only are the feds out to find *him*." He hitched his chin toward Knox before angling it toward Julia. "But they'll be lifting every rock and cutting down every tree to find *her*."

"You're right about that." Concern creased Julia's forehead when she looked around the little cabin. "The running generator tells me this place isn't hooked up to the electrical grid. The rain barrels out front say the same goes for any connection to a municipal water system." Her gaze landed first on Hew and then on Britt. "Is there any way this property can be traced back to anyone sitting in this room?"

"None," Britt assured her.

"Is there any way this property can be traced back to someone any of you just happen to *know*? If so, the techs back at the bureau will unearth that connection."

This time, it was Hew who said, "None." He rolled the word around on his tongue like he was tasting it.

She blew out a windy breath. "Okay, then. We're in for the long haul. We stay put until your white hat hacker comes through."

Britt blinked. Now that he'd presented her with the proof of Knox's innocence, he expected her to ask him to make good on his promise to take her to the nearest phone. "You don't want me to take you into Traverse City?"

Her nose wrinkled like she smelled sulfur. "I hate thinking about my associates out there not knowing where I am. And I hate it worse that someone will inform my family that I'm missing. That'll worry them like crazy. And poor Sean will have to go to my place to feed my animals. Gunpowder hates him and will try to peck his eyes out. And Chewy? Chewy will bite his ankles if he doesn't get the wet dog food to dry dog food ratio just right."

Julia realized she was naming people and animals the rest of them didn't know. Er…*shouldn't* know. *Britt* knew because he'd been…you know… *stalking* her.

"Sean is my brother and the only one not on duty tonight. My father and my three brothers are all firemen," she explained. "Chewy, short for Chewbacca, is my rescue Chihuahua who sounds like a Wookie and is particular about everything from his food to his dog bed to his favorite blanket on the corner of the couch. If it's not folded in exact fourths, and if it has even the slightest wrinkle, he'll make that rrhhhaawwww sound until you smooth it out."

Sabrina eyed Julia with a new appreciation.

And Britt understood the change in her opinion. Until now, Julia had been nothing if not professional—the consummate FBI agent. But this peek into her private life humanized her. It spoke of who she was beyond the badge: a bleeding-heart animal rescuer, a sarcastic sister who kept her brothers on their toes, a loving daughter…

"And who's Gunpowder?" Sabrina asked quietly.

"Gunpowder's her African grey parrot," he supplied helpfully. "What are his favorite phrases again?" He looked at Julia expectantly.

"Sugar tits and dick breath," she supplied automatically. But her eyes were narrowed on him. "How did you know that?"

His heart skipped a beat. Had he just given himself away? *Again?* Then he remembered. "You told us about Gunpowder during the Senator McClean case. You said you adopted the bird after you put his previous owner behind bars."

"The weapons dealer," she nodded, the flame of suspicion guttering in her eyes. "Right."

Britt breathed a silent sigh of relief.

"Hence the bird's colorful vocabulary," Hew said. Then he lifted an eyebrow. "Unless *you're* the one who taught him sugar tits and dick breath?"

Julia rolled her eyes. "No." Then she grimaced. "But I *do* tend to overuse the phrase *cockwaffle*, especially in reference to Ren. He's my *other* dog, a three-legged pitbull mix who gets the zoomies, can't control his momentum on my hardwood floors, and inevitably crashes into something and makes a mess. I guess when that happens, I tend to yell *cockwaffle!* Now Gunpowder thinks Ren's *name* is Cockwaffle. So anytime Ren enters the room, Gunpower says, *Hello, Cockwaffle.* Followed by a squawk." She made a face. "It's no wonder my sisters-in-law ask me to come to *their* houses to babysit instead of bringing my nieces and nephews to my place."

Britt realized he was grinning at Julia like an idiot when he caught his brother giving him a considering look.

He quickly changed the subject. "I'm sorry for the worry it'll cause your family. And I'm sorry for your brother's ankles and eyes. But I appreciate that you're willing to remain here with us."

Julia shrugged. "If I go back, there will be questions. Questions I can't answer without putting all of you in danger."

Britt could see her lips were still moving. But he couldn't make out her words. All he could hear was his own heartbeat, fast and fierce and hungry.

Julia was staying. With him.

The sensation that bloomed to life inside his chest was the same one he would have felt had he won a prize.

The greatest prize of all.

CHAPTER 19

Hew couldn't sleep.

He blamed the lumpy mattress on the trundle he'd pulled from beneath the daybed. Springs poked through the foam to stab into his backbone, and his feet hung over the edge.

Also, he was cold. He'd drawn the short straw when it came to the shower line. By the time it was his turn to wash off the dust from the road, there hadn't remained one single drop of hot water. He'd been chilled to the bone by the time he toweled off, and he hadn't managed to warm up since. The paper-thin quilt he pulled up to his chin might as well be a sheet of air for all the good it did him.

As if the lumpy, too-short mattress and the brewing bout of hypothermia weren't enough, Knox Rollins snored. Not a subtle sawing of logs. Oh, no. It was a full-on lumberjack's chainsaw of sound.

Hew wasn't sure how Sabrina was sleeping through it.

Is she sleeping through it? he wondered, cocking his ear toward the bed above him.

No whisper of breath. No rustle of sheets. No squeak of the bedframe.

Hopefully, that meant she was getting some rest. Because by the time she'd emerged from the bathroom, her hair freshly washed and her face freshly scrubbed, she'd epitomized the phrase *the walking dead*.

If exhaustion were a person, it would be Sabrina Greenlee.

Holding his breath, he listened harder. But it was impossible to hear anything over the roar of Knox's obstructed airway.

Seriously, the man needed to see a specialist. Maybe get a mouthguard or one of those fancy-dancy CPAP machines that made a person look like they'd been attacked by a facehugger from the *Alien* movies.

Hew tried to drown out the noise by shoving his pillow over his head. It helped. Sort of. *Not enough.*

Sighing heavily, he slipped the pillow back beneath his skull, gritted his teeth, and considered marching into the living room and yanking Britt up by his short hairs. After all, it had been *Britt* who'd assigned them all their sleeping arrangements.

Sabrina, Knox, and Hew had all been told to bunk out in the bedroom, with Sabrina in the queen bed, Knox on the daybed shoved into the back corner, and Hew on the trundle. Julia and Britt were in the living room, with Julia on the sofa and Britt on a pallet on the floor in front of the fireplace.

Initially, Hew had thought Britt was taking one for the team, sacrificing himself to the floor's uncompromising hardness while the rest of them had soft spots to sleep in. Now, he realized the rat bastard had played them all and had saved the best piece of real estate for himself.

A warm, roaring fire? An entire wall away from Knox who *had* to be rattling the shingles on the roof?

Yeah. That sounds like heaven.

Hew was about to throw back the thin quilt and remedy the situation, but Sabrina's soft words cut through the darkness. "You're quiet. But you have an unquiet mind."

He blinked in surprise. "What makes you say that?" he whispered.

She was silent for a moment as if contemplating her answer. Then, "It's the way your eyes take in every detail of everything happening around you even when you're pretending to be bored to death."

Huh. Well, how about that?

Most people thought just because he preferred to sit in a corner and watch a conversation rather than join in, or just because he liked finding a quiet spot to read, that meant he was a Zen master. That he had a still mind to match his still mouth and body. But, in reality, the opposite was true.

If he was awake, his brain raced a mile a minute…cataloging, *calculating*. The only time he got a break was when he was asleep. And even then, he would come awake at the slightest noise, the subtlest movement.

Of course, that is probably a consequence of my upbringing.

"Plus," she continued to whisper. "I can hear the wheels turning in your head. They're spinning so fast they're emitting a low hum."

He chuckled. "Not sure how you can hear anything above Sir Snores A Lot."

He couldn't see her smile, but he could hear it in her voice. "And just think, this is your first night with him. Imagine if you were me, and this was night number three."

I'd rather someone put my balls in a vice, he thought uncharitably.

Aloud, he said, "No wonder you look like you've been through the Crusades and back." He realized his mistake as soon as he made it. No woman liked to be told she looked like hammered shit. "I mean, you're beautiful, of course. It's just that your exhaustion is palpable. You can hear my mind spinning, and I can feel your fatigue. We make quite a pair."

"Yeah." She released a sleepy sigh. "I *want* to sleep. I just can't."

"Who could with all this racket?"

"No." He could hear a subtle rustle and knew it was the sound of her hair shushing against the pillow as she shook her head. "It's not that. Or… it's not *just* that. Every time I close my eyes, I see…him."

His heart softened. "Your brother?"

"No," she countered immediately. "I refuse to let my mind go there. I'm not ready for that. Not yet."

He'd never had a family, so he didn't know what it was to lose someone who shared his blood. But he'd flown enough missions with good men who hadn't returned from their assignment. He could sympathize with the need to push away the horror. To shove it all into a little box covered in razor blades that threatened to slice his fingers to ribbons if he ever tried to open it.

He hated even uttering the words. They sat on his tongue like poison pills. But it was clear she wanted to talk about it, and he felt honored she'd decided to talk about it with *him*. "So, then, you see the face of the man who…" He trailed off, unable to speak the rest of the thought aloud.

He marveled at women—their softness and grace, the sound of

their laughter, the way they moved. Nothing in the whole world was as wonderful, mysterious, frustrating, and fascinating as a woman. And he could not understand how *any* man could countenance the thought of defiling something so beautiful.

"The one who attacked me," she whispered, and the thickness in her voice had him curling the quilt into his fists. "When I close my eyes, I see the look on his face when he grabbed the back of my head and told me he was going to enjoy making me scream and making Cooper watch. I taste the marijuana on his lips when he shoved his tongue down my throat. I smell his cheap cologne and his filthy body odor when he unbuttoned his fly and—"

Her voice cracked like it'd been slammed against a sharp edge. He wanted to climb into bed with her. Hold her tight so he could help keep her demons at bay. But the last thing she needed—indeed, the last thing she likely wanted—was for another hairy, heavy-handed man to touch her.

Instead, he reached his hand over the side of the mattress, palm-up. A silent offering.

For the span of a dozen heartbeats, she didn't speak, didn't move. He wondered if she'd seen his gesture. And then he wondered if she'd seen his gesture and had chosen to ignore it.

He was about to drop his hand when it happened.

Her cool, slender fingers threaded through his. So slowly. So softly. So tentatively that he dared not move. Barely dared to breathe.

When her palm kissed his, his first thought was relief that she'd accepted what little comfort he could offer. His second thought was that her hand felt tiny and fragile inside his own. His third thought?

Well, it wasn't really a thought. It was more of a physical response.

He shivered. And it had nothing to do with the cold shower or the paper-thin quilt.

Carefully, looking for any indication that she might disapprove, he slowly smoothed his thumb along the soft skin on the side of her hand. One. Twice. Three times. And then on methodical repeat when she didn't snatch her hand away.

"Thank you," she breathed, and he felt her strength as clearly as he felt her brittleness. She was holding herself together by sheer force of will.

He knew how much that hurt. It was painful to shore up the broken pieces of one's heart with nothing but the glue of grit and guts because the alternative was to fall apart. And once that happened, once the fragments were allowed to split and splinter, they might never be back together again.

"What that man did to you—" He was cut off when Knox let loose with a series of machine gun snores. He was about to punch the sonofabitch in the face with his free hand. But Knox rolled onto his side, and his snoring was suddenly reduced to deep, sonorous breaths.

Thank Christ for small miracles, Hew thought irritably before returning his attention to the feel of Sabrina's hand inside his own. To the subtle sound of her ragged breaths that told him she was once more fighting back tears.

"What that man did to you doesn't define you, Sabrina," he assured her. "No more than the sexual assault I suffered in foster care defines me. Those things happened *to* us. But they aren't *us*."

"Y-you were in foster care?" He could hear the interest in her tone despite the sogginess of her voice.

"My whole life," he told her. "I never knew my parents."

"I'm sorry," she breathed.

"I'm not." His response was instantaneous. "It's impossible to miss something you never had."

A small silence followed that pronouncement, and he wondered if he'd been too blunt. Britt had once accused him of being as subtle as a sledgehammer.

"I knew both of my parents," she admitted quietly. "But sometimes I wish I hadn't. If I'd never known them, I'd never have had to admit they loved their friends and their drugs and their booze more than they ever loved me or Cooper. I'd never have known what it was to wait for them to walk through the front door because they'd been gone for five days and we were down to our last can of corn and our last sleeve of saltines."

He heard the old hurt in her voice. What Fat Eddy had done to her was a fresh cut that openly bled. But what she'd experienced at the hands of her parents was a bone-deep wound that would never fully heal. It would continue to ache and fester for the rest of her life.

He knew all about both kinds of wounds.

"You talk about them in the past tense. Are they—"

"Dead," she finished for him. "Drowned. It was the summer after I graduated high school. They were with their usual group of deadbeats down by the bay. They were all drunk and high and when my mom jumped off the dock, she didn't come back up. My dad jumped in after her and had to be pulled out of the water by his friends. Come to find out, a big, waterlogged tree had washed under the dock's pilings. Mom impaled herself on a branch. Dad sucked water into his lungs trying to save her. He lived for nearly twenty-four hours, but eventually succumbed."

"Dry drowning?"

Her hesitation told him she was shocked he knew what had happened. "Yeah. Although the doctors in the emergency room called it pulmonary edema."

He opened his mouth to express his condolences, but she rushed ahead. "What about your folks? You said you never knew them?"

"Gunned down by a mass shooter at a concert when they were both just eighteen. Dead before they'd really been given the chance to live."

He didn't tell her the rest of the story. Didn't want to burden her with the horror of it. People tended to get weird around him when they knew.

"So we're both orphans," she whispered, her tone heavy with sadness.

"Like I said," he gently squeezed her hand, "we're a pair."

Her only response was a subtle tightening of her grip. And then… silence.

One heartbeat became two. Two heartbeats became ten. Until, finally, he stopped counting.

Has she fallen asleep, he wondered?

A part of him hoped so. He could lie there and hold her hand all night if she'd fallen asleep. The thought of that filled him with…something.

Something he couldn't name.

Then her soft voice reached through the darkness once again. "Will you come lie beside me?"

He was sure he'd misheard her. "Huh?" *Wow, Hew. Spoken like a true scholar.* "I mean, what did you say?"

Her response came quickly then. Each word was edged with uncertainty. "I know it's a weird request. We're strangers. And I'll understand if you don't feel comfortable. But every time I'm about to doze off, I have that falling sensation, and I jerk myself awake. It's been happening over and over since… Well, since it happened. And I feel like maybe if someone is next to me, someone who can *ground* me, then I might be able to get some sleep." Her voice hitched on a repressed sob. "I'm so tired. I didn't know it was possible to be this tired. No one tells you that at some point exhaustion becomes physical pain and I—"

She stopped midsentence when he stood.

"You want me to stay on top of the covers?" he asked.

The room was dim, but it wasn't completely dark. He saw when she threw back the coverlet in silent welcome. There was relief in her voice when she said, "Under them as long as you're comfortable? I'm cold and I—"

Again, she stopped midsentence when he slid between the sheets, hastily pulling up the coverlet before spreading the thin quilt he'd brought with him atop the bed for added warmth.

His weight depressed the mattress, forcing her to slide in his direction. Her hip touched his as soon as he lay back against the pillow.

He wanted to take her hand. He wanted—

It didn't matter what he wanted.

All that mattered was what *she* wanted.

"Sh-should we stay like this?" His voice sounded like his hot chocolate had been laced with glass shards. "Or do you want me to hold your hand again? Or maybe—"

"Can I…hold you?" she interrupted.

He blinked in surprise.

"I feel like if I can hold onto something solid, maybe I won't feel like I'm falling anymore. You're the most solid thing I've ever seen."

And she'll be in charge, he thought. *Any physical touch will be* her *choice. It's a way for her to reclaim some of the power Fat Eddy that fucking fuckhead took from her.*

He lifted his arm, welcoming her to curl against his side. But she shook her head. "Will you face away from me? I want to be the big spoon."

He wasn't sure why a smile of delight curved his mouth. Maybe it was because he dwarfed her and the idea of her being a big *anything* compared to him was laughable. But he suspected the real reason he was grinning as he turned onto his side was he'd never gotten to be the little spoon before. No woman had ever even suggested it. And the idea of being *held* instead of always having to do the holding was oddly appealing.

She moved her pillow close to his. Then, carefully, tentatively, she fitted herself against his back. Her hips tucked close around his butt. Her legs curled tightly along the backs of his. And she slid her hand under his top arm so she could press her palm flat against his chest.

He felt the warmth of her breath on the back of his neck and expected his body to respond in its usual way to the touch of a beautiful woman. But to his surprise, he didn't experience that same punch of lust that had accosted him when she'd been on his lap in the pantry. Instead, all he felt was…comfort.

Her body heat seeped into him. With her hand over his heart, he could count the beats and they were slow and steady and sure. It felt like…what Black Knights Inc. felt like. It felt safe and sort of like…*home.*

Or maybe that was only his imagination.

He'd never had a home. How could he possibly know what one felt like?

For long moments, neither of them moved. Neither of them spoke. Then, her whispered words fell hot upon his neck. "I'm sorry for what happened to you. In foster care, I mean."

He swallowed convulsively. "I'm sorry for what happened to you, too, Sabrina."

She squeezed him. Just a little. Then she relaxed, and within seconds, her breaths evened out.

He lay there in the darkness. No longer cold. No longer wanting to change places with Britt.

He lay there in the darkness and thought…

This is what it's supposed to feel like.

He wasn't sure what *this* was, exactly. All he knew was that it felt right.

CHAPTER 20

The flickering flames in the fireplace made shadows dance across the ceiling. Julia stared at them and tried not to think about how Sergeant Britt Rollins was only three feet away.

Sergeant Britt Rollins, who *hadn't* lied to her even if he'd played with semantics. Sergeant Britt Rollins, who had proved himself loyal and honorable at every turn. Sergeant Britt Rollins, who had trusted her to hear the evidence of his brother's innocence and come to the correct conclusion concerning what to do with that information. Sergeant Britt Rollins, who had emerged from the shower in a tight black undershirt that emphasized the breadth of his chest and gray sweatpants that emphasized the breadth of…well…*not* his chest.

Hubba, hubba, and holy screaming ovaries!

He wasn't asleep. That much she discerned from the quiet way he breathed. But neither had he said anything since they'd claimed their places for the night.

She kept expecting him to say…*something*.

Or maybe she just *wanted* him to say something because she loved the sound of his voice. Loved that deep, melodic Lowcountry drawl that was the auditory equivalent of sweet sun tea.

How many times had she fantasized about him whispering naughty words that would make her face flush and her blood rush? How many times had she heard his voice in her dreams only to wake up hot and bothered and unable to get back to sleep without first reaching into her bedside drawer for a little battery-powered relief?

Too many times to count.

And speaking of being hot.

A bead of sweat slipped between her breasts and had her kicking off the colorful afghan blanket she'd pulled from the back of the sofa.

The coolness of the room's air was a blessed relief against her bare toes. But it wasn't enough. She couldn't get comfortable. She was still too hot. Plus, someone was snoring in the next room. And the pair of flannel pajamas Britt had supplied her with—a donation from whoever owned the cabin—were too tight.

Or maybe that's just my skin, she thought.

She had the oddest feeling. Like something inside her needed to burst free. Like the very essence of her being was too confined and needed an escape and—

"Something on your mind, Agent O'Toole?" Britt's deliciously low voice drifted across the space between them.

You, she could have told him. *You're on my mind.*

Instead, she said, "Agent O'Toole, huh? We're back to being all professional and standoffish with each other?"

"Isn't that what you want?"

"No." The word was out of her mouth before she could stop it.

His voice dropped to a lower octave. When he said the words, "Then what *do* you want?" she could feel her heartbeat in the tips of her breasts. And in places a lot farther south.

You, she could've said. *I want you, you.*

But she'd already made that obvious when she'd tried to eat his face off and rub herself to completion against the ridge that'd risen behind his fly. She'd made her want of him obvious, and then he'd soundly rejected her.

Not really rejected *you,* a voice of reason argued. *Just pointed out that he's not the kind of man you're looking for.*

Except, despite all her logic and reason, she couldn't shake the feeling that he was *precisely* what she was looking for.

Of course, those were her ovaries talking and not her brain. He felt precisely like what she was looking for because they had chemistry. Careless, carnal, combustible chemistry. And that was an intoxicating thing that muddled her mind and made her want to ignore logic and reason and simply…*live*.

Live in the moment. Revel in the now. Go with her gut…er…rather her hormones.

Instead of answering him, she said, "I'm just restless, I guess. There's nothing worse than being up against a ghost. I can deal with an enemy I know. But an enemy I don't know?" She shook her head.

Silence followed her pronouncement. For a moment, she wondered if he'd call her out for so soundly changing the subject. But eventually, he said, "If anyone can find a ghost, it's Ozzie."

"The FBI has firewalls inside their firewalls," she told him, glad he'd followed her down this new conversational path. Mainly because the old one had been veering into treacherous territory and making her contemplate dangerous things. "I suspect the IRS is even more secure."

"And Ozzie is a virtual fire jumper. If the evidence is there to be found, Ozzie will find it."

"But what if finding it takes weeks instead of days? I can't stay here that long. I can't worry my family and coworkers like that. I'll need to—"

"Don't borrow tomorrow's troubles," he interrupted.

She scoffed. "My whole *career* is about thinking one step ahead. Whoever outed your brother and Mr. Greenlee to the cartel is playing a dangerous game. They have to know that. Which means they're probably too smart to have left behind a digital footprint."

"Nah." She heard a rustling and lifted her chin to find he'd sat up on his pallet. When he leaned his elbows against the stone hearth behind him, the fire at his back cast his form in silhouette. The little tuft of hair over his temple stuck up straight. She had the nearly overwhelming urge to run her hand over it. And then run her hand over *so* much more. "You don't have to be smart to be dangerous," he explained. "You don't avoid a black widow spider because it's smart."

She sat up as well. Sleep wasn't possible with her mind spinning in circles and her chest tight with worry. It *definitely* wasn't possible with Sergeant Britt Rollins only three feet away.

Three feet away and wearing gray sweatpants.

Had he done that on purpose? Did he know gray sweatpants were catnip for women?

Talk about MEOW!

She needed a distraction. "Would you have really killed the tactical team guys if they'd found us?"

She watched as his lips pulled wide in a Cheshire cat smile. "Never said I'd kill them."

"Yes, you did. You said—"

"That I'd shoot them," he interrupted. "Shooting someone and killing them are two very different things. If they were synonymous, I'd be pushing up daisies."

Her momentary relief that he wasn't the type of man to go around murdering innocent agents for doing their job was immediately replaced by a keen sense of curiosity. "You've been shot?"

"Mmm." He nodded slowly.

"Where?" The question was out of her mouth before she realized how inappropriate it might be.

What if he'd been shot somewhere embarrassing? Like his ass? Or his balls? Or his—

Her thoughts screeched to a halt when he stood and sauntered casually over to the sofa. He sat down beside her. Not at the other end of the sofa. Nope. He chose the cushion right next to her.

She'd barely recovered her breath from his proximity when he lifted his T-shirt, and she forgot how to breathe entirely.

He was... *beautiful*.

Her brothers were overgrown and bulky. Her last boyfriend had been a carbon copy of that, strapping in a brutish sort of way. But beautiful? No. That wasn't a word she'd have used to describe any of the men in her life.

It was the only word to describe Britt.

His skin was the color of light caramel. His hips were lean, and his stomach was corrugated. Flat brown nipples sat upon square pectoral muscles. And as if this particular sundae needed a cherry, he had a light smattering of crinkly black hair that ran up the centerline of his body until it fanned out in perfect symmetry across his wide chest.

He was Michelangelo's *David* made flesh. A finely-crafted marble statue sprung to life. *Art.*

He was the kind of gorgeous mere mortals like her could only admire from afar. Except, funny thing was, he kept using every excuse to get close to her.

She followed his hand as he pointed to a wound on his flank. It was the shape of a cigarette burn, only about three times bigger. It crinkled slightly with each of his breaths.

"So you weren't able to melt *this* one," she murmured.

"Huh?"

"Nothing." She shook her head. "Just a random thought I had earlier."

Before she thought of how inappropriate it was to touch him without his consent, she reached forward and slowly ran her fingertips over the remnants of the injury. He hissed as his stomach muscles accordioned. She yanked back her hand as if she'd been burned.

And maybe she had.

His flesh was flaming hot to the touch.

"Sorry," she whispered, her gaze shooting up to find his eyes fixed on her face. His expression was…

Ruthless maybe? *Barbaric?*

Both came close. Neither was exactly right.

She shivered. "I'm sorry," she said again, her voice not sounding like hers. It was lower. *Shakier.* "I shouldn't have done that. Does it still hurt?"

"No."

One word, gritted through his teeth.

She frowned. "Then why did you—"

She stopped when he dropped his shirt. She couldn't decide if she was sorry or relieved she could no longer see all that glorious, golden flesh.

For long moments, the room was quiet. The only noises to break the silence were the gentle crackle of the fireplace, the soft snores coming from the bedroom next door, and the ragged sound of her own breathing as she searched his face.

"When you touch me, Julia, I feel like I'm falling," he finally confessed, his voice little more than a low, gravelly whisper.

Julia…

She would never get tired of hearing him say her name.

Her whole life, people had pronounced it *jew-lee-uh.* But his drawl turned it into the much softer-sounding *jewel-yuh.*

"Is that a good or bad feeling?" she asked breathlessly.

"Good. Too good. I don't want you to stop. I want you to keep going until you've touched every part of me, and I've fallen through the center of the earth."

His voice had thickened. Her blood thickened in direct response, and she couldn't stop the small, triumphant smile that pulled at the corners of her mouth.

It was a heady thing to be wanted by a man like him.

She had a wildly inappropriate impulse. An impulse she should definitely ignore. But it was like her hand had a mind of its own when it splayed over his chest, right above his heart.

Warm…

He was so unbelievably warm.

Hard…

His muscles felt as unforgiving as titanium beneath her fingers.

He placed his hand over hers. She thought he did it to pull her away. But a split-second later, she knew the opposite was true.

He pressed her palm harder into his flesh. Hard enough that she could feel the *lub-dub* of his heart as it kicked up a notch. If she were the romantic kind, the *reckless* kind, she'd say the organ was begging to be claimed.

Good thing she was the realistic, pragmatic sort instead.

"You don't have any idea what you do to me, do you?" he said, softly tracing her fingers.

She did know. Because everything he felt, she felt too.

She didn't confess as much. Instead, she whispered, "Tell me," as her pulse pounded out of control.

What the hell do you think you're doing? the little voice demanded.

Throwing caution to the wind, she silently answered.

She tried to be so in control of every aspect of her life. So *smart* in every decision she made. But now, with this man, she wanted to be careless. She wanted to be wild. She wanted to act on impulse and damn the consequences.

He wanted a Miss Right Now? Well, she could be that woman. She could pretend, just for tonight, that right now was enough.

He swallowed hard, closing his eyes like he was trying to find the words. When he finally spoke, she listened closely, memorizing each word because each word was more enchanting than the last. She might live her whole life and never hear another man speak to her like he spoke to her.

"It's impossible to describe the chaos you create inside me." His voice was raw and unsteady. "Each of your touches is like a lightning strike. They leave me destroyed. And yet…I want to beg you for more."

She swallowed convulsively. Her breaths came sharp and fast.

"It's like…fire and ice, all at once," he continued, the blue of his eyes piercing deep inside her. Into places she should protect from him. Into places she imprudently left wide open so they could welcome him in. "Every part of me aches for you, and when you touch me…it's like nothing else exists. It's like…" He let out a breathless laugh, shaking his head. "God, it's like drowning, but I don't want to come up for air."

His words set something free inside her. Freed her from the fear of what giving in to her basest instincts might do. Freed her from the pressure of always doing the right thing, the *smart* thing. Freed her from caring about what tomorrow might hold because the only thing that mattered was the here and now.

"Kiss me, Britt. Kiss me like you kissed me this morning."

His pupils dilated until they nearly eclipsed the blue of his irises. "I thought we agreed this morning would be the only time—"

"I don't care about that," she interrupted. "Someone smart once said we only regret the decisions we don't make and the chances we don't take. I don't want to regret not exploring whatever this thing is between us. Even if it's only for one night."

His hand stilled atop hers. For a moment, she thought he might not agree to her bargain. For a moment, she thought she might've taken a shot…and missed entirely.

Then, it was like her words had set something free inside him, too. Because the muscles in his jaw hardened. His gaze turned decidedly predatory. And there was no mistaking the determination in his tone when he warned, "Make sure you understand what you're saying, what you're agreeing to. This…" He lifted his hand away from hers so he could place his wide palm above her left breast. After finding the place where her pajama top parted, he ran a callused thumb along the ridge of her collarbone. So gently. So studiously. As if he'd never touched a woman before.

Which she knew was a lie.

The way Britt kissed, the way he knew how to use his hands and his body to give pleasure, told her there were *myriads* of women left in his wake. *Satisfied* women.

She might've been jealous of them if she'd had time to think about them. But she didn't. Because he lifted his hand from her chest to her face.

Cupping her jaw, he dragged the pad of his thumb over her bottom lip. When her tongue darted out to follow the caress, his eyes sharpened until she was reminded of a jungle cat spotting its prey.

His voice was lower, rougher when he finished. "This is all it'll ever be. This physical…*thing* between us. It'll never be more. It'll never be what you're looking for."

"Then, let it be this." She leaned forward until her lips were a whisper away from his.

The inches between them felt like kindling. And the spark that would set that kindling ablaze would be one of them moving.

She waited for him to be the one. Waited with bated breath and her blood rushing in her ears. Waited until she couldn't wait anymore.

When she brushed her mouth across his, every thought in her head dissolved into a heated blur, leaving only the sensation of his hot breath mingling with her own and the sweet, agonizing thrill of finally allowing herself to be consumed by the fire that had raged between them since the first moment they met.

CHAPTER 21

Damned if Britt wasn't kissing Agent Julia O'Toole. *Again.* Despite his best intentions. Despite knowing how *dangerous* this whole thing could be. To himself. To *her.* He was kissing her.

Or…maybe she was kissing him.

It was hard to tell.

Half his brain was yelling, *Stop! End this before it burns out of control!*

But the other half of his brain? Oh, *that* half was screaming something else entirely. Something that started with *oh* and ended with *yeah* and had a *hell* thrown in there somewhere in the middle.

He liked the second half of his brain much better than the first half. Decided the second half was obviously the intelligent half, and the first half could go take a flying leap.

Of course, the choice of which half of his brain to listen to went up in a puff of smoke when Julia opened her mouth wider to the press of his tongue. It was the sweetest of invitations. The sexiest of requests. One he didn't refuse.

He did the *opposite* of refuse, in fact. He jumped in *whole-hog,* as his father had liked to say.

Their sweet, soft kiss became a fight for supremacy. Their lips and teeth devoured. Their tongues clashed. Their hands tugged in desperation.

It was like they warred to get closer. Battled to experience all the other had to offer.

And what Julia offered was unbearable softness. Unbelievable warmth.

She was liquid silk in his arms. Her mouth was like hot sugar that melted against his tongue. The smell of her, that festive scent, like cherries and almonds and hot vanilla, tunneled up his nose and reminded him of the holidays.

It made sense, he supposed. Julia O'Toole was Christmas morning, Thanksgiving dinner, and Easter Sunday all rolled into one diminutive blond package. She was the sweetest gift and the greatest prize and… something more. Something he couldn't name.

All he knew for sure was that he wanted more, more, *more*. More of her taste. More of her touch. More of her mind and body and soul.

No matter how hard he pulled her against him, or how strongly she clasped him to her, it wasn't enough. Wasn't *close* to enough.

He wanted to dissolve into all her warmth and softness. Wanted to lose himself in her. And good lord, maybe she was clouding his memory, but he couldn't remember anyone ever being this hot. Anything ever being this fast. This crazy.

She sucked his tongue, laving along its length with her own. He nipped at her luscious lips, kissing and stroking over and over. And all the while, they rocked against each other. *Rubbed* against each other.

He could feel the hard points of her breasts rasping against his chest. Feel the heated dew that slicked her skin as her passion rose in direct proportion to his own.

She was flint and he was steel. She was flame and he was tinder. Together they were a conflagration. A wild, ferocious inferno that would soon burn out of control if he didn't throw some water over the blaze.

At the rate they were going, it would all be over in minutes. He'd rip off those flannel pajama bottoms, release his raging cock, and pull her into his lap. He'd impale her onto himself and fuck up into her hot wetness over and over again. It would be hard and fast and…

Holy shit!

How had he ever thought he could deny himself this woman? How had he ever thought he'd be satisfied to simply watch her from the shadows?

They'd been destined to come here from the moment they set eyes on each other. To come together. From the first time they'd shaken hands, when their fingertips had touched and electricity had sparked, that invisible thread had been pulling them inexorably closer, steadily drawing them to this very spot.

This… This was meant to be. They were meant to find each other and know how hot passion could burn. They were meant to fire hot and flame out, like a shooting star.

The low moan at the back of her throat seemed to reverberate down into his balls, making him highly aware of how tight and heavy they were. It was enough of a distraction to have some good sense returning.

If this was all it would ever be, if all they had was this one night, he wouldn't rush.

He would revel.

He would do everything he'd been dreaming of doing. He would touch every part of her. Taste each inch of her. Make her finish with his fingers and his mouth and his cock until every orgasm she had going forward reminded her of him.

Yes, even though he wasn't the one for her, he wanted to be the one she remembered. The one she thought about on nights she was alone. The one who filled her fantasies when she rubbed herself to completion.

Maybe that was selfish. Maybe a better man wouldn't want that for her. But he didn't care.

All that mattered was making this night count.

All that mattered was making her his for these few, fleeting hours in the hopes she'd carry him with her through all the years to come. Because he knew he'd be carrying her with him for the rest of his life.

Pulling his mouth from hers took all the self-control he could muster. Then, he pressed his forehead to hers as their ragged breaths mingled.

"Don't stop." Her warm words feathered over his hungry lips.

"There's no way I'm stopping." His voice sounded like he'd dragged his vocal cords over shattered glass. "Not unless you tell me to. And if you do, I'll likely walk funny for the next three weeks."

She pulled back to study him. The firelight showed her eyes weren't one shade of brown but hundreds. Caramel and toffy, chocolate and butterscotch. He could spend a lifetime looking into her eyes and never name all the sweetness he saw there.

"Then why did you pull away?" she whispered, her cheeks rosy with the warmth of passion.

"Because we're going too fast. I don't want to miss out on anything. I want to experience it all." He brushed a strand of hair back behind her ear. "Will you let me?"

Her throat worked over a hard swallow. When she exhaled, it was ragged and smelled of hot chocolate. "I'll let you do anything you want, Britt."

"Then come with me." He stood from the sofa and offered his hand.

She accepted without hesitation, and he felt a punch of satisfaction. When she obediently followed him to the pallet in front of the fireplace, lying down atop the soft quilt per his whispered instructions, he felt a wave of lust. But it was the moment she lifted a hand, silently beckoning him to join her, that made him feel something entirely new.

Something he'd never felt before.

He recognized it for what it was, though. And he wasn't proud to admit it wasn't a modern or an enlightened emotion. It was animalistic. Primal.

He wanted to *claim*. He wanted to mate. He wanted to possess her body and soul until every inch of her was imprinted with him. He wanted…

Her.

That was the simple truth of it. He wanted her more than he'd ever wanted anything in his whole damn life. And every second he wasn't touching her, wasn't kissing her, wasn't making her moan his name in ecstasy, was time wasted.

Quickly crossing to the bedroom door, he shoved the wooden doorstop beneath the crack. It wouldn't stop the bedroom's occupants from exiting the room, but it would slow them down enough to allow Britt and Julia to cover themselves.

Then he turned to make his way back to the pallet and the woman who waited for him with open arms and a vixen's smile.

CHAPTER 22

The flames in the hearth crackled softly. But it was the fire inside Julia that held her attention. It moved through her veins like molten honey—liquid and glowing.

Her heart thrummed inside her chest with a wild, insistent beat. Her breaths came fast and shallow, the air filling her lungs tinged with the taste of the burning wood and the lingering flavor of his kiss.

The man had the most delicious mouth. His breath was hot and sultry, like a summer night. And his taste? Oh, it was intoxicating. Salty and sweet and potent, like buttered bourbon. She wanted to drink from him until she was drunk.

She already *felt* drunk. Or maybe *drugged* was a better word for it.

Her limbs were heavy. Her mind was fuzzy. But at the same time, she was keenly aware of every inch of her flesh. Aware of how her arms tingled. How her legs prickled. How the flannel of the pajamas rubbed across her hard nipples with a painful pleasure.

All of it was because of him. All the lazy stupor and the heightened senses. They were a product of his touch and his kisses. Of the wicked wantonness of his words and the unquestioning truth that he planned to make all her fantasies into reality.

He towered above her, every inch of him a study in strength and masculine beauty. His dark hair was unruly—as usual—the thick waves framing the angles of his face and his cowlick sticking up straight to soften his otherwise stern countenance. His close-cut beard followed the hard lines of his jaw.

And his eyes?

My god. I've never seen eyes like his.

They were deep, endless pools. She wanted to drown in them.

Whatever happened after this night was inconsequential. Because *this* night was everything. *This* night was going to show her what true passion was, what true chemistry was. And that would be enough.

I'll make it be enough.

"Are you going to stand there all night?" Her voice was deep with desire. "Or are you going to join me down here so I can get my hands on you again?" The smile she gave him was intentionally coquettish. She let her eyes drop to the hard ridge pressing against the gray cotton of his sweatpants. "And so I can get my *mouth* on you," she added with a practiced purr.

His rigid cock flexed, stretching the fabric tight and giving her a perfect view of his shape and dimensions. Her throat went desert dry at the same time a rush of wetness slicked between her thighs.

He was…not a small man.

"Oh, I'm very much looking forward to the time you get your hands and mouth on me." His gaze roamed down her body and stopped at the junction of her legs. His eyes narrowed as if he knew how wet she was. His nostrils flare as if he could smell her desire. "But before that happens, I plan to undress you slowly. To lick and suck and kiss every inch of your skin as I uncover it."

Despite the warmth of the fire and the hotness of her blood, goosebumps peppered her skin.

He reached over his head, grabbed the collar of his shirt, and peeled the cotton away from his body in one practiced move.

She gasped at his beauty, at the shadows that danced across his tan skin, accentuating the ridges of muscle beneath. The black ink of the eagle feather tattoo on his forearm stood out in sharp relief and she wanted to ask after it, ask what it represented because she'd noted many of the men who worked at Black Knights Inc. sported a similar tattoo. She was distracted from her question, however, when he bent at the waist and pulled off his sweatpants.

He stood to his full height then, and he was…

Nude.

Holy shit, Sergeant Britt Rollins was nude.

And, suddenly, *beautiful* didn't begin to describe him. It didn't capture the breadth of his shoulders or the narrowness of his hips. It didn't encapsulate the sheer *manliness* of his form. And it didn't begin to cover how nervous she felt once she got a good, long look at what she'd be working with.

Emphasis on good *and* long, she thought a little hysterically.

His cock was so hard it thrust from his body at an angle that defied gravity. The shaft was heaviest in the middle. Thick veins snarled up his length, turgid and pulsing. And his plump head was so engorged the skin covering it was shiny.

"G-good lord," she breathed, and then swallowed convulsively.

When he reached down and unabashedly gave himself a single stroke, the desire that slammed into her was a tangible force. It made her blood flow like fire and her skin tingle like it was kissed by Fourth of July sparklers.

"This is what you do to me." His eyes were penetrating.

A flutter of uncertainty twisted in her stomach. But it was quickly drowned out by the waves of lust and anticipation that washed over her.

Sitting up, she automatically reached for the rigid column of flesh that protruded so proudly and begged so unabashedly for her attention. But she stopped when he shook his head. "Not yet."

She glanced up and found his bearded jaw set at a hard angle. His chest worked over harsh breaths. And his gaze was hot and unwavering.

"Why not?" Her fingers itched to touch that rigid length of silk-covered steel. She knew the flesh would be burning hot.

"Because the anticipation is half the fun." His tone was arrogant, as if he knew more about pleasing her than she knew about pleasing herself. "Let me show you." He joined her on the pallet then, encouraging her to lie back as he stretched his long, naked length out beside her.

She wanted to run her hands all over him. Wanted to test the resiliency of his skin. Wanted to map every hard ridge and muscled contour. Wanted to fling off her pajama bottoms, climb on top of him, and skewer herself on that hard column of flesh that was as threatening as it was impressive.

He didn't let her.

When she tried to turn toward him, he gently pressed her shoulders into the coverlet and whispered, "Stay still. Let me unwrap you like the gift that you are."

She shivered at the idea. "Were you the type of kid who ripped into his Christmas presents? Or the type who carefully unwrapped each one to keep the paper intact?"

His smile was utterly uncivilized. It matched the jagged scar on his temple. "As I said, the anticipation is half the fun. Now, close your eyes."

Part of her balked at the idea. If she closed her eyes, she wouldn't be able to keep ogling all his glorious male flesh. But another part of her thrilled at the thought of letting him take the lead, giving him the reins to her pleasure and simply allowing herself to go along for the ride.

Her breath sawed out of her when she did as instructed and two words rumbled from the depths of his chest, "Good girl."

Holy hell!

The air around her felt electric, charged with that intangible something pulled tight between them. It was like a live wire, fizzing and crackling. She gave into the danger of it, knowing that it might burn her.

But the reward would be worth the risk.

Then, all her thoughts vanished when she felt the air around her move because he reached out his hand. A second later, his fingers skimmed her cheek so lightly she almost didn't feel it. Her body reacted as if he'd branded her; however, a harsh shudder ran down her spine.

Gently, he turned her head until she faced him. Her eyelids fluttered but remained closed when he brushed his thumb over her bottom lip.

"You're so goddamned beautiful." The timbre of his voice was raw and all-consuming. And then his mouth was on hers.

It wasn't a frenzied kiss. Not like the one they'd shared in the kitchen that morning. Not like the one they'd just shared on the couch.

This was a slow kiss. A mapping kiss. This kiss was pure, *thorough* seduction. And by the time he pulled his lips from hers, she was panting and mewling and begging him to touch her.

She needed his touch more than she needed her next breath.

He seemed to sense it because, in the next instant, his fingers moved from her face down to her neck and settled at the top button on her pajamas.

She bit her lip in agonized anticipation when she felt the first button slip free, followed by the second and the third. When he spread the halves of the top wide, the room's coolness coupled with the heat of his gaze—even though she couldn't see them, she could feel his eyes on her—and made her shudder. Her nipples furled into even tighter buds. Her stomach began to quiver.

"So goddamned beautiful," he repeated reverently, his hot breath feathering over the nipple closest to him.

She couldn't help herself; she reached for him. But he caught her hand before it could make contact.

"Not yet," he scolded again, manacling her wrists above her head.

She was aware of how exposed she was to him, with her arms raised and her breasts lifted high in invitation. But instead of feeling nervous or embarrassed, she only felt excitement.

Excitement, anticipation, and an odd sort of trust that, despite his high-handedness—*or maybe because of it?*—he would give her pleasure unlike anything she'd ever known.

She dared to open her eyes and found his gaze locked on her breasts. His irises swirled like whirlpools. The muscle in his jaw twitched with hunger. And his expression? There was no quarter there, only a dark, ravenous need that made her throat go dry.

He wasn't looking at her face. So she wasn't sure how he knew she'd opened her eyes. Maybe he had a sixth sense about such things.

"Close them," he growled. "I want you to keep them closed so all your focus is on *feeling* what I'm doing to you."

She nodded and dutifully squeezed her eyes shut.

He rewarded her obedience by sucking her nipple into the heated haven of his mouth.

"Britt!" she gasped his name, her toes curling in pure pleasure.

"Easy." His breath was hot against her nipple. His tongue was hotter when he flicked it out to tease the tip. "Trust me, okay? I'm going to make you feel so good."

I do trust you, she thought. *For whatever reason, I trust you completely.*

She nodded her agreement, and he focused his whole attention—and his entire mouth—on her breasts. He knew precisely what to do. How to suck, how to flick his tongue, how to nibble with his lips to delight her and have her blood pooling hot and heavy in her sex.

She fully gave herself over to him. Fully allowed herself to do nothing but passively participate in the pleasure he pressed on her body as, true to his word, he slowly undressed her and kissed and nibbled and sucked on every new inch of flesh as he uncovered it.

By the time she was fully naked, no part of her had been left unexplored. From her earlobes to her belly button, from the backs of her knees to the turn of her ankles, he'd used his hands and mouth to map her body.

Well, there's one *part he hasn't explored*, she thought a little desperately.

It was the part that ached the most, the part that needed attention the most.

The man was a tease. Wonderfully, terribly deliberate in how he went about her seduction. So that now, every single one of her nerve endings thrummed with lust. And he had but to skate the tips of his fingers along her skin and sparks of utter delight would go shooting through her entire system.

She could feel the heat of his body along her side. Feel the branding pulse of his hot, heavy cock against her hip.

She *so* wanted to wrap her fingers around him, feel him throb in her palm while she ran her thumb over his tip to catch the drop of desire that would bead there. But anytime she tried, he scolded her and repositioned her hands above her head, holding her captive and forcing her to submit to his relentless assault.

 The anticipation of what was to come had her teetering on the edge. She was desperate for the fall. And when he finally, *finally* cupped his hand against her sex, a soft, broken sound escaped her throat.

It wasn't a sigh. It wasn't a moan or a panting gasp. Somehow, it was a mixture of all three.

"Is this what you want?" His words were low and hot as they swirled in her ear. "You want me to rub this pretty pussy until you scream?"

Jesus.

Dominant *and* dirty talking? Sergeant Britt Rollins was a fantasy come true. A brooding romance novel hero in real life. Every woman's wet dream in biker boots and Marvel T-shirts.

"Please," she rasped, pumping her hips in a desperate bid to force him to give her the friction she needed. "Please, touch me, Britt."

A low rumble of approval sounded in his chest. "Then open your eyes," he commanded. "I want you looking at me when I make you cum for the first time."

Her eyelids felt weighted by anchors. But she managed to crack them open and find him looming over her. There was satisfaction in his face. Satisfaction and hunger unlike anything she'd seen before.

Daring to reach for him, she was delighted when he didn't stop her from cupping a hand against the beard on his jaw. Nor did he stop her when she used her other hand to tangle in his hair.

"I want you so much," she told him boldly. "I need you more than I've ever needed anyone."

"Good," was all he said before allowing her to pull his mouth to hers.

There was nothing gentle about the way he kissed her then. It was raw and desperate. A claim as much as a kiss.

She met him with equal fervor, her own hunger fully unleashed.

And then he did it. *Finally.* He slipped his fingers between her folds and unerringly found the bundle of nerves that needed his touch the most.

She hissed. She was so sensitive; the pleasure was painful.

"So hot," he hummed against her lips. "So wet."

And then neither of them spoke for long moments as he reclaimed her mouth and expertly worked her with his fingers. He set up a remarkable, maddening rhythm, alternating gently rubbing her greedy clit and then slipping his fingers inside her, stroking her in a lazy come-hither motion that soon had her mewling mindlessly while her hips bucked and begged for more.

Time and time again he pushed her close to the edge only to slow down and back her away from it. Time and time again, her womb coiled on the brink of release and then ached in misery when he didn't give it to her.

"Britt! Please!" she pleaded, her eyes open but sightless.

"All right then," he growled into her mouth while expertly stroking her. "Cum for me."

And she did.

Her body was no longer her own. It was his to command. And like a good soldier, it obeyed without question.

Her climax slammed through her so violently that her back arched off the pallet. The tendons in her neck strained. It was a good thing his mouth was on hers. He was able to swallow her scream of unimaginable pleasure.

Pulse after pulse of unending satisfaction pumped through her. He managed to draw out her bliss for innumerable moments. And only when her body couldn't take any more, only when her thighs instinctively closed around his marauding hand because she was completely spent and so sensitive she felt like one huge, raw nerve, did he relent.

When he pulled his fingers from inside her, she didn't know if she was groaning or if it was him. Maybe it was the both of them.

Her vision slowly returned, and she found herself staring into his lust-laden eyes. She wasn't surprised to find his gaze was a pure blue flame, hotter than the fire in the hearth. More dangerous to her heart than anything she'd ever seen.

"Good girl," he praised again. Then, he stuck his fingers into his mouth, his lids fluttering slightly as he savored her taste.

CHAPTER 23

Julia was…
Hell.
He had no words.
Learning her body was a pleasure unlike any he'd known. Her skin was smooth and impossibly soft beneath his fingertips—a silken expanse he felt honored to touch. Tasting her flesh was pure joy. She was sweet and salty and everything a woman should be. And watching her come undone was the most beautiful sight he'd ever seen.
Julia in the throes of orgasm…
My god… he thought reverently.
He wanted nothing more than to kiss his way back down her body, toss her legs over his shoulders, and bury his mouth in her womanhood. That trick with his fingers had only been an appetizer; he was hungry for a whole meal. But he knew she was too sensitive. He knew she needed time to recover.
And so he satisfied himself by simply rubbing soothing circles around her belly button as his eyes traced the curves of her body, committing each one to memory.
For such a small woman, she had ample breasts. They were teardrop-shaped, heavier at the bottom than the top. When her arms were above her

head, they stood proud and firm from her chest. When her arms were at her sides, like now, they lay against her rib cage in luscious mounds that invited his touch, his kiss.

Because she was a natural blonde, he'd expected her nipples to be cotton candy pink. But they were the most delicious chocolaty brown. They matched the sweetness of her eyes. And they were oh-so-responsive. The way they pinched and hardened at the slightest rasp of his fingertips, at the gentlest probe of his tongue, was enough to make him feel ten feet tall and fireproof.

And speaking of the fire…

The flickering light played with the drastic dip of her waist, cast dancing shadows over the dramatic flare of her hips, and sparkled like gold dust in the small triangle of dark blond hair at the top of her sex.

She was a goddess. Ethereal. Too perfect for this world.

And yet…she was here. She was lying beside him, trusting him to take her further than she'd ever been taken before.

When her breathing returned to normal, when the dew on her skin began to dry, he dragged his gaze back up the length of her body—he couldn't get enough of looking at her, every inch of her was meant to entice a man's hunger. He found her eyes on his face. They were gleaming with lazy satisfaction.

She patted his shoulder. "Thank you. I really needed that."

"My pleasure," he assured her, his lips twitching.

"Nope." She shook her head, and he loved how her hair was spread over the pillow like a golden curtain. "Pretty sure that was *my* pleasure."

He chuckled because…

There she is. There's the funny, confident, dynamic woman who put me under her spell on day one.

He let his hand trail up her stomach, stopping when his fingers brushed the underside of her breast, delighting when her nipple instantly hardened in anticipation of his touch.

"And just think"—he used one finger to trace a path around her nipple, watching her stomach quiver in response—"we're just getting started."

"Why do I get the feeling you're going to be the death of me?"

"*Attack of the Clones*," he said, having accurately guessed which movie the quote was from.

"Wow." She ran a finger over his collarbone, then down until she mirrored his caresses. Her finger circled his nipple, and he felt the skin there furl tight under her touch. "You're pretty good at that."

"At what? Recognizing *Star Wars* quotes are playing with your lovely little nipples?"

"Yes," was her one-word answer.

He grinned, loving this side of her. This sated, satisfied, playful side.

"Does that mean you're ready for me to resume playing with *all* of you?"

"When do *I* get to play with *you*?" She pretended to pout. He didn't ignore the urge to bend down and nip at her protruding lower lip.

He meant for it to be a quick, teasing kiss. But she stopped him with a hand on the back of his head.

Her eager tongue darted into his mouth. And before long, his desire to slowly rebuild her passion was supplanted by the fire still raging unchecked inside him.

He wasn't slow or studied this time as he skated his hands and mouth all over her body. He *knew* her now. Knew what would make her gasp. What would make her squirm.

By the time he worked his mouth down her body, she was doing both.

"Show me where you want my tongue," he growled from between her legs. The scent of her was that of a wonderfully ripe woman, sweet and earthy. His dick responded by throbbing hard against the coverlet. He pressed himself into the fabric, searching for relief.

He found none.

The only relief would come when he was sheathed in her tight, hot body. But he wasn't ready for that. First, he wanted to taste her. Wanted to fill his mouth with her soft, wet folds. Wanted stab his tongue into her honeyed core.

He growled his approval when she reached down to spread her herself, showing him her pink, glistening center.

"Here," she husked, her middle finger circling the engorged head of her clit as it peeked from its fleshy hood. "I want your mouth right here."

She didn't have to tell him twice.

He hooked her knees over his shoulders and feasted. Feasted on her scent. Feasted on her flavor. Feasted on the hot, soft feel of her against his mouth.

As he worked her with his tongue and lips, keeping her thrusting hips pinned to the pallet with his hands, he rode the waves of desire that crashed through him like so many tsunamis, each one fiercer and more relentless than the one before it.

Before long, he could feel her heartbeat against his lips. He could taste her looming orgasm on his tongue. He could hear how her soft sighs turned into sharp, whimpering pants.

She was close.

So damn close.

It took herculean effort to pull away from her. But he managed it.

"Whaaa?" Her cry of confused anguish matched the look in her eyes when he quickly turned for the duffel bag he'd left near the end of the sofa.

"The next time you cum, I want to feel it all around me." His voice was a raw rasp as he unzipped the bag, found his wallet, and pulled a foil pack from within. "I want to feel your sweet pussy as it grasps my cock."

Lust glazed her eyes as she watched him. Her hands played with her nipples, and her thighs unabashedly rubbed together as if she couldn't stand the lack of stimulation.

"That's right," he told her, his eyes flaming brighter than the fire in the hearth. "Keep touching yourself. Keep yourself right on the edge for me."

Two of her fingers disappeared into her body. His own body responded by throbbing so hard he hissed. He hissed again as he fisted the condom down his length. And then he was groaning as he lowered himself onto her.

Her arms were instantly around his back. Her legs hooked around his so that her heels fit into the backs of his knees.

It was heaven to feel her nipples scraping through his chest hair. It was nirvana to feel her hips cradling his own. But it was something too huge and too powerful to name to feel her wet, greedy entrance sucking at the head of his dick when he guided himself into her.

They both gasped at that initial touch. That first inch.

"So fucking hot," he whispered against her lips, feeling a drop of sweat bead on his forehead. "So fucking tight," he added when he nudged his hips forward and embedded himself another inch.

She caught his tongue between her teeth. Not hard enough to hurt. Just hard enough to issue a warning.

Received loud and clear, he thought as he stopped his advance.

He'd been in enough foxholes and locker rooms to know he wasn't your average joe. And she was swollen and achy from her last orgasm. He needed to go slow, coax her body into accepting him.

He carefully pressed forward, ever so slightly, ever so slowly. It was heaven to feel her walls flutter around him. It was hell having to hold back when his body and every animal instinct he possessed urged him to thrust and rut and fuck.

He watched her face as he continued his slow assault, his vision dimming around the edges and coalescing into pleasure when he saw her concentration melt into bliss. After long, torturous moments, he was seated to the hilt, his balls resting against the smooth curve of her ass, his head smashed tight against the barrier of her cervix.

They moaned in unison.

"You okay?" he asked through a clenched jaw.

Her answer was a desperate nod.

"Good. Because I'm going to fuck you now, Julia," he promised, lowering his lips to hers. "I'm going to fuck you and feel you cream all over my cock."

Her whimper was all the agreement he needed.

His thrusts were slow and measured to start. He gritted his teeth against the indescribable friction. And only when he felt her walls begin to spasm did he increase his rhythm.

Her heels found a spot beneath his ass, urging him ever onward. Her hands ran from his shoulders to his hips and back again, encouraging him faster, harder.

By the time he felt the first spasm of her orgasm, his shaft was screaming with pleasure and his balls were ready to explode.

He slammed his mouth over hers to muffle her scream. And then her gripping, undulating, seemingly endless orgasm pulled him over the edge with her.

His grunt of pleasure wasn't studied or sexy. It was a crude, animalistic sound as jet after jet of lightning-bright lust shot from his body and left him breathless, sightless, weightless as the world fell away and he was lost in a place where only ecstasy existed.

Ecstasy and that ineffable, nameless *thing* that existed between them. Even then, even with their bodies fused and their orgasms mingling, he could feel the pull of it. It was stronger than before—if that was possible.

Stronger and softer and more delicious.

More dangerous.

He had no idea how long they lay there after the last waves of lust blew through them. It could've been minutes or hours. All he knew was that by the time he came back to himself, by the time he realized he was still embedded deep inside her and her breaths were no longer coming in desperate, shallow gasps, the fire had burned down to glowing embers.

He shoved up on his elbows, careful to keep his hips still—he loved the way her little aftershocks fluttered along his shaft. Glancing down into her face, he saw her eyes were shut, her cheeks were red and rosy, and a small, satisfied smile played at her lips.

"You look very pleased with yourself." He brushed a damp lock of hair back from her forehead.

"I *am* very pleased with myself." Her eyes fluttered open. The look in them was purely feline.

The wolf in him answered with a growl. He nuzzled his nose into the crook of her shoulder to inhale her scent: soap, a lingering hint of her perfume, and the smell of a sexy, sultry, satisfied woman. "I'm very pleased with you too."

"I know." He could hear the teasing in her tone as she tunneled her fingers into his hair. "I was there. I felt how pleased you were with me."

God, he thought. *I could worship her like this forever.*

CHAPTER 24

"What's wrong with the month of March?"

Julia had been on the verge of sleep. After Britt disposed of the condom, he'd rejoined her on the pallet. With the smoldering embers at her back and his warmth pressed all along her front because she'd thrown a leg over his thighs and cradled her head in the nook of his shoulder —that space on a man's body was perfectly formed to hold a woman's cheek—she'd been content to give in to the pull of slumber.

"Mmm?" she asked sleepily, loving the tickle of his chest hair against her cheek. Loving the solid *lub-dub* of his heartbeat against her ear.

"March," he said again. "You said you hate orange marmalade, the month of March, and going to the dentist. I get the dentist. *No* one likes going to the dentist. The sound of the tools scraping against your teeth is just…" He shuddered dramatically. "And orange marmalade is understandable. I mean, I don't *hate* it. But I'd much rather slather strawberry jam or grape jelly on a piece of toast. But March? What's wrong with March?"

She wrinkled her nose. "What's *right* with March is the better question. It's bitterly cold. The snow on the ground is so old it's gray. And everyone is cranky as hell because they can't go outside without first putting on three layers of clothes. Statistics say violent crime peaks in Chicago over the summer. But I bet dollars to doughnuts that *non*violent crime, the petty stuff, all the misdemeanors and misconduct that stems from a general sense of malaise and irritation, happens in the month of March."

When he hummed, she felt it vibrate against her cheek. "I reckon that's the difference between a Southerner and a Midwesterner."

"How so?" She snuggled closer, loving how his arm automatically tightened around her waist.

"In Charleston, March is the *best* month. The gray winter days are behind you, but summer's hot soupy days are still weeks off. March is when the flowers bloom. When you can sit outside and drink sweet tea without having to coat yourself in mosquito repellent. When you don't have to worry about a hurricane blowing in while you're fishing on the marshes."

It was her turn to hum her appreciation. "That sounds lovely."

"Have you ever been to Charleston?"

"Hmm-mmm." She shook her head slightly and was rewarded with a warm kiss pressed to the crown of her head. "But I've heard good things."

She thought he might invite her to go there with him. Thought he might want to show her his hometown. She was a little disappointed when all he said was, "It's worth the trip for the food alone."

Right.

Because they weren't a couple. There wouldn't be any trips. Hell, there wouldn't be any nights beyond this one.

Slam, bam, thank-you-ma'am. Isn't that what I agreed to? she thought a little despondently.

Then she thought, *No. Don't mourn what you won't have. Revel in what you do have. You're in a cozy cabin in the woods. There's a warm fire at your back, and you're lying in the arms of the world's sexiest man. Things could be worse.*

"What's your favorite Charleston staple?" she asked, lazily drawing a shape around his navel up to his pecs and back down again.

"She crab soup," he answered automatically.

"I'm assuming that's different from *he* crab soup?" she quipped, proud of her own wit.

"It's a crab bisque made from female crabs. It's orange because of the roe they carry."

That had her pushing up on her elbow to blink down into his handsome face. The glowing embers in the hearth turned his tanned skin to burnished gold and made his blue eyes darken to the color of the sea before a storm.

"Roe as in *eggs*? It's a soup made from pregnant crabs?"

He bit his cheek to keep from laughing at the horror on her face. "So let me see if I have this straight. You'd be fine if it were soup made from regular old crabs, male or female, but if it's female crabs carrying eggs, *that's* the bridge too far?"

"*Yes*," she declared with a staunch dip of her chin.

He chuckled lowly. She felt the reverberation in her own chest, and it was such a delicious sensation.

Not as delicious as all the things he'd done to her over the last hour or so—truly, the man was a marvel. But wonderfully nice all the same.

"Tell me," he said once he'd sobered. "Do you eat crab legs?"

She narrowed her eyes. "Yes."

"Have you ever had caviar?"

"Once at a Southside fireman's gala that my dad and my brothers made me go to." She curled her lip. "I didn't care for it. Too salty."

"So you'll eat crabs. And you'll eat eggs. But a soup made with the crabs and their eggs is gross?"

"Don't try to use logic when this is clearly an emotional topic. Soup made with pregnant crabs just *feels* wrong."

He bit his bottom lip to contain his wide grin before nodding dutifully. "Noted. No logic. Pure emotion." Then he tilted his head. "So what's your favorite Chicago staple?"

She liked this part. The lazy, sated, getting-to-know-each-other part.

At least, she liked it with *him*.

She'd dated men who were complete shit at it. Men who rolled over and fell asleep directly after orgasm. Or men who stayed awake long enough for her to ask them questions, get one-word answers, and eventually realize they had no interest in her beyond what her body could offer them. They were *far* worse than the straight-to-sleep guys. At least the straight-to-sleep guys were honest.

But Britt?

He was genuinely curious about her. Genuinely funny and kind and smart. And unfortunately, instead of the sex having scratched her itch for him, it'd only inflamed it.

She wanted more. More of the sex. More of this pillow talk. More of him.

All of him.

It hit her then.

That...*thing* that existed between them, that chemistry or compatibility or...what was the word he'd used? Oh, right. *Affinity.* It went beyond the physical.

They were a mental match, too. Her intelligence aligned with his; she enjoyed his wit as much as he seemed to enjoy hers. They *got* each other. Simpatico.

Stir those things together in a pot, throw in a dash of Southern charm, and top it with his penchant for loyalty and honesty, and what she had was a big ol' recipe for falling in love.

Yes, she thought forlornly. *It'd be so easy to fall in love with Sergeant Britt Rollins.*

Perhaps he'd sensed that from the start. Sensed that their mutual attraction would extend beyond the bedroom. Maybe that's why he'd been so quick to poo-poo her offer for drinks. He'd wanted to head her off at the pass before she'd had the chance to take the leap over the ledge and—

"Did you fall asleep with your eyes open?"

His question had her thoughts flying back to the present. "Oh." She shook her head. "Sorry. I spaced out there for a second."

"Where did you go?" A little line formed between his eyebrows.

Had she mentioned how lovely his eyebrows were? Jet black, slightly arched, thick without being overgrown?

Gah! Now she was waxing poetic about his eyebrows?

Damn, I've got it bad.

Although the truth was, she'd *had* it bad for him from the beginning. Now, it was just worse.

"Off in a direction that's not worth mentioning," she assured him. He'd made it clear he had *no* interest in a relationship. Mentioning how easy it would be for her to fall in love with him was a moot point. "What was the question again?"

He narrowed his eyes like he wanted to press her. But decided not to—thankfully—because he said, "I was asking about your favorite Chicago staple."

"A steak sweet. Hands down."

He lifted an eyebrow. "And that is...?"

"It's a steak sandwich dipped in a sweet sauce made at one place and one place only. Home of the Hoagy. It's on 111th Street. It's a big, sloppy mess to eat, but it's worth every stain you get on your shirt."

Maybe when we get back to Chicago, we can go there.

The words were perched on the tip of her tongue. She swallowed them down because…*one night only.*

"I'll have to give it a try."

She parroted his earlier words back to him. "It's worth the trip."

After resuming her previous position, she was free to run her hand over his torso. His crinkly chest hair tickled her palm. His left nipple hardened under her fingertips. And when she slid her hand down his belly, she smiled softly at how his stomach muscles tensed.

If all they had was the one night, she wasn't going to waste it on sleep.

Before she could wrap her hands around him, however, her fingers brushed lightly over the puckered wound on his flank. She was instantly distracted.

She practiced with her service weapon twice a week. She'd seen plenty of death by way of a round traveling at 1300 miles per hour. But she'd never met anyone who'd actually been shot.

Despite what the movies would have everyone believe, most FBI agents didn't spend their careers dodging bullets. In fact, *most* of her colleagues had never fired their service weapon in the line of duty.

"How did this happen?" She pushed back onto her elbow.

He met her gaze full-on, but his expression was shuttered.

"Oh." She nodded. "Is this one of those super-secret soldier things that's been buried in a file in the basement of the Pentagon?"

He took a moment, seeming to consider. Then he shrugged one shoulder. "It's a part of my past that's been 'redacted out the wazoo,' as you so eloquently put it."

"So, then, yes."

"Let's just say it involved a raid on an enemy compound, and I darted left when I should've dodged right."

It wasn't anything close to a real answer. But she understood what it was to be the keeper of classified information. She didn't press him further. Instead, she changed gears.

"And this?" She ran a gentle finger over the scar on his forehead. "Is this another injury from the blacked-out part of your file?"

He grimaced and shook his head. "*That* is a souvenir from my misspent youth." When she lifted an intrigued eyebrow, he continued. "You know I told you Knox got his start by boosting cars?"

She nodded.

"Well, sometimes I tagged along. And this..." He reached up and tapped the damaged skin. "Is from when we crashed a Jaguar into a guardrail while running from the police. Knox walked away with a broken arm. And I came away needing about twenty stitches. We didn't have medical insurance, though. So Knox made a homemade splint with a set of drumsticks, and I made do with butterfly bandages."

It explained the uneven, jagged edges of the wound.

"And hence, your love of adrenaline was kindled."

He chuckled and shook his head. "To quote Lady Gaga, I was born this way. The Rollins men come hardwired for action and intrigue. Knox feeds his hunt for dopamine with shady shit. I feed mine with harrowing missions and mayhem."

"You *fed* it," she corrected.

Something shifted behind his eyes. "Right." He nodded. "Past tense."

Her investigator's instincts kicked in along with her curiosity. "Something tells me it's *not* past tense?"

"I satisfy myself with fast rides down narrow country lanes, base jumping, hang gliding, and tossing myself out of the occasional airplane." He shrugged again. "It's not *quite* as thrilling as dodging—and sometimes not dodging—bullets. But it'll do in a pinch. And then there's this." He reached up to kiss her mouth, his lips lingering until her toes curled. "This is *quite* the adrenaline rush."

"Mmm." She hummed against his mouth. Then she was reminded of the kiss they'd shared in the kitchen, and she pulled back to skewer him with a hard stare. "Is *that* why you kissed me this morning? Because you were looking for a hit of dopamine?"

He had the grace to grimace. "I've wanted to kiss you since the first moment I saw you. But this morning, I used that as an excuse to keep you from going into the pantry looking for Peanut's cat treats."

She narrowed her eyes. "Because..." She drew out the word.

"Because that's where Knox and Sabrina were hiding. Peanut, that damned cat, almost blew the whole thing."

"Scoundrel!" She slapped his shoulder. "Villain!" she added for emphasis. "They were in the pantry? Just five feet away from me the whole time?"

"I know." He nodded, looking guilty. "It was a lowdown, dirty trick. But I can't regret it." He shook his head. "Don't ask me to regret it. It's one of my life's highlights."

She opened her mouth to question him further, but he stopped her by palming her ass and pulling her harder against him. A fresh flame of desire ignited low in her belly.

"I got the impression, before you got distracted by my bullet wound, that you were thinking about round number two. Did I read that wrong?"

She bit her lip and lifted a teasing eyebrow. "No, you did not."

"Good," he rumbled. "Then let's use our mouths for something better than talking. What do you say?"

"I say I like the way you think." When he went to push her onto her back, she stopped him. "Hang on a minute. It's *my* turn to play with *you*."

Desire sparked in his eyes and had a smile playing with the corners of his mouth. He folded his hands behind his head. His tone was indulgent and arrogant when he said, "Go on then. Do your worst."

She did.

Oh, she definitely did.

By the time she straddled his hips and lowered herself onto the part of him she'd paid particular attention to, his indulgence had been replaced with a burning need, and his arrogance had been replaced with gasping pleas for mercy.

CHAPTER 25

J ulia came awake to the sound of Britt and Hew arguing.
"Okay, fine," Hew said. "I may have rushed to judgment on that one."

"You took the fucking Concorde jet to judgment, my brother," Britt countered.

"I know you're not an aircraft guy. But the Concorde was decommissioned over twenty years ago. Your analogy is dated."

She hadn't opened her eyes. So she couldn't see him do it. But she knew Britt rolled his eyes by the sound of his voice. "Everyone knows that, Hew. Y'all flyboys aren't as hot as you think you are."

"Really?" Hew feigned surprise. "I find that hard to believe. I do own a mirror, after all."

Julia recognized an ongoing game of one-upmanship when she heard it. She and her brothers played all the time. And since she'd only gotten… she went to grab her phone and then remembered she'd chucked it… *maybe* two hours of sleep, that meant she was cranky, in desperate need of coffee, and in *no* mood to listen to verbal sparring.

Before Britt could respond, she lifted a hand above the sofa to stab a finger into the air. "Will you two shut up! Some of us can't stand conversation until we've mainlined coffee!"

After their second round of lovemaking, she had re-donned her pajamas and retaken her place on the sofa after removing the doorstop from beneath the bedroom door. She would have *loved* to remain in Britt's arms. But she was an FBI agent who was still officially on the clock. She wanted to maintain at least a modicum of professionalism in the eyes of the others, even if that ship had long since sailed when it came to Britt.

She hadn't expected to get any sleep at all, honestly. But the previous day and the long, luxurious night had caught up with her. At some point, she'd succumbed to the pull of slumber.

Now, she sat up, pushed her hair out of her eyes, and blinked blearily toward the kitchen.

Hew stopped with a mug halfway to his mouth. "Jesus, woman. What does the other guy look like?"

She was a restless sleeper. She always woke up with a rat's nest for a hairdo. Plus, she could *feel* the bags under her eyes and the pillow marks cutting lines into her cheek.

"You're hilarious," she told him grouchily. "When's open mic night at the comedy club?"

He made a face and turned to Britt. "She's not a morning person, I take it?"

Ignoring him, Britt strode from the kitchen with a steaming mug of coffee in hand. When he dutifully placed it on the coffee table, she nearly broke a nail snatching it up.

It was piping hot, thick as motor oil, and strong enough to make her teeth grow hair.

In other words, *perfection*.

She hummed her appreciation after the first sip.

"Morning." Knox stumbled out of the bedroom with a yawn wide enough to make his jaw crack. "I smell coffee."

"Fresh pot on the counter," Britt informed him.

"Did someone say coffee?" Sabrina entered the living room looking *far* more rested than she had the day before. She wore jeans and a crisp flannel. Her hair was pulled back in a sleek ponytail. And her face looked fresh and completely free of pillowcase lines.

Apparently, *she* wasn't a restless sleeper.

Grr.

Julia wasn't the jealous type, but she felt a little punch of petulance that anyone should wake up looking like Sabrina while *she* woke up looking like she'd gone ten rounds with a hurricane and lost.

Hoping to succor her sour mood with that sweet, sweet cure-all known as caffeine, she took another long sip and watched Hew rush to help Sabrina pull down a mug from the cupboard.

The quiet *thanks* Sabrina gave him was coupled with a shy…knowing?… look that made Julia lift an eyebrow.

Was something brewing between Cooper Greenlee's dark-eyed sister and the auburn-haired behemoth? And if something *was* brewing, was it a foxhole Hemingway thing or something more?

The thought of it possibly being something more made the green-eyed monster hop back on Julia's shoulder. Why did *Sabrina* get the guy when all Julia got was laid?

No, she scolded herself. *Be grateful for the night you had. You'll hold the memory dear for the rest of your life and—*

A loud *buzzing* cut into her thoughts. She glanced around curiously.

Hew pulled a phone from his pocket and held it to his ear. "Oz, man, what do you know?"

She watched Hew's serene expression grow increasingly troubled as he listened to whatever was said on the other end of the call. Every instinct she possessed went on high alert, and she'd already stood from the sofa when Hew cursed, "Fuck. How long?" Then he immediately added, "Never mind. They're here."

He promptly dropped the phone on the floor and, to Julia's surprise, began stomping it to bits.

"What in the world?" She blinked. "Who's here?"

Then she heard it, the subtle *whomp-whomp-whomp* of helicopter blades slicing through the morning air. Her heart sank.

"Don't tell me you didn't think to use an encrypted phone." She pointed to the shattered plastic and twisted metal that lay on the floor at Hew's feet. "I told you the techs in the bureau could trace—"

Hew cut her off. "I smashed the phone to make sure your friends don't try to use it as evidence against Black Knights Inc. And for the record, they didn't trace *us*. They traced *you*."

"Me?" She blinked incredulously. "How? I yeeted *my* phone back at the farm and—"

Again, Hew didn't let her finish. "Something about your family and a tracking device and a fanny pack. Ozzie kept tabs on online bureau chatter and just saw that your coworkers were coming here."

Julia felt all the blood drain from her head.

She stubbed her toe on the leg of the coffee table as she raced for the pile of clothes she'd left behind the sofa. Hopping on one foot and cursing up a storm, she snatched her fanny pack off the ground, unzipped it, and used the sensitive pads of her fingers to feel around the pack's lining.

She screwed her eyes shut when she located the telltale lump of a small tracking device.

"My father," she breathed, turning to the gathered group and shaking her head apologetically. "He worries, you know? Because this is a dangerous job? And when he bought me this for Christmas, I never thought to—"

"We don't have time for explanations. Your friends are here." Britt silenced her by slashing his hand through the air as Knox began to pace the floor like a trapped animal. Hew pulled a weapon from the back of his pants and carefully placed it on the bar. And poor Sabrina's eyes were round as saucers and fixed on the front door.

"They're not my *friends*," Julia insisted. "They're my colleagues."

"Whatever. The important part is now it's going to be up to *you* to keep my brother alive." The look on his face was a far cry from the one he'd been wearing the night before.

That look had said he thought she was the most beautiful thing he'd ever seen. *This* look said he wanted to wring her neck with his bare hands.

And who could blame him?

He'd gone to all this trouble to keep his brother safe and out of the hands of the feds, and now, because of *her*, all his well-laid plans had gone up in smoke.

"Whatever happens over the next few hours," he continued, his gaze hard enough to cut, "you don't let Knox out of your sight. You hear me? We still don't know who the rat is. We still don't know if they'll try to tie up loose ends by killing witnesses. So you better make sure—"

What little bit of tranquility had remained inside the cabin shattered like glass.

The front door slammed open with an explosive crack, wood splintering, as four tactical team members stormed inside. They were geared head-to-toe in black and Kevlar, and all their weapons were up and at the ready.

"FBI! Everyone down! Faces on the floor! Hands where we can see them!"

Sabrina sprawled on the floor in an instant. Knox was a little slower to drop to his knees and prone himself out on the rug. Hew leisurely folded his legs until he was seated, and then he took his time lacing his fingers behind his head. But Britt? He was the slowest of all.

"Down! Now!" barked the lead agent as he aimed his weapon at Britt's broad chest. Julia noticed Britt's T-shirt was printed with the words: Heavy Metal. And beneath that was Iron Man's face.

"Sure thing, brother." Britt dropped to his knees. "I was just appreciating the way y'all came busting in here with the guns and jawlines. Very intimidating. Very *ooh-rah*."

"This is a mistake!" Julia shouted, hoping her voice cut through the din of the other agents barking orders. "You don't understand—"

"Are you okay, ma'am?" asked the agent who had already wrenched Sabrina's hands behind her back so he could secure them with a zip tie.

"I'm fine. This isn't what—"

Dillan burst through the open door. "Oh, thank god!" He raced to her side and placed a hand on her shoulder. To her surprise, there was real relief in his eyes.

Under other circumstances, she would've teased him for his worry. Under these circumstances, she needed him to understand that cuffing and stuffing Britt and the others was a mistake.

Before she could get out a word of explanation, however, Dillan continued. "We spent half the night looking for you. And then, when we couldn't find you and had to inform your family, your dad told us—"

"I *know* what he told you. I know what he did. But, Dillan, listen. I have to make sure you understand what's—"

Agents Keplar and Maddox marched inside, looking windblown and angry. And just like that, the little cabin was packed to the seams. Julia didn't think one more body could squeeze inside.

"Ouch!" Sabrina cried when the agent who'd cuffed her dragged her to her feet by wrapping a hard hand around her upper arm.

"Be gentle with her, you fucker!" Hew shouted, his face as red as his hair. His next words were muffled because an agent shoved him face-first into the rug. A second later, Hew's hands were pulled behind his back. A zip tie hissed tight around his thick wrists until the plastic bit into his skin.

"All secure," confirmed the agent who'd cuffed Britt.

Britt was still on his knees, his blue eyes shooting daggers at Julia and prompting her to lift her voice above the chaos again. She did exactly that.

"Everybody, stop talking! Stop moving!" she screamed loud enough to fray a vocal cord.

That had every eye in the room landing on her. On her rat's nest hair. On her borrowed flannel pajamas—somehow, she was the only one still in sleepwear.

Awesome. Way to look professional, Jules.

Pushing her hair out of her face and pulling her shoulders back, she turned her attention first to her partner and then to the agents from South Carolina.

"There's no need for this." She waved a hand to indicate the four people trussed up like Thanksgiving turkeys. "Everyone in this room is innocent and will come with you willingly."

"Innocent?" Agent Keplar sputtered. "How the hell can you know—"

"Because *that*"—Julia interrupted and pointed to Sabrina—"is Cooper Greenlee's sister. And she'll be happy to confirm she was there the night her brother was killed. Knox Rollins wasn't the one to do it. A cartel member named Eddy Torres was."

She pinned her gaze on Agent Keplar before delivering the coup de grâce. "Your joint sting operation has a fox in the henhouse. Someone tipped off the cartel and told them who Rollins and Greenlee were *actually* working for."

Keplar's jaw tightened. But Julia couldn't tell if it was from surprise or anger or mental machinations.

CHAPTER 26

FBI Regional Headquarters, Chicago
Eight hours later...

B
ritt paced the length of the lobby, ignoring the concerned look of the guard manning the desk.

Yes, his pacing made him appear a little unhinged. Yes, his hair was in disarray thanks to the helicopter ride back to Chicago. Yes, he hadn't been given anything to eat since the cabin, and even though he'd been given unlimited cups of coffee, the swill had been so weak it might as well have been foul-flavored tea.

So yes, he was gaunt with hunger and pale from lack of adequate caffeine intake. And yes, he'd been stuck in an interrogation room for five of the last eight hours, where he'd been forced to give his statement over and over again to different agents who hoped to trip him up just in case he wasn't telling the truth about any part of the story.

News flash. He *was* telling the truth.

Well...the truth about what happened from the moment Knox showed up at my door, he silently amended. During all his myriad interrogations, there was *one* lie he'd held to. It was the lie about being nothing more than a simple motorcycle mechanic.

Given all of that, to say he was in a nasty mood was the understatement of the century. He wanted to breathe fire and bust heads. So yes, he didn't give a flying fuck if the guard at the desk thought he was one sandwich short of a picnic.

After his time in the hot seat wrapped up, he'd been escorted to the lobby and told to wait. Ten minutes later, Hew had joined him, looking as retched and exhausted as Britt felt. But unlike Britt, Hew had chosen to lower his bulk onto one of the faux leather benches, cross his arms over his chest, and doze.

One of the great tricks spec-ops guys learned early in their careers was how to sleep in impossible positions in wildly unconventional locations. Britt had once caught some much-needed Zs inside an open-air Chinook helicopter flying through a thunderstorm. When he'd still been with the Army, it'd been standard practice for him to take a quick nap inside his transport Humvee while it bounced over uneven terrain. And he'd spent plenty of nights hanging off the side of a mountain on a portaledge—a suspended cot—at altitudes high enough to give a bighorn sheep a nosebleed.

But no matter how badly he might *need* sleep—*and thanks to Julia and her insatiable appetite, lord knows I could do with forty winks*—he couldn't calm down enough to make shuteye an option.

Not that he'd trade his night with the sexy, blond agent for sleep.

Hell, no.

He'd have happily died of sleep deprivation rather than pass up the opportunity to get to know Julia O'Toole in the biblical sense.

Like the stories in the bible, the experience had been... *transcendent.*

He stopped pacing long enough to admire how the late afternoon sun glinted off the surrounding skyscrapers as his mind filled with scenes from the night before. He recalled how the real world had fallen away, and he'd been left with nothing but sensation when she'd first wrapped her succulent mouth around the head of his dick. He remembered how he'd forgotten every pleasurable sensation he'd ever experienced in his life the instant she straddled his hips and lowered herself onto him because nothing had ever felt as good as Julia's hot, silky walls closing around his length. And he recollected how he'd been instantly lost to her, to the fire between them, as she'd ridden them both to completion.

The memories alone were enough to have his heart beating so hard he could feel it at his fingertips. In his toes. And in, er, other places that didn't do him any good since he was stuck in the feds' lobby.

He'd hated watching her get dressed, watching all that lovely soft flesh disappear into those flannel pajamas. He'd hated it worse when she insisted on returning to the couch. But what he'd hated the worst of all was knowing it was over.

Knowing their night together was over.

It's good that it's done, he told himself now. *It'd be too easy to keep going, to take the leap...and then land on a bed of broken glass.*

He resumed his pacing, hoping by moving his muscles that he'd burn off the toxic blend of emotions sliding like oil through his veins and—

"You're burning calories you don't have," Hew's voice cut into his thoughts. "And you're making the guard anxious." Hew cracked open one eye and patted the space on the bench beside him. "Why don't you come over here and take a load off?"

"Can't." Britt shook his head. "Too keyed up."

"Agent O'Toole will make sure Knox is safe."

"I know." Britt nodded. And he *did* know. He trusted Julia to do as he asked, to stay with Knox until they figured out who in the joint task force had outed him.

"Then what's got you so wound up?" Hew sat up, stretching his neck from side to side. "You jonesing for another hit of the little blond fed? You got it that bad?"

That was enough to stop Britt in his tracks. He slid Hew a calculating glance.

Hew responded with a chuckle. "Don't worry. Your brother was sawing logs like a woodsman preparing for winter. And Sabrina's exhaustion finally got the better of her. I'm the only one who heard you and Agent O'Toole smashing naughty bits in the living room."

"We weren't *smashing naughty bits,*" Britt grumbled.

"No?" Hew raised a bushy eyebrow. "Then what would you call it? Doing some aggressive naked cuddling? Going to Pound Town in the fuck truck?"

"She's more than a piece of ass," Britt hissed, making sure his voice didn't carry to the guard at the desk.

"Sure." Hew shrugged. "She's smart and funny and seems to be good at her job."

"She's *great* at her job," he insisted, unsure why he felt the need to defend her.

Now, both of Hew's eyebrows tried to disappear under the shock of auburn hair falling over his forehead. "This is serious, isn't it? I mean, I knew when you were stalking her that she—"

"I wasn't stalking her," Britt insisted, mostly out of habit.

Hew was having none of it. "*Yes.* You were. And it's because she's different from the other women I've seen you with."

Hoping to distract his teammate, Britt kissed his finger and pointed it at the sky. "This one goes out to all the ladies I've known before. Don't listen to him. You were all magnificent in your own ways."

Ignoring his attempt at levity, Hew continued, "*You're* different when you're around her."

That had Britt blinking. "How so?"

"You're less restless. More relaxed. It's like she calms down all that edgy energy inside you."

Britt scoffed. "Please. You're making castles in the sky."

"I'm not," Hew insisted.

"Then you're one chromosome away from having the brains of a kumquat. Julia is great. But she's nothing special." He bit off the last word because uttering it was offensive. Julia *was* special. The *most* special. But he couldn't have Hew—

His thoughts stopped when Hew started waving his hands in front of his face and coughing.

"What's that?" he demanded. "What are you doing?"

"Sorry," Hew said. "It's just getting hard to breathe with all the bullshit flying around."

Britt ground his teeth so hard he heard enamel crack. "Okay, fine. She *is* special. She's the most amazing woman I know. And that's saying something, considering I know women like Becky, Eliza, and Grace. But that doesn't change the fact that I'm me and have nothing to offer her."

Hew frowned. "What do you mean? You're smart. Some people think you're funny—although I'm not sure I agree with that one. And you're as loyal as a damned dog."

"But my heart is a closed fist," Britt countered.

"What the fuck does *that* mean?"

"It means I'm not open to love. When I love someone, it costs me my peace. And that's too damned expensive."

Hew blinked. Then he blinked again. When he opened his mouth, Britt jumped in to stop him from saying whatever he was about to say. "What happened between me and Julia last night isn't a topic I want to discuss. And I'm even less interested in talking about what's not going to happen between me and Julia going forward."

"Right." Hew nodded, seeming to analyze Britt's expression, which he hoped clearly indicated the subject was closed for business. "Far be it from me to stick my nose in anyone's rose. And just so we're clear, the extent to which I don't give a shit about your sex life cannot be measured."

"Good." Britt nodded. "Great."

"Good." Hew sarcastically mirrored the harsh dip of Britt's chin. "Great."

Britt was about to say something appropriately scathing, but one of the elevators *dinged*. When the silver doors slid open, they revealed Agent Dillan Douglas.

Britt's annoyance and frustration were instantly transferred from Hew to Julia's partner. The sonofabitch had a face that'd been forged from steel. It was all hard angles and smooth expanses. Plus, the self-satisfied look Douglas always wore seemed to scream that he was the winner of the big dick lottery as well as the inheritor of a sizeable trust fund.

How long before Julia succumbed to those good looks and all that swagger? How long before Agent Dillan Douglas convinced her they'd be good partners *outside* the office?

The thought was enough to have Britt's jaw sawing back and forth.

Douglas spotted Hew and immediately headed in his direction. By the time he reached Hew's bench, Hew had gained his feet, and Britt had taken up a position next to him.

"Where's my brother?" Britt demanded.

"Where's Sabrina?" Hew asked before the last syllable left Britt's lips.

"Both are still upstairs being questioned," Douglas declared.

"I want to talk to Julia," Britt insisted. He needed to know what was going on with Knox. He needed to know what they planned to do to keep Knox—

His thoughts were interrupted when Hew said, "And I want to talk to Sabrina."

Britt shot his teammate a curious glance. But Hew's impassive face gave nothing away.

"Agent O'Toole is with your brother and will come down to fill you in on what's happening with him when she has the chance," Douglas assured Britt. "And Miss Greenlee is still talking with Agents Keplar and Maddox."

Hew seemed to grow six inches. His tone was menacing when he said, "You think that's a good idea? One of those sonsofbitches could be the rat and—"

"Never mind that." Douglas lifted the phone in his hand. "There's a call for you two."

"A call?" Hew's chin jerked back.

"Who is it?" Britt asked as an odd sense of foreboding gripped the back of his neck.

Douglas wiggled the phone. "It's your blond-haired designer. I don't know how the sonofabitch found my personal cell phone number. But here we are. And he's demanding to talk to you. He says it's urgent."

"Right." Britt snatched the phone from the fed's hand before Hew could do the honors. "Ozzie, my man, what have you got?" he said into the phone's microphone.

"I have been eating at a buffet of the bizarre for twenty-four hours." Ozzie's tone was brisk. "Every firewall I've jumped, every code I've cracked has made me itchy, like someone is watching my every keystroke. But I haven't been able to figure out who it is. And then *they* made themselves known."

Britt frowned. "What do you mean *they*?"

"Kerberos."

"Jesus," Britt breathed. The hairs on his scalp lifted so fast and so high it was a wonder they didn't jettison themselves right off his head.

For a long time, Kerberos was thought to be a myth, a secret hacktivist organization dreamed up by computer nerds who liked the idea of an all-seeing, all-knowing group that policed the dark web and brought the bad guys to justice.

But the Black Knights had come to know that Kerberos was, in fact, real. There *was* a group of vigilante computer geeks out there who remained anonymous and who seemed to find information even highly skilled white hat hackers like Ozzie couldn't.

"What did they say?" he asked Ozzie now.

As Ozzie outlined what he'd learned from the supermen of cyberspace, gunpowder began to fill Britt's veins, and his heart began to thunder in the rhythm of a war march. By the time he told Ozzie, "Got it. Thanks for the call," he felt as focused and as ferocious as he did when he was dropped into a hot zone behind enemy lines.

The *ding* of the elevator bank diverted his attention.

When his eyes landed on the group of people exiting through the silver doors, the center of his sight began to crackle like disco lights, and the edges of his vision began to darken. The feds had confiscated his and Hew's sidearms and had yet to return them. Which left only Agent Douglas.

"Take out your weapon," he growled to Julia's partner as all the restless energy Hew spoke of coalesced into a chilling stillness inside him.

"Wh-what?" Douglas sputtered in confusion.

"Take. Out. Your. *Weapon*," Britt snarled each word, not daring to take his eyes off the approaching group.

When the fed only blinked, Britt growled, "Fine. I'll do it myself."

Before Agent Douglas could object—or offer any resistance—Britt reached into the man's jacket and snatched his service weapon from its holster.

A split second later, he aimed his sights between the eyes of the rat.

"What the hell?" Julia, who at some point had changed into another one of her formless pantsuits, stopped in her tracks and stared at him incredulously. Knox, Sabrina, and the agents from South Carolina all followed Julia's lead and abruptly halted their journey across the lobby.

The guard at the desk jumped up and pulled his service weapon, pointing it shakily at Britt's chest.

"Drop it!" he yelled in a thick Chicago accent that reminded Britt of that old Saturday Night Live skit starring the late, great Chris Farley. *Da Bears.* "Drop it now!" the guard added, his voice as shaky as the gun in his hand.

"What the fuck are you doing?" Agent Douglas demanded from beside him.

"Britt, brother, go easy," Hew cautioned from behind him.

Britt ignored them both as he stared hard at the one responsible for all this trouble. The one responsible for Sabrina's assault, for his brother's flight north, and for Cooper Greenlee's death.

"You move," he snarled, his nostrils flaring wide as his vision tunneled onto his target, "and I'll put three holes in your head like a fucking bowling ball."

CHAPTER 27

JD Maddox blinked in confusion at the motorcycle mechanic.

Although, he supposed having a gun aimed at his head was just the icing on the week's shitty-assed cake.

Nothing had gone right since he told his superiors inside the cartel that it was time to move on the FBI's assets. First, Cooper Greenlee's sister had been at her brother's house. Second, Fat Eddy had fucked up the hit by getting his jollies off before finishing the job. Third, Knox and Sabrina had escaped north. And finally, that damned blond bitch hadn't left Knox Rollins alone for one second so that JD could inject him with the poison he had in a tiny syringe in his pocket.

And now this, he thought angrily, having reached his wit's end.

He had no idea why the mechanic had suddenly gone batshit, but he had neither the time nor patience for it. He had to find a way to get that poison into Knox before the sonofabitch turned state's evidence.

"Stop waving that iron in my face," he called across the lobby to the mechanic. The air inside the cavernous space was so thick with tension that it was hard to breathe. "Have you lost your damned mind?"

"No." Britt Rollins shook his head. "But you take one step in the wrong direction, and you'll lose yours. I'll splatter your gray matter all over the wall behind you, Wilkes."

The name was spat across the tiled floor like a venomous snake. JD felt the impact of it like a pair of fangs lodged deep in his chest.

Wilkes…

Not Maddox.

How the hell does he know?

"Drop your weapon!" the guard at the front desk shouted at the younger Rollins brother again.

"He's crazy!" JD hollered, pointing at the mechanic. His thoughts spiraled, a whirlpool of disbelief and panic. "Take him down before he takes one of us down!"

"No!" Agent O'Toole cried while Keplar yelled, "Belay that order!"

JD didn't care for the speculation in his partner's eyes when Keplar turned to him and asked lowly, "What's he talking about? Why did he call you Wilkes?"

"H-how the hell should I know?" JD sputtered, turning back to find the weapon in Rollins's hand was rock steady.

But it was the certainty in Rollins's voice that terrified him more than anything. The certainty and the *facts* he stated. Facts no one outside of a handful of folks *very* high up in the drug trafficking syndicate knew. "Jordan Ray Wilkes. That's your real name, right? The one your mother gave you at birth? The one you used before the cartel set you up to be their inside man?"

Sonofabitch!

JD's meticulously constructed life was gone, obliterated in a single moment.

But how? How does the mechanic know when even the FBI is in the dark?

Of course, the answer to that question was of little importance. What was most important was what JD did in the next thirty seconds.

His cover was blown, and his true identity was revealed. The jig was up, and fifteen years of carefully crafted work now circled the drain.

Time to GTFO.

If he could make it out of the building, he had a chance. He knew the FBI's protocols. He could beat them.

His pulse thundered in his ears as he looked to his left at Julia O'Toole. She might be just the ticket. He'd seen how she kept glancing at Britt Rollins on the flight from Traverse City to Chicago. The blond fed had a thing for the mechanic.

The question was, did the mechanic have a thing for her? And would that thing be enough to stay the bastard's hand?

Only one way to find out.

Grabbing Julia's wrist, JD yanked her in front of him. In the same move, he pulled the syringe from his pocket.

O'Toole gasped, but the sound was cut short when he pressed the cold steel of the needle against the tender skin of her neck.

"No!" Britt Rollins yelled at the same time Keplar snarled lowly, "You motherfucker!" His pudgy hand reached for his pistol. "It was *you*? *You're* the one who gave up my assets?"

"Don't even think about it, Ryan," JD spat, using Keplar's first name. No point in standing on ceremony now. "You so much as twitch, and I'll shove this shit into her veins. She'll be dead in sixty seconds."

"Why?" Keplar demanded, his face red as the proverbial beet. "Why would you turn on the bureau?"

JD snorted. "I never turned on the bureau, you idiot." There was no use denying it. The cat was out of the bag, and it wasn't getting shoved back inside. Besides, it felt good to inform Keplar he'd been partnered with a cartel plant. It felt good letting the arrogant asshole know he'd been duped from the jump. "Don't you get it? I was never *with* the bureau. I was always with the cartel."

Keplar blinked rapidly as if he couldn't comprehend that one simple truth.

"You so much as prick her skin, and I'll plant lead into your brainpan," Rollins snarled, still steadily aiming in JD's direction even though O'Toole now blocked a clean shot.

JD laughed, but there wasn't a drop of humor in it. "You think you're good enough to hit me and miss Little Miss Human Shield here?"

Rollins didn't need to say anything. He didn't pull his trigger, and that was answer enough.

"You knew Knox was innocent all along," Keplar gritted through his teeth, taking *forever* to figure out what everyone else in the lobby had surmised when JD grabbed the blond. "You knew he was innocent because *you* were the one who blew his cover. And yet you were gung-ho to help me find him. *Why?*"

JD chanced a glance at his former partner in exasperation. It was clear he needed to spell things out. "I knew if you didn't find him and kill him in your hurry to mete out justice, you'd haul him in, and I'd get the chance to give him a heart attack with this lovely little elixir concocted by our own Central Intelligence Agency. I've been told it denatures in the body in under an hour and therefore can't be detected on autopsy. So helping you catch him was a win-win for me. Either you'd do the dirty work, or I would. But the end result would be Knox Rollins in a body bag and unable to tell a jury what he knows."

"You're a sonofabitch," Keplar snarled.

"Takes one to know one, asshole." JD knew it was childish, but he couldn't resist getting in a dig. He'd been eating the shit Keplar fed him for months, and, in an odd way, it felt good not to have to pretend to kowtow to the fat fuck.

"Get back," Keplar told Sabrina and Knox, motioning with his meaty hand. "Back toward the guard desk and—"

"I don't think so." JD pressed the needle harder against O'Toole's neck, hard enough that she whimpered in fear. "I'm the one calling the shots here."

His breaths came in short, ragged gasps, his mind flying through the next steps. The mechanic was armed. Keplar was armed. O'Toole and the guard were both armed. JD's first order of business was to change all that, to restack the odds in *his* favor.

"Take out your weapon, Agent O'Toole," he whispered close to her ear. "Two fingers only."

She'd instinctively lifted her hands in front of her the moment she felt the needle at her throat. Now, he saw them shake.

"Nice and easy," he coached her as she slowly reached into her jacket with one hand.

The lobby was so quiet that he could have heard a pin drop. He *did* hear the guard's ragged breathing and the *snick* as O'Toole thumbed off the snap on her holster.

She used her thumb and forefinger to free the weapon.

"Very good," he praised, wondering if that was *her* heart he was feeling beating hard or his own. Maybe both. "Now, drop it on the floor and kick it across the room."

She did as instructed, and he felt a little spurt of satisfaction when the pistol came to rest against the far wall.

Keeping his eye on Rollins—the man's finger hadn't so much as twitched on the trigger —he turned slightly toward Keplar.

"Your turn, Ryan." He did his best to regulate his breaths since he couldn't stop the thundering of his heart. He needed to get out. And *quick*. Because he might have the situation under control now, but that could change in a heartbeat if one more person walked into the lobby. "Take out your pistol and send it over to join O'Toole's."

He could see the hesitation on his former partner's face. He'd worked with Keplar long enough to know that taking orders from a junior agent—even in *this* circumstance—grated. But, eventually, Keplar pulled out his gun.

The older man's knees cracked when he bent to place the six-shooter on the floor. They cracked again when he stood and gingerly kicked the weapon away.

It didn't sail to the far wall like O'Toole's had. But it was out of reach, and that's really all JD wanted.

"Now you," JD snarled at the mechanic.

"You're not going to inject her," Britt Rollins grumbled. "You know if you do, I'll shoot you."

JD's galloping heart stuttered. Had he read the situation wrong? Did Rollins *not* share Agent O'Toole's softer feelings?

Again, there's only one way to find out.

"Is that a risk you're willing to take?" he challenged as he subtly, ever so gently tightened his grip on the syringe.

The mechanic's eagle-eyed gaze sharpened. JD knew he'd hit the nail on the head when, with a harsh curse, Rollins crouched and placed his gun on the floor before kicking it toward the far wall.

JD couldn't resist getting in one good jab. "That's a good little grease monkey." He winked before transferring his attention to the guard.

He wasn't actually concerned the man at the desk would shoot him. The asshole's hands were shaking so badly that even if he squeezed his trigger, JD figured his shot would veer off in some crazy direction.

Still…the twitchy fuck would have the upper hand if he was the only one armed. And JD needed to be the one with the upper hand if this was going to work.

"You too." He hitched his chin toward the uniformed man. "Drop your weapon."

The guard glanced around as if looking for permission from the others.

"Don't look at them," JD snapped. "Look at me. And do as you're told or any death that happens today will be on *your* hands."

The guard's large Adam's apple bobbed as he gingerly placed his weapon atop the desk.

"Now, back away with your hands in the air," JD commanded.

Once the guard obeyed, he glanced around the room at all the hands lifted in the air.

Progress, he thought, and then he moved on to the next stage of his plan.

"Right. Now, I'm the only one who will be moving, capiche? If one of you fuckers so much as blinks before I make it to the front door, Agent O'Toole gets it in the throat."

"Go ahead and run like the rat you are, Wilkes," Rollins taunted, his voice dripping with malice. "You won't get far. Not from me."

"Not from me either," Keplar swore. His face was shiny with sweat.

JD figured his former partner was about ten seconds away from having a massive coronary. And that'd be just fine. One less shithead to deal with.

"I do enjoy a good game of cat and mouse," he sneered as he shuffled sideways, keeping his back to the wall of windows and dragging O'Toole with him.

An SUV was parked out front. They had called for it earlier to transport Knox and Sabrina to a safe house. Now, it would be his getaway vehicle.

He'd need to ditch it within a mile or two. No doubt it came equipped with a tracker. But as long as he put some distance between himself and the field office, he could disappear into the city.

It was funny. Most people thought when criminals went on the run, they chose to vanish inside dense forests. But the truth was a big city—and the millions of faces inside it—offered far better camouflage.

With the cartel's help, and with the money he'd squirreled away over the last decade and a half, he could cross an ocean and buy himself a new face, a new life, and a new name.

It wasn't how he'd hoped to end his career as a federal. He'd hoped to keep playing his part until he could retire with a government pension *and* the cartel's cash. But he'd always known discovery was a possibility. And he'd planned accordingly.

He just needed to escape this fucking lobby.

The glass doors leading to the street seemed a million miles away. He could feel the seconds ticking down, the world closing around him. His hands were clammy, his mind a blur of calculations. Each step toward the exit felt heavier than the last, but he couldn't stop. He couldn't falter even though Agent O'Toole wasn't exactly cooperating.

She kept tripping over her duty shoes. Whether that was because she was being intentionally rebellious or because she was clumsy with fear, he couldn't say. Either way, he snarled in her ear, "Pick up your damn feet, woman."

What he silently added was, *I refuse to die here. Not today.*

He was almost to the door—and a bright burst of victory fired through his veins—when O'Toole suddenly became a dead weight.

He struggled to keep hold of her. She was just a little thing, after all. But even a little thing was too much for him to handle one-handed.

She hit the ground like a sack of rocks, and the room exploded into chaos.

Keplar and Britt Rollins raced for their weapons. Sabrina and Knox dashed toward the safety of the elevator bank with the auburn-haired behemoth hot on their heels. But it was the guard who, surprisingly, sprung into action and took the first shot.

Boom!

JD heard the pistol's report at the same time he saw the muzzle flash from the corner of his eye. He immediately realized he'd underestimated the man.

The force of the bullet punched into his thigh like a molten hammer. The impact had the syringe flying out of his hand and sent him sprawling as agony shot through him, white-hot and relentless.

His hand instinctively pressed against the wound. Warm blood bubbled up between his fingers as a sticky, scarlet flood oozed down his pant leg.

His vision blurred. His head swam. Fragments of his life surged to the surface—fractured memories of his mother introducing him to the cartel's kingpin, long nights spent hammering out his new identity, and the beautiful line of zeros stacked up behind the lead number in his offshore bank account because the cartel had been *very* generous to him over the years.

The wound wasn't fatal.

He could still get to the money.

He could still make it out of this.

He pushed to his feet and… *Boom!* A second shot rang out.

Bracing himself for the impact, he blinked when it didn't come. Instead, a scream tore through the lobby. He turned to see Agent Julia O'Toole grip her chest as a dark stain bloomed beneath her blouse.

The guard's luck had run out. His aim was no longer true.

That worked out fine for JD since Britt Rollins roared his dismay alongside Agent Douglas. Both men ran for Agent O'Toole. Neither cared about JD or the fact he'd regained his feet.

He could count his heartbeats roaring in his ears, fast and furious. His fingers trembled as his blood-slicked hand found the door handle. Freedom was just a breath away.

I made it!

Another explosion shattered the air.

This time, when he felt it—the searing, devastating impact between his shoulder blades—he knew it was over. He knew *he* was over.

The bullet tore through muscle and bone before erupting out of his chest in a red mist. The iron-rich smell of his own blood filled his nostrils. And the force of the impact flung him forward.

He crumpled to the ground, half in and half out of the doorway.

The cool afternoon air kissed his cheek, mocking the warmth that quickly drained from his body.

Strange. From the very beginning, he'd known he'd been playing a dangerous game. From the very beginning, he'd known that game could end in his death. But call it vanity or arrogance or pride—*hell, call it all three*—but he'd truly believed he'd make it out alive.

How did this happen? How did I end up here?

He'd never know the answers to those questions. And as his vision dimmed, he barely registered the heavy footsteps pounding toward him. Then, a dark shadow fell over him, and he had just enough strength to flip from his side to his back.

The first thing his waning eyesight registered was the raised weapon. Smoke coiled lazily from the barrel. The second thing he saw was…

Ryan Keplar.

As his life's blood ebbed away, mercifully taking his searing agony with it, he locked eyes with the man who had just signed his death warrant. Keplar's face was a mask of resolve, devoid of any regret.

Not that JD expected any. Keplar was a heartless bastard, after all.

"Y-you're a sonofabitch," he managed to cough around the hot, metallic blood that filled his mouth.

The last thing he saw before everything tilted and his world faded to black was Keplar's joyless smile. The last things he heard were his own words thrown back at him. "Takes one to know one, asshole."

CHAPTER 28

Northwestern Memorial Hospital
Eight days later…

Julia came awake to the sound of her brothers' bickering.

"Stop giving me the evil eye," Sean, her middle brother, said. "I think it's a law or something that you can only use it if you're Italian. And last I checked, we're Irish."

"I'm not giving you the evil eye," Patrick, her oldest brother, countered. "I'm looking at you with pity because all this bluster is *obviously* you compensating for an embarrassingly tiny set of sex organs."

"Ha!" Sean snorted. "Please. I'm hung like a horse. It runs in the family. Too bad that particular gene skipped *you*, though."

"I hope *both* your lives are plagued by stray Lego pieces, wet socks, and chronic hangnails," Oscar, her youngest brother, interjected.

"Oh, ho!" Patrick crowed. "Lord Dickbreath of Doucheville has deigned to join the conversation."

"You see this?" Oscar asked, and Julia cracked a lid to discover that her youngest brother was flipping off her oldest brother. "This is my asshole antenna. I'm happy to report you're coming in loud and clear, Pat."

Patrick frowned. "I'm a ball's hair away from breaking that antenna."

"And I'll tear you *both* new assholes you can fit entire deep-dish pizzas in," Sean declared, wearing a shit-eating grin.

Usually, Julia appreciated the middle school banter of her overgrown brothers. But her doctor had been slowly weaning her off her high-powered pain medications in preparation for discharging her later in the day. As a result, the wound through her shoulder had grown teeth that relentlessly gnawed at her. The IV needle in the back of her hand smarted and burned. And to top it all off, she was working on a nagging headache.

All that to say, she could do without the name-calling and dick jokes.

"Will you three shut up?" She wrestled with the pillow behind her head in an effort to sit up. "I'm in sorry enough shape as it is. I don't need visuals of your nether regions dancing in my head."

As a group, her brothers raced to her bedside. Sean pushed the button that folded the bed like a taco shell to aid in her bid to get vertical. Patrick tucked the flimsy, over-washed hospital sheet tighter around her socked feet before pulling the quilt their mother had brought from home over her lap. And Oscar patted her hand solicitously.

She could smell their Old Spice deodorant. She wasn't sure if it was a firefighter thing or a Southsider thing, but most of the men she'd grown up around insisted on that brand. And thus, they all smelled like spice and cedarwood.

But it's better than the overpowering scents of bleach and antiseptic, she thought, feeling sick and tired of being sick and tired in the hospital. She wanted to go home. Wanted her bed and her animals and her Keurig.

"How are you feeling?" Sean asked, brushing her hair back from her face and wrinkling his nose when his fingers came away greasy.

"I feel like I've been shot." The look she gave him was withering. "And I feel like I haven't showered in a week."

The sponge bath the nurse had given her had been glorious. But the lovely woman hadn't touched her hair, and *that* was what needed water and soap the most.

Her mother had promised to help her wash her greasy scalp and ratted mop in the kitchen sink once she was home and ready to tackle the task.

"That's because you *haven't* showered in a week," Oscar supplied helpfully.

Her withering look was transferred to her youngest brother. "I *know* that. I was being sarcastic."

Never one to miss a chance to razz one of his brothers, Patrick quickly lifted a hand to shade his eyes. "Your stupidity is blinding me, Oscar. Please turn it off."

"Never tell me to hide my light under a bushel, Pat." Oscar's smile said he was quite pleased with that comeback.

"Ugh." Julia waved her hand in front of her face. "Back up. All of you. There's so much testosterone flying around me right now that I feel like I'm sitting inside a testicle."

"Is this a bad time?"

The four siblings turned to find Agent Dillan Douglas standing in the doorway. He was dressed in his usual tailored suit. His eyebrows formed two perfect arches above the lenses of his sunglasses before he pulled them off his face and smiled at the gathered group.

"God, no." Julia shook her head. "Come in. Come in." She turned to her brothers. "And you three, go away. FBI business and whatnot."

Patrick rolled his eyes. "Yeah, yeah. You're a big shot. We get it."

"It's more like I'm tired of being fussed over. I swear, you guys are worse than Mom."

Oscar fluffed imaginary hair. "I take that as a compliment. Mom's the best."

"Shoo!" She waved them out and waited until they'd lumbered through the door before motioning for her partner to pull up the hard, plastic chair beside the bed.

Dillan scooted close enough to place a hand on her forearm. "You're being discharged today?"

"So they say." She winced when she moved her injured arm into a more comfortable position. "Quite honestly, I think they're kicking me out so my family will stop using this place as a second home."

Dillan's lips twitched. "I heard your father nearly came to blows with the head nurse that first night when she tried to force everyone out of your room."

Julia made a face. "Dad's been sleeping in that chair." She hitched her chin toward the uncomfortable-looking armchair pushed into the corner. "And they had to bring in a cot for Mom. As for those three?" She inclined her head toward the empty doorway where her brothers had disappeared. "When they haven't been on shift, they've been here, driving the hospital staff crazy."

"Not to mention the Black Knights."

That had her blinking at him. "What?"

"Yup." He nodded. "Those few days, this room was packed to the gills with well-wishers from BKI." He pointed to all the vases that lined the windowsill and the little table beside her bed. "What? Did you think it was your family who turned this place into a flower shop?"

Honestly? Yeah. Or, rather, she hadn't really thought about it.

Her eyes scanned the flowers now, and she saw cards attached to little plastic sticks. Were any of them from Britt? And, if so, what had he written?

A little bubble of hope formed in her throat. It made her voice sound full when she said, "I...I had no idea."

He nodded. "You were pretty out of it. And then when it became clear you were going to make it, your mother, in the nicest way possible, " he quickly added. "Well, she told those of us who aren't family to bug off and give you time to heal." He widened his eyes. "I see where you get it from. She's terrifying."

A chuckle burbled in the back of her throat as she imagined her diminutive mother standing with her hands on her hips and issuing decrees like a monarch. Then, she grimaced. "Don't make me laugh. It hurts when I laugh."

"Right." He nodded solemnly. "Only serious topics from here on out."

She wanted to ask him if Britt had been in attendance when the Black Knights visited. She wanted to ask if he *had* been in attendance if he'd seemed overly worried about her, or just the right amount of worried. You know, like a *friendly* amount of worried as opposed to a *more* than friendly amount of worried. But she didn't want to sound desperate.

And considering Britt owed her nothing, and considering she'd only agreed to that one night, it wasn't worth opening herself up to Dillan's speculation.

Plus, she needed to stop thinking about Sergeant Britt Rollins. She needed to stop dreaming about him.

For three nights now, she'd been plagued by soft, wonderous fantasies of the two of them making coffee together in the kitchen, putting ornaments on a tree in the living room come Christmas, and snuggling by a fire while her animals lounged around them.

She blamed the illusions on the pain meds. Because the alternative was that it'd only taken one night for her to fall head over heels in love, and she refused to allow *that* to be true.

It would be too sad, too…*torturous.*

It has to be the pain meds, she silently assured herself. *And now that I'm done with the meds, it's back to life, back to reality.*

The reality where she ignored that *thing* that existed between her and Britt. The reality where they went back to being strangers.

A hollow feeling blossomed in the center of her chest.

"Speaking of serious topics." She stared hard at Dillan. "What happened to Agent Maddox? Or…Wilkes, right? That's his real name?"

The last thing she remembered was Britt falling to his knees beside her, his face a mask of misery and shock as he pressed his hands against her chest to stop the flow of blood. His words barely made it through his iron-clenched jaw when he'd said, *"Easy. You're okay. Hang in there. You're going to be okay."* And then? Lights out.

"You don't remember asking me about this five days ago?" Dillan lifted an eyebrow.

She racked her brain and came up blank. "I don't know if you know this, but they had me on some pretty intense narcotics. I can hardly remember what I had for breakfast this morning, much less what we talked about five days ago."

He nodded. "You *were* slurring your words quite a bit. And half the time your eyes were closed."

"Well, my *brain* must have been closed the entire time." She made a rolling motion with her hand. "So spill. Tell me everything I've missed."

He took a deep breath before giving her the sordid tale of Jordan Ray Wilkes. Apparently, the man they'd known as Agent Maddox had been the stepson of one of the cartel's major players. When he turned eighteen, the cartel set him up with a new identity and sent him off to college with one directive and one directive only. *Get an education. Get accepted into the FBI training program at Quantico. And get a job as an agent so the drug trafficking organization stays privy to any investigations, busts, and stings.*

"Holy shit," Julia breathed when Dillan was done. "I can't believe his false identity held up under the background check. The bureau is scrupulous."

"Get this, there *was* a JD Maddox. He actually *looked* a little like Wilkes. But he died in a car crash at eighteen. The cartel managed to scrub the kid's death from the internet, though. It was easy to have Wilkes pick up where the real Maddox left off."

"You think the cartel had the *real* Maddox murdered?" Her lip curled at the thought of such unabashed cruelty.

Dillan shrugged. "I mean, it seems awfully coincidental if they didn't. But we'll never know. The kid's car went off the Cooper River Bridge. It was listed as an accident, so no autopsy was done. And the vehicle has long since been dragged out of the bay and crushed, so there's no way to go back and check for foul play."

"Holy shit," she breathed again, her mind racing in a million directions. "He fooled me. I'm usually better at reading people. But he fooled me."

"Don't feel too bad. He fooled *everyone*."

She remembered her initial question. "So what's happening with him?"

"What do you mean?"

"Is he trying to cut a deal or—"

"He's dead. Agent Keplar blew a hole right through him a split second after that idiot guard blew a hole through you."

"Not *through*." She grimaced. "I'm told that's why there was so much bleeding. The round entered and bounced around for a bit."

Dillan's face paled. He replaced his hand on her arm, squeezing it. "I'm glad you're going to be okay."

She saw the sincerity in his eyes and figured now was the time to lighten the mood. "Who are you, and what have you done with my partner?"

"What can I say?" He lifted his hands. "Watching you take a round to the shoulder put things in perspective."

"Well, I prefer it when things are *out* of perspective. It won't be any fun bossing you around if my bossing you around doesn't annoy the ever-living hell out of you."

"Oh, don't you worry about that. Once you're back up and running on all cylinders, guaranteed I will find you as annoying as ever. Probably *more* so since your ego will be overinflated because you've been shot. I'm sure the bureau has a commendation lined up for you."

"You think it'll be a star?" She smiled evilly, alluding to one of the four medals the FBI bestowed on its agents for injury, bravery, achievement, or valor. "I'll put it in one of those fancy plastic cases and sit it on my desk. You'll have to look at it every day and remember I'm a bigger badass than you are."

"See?" He feigned a frown. "I'm annoyed already."

"Good. Then, all is right with the world."

He laughed before sobering. "In all seriousness, I wanted to murder that damned front desk guard."

She tried to be mad at the man who'd shot her, but she didn't have the strength for vitriol. "What's going to happen to him?"

"He's currently on paid leave." Dillan made a face. "I think the bureau is sending him out for more training."

"I'm glad they didn't fire him." She took a deep breath that hurt more than she let on. "None of us knows how we'll handle a situation like that until we're in it. Then, if we're not cut out for it, it's too late."

"You're a big softy," Dillan accused, but his tone had no real distaste.

"Mmm. Maybe." She shrugged her good shoulder along with her eyebrows. Then, those same eyebrows pulled into a vee. "Wait a minute. If the bureau didn't sniff out Wilkes's real identity for a full fifteen years, how did Britt Rollins figure it out? Did Ozzie—"

Dillan cut her off with a shake of his head. "Nope. It wasn't the amateur hacker they have on staff over there at the motorcycle shop. According to Ozzie, it was Kerberos."

The hairs on the back of her neck lifted. She hissed the three syllables like a curse. "*Kerberos?*"

Dillan's eyes were wide at the connotation. "Apparently, they were monitoring Ozzie's attempt to get the goods on the people associated with the joint operation. They figured out what he was really after and contacted him to give him the lowdown on Wilkes. They sent him microfiche images from the local newspapers regarding the real Maddox's death. Sent him Wilkes's birth certificate, graduation announcement, and the marriage license between the cartel lieutenant and Wilkes's mother. They laid it all out for him like it was a Sunday dinner."

"Wh-why would they do that?" She shook her head. The vigilante hackers were a thorn in the bureau's side because they found ways to hack into the FBI's system and uncover information they had no business uncovering. But they were also a boon to all those who believed in truth and justice because they exposed corruption and malfeasance in ways the bureau couldn't. It was safe to say most feds had a love/hate relationship with the anonymous group. "I mean, their whole mantra is *we are the ears that listen in the darkness. We are the eyes that witness secret sins. We are the guardians against tyranny and fascism.* Isn't this small potatoes for them? They usually go after politicians and corporations. Not some two-bit rat inside the FBI."

"Your guess is as good as mine." Dillan shrugged. "It's not like we can get online and ask them why they decided to help."

"Right." She nodded. Then she winced when a stab of white-hot pain sliced into her. It was odd. The wound ached constantly. But occasionally, it was like someone shoved a sword through her shoulder.

The doctor said it was normal. Just injured nerves making their presence known. But *damn.*

A line appeared between Dillan's eyebrows. "You were smart to do what you did."

"Hmm?" She tried rearranging her bandage so it wasn't cutting into her armpit. "What did I do?"

"You hit the deck and gave us time to take down Wilkes. At great risk to yourself. He could've stabbed you with that needle."

"He made the mistake of paying more attention to getting to the front door than he did to me. He moved the syringe away from my neck enough for me to think it was worth becoming a human sandbag."

"Still." Dillan shook his head. "You got balls, kid."

"And that's why they pay me the big bucks."

When he rolled his eyes, she laughed. Then she grimaced and grabbed her injured shoulder.

His expression was instantly concerned. "Do I need to call the nurse?"

"Hell, no." She shook her head. "If I complain too much about the pain, they'll keep me another night. And I need to get home. It's only a matter of time before one of my pets turns feral and decides to murder whichever one of my brothers happens to be at my house feeding them."

"Don't worry about that," Sean said from the doorway. He had two cups of coffee in hand. Julia's stomach growled when the sweet smell drifted across the room. "That motorcycle mechanic who was hanging around here for days after they brought you in is the one who's been seeing after your menagerie of furry and winged friends."

Julia blinked uncomprehendingly.

"I'll check on you in a couple of days," Dillan said, giving her arm one more squeeze before making his way to the door. He dipped his chin at her brother and added, "Take care of our girl in the meantime. She's a serious pain in the ass. But she's a fine investigator, and the bureau needs her."

"We'll make sure she's fed and clothed," Sean assured him.

"And bathed." Dillan wrinkled his nose and whispered conspiratorially, "I worry there's no saving that hair. Someone might have to shave her head."

Julia rolled her eyes. "*Goodbye*, Agent Douglas."

He turned and flashed her a grin that would melt the panties off most women. Thankfully, she was immune. "Get well soon. Stuart Brown is missing you terribly."

"Please," she scoffed. "Stu only wants me because he can't have me."

"True. But I'm getting tired of his hangdog glances at your empty desk. So come back as quickly as you can."

"That's the plan," she assured him.

He lifted a hand in farewell before stepping past her brother and disappearing into the hallway.

"Gimme." She made grabby fingers at the coffee in her brother's hand.

He sauntered over and obligingly offered her the paper cup.

After greedily accepting it, greedily gulping down her first sip—and making a face because it was tepid and weak—she fixed her gaze on her brother. "How is it that Britt Rollins is caring for my animals?"

She tried to keep her tone light. But her heart beat so hard she could feel it in her injury.

Sean shrugged. "He volunteered." When he saw that his answer wouldn't cut it, he added, "When Mom was kicking everyone out of your room but family, Britt asked if there was anything he could do to help. Since Mom and Dad were determined to stay here with you, and since me and the boys were pulling forty-eight-hour shifts, she happily handed off your house key to Mr. Helpful and told him he could pet sit and house sit if he really wanted to be of service."

He frowned at her. "Why? Is that a problem? I mean, he's got to be a stand-up guy because, according to the daily check-ins he's been exchanging with Mom, he's taught Gunpowder to say *chicken butt* instead of *dick breath*. And apparently, Chewy is in love with him and lets him carry him around everywhere *without* biting the shit out of him with his little needle Chihuahua teeth."

The thought of Britt inside her personal space, caring for her animals, should have made her feel strange. And yet...the opposite was true.

What she felt was a spark of hope that maybe her soft dreams of the two of them together weren't because of the drugs but because he'd changed his mind. Maybe their first night together wasn't going to be their last night together, after all.

"Go ask the nurse if they can discharge me early," she instructed, taking another sip of her coffee and hissing at the weak flavor.

Sean lifted an eyebrow. "In a sudden hurry to get home? Is there something you want to tell me about you and Mr. Motorcycle Mechanic?"

Aloud, all she said was, "I need my own coffee and my own coffee maker. This stuff is swill."

But silently, she thought, *I sure hope so.*

CHAPTER 29

Julia O'Toole's house, Beverly neighborhood

Britt reread the letter he'd written to Julia for the fifth time as he scratched Chewy's head.

Ren was on the floor at his feet. The three-legged pit bull liked to curl between the legs of the kitchen table chairs. Binks, Julia's overly independent cat, sat in his favorite spot on the windowsill, chattering at the birds in the oak tree in the backyard. And Gunpowder perched on the chair next to Britt. The parrot tilted his head like only birds and reptiles do, eyeing Britt's handwriting as if his walnut-sized bird brain had some opinions about what was written.

For a week, Britt had been part of Julia's life in a way he'd never imagined. Been part of her *world* in a way that only made him adore her more.

She organized her closet by color. She kept an extra toothbrush in the shower. And she collected *Star Wars* figurines that she proudly displayed in the china cabinet instead of…you know…actual *china*.

She had a dozen half-dead plants spread throughout the house, which he'd tried his best to nurse back to health. She liked family photographs. The hallway to her bedroom was adorned with pictures of the O'Tooles, some posed, some candid. And she preferred records to digital music—her vinyl collection was a thing of beauty.

It was all so domestic. So homey. So...*familial*.

And that was before he got to her *family*. Her brothers were big brutes who loved slinging insults at each other. Her father was a tough old bird who mixed it up with his sons like he was decades younger than he was. And her mother? Well, somehow, despite being as petite and perfect as Julia herself, Nora O'Toole ruled over all of them with an iron hand encased in velvet.

The O'Tooles were big and boisterous and bonded. They loved each other so easily and so deeply and so thoroughly that he couldn't help being a little envious.

However, hard on the heels of that envy came fear. Always fear.

Fear for what would happen to them should tragedy strike. Fear for the depths of the grief they'd suffer, the magnitude of the pain they'd be forced to endure should life do what life always does and end for one of them.

That thought alone was enough to have a pit forming in his stomach and a cold fist squeezing his heart. That thought alone was enough to make him pick up his pen and sign the letter with a flourish.

You're doing the right thing, he assured himself as he folded the sheet in half.

"Sugar tits!" Gunpowder squawked when Britt propped the note against the salt and pepper shakers in the center of the kitchen table.

Britt frowned at the bird. "I know it's not poetry or anything. Fisher could have written it so much better. But it says the important stuff, right?"

"Chicken butt."

"I suppose that's better than dick breath." He sighed, pushing up from the table to take one more tour around the house.

He was slow about it, letting his eyes and fingers drift over her things. Committing it all to memory since it would be the last time he stepped foot inside.

He held the ends of the scarf she'd draped over the side of her vanity mirror, testing the silky fabric and thinking that as soft as it was, it wasn't nearly as soft as Julia's skin. He smoothed the duvet cover over her bed, refusing to allow himself fantasies of joining her under it. He popped the top on her perfume bottle and lifted it to his nose. Closing his eyes, he pulled the festive scent deep into his lungs.

When he was satisfied everything was as lovely as he could make for her return, he placed the house keys her mother had given him on the kitchen table beside the letter, set Chewy in his favorite spot on the couch, and gave Ren a scratch behind the ears.

"Bye, bitch!" Gunpowder had flown in from the kitchen to perch on the back of the sofa.

"Bye bitch to you too." Britt chuckled. But the laugh died quickly in his throat as he softly closed the door behind him and headed down the walk to the production bike he'd been riding since his own beloved Haint had been hauled out of the Michigan woods and hoisted onto a bike lift at BKI.

As he thumbed on the ignition, his heart felt heavy. The motorcycle rumbled to life, but he barely registered the healthy roar of the engine.

Binks had followed the others into the living room. Now, the cat perched in the front window, his yellow eyes watching Britt closely, his fluffy tail flicking against the glass. Two of Ren's outdoor dog chews showed up in colorful contrast to the fading green of the grass on the front lawn. And the swing hanging from the buckeye tree—no doubt put there for when Julia's nieces and nephews visited—swayed slightly in the breeze.

It was all so painfully ordinary, so perfectly *common*. Its simplicity cut deeper than any wound he'd ever taken.

It was an unfortunate twist of fate that he could *long* for a thing almost as much as the thought of actually *having* that thing scared him to death and sent him running for the hills.

The fall air was crisp and sharp with the scent of wet leaves, but it did nothing to douse the flame burning in the center of his chest. He clung to the ache, letting it radiate through him.

It was a warning. An ominous taste of what he would feel should he ever consider throwing caution to the wind and taking a chance on the kind of life, the kind of *love* most people sought as a matter of course.

The utter *devastation* he'd felt when he saw Julia take a bullet, the hours of terror he'd lived through when she'd been rushed into surgery and no one knew the extent of her injury, had proved to him that he didn't have what it took to be…*normal*. To want what *normal* people wanted.

Because the loss associated with a normal life was just too much.

I wish I were braver, he thought. *Someone who could give her what she deserves.*

He wasn't that man, though. He knew it as surely as he knew the weight of his handgun when it was fully loaded.

His fingers hesitated on the clutch as if some part of him—the part she had carved her name into—begged him to stay. But the other part, the part that knew the truth about himself, urged him to go.

As the tires rolled forward, as he left her wholesome little bungalow behind, it felt like he was leaving a piece of himself there on the lawn next to the dog chews and the whispered welcome of a life he'd never have the courage to claim.

CHAPTER 30

*Black Knights Inc.
Three months later...*

Julia stood outside the gates of Black Knights Inc. and stared up at the building's imposing brick façade.

Is Britt inside? she wondered, rubbing a gloved hand against the ache in her chest.

The pain had nothing to do with her still sometimes tender injury and everything to do with the days and weeks and months since she'd come home from the hospital to a sparkling clean house, watered plants, well-fed pets, and...Britt's goodbye letter.

He hadn't *said* the word goodbye in the letter. But his farewell might as well have leaped off the page and slapped her across the face. It didn't take an FBI agent's ability to read between the lines to pick up on what he'd been laying down. And even now, even all these weeks later, she could still recall every line.

Probably because she'd read and reread the letter so many times that the paper was beginning to thin around the edges, and the ink was starting to smudge.

Was it because she was a glutton for punishment? Or was it because, despite the finality of his words, one line—one particularly *beautiful* line—had given her hope?

Dear Julia… He'd begun, and her heart had fluttered at the sight of her name scrawled in his handwriting. In her head, she could hear his voice saying *jewel-yuh.*

I cannot tell you what an honor it's been getting to know you over the hours we've spent together. Hours that were too fleeting but perhaps made more magical because of their briefness and transience.

You are an amazing woman. Your beauty and brains are only outdone by your courage and kindness. It has been my privilege to watch you work, to see you rise to every occasion, to touch you, kiss you, and hold you during those miraculous moments in front of the fire.

I know your recovery will be painful and frustrating. But if anyone can come back better than before, it's you. With the help of those who love you—and lord knows, that's everyone who meets you—you will have a fantastic life and an illustrious career.

I'm rooting for you. Always. And I hope you find someone who sees you the way I do, someone who is everything I cannot be. You deserve the world, and I hope you never settle for less.

Take care of yourself. Be happy.
With all that I am,
Britt

"With the help of those who love you," she whispered to herself, "and that's everyone who's ever met you…"

That was the line. The one she kept coming back to. The one she thought about when she put her head on her pillow at night and the one that came to her the moment she woke up every morning.

Did he include himself in that statement? And if he did, then what did that mean for—

"You're free to go inside."

The words drew her from her ruminations. She glanced at the redheaded Goliath in the guardhouse and nodded her appreciation.

"Miss Greenlee says she'll meet you at the front door," he continued, hitching his chin back over his shoulder toward the snowy expanse between the front gate and the factory building.

"Thanks!" She waved a gloved hand and tightened her stocking cap around her ears.

Her progress was slow and tiresome. The snow tugged at her boots and shorted her steps as she made her way across the grounds between the front gate and the motorcycle shop. Bitter wind tried to tunnel beneath her coat. She flipped up the collar and adjusted her scarf to cover her chin.

The night before had seen the city assaulted by an early-season blizzard. The storm had swung down from Canada to deposit eighteen inches of the white stuff. And even now, lazy flakes drifted from the hulking sky to stick in her eyelashes and melt on her cheeks.

The smell of snow in the city always carried a crisp, metallic sharpness. Clean but tinged with the faintest blend of steel, like the bridges that spanned the river and the trusses that held up the skyscrapers.

Of course, when the front door swung open, hitting her with a blast of warmth, all she smelled was strong coffee, engine grease, and automotive paint.

Ah, Black Knights Inc., she thought fondly. *Some things never change.*

"What in the world brings you out in this weather?" Sabrina Greenlee waved Julia inside. The woman looked about a billion times better than she had the last time Julia had seen her.

While Julia had been in the hospital recovering, her colleagues at the Federal Bureau of Investigations had determined Sabrina didn't know enough about the cartel to warrant the expense of putting her into witness protection. Dillan said he'd fought for Sabrina and had made the case that the poor woman couldn't go back to Charleston because she knew the identities of three of the cartel's hitmen. But the higher-ups in the chain of command had determined that wasn't their problem.

Julia hadn't been apprised of the situation until *after* the fact. Which was a good thing because she'd have raised enough hell to get fired.

One of the only things she didn't like about her job was that it could be soulless. As a government entity, the FBI was subject to the almighty whims of the federal budget. And *that* sometimes meant they made choices based on a buck and not the best interests of those they'd sworn to serve and protect.

Thankfully, the Black Knights had come to the rescue. They'd agreed to house and hire Sabrina as their shiny new marketing, advertising, and social media guru. And Julia figured that was probably better than WITSEC.

Heaven knew the Black Knights had the setup to keep Sabrina safe.

Their security was enough to make a warden at a supermax envious.

After stomping the snow from her booted feet, Julia whipped off her hat and gloves and breathed a sigh of relief when the large metal door clanged shut behind her. Even though she tried to stop herself, her eyes darted around the place, searching for Britt's familiar form. For those icy-blue eyes and that adorably sexy cowlick.

Hew and Graham worked on a bike at the back of the shop—both men hunched over a particularly sparkly section of chrome. Julia couldn't hear what they were saying but could tell they were engaged in a friendly argument. And, if they were anything like her brothers—which she'd learned they were—no doubt they were disparaging the size of each other's manly bits.

Becky looked over a drawing spread atop one of the bike lifts, a pencil in her hand and a lollipop stick protruding from her mouth. She made a note on the drawing, slipped the pencil behind her ear, and then yelled for Hew and Graham to "Cut it out, you big buffoons! Or go get the ruler and end this argument once and for all."

Julia hid a smile that she'd been right on the money regarding the men's conversation.

"Men." Sabrina rolled her eyes.

"Having three brothers allows me to say this with my whole chest," Julia whispered from the side of her mouth. "They are forever stunted at the emotional age of fourteen and—"

Graham's response to Becky interrupted her. "Ruler? More like a yardstick!"

Becky guffawed. Whatever her comeback was, Julia missed it because she was back to scanning the room.

She could see the back of Ozzie's head. He was at his usual spot in front of the bank of computers on the second floor. Skid Row hummed from the speakers, singing "I Remember You" at a decibel level that, surprisingly, didn't endanger anyone's ability to hear.

Frank Knight leaned over the railing. He had a cell phone pressed to his ear while wearing his standard issue expression—the one that said he snacked on puppies and babies in his spare time.

But no Britt.

Julia felt like her entire body drooped with disappointment as, one by one, the Black Knights noticed her arrival and waved their hellos. She lifted a hand in greeting before she turned back to see Sabrina nervously twisting her fingers together.

"Right." She nodded. "How about I tell you why I've come over a hot cup of coffee?"

"Of course." Sabrina motioned for Julia to follow her to the kitchen.

Two minutes later, Julia found herself sitting at the center island. She'd shed the rest of her outerwear and now gratefully curled her hands around a warm mug of caffeinated heaven.

She tried not to remember how Britt had pushed her against the door to the pantry, tried not to remember how hot and hungry his mouth had been, how hard and ready his body had been. Tried and failed.

She wasn't sure how her news was going to land. So she figured she'd start with a softball. "You're looking well," she told Sabrina, who offered her a shy smile as she stood across the island from Julia.

"Eliza's quite the cook."

Julia chuckled. "I've had the pleasure of sampling her pastries. If I lived here, I'd weigh three hundred pounds."

Sabrina patted her still-flat stomach. "I'm working on it." Then, she grew serious. "How's Knox?"

"Still being held in a safe house, waiting for the day he'll take the stand and turn state's evidence against the cartel."

"And after that's done?"

"Agent Keplar will find him a nice spot in the WITSEC program. Knox Rollins will disappear from this timeline and a new man will be born in his place."

Sabrina's forehead wrinkled. "That'll break Britt's heart. Knox is the only family he has left."

Julia swallowed the knot that lodged in her throat, biting her tongue against asking after Britt since Sabrina had brought up the subject. "I hate it, too. But I think Sergeant Rollins would rather know his brother is alive and well rather than…the alternative."

"I suppose you're right." Sabrina sighed heavily.

Julia took a sip of coffee, luxuriated in the bitterness of the strong brew, and then said what she'd really come to say. "Eddy Torres is dead."

Sabrina blinked uncomprehendingly.

Julia emphasized, "The man who killed your brother, the man who brutalized you, is dead."

"H-how?" Sabrina's voice was a bare rasp.

"Shot in the head."

"Why? *Who?*"

All Julia could do was shrug. "Ballistics came back clean. Maybe his own guys offed him after he bungled the job with Knox and your brother? Maybe a rival gang caught up with him and did the honors? With a guy like him, it's impossible to say. But I wanted you to be the first to know."

"Thank you." All the blood had drained from Sabrina's face. Even still, she didn't come close to resembling the weak, wounded creature Julia had met months earlier.

Black Knights Inc. was good for Sabrina. Not that Julia was surprised. Black Knights Inc. seemed to be good for everyone lucky enough to live and work there.

"I really appreciate you coming all this way in the snow to tell me," Sabrina added.

"Tell you what?" Hew sauntered into the kitchen and made a beeline for the refrigerator. He pulled out a carton of strawberry yogurt that looked impossibly tiny in his huge hands.

Peanut appeared from nowhere.

Julia wasn't surprised. Her own animals had a Pavlovian response to the opening of the refrigerator door. Nor was she surprised when the grizzled-looking tomcat ran figure eights around Hew's ankles in a feline bid for treats.

"Agent O'Toole made good on her promise." Sabrina automatically reached into a drawer to find a spoon to hand to Hew. "She came to tell me Eddy Torres is dead. Shot in the head."

Hew stopped in the middle of peeling back the foil on the yogurt, his moss-green eyes darting to Julia's face. "No shit?"

Julia nodded. "They pulled him out of a marsh last week. He'd been there a while. They had to run his DNA to identify him. Results came in this morning."

"Good riddance to bad rubbish," Hew spat, stabbing the spoon into the yogurt in punctuation. He pulled out a small spoonful and purposefully dropped it on the floor at his feet. Peanut pounced on the glob like he hadn't been fed in a week. "I hope the sonofabitch suffered before they put his lights out."

Sabrina placed a comforting hand on his forearm, and Julia watched in astonishment as every muscle in Hew's body softened.

"It's over," Sabrina whispered, her eyes glistening up at Hew. "He's gone. The boogeyman is gone."

"Maybe now you'll stop having those nightmares." Hew's expression was filled with so much tenderness as he stared down at Sabrina that Julia had to look away.

So...in the end, Sabrina did *get the guy, and all I got was laid*, she thought, and then immediately scolded herself for being a jealous bitch. Sabrina had been through hell and *deserved* all the love and happiness she could find.

After gulping down half the contents of her mug, Julia grabbed her coat from the barstool beside her and pushed to a stand.

"I need to get back to the office," she announced. "If I'm gone too long, Agent Douglas hides my FBI star, and then I spend half the day looking for it."

"An FBI star, eh?" Hew's New England accent sounded particularly strong in that sentence. "Congratulations."

"Thanks." She grimaced. "It wasn't like I had to do much to get it. Just be in the wrong place at the wrong time when a guy with a gun decided to start spraying bullets."

"It's no small thing getting wounded in the line of duty," Hew returned. "I'm glad the bureau gave you the recognition you deserve."

Uncomfortable with compliments, Julia fell back on humor. "Thank you, Chief Birch." She snapped him a jaunty salute. "That means a lot coming from a Nightstalker."

"*Former* Nightstalker," he corrected.

"No such thing." Julia shook her head. "Just like there's no such thing as a *former* fed. It gets in your blood and stays there even after you take off the badge. Or, in your case, take off the uniform."

"I suppose you're right," he conceded with a dip of his mile-wide chin.

"I'll walk you to the door." Sabrina motioned for Julia to follow her from the kitchen. Hew stayed behind to finish his yogurt.

As they exited the short hallway, Julia slipped into her coat and scarf while sneaking surreptitious glances around the shop.

Still no sign of Britt. But Sam had joined Graham at the bike lift in the back. He waved when he saw her. She lifted a hand and then watched him flip down the visor on his welding helmet.

She was too busy shoving on her stocking cap to see the moment he fired up his torch and went to work. But by the time she and Sabrina made it to the front door, the smell of burning metal filled her nose.

Julia held her gloves in her left hand and extended her right. "I'm happy you found a soft place to land," she told Sabrina, feeling the subtle strength in the woman's grip. "And I'm sorry the bureau wasn't willing to do more to keep you safe. We can be real bastards sometimes."

Sabrina's soft smile said it all. "I think things worked out for the best. I'm happy here."

Julia felt the green-eyed monster try to hop on her shoulder again. But she flicked him across the room with an imaginary finger. When she told Sabrina, "I'm so glad for you," she meant it.

After pulling on her gloves, she allowed herself one more glance around the shop. One more chance to possibly catch sight of Sergeant Britt Rollins.

"He's not here," Sabrina said softly.

Julia didn't bother pretending to be ignorant and asking *who*. They both knew who she was looking for.

"Where is he?"

"On week one of a three-week mountain climbing expedition." Sabrina's expression was sympathetic. "You know Britt. When he's not building bikes, he's looking for his next big adrenaline rush."

Julia tried for a breezy tone. Tried and failed. "Actually, I don't know Britt at all."

Something moved across Sabrina's face then. It looked a lot like pity. "Is there anything you want me to tell him? You know, once he gets home?"

Julia grabbed the door handle and opened the shop to the frigid day outside. The air that rushed in instantly chilled her cheeks. As she stepped past Sabrina, she murmured, "Thank you. But I think everything that needs to be said has been said."

She didn't turn back to look at the old factory building as she made her way across the snow-covered grounds, waved at the redhead in the guardhouse, and hopped into the SUV she'd parked by the curb. She didn't turn back because there was nothing for her to see there. Nothing *for* her there.

It's done. Finished.

Whatever she'd had with Britt Rollins, whatever she'd *hoped* to have with him, was over. And if her heart was broken, she had no one to blame but herself.

He told me the truth from the beginning. I'm just the idiot who thought he might change his mind.

CHAPTER 31

Mount Fitz Roy, on the border between Argentina and Chile

Britt sat on a rough slab of stone, his mountaineering boots—with their metal crampons—dangling over the edge of a cliff.

The horizon stretched endlessly, waves of jagged peaks rolling into the distance, their snow-capped summits glistening like shards of glass as the sun rose over Patagonia. The air was crisp and biting, tinged with the scent of ice and stone. And it was quiet at this elevation. No cries of eagles. No rustle of trees. Only the sound of distant glaciers cracking and the gentle shush of rivers rushing far below.

Usually, the sheer majesty of the place would have filled him with exhilaration. Usually, he would have been grinning like a kid, thrilled to test his limits against Mother Nature and her cruel, uncaring creations.

But not today.

Not today. Not yesterday. And not the three days before that.

He shifted uncomfortably, the coarse fabric of his hiking pants scratching against his legs. He stretched his neck from side to side, but the tension remained. He concentrated hard on the beauty around him, but his mind's eye kept focusing elsewhere.

The itch under his skin wasn't from the dry air or the lingering chill of dawn. It was something deeper, more persistent. It gnawed at him from the inside like a rat stuck in a gunny sack.

He missed Julia.

For three months, he'd tried to convince himself otherwise.

The mission in the Middle East had been a godsend, a welcome distraction that demanded every ounce of his focus. Staying alive and keeping his teammates alive had left no room for wandering thoughts. But she'd been all he could think about the second he'd stepped off the plane back in Chicago.

He'd thought restoring Haint would help. He'd hoped throwing himself into the work of repairing and repainting his beloved bike would chase her from his mind.

It hadn't. If anything, it had only made things worse.

She'd been there every quiet moment as he'd popped out dents, every dull hour as he'd sanded and prepped. In his head, in his heart, in the very fabric of his being…there she was.

The sound of her laughter haunted him. Her wide, sunny smile projected itself onto the backs of his eyelids whenever he closed his eyes. And his dreams? Oh, they were filled with her. Filled with the scent of her, the softness of her, the *warmth* of her.

When the temptation to see her had become too much, when he'd found himself hovering on the edge of doing something stupid, he'd run for the hills. *Literally.*

Patagonia had seemed like the perfect escape. As far from Chicago and Agent Julia O'Toole as he could get.

But 5,500 miles and some of the most breathtaking scenery on earth hadn't done a damn thing to quiet the longing inside him.

The sun crept higher, bathing the landscape in warmth, but he felt no comfort in it. He didn't just want to see Julia again. He needed to. Pretending otherwise was pointless. And lying to himself had become exhausting.

He exhaled slowly and watched his breath turn to mist in the cold air.

Time to go home.

CHAPTER 32

South Riverside Plaza, Chicago
Ten days later...

The warm, rich scent of roasted coffee beans mixed with the smells of spiced chai and freshly baked pastries. The hum of conversation blended with the hiss of the expresso machine and the clatter of ceramic mugs.

Julia welcomed the familiarity of her favorite coffee shop as she shuffled forward in the slow-moving line.

Let it snow, let it snow, let it snow, she hummed to herself as she glanced out the window. Flurries danced in the air and landed on the shoulders of the passersby. The forecast called for another six inches of the white stuff, and she mentally braced herself for more of what had already been a long, hard winter.

Tucking her hands into her coat pockets because the biting chill of the outdoors still lingered in her fingertips, she couldn't wait to wrap her hands around the cup of hot coffee. Anticipation of the liquid warmth as it slid down her throat and the zing she'd feel once the jolt of caffeine hit her bloodstream had her eagerly stepping forward when it was her turn.

"Good morning, Chaz." She smiled at the barista.

He flashed her an easy grin, showing off his perfect teeth and even more perfect dimples. "Morning, Julia. The usual?" His voice was warm and teasing because they went through this every day.

"Some day, I might surprise you and order something different. But today is not that day."

"I like a woman who's consistent." He wiggled his eyebrows as he rang up her order. "In fact, it's one of my favorite qualities."

She chuckled and shook her head, handing over her credit card. "Why are you working here? Seriously, with that jawline and that hair, you should be doing commercials for luxury shampoos."

"And miss the chance to see your beautiful face every morning?" He blinked dramatically. "Never."

She could almost hear her sister-in-law Annie's voice in her head, urging her to *live a little*.

Annie had been the first person in her family to realize it was something *other* than the bullet wound that, for weeks, had made Julia putter around her house in *a blue funk*, as her mother called it. One evening, after Annie had come by to drop off groceries, Julia had confessed what happened between her and Britt Rollins. When she'd shown Annie Britt's letter, Annie had held her while she'd cried in self-pity and disappointment.

And it was Annie who, just last night, pulled her aside to brazenly inform her that *the only way to get over someone is to get under someone else*.

A guy like Chaz wasn't the type Julia would take home to meet the parents—he wasn't the type to *want* that—but he sure seemed like he'd make a great distraction.

Distraction.

That was the ticket. She needed to distract herself. To move on. To forget.

Unfortunately, all she could think about as Chaz turned to make her drink was Britt.

No matter how hard she tried, the memory of him refused to fade. When things were quiet, she heard his laugh, that low, delicious rumble. When she closed her eyes, she saw how his brow furrowed in concentration, how those three perfect lines on his forehead went wonky at the edges because of his scar. She remembered feeling the weight of his presence in a room, how it seemed like gravity itself shifted around him.

Go away! she silently cried to the memories. *Go away and give me some damned peace!*

But it was useless. The way she felt about Britt lingered just as her memories of him lingered. He was a song she couldn't shake. An earworm of the heart, and she was sick and tired of trying to—

"Voila!" Chaz pulled her back to the present as he slid a paper coffee sleeve over her freshly poured beverage.

"Thank you." She grinned at him. "You're a lifesaver."

"You say that every day."

"It's true every day."

He chuckled. "So if we're keeping things consistent, now's when I ask you out. And now's when you crush my spirit by refusing." He leaned on the counter, all confidence and charm and *perfect* looks.

The usual words hovered on the tip of her tongue. But instead of her pat refusal, she heard herself say, "You know what? Yes. How about we meet for drinks tonight?"

Chaz blinked. "You're joking."

"Serious as a heart attack," she assured him.

"The Drawing Room on Michigan Avenue? Seven PM? I'll make reservations," he blurted, like he worried she might change her mind if he dared to hesitate.

"The Drawing Room it is." She nodded, her heart pounding for reasons she didn't dare unpack.

As Chaz scribbled something on her coffee cup, she felt it again. That prickle of awareness that made the hairs on the back of her neck rise.

She was being watched. Or at least that's what her lizard brain told her.

It had been months since she'd last felt the odd sensation. But this past week, it had returned with a vengeance.

She craned her head over her shoulder, quickly scanning the room.

No one stood out. The place was packed with the usual morning rush—a mix of office workers looking for their liquid wakeup call, students typing furiously on laptops, and the occasional country tourist who seemed overwhelmed by the sea of people.

She glanced toward the front door just as it closed behind a man stepping out onto the snowy sidewalk. Broad shoulders, hair so dark it was almost black, an easy, loose-hipped stride.

Britt? Her heart stuttered.

Don't be ridiculous, her inner voice scolded. *You've been imagining him everywhere lately.*

That was true. Every time she turned a corner, she thought she got a glimpse of his profile. She thought she spied his leather jacket every time she peeked behind her.

But it was never him.

Still, the prickle on her neck remained as she took the coffee from Chaz and promised him, "I'll see you this evening."

Rubbing her gloved hand absently over her nape, she turned and headed outside.

The cold hit her like a slap, and she pulled her stocking cap tighter over her ears. The sidewalk bustled with people bundled in coats and scarves, their breath visible in the air as it crystallized into white mist.

Despite knowing it would amount to nothing, despite telling herself she was a fool, she glanced up and down the sidewalk, scanning the river of flowing humanity.

There.

The broad back. The dark hair. The—her breath caught and then leaked out of her on a slow sigh—cowlick.

The same damn cowlick I've been dreaming about for months.

It *was* Britt.

Before she could think, her feet were moving. She started off at a fast walk. But soon, she broke into a run, dodging pedestrians and sloshing her coffee so that liquid burst through the little hole in the lid to spill down the sides of the cup.

She didn't care that it wetted her favorite pair of leather gloves.

"Britt!" she called, her voice cutting through the city's noise.

The cold bit into her cheeks as her boots crunched over the salt-dusted pavement. Snowflakes swirled around her, carried by the sharp Chicago wind. But all she could see was Britt. His brisk steps, his jean-clad ass, the way his leather coat stretched tight against his back.

"Britt!" she called again. But he didn't stop. He didn't stop until she caught up with him and *made* him stop by grabbing his arm and spinning him to face her.

The sight of him sent warmth rushing through her veins despite the frigid air.

His hair was longer than the last time she'd seen him. It was like he'd forgotten to tame it in the intervening months and had let it grow wild. His beard was longer, too, flecked with snow as it framed his square jaw. But it was his eyes that had her breath sawing from her lungs. Their piercing blue was made even more vivid by the cold light of the winter day.

"Didn't you hear me calling you?" she asked breathlessly. Although, she wasn't sure if she was breathless because she'd run down the sidewalk or because of the way he was looking at her.

He was so completely still that it was unnerving. And the expression he wore was...what was the word? Acute? Intense? *Voracious?*

Instead of answering her question, his eyes scanned her face. "What was different about today?" His deep voice and Lowcountry accent licked at her ears.

"What do you mean?" She blinked her confusion.

"Why did you decide to go out with that tiny-dicked barista today when you've turned him down every other day?"

Her chin jerked back at his bluntness. "He doesn't have a tiny dick," she countered automatically.

His expression darkened, and she was reminded of a thunderstorm moving across Lake Michigan. "How would you know he doesn't?"

She crossed her arms over her chest, careful not to smash her coffee. "How would you know he *does*?"

Then it hit her. That strange, nagging sensation she'd felt for the last week, like someone was watching her. And then more pieces slotted into place. Like his comment *months* ago about her driving. Like his comment about her pets and other things she hadn't paid much attention to until, suddenly, in that moment, it all made sense.

Her eyes widened at the realization. "It was *you!*" She pointed a finger at his face. "You're the one who's been following me, making me think I'm going crazy. And not just the last few days, either. Before, too. Before your brother came to town."

She searched his face, expecting him to deny it. Instead, he remained silent. His jaw clenched. His eyes steady on hers.

His *lack* of response was all the confirmation she needed.

"Why?" she demanded, her heart pounding so hard that it drowned out the din of the city.

When he still refused to answer, she grabbed his sleeve and yanked him into the nearest alleyway, away from passersby's prying eyes and eavesdropping ears.

The hum of humanity, traffic, and conversation faded as she dragged him toward the dumpsters at the end of the alley. By the time she stopped, all she could hear were her ragged breaths and the distant rumble of a train.

Now that they were alone, she became acutely aware of him. Of the heat radiating from his body—it rose from his collar as steam. Of the exotic, spicy scent of his aftershave as it wafted in the air between them. Of their connection, that live wire of awareness that snapped taut whenever they were within five feet of each other.

She saw something that made her stomach flip as she searched his gaze. It was a strange mixture of guilt and longing and…something darker. Something she didn't have a name for.

"Why?" she asked again. Her voice was softer than it'd been on the sidewalk, though it was no less insistent.

Instead of answering, he asked, "How are you?"

She blinked.

"After your injury, I mean," he clarified. "Have you regained full movement? Are you still in any pain?"

She might have ignored him and demanded he answer *her* question first. But she could hear the deep concern in his voice, see the sharp anxiety in his eyes.

"I'm fine." She lifted her arm above her head to prove it. "I'm still working on regaining strength in this arm. And my shoulder aches when there's a change in the weather. But that's it."

"Good." He nodded, his relief clear in the way his shoulders relaxed. "That's good. I wanted to check in on you after you got back from the hospital. But I wasn't sure you'd want me to after…the letter. I reckoned we'd put a period on things, and it was best to leave it at that. But I've thought about you. Worried about you."

"We'll talk about the letter later," she told him, her voice sounding stronger than she felt. Her breaths were coming short and quick, and her knees felt like they were made of whipped cream. "For now, I want to know why you've been following me. And don't try to say it's because you wanted to assure yourself I'd recovered. You were watching me before."

She searched his gaze. But, as usual, his expression told her nothing about what was going on in his head. She realized he wouldn't answer her when his lips pressed into a thin line.

If he'd been one of her brothers, she'd have given him a titty twister until he relented. But since he was Sergeant Britt Rollins, she satisfied herself by grabbing the collar on his coat and yanking his face down to hers. "Why?" she demanded harshly, her mouth mere inches from his. "Tell me the truth. I deserve it."

His hands were jammed into his coat pockets as if bracing against the cold—or maybe he was bracing against the information she was determined to drag out of him.

He hesitated for a second more. Then he closed his eyes and admitted lowly, "Because I can't help myself." He exhaled, his breath curling in the cold air and brushing against her face as he slowly reopened those whirlpool eyes. "Because you're in my blood. You've *been* in my damned blood since the first moment I laid eyes on you. And no matter how hard I've tried, I can't get you out."

Her heart pounded harder with each word. By the time he paused, her ribs ached.

"I can't get you out, but I can't have you." She could see the anguish in him, the way it twisted his delicious mouth. "So…I watch. I watch because it's the closest I can let myself get to you."

The ache in his voice meant that it took everything in her not to close the distance that separated them and kiss him. Heavens, how she wanted to. How she wanted to kiss him and hold him and reassure him that whatever was holding him back wasn't worth the struggle. Assure him that everything would work out if he would just give in.

Instead, a cooler head prevailed. "Explain to me again why you don't believe in happily-ever-afters," she demanded.

The muscle under his eye twitched. "It's not that I don't believe in them. It's that they're not for me."

"Why?"

He pulled out of her grasp abruptly, taking a few steps down the alleyway before turning back. His hands dragged through his hair, leaving his cowlick standing straight.

Like always, the sight made her chest tighten. The urge to smooth that tuft of hair down was absurdly strong. But she didn't move.

If she touched him, she might not be able to stop. And she couldn't let herself be distracted. She needed answers. She needed the truth. Something very important was about to happen here. She could feel it.

"Because I know what it's like to love someone." His voice was hoarse. "And I know what it's like to lose them. I know what it's like to be the *reason* they're gone." His voice cracked and the sound opened up an answering fissure in her own heart. "I can't do it." He shook his head. "I can't let myself fall in love with a woman only to lose her. It was bad enough what I went through when you got shot."

Love…

Even though it hadn't been directed at her—not exactly—the word still made her light-headed. She felt like the ground had dropped from beneath her feet.

"Who says you have to lose?" Her voice was barely louder than the wind threading through the alleyway.

"It's a risk." He made a slicing motion with his hand. "One I won't take."

She opened her mouth to argue. To press him. To make him see that every risk was worth it when it came to love. But something stopped her.

Instinct maybe? All her FBI training on how to handle an uncooperative witness?

They were balancing on a precipice here. She could feel it as surely as she felt the hammering of her heart.

He wasn't ready to hear her arguments against everything he was saying. Not at this moment. Not in this place. And that was fine because she needed time to plan. Time to gather her thoughts. Time to choose her words carefully.

"Come to my house tomorrow night," she told him.

"What?" His chin jerked back.

"My house," she repeated. "I want to talk to you about this. I want to understand. You owe it to me to help me understand."

He didn't naysay her. Instead, he challenged. "Why tomorrow night? Why not tonight?"

She wished she was the type of woman to flake out on an obligation. But she wasn't. If she said she was going to do a thing, she did the damn thing.

"You know why. You were there. You heard me make plans with Chaz."

He hitched his chin toward her cup, where Chaz's phone number was scrawled across the coffee sleeve.

"You're too good for him," he said from between gritted teeth.

"Pfft." She rolled her eyes. "*He's* too good for *me*. I mean, have you *seen* him?"

"Enough to know he'd got more brawn than brains."

"If he were as smart as he is good-looking, then we'd know for sure God has favorites."

The muscle beneath his eye kept twitching. But now, it was joined by the muscles on either side of his jaw.

"You're jealous," she accused, trying not to sound too jubilant even though she imagined doing a happy dance complete with finger guns and hip thrusts. Feigning impatience, she added, "But I don't have time for it; I have to get to work." She turned and headed toward the alley's mouth.

"Julia—" he started, but she cut him off.

"My place!" she called over her shoulder without looking back. "Tomorrow night. Seven P.M. Don't be late!"

She didn't wait for his excuses or protests. She kept her steps purposeful even as her legs trembled beneath her.

As she exited the alley and headed toward FBI headquarters, the city closed around her again, the noise, the cold, and the rush of bodies.

None of that could drown out the thundering of her heart, though. None of it could touch the hope *in* her heart.

CHAPTER 33

Black Knights Inc.
The following day...

Hew stepped into the kitchen, breathing deeply of the warm scent of coffee and the flowery-smelling cleaner Eliza used on the soapstone countertops.

Britt paced the length of the center island—long, deliberate strides that did nothing to loosen the tightness in his shoulders. His hands clenched and unclenched at his sides. And he kept muttering something to himself that sounded a little like, *"You're a damned idiot."*

Hew quirked an eyebrow but said nothing. He headed straight to the refrigerator. After pulling out two packs of string cheese, he shut the door with a satisfying *thud* and, right on cue, Peanut appeared from out of nowhere to wind around his ankles.

Peeling open one of the wrappers, he leaned against the counter, took a contemplative bite, and finally broke the silence. "I can't help but notice you have an overabundance of restless energy today. Even for you. I also can't help but notice you have that rarely-seen thinking line between your eyebrows. Something you want to share with the class?"

Britt shot him a look, halting for half a beat. "Not really." There was no missing the annoyance in his voice as he resumed his pacing.

Hew finished his first piece of cheese while watching his teammate with quiet amusement. It was only after he'd unwrapped the second piece—and dutifully dropped a long string for Peanut to pounce on—that he said, "This wouldn't have anything to do with your date tonight with one lovely little blond agent, would it?"

That had Britt skidding to a stop. "Who told you?"

"Becky," Hew supplied casually as he took another bite of cheese.

Britt groaned. "I should've known she couldn't keep a secret. That's the last time I ask to borrow her car."

Unperturbed, Hew continued to needle. "So it's true. You *do* have a date with Agent O'Toole?"

"It's not a date. I'm going to her house."

"Even better!" Hew wiggled his eyebrows.

"No!" Britt's protest echoed around the kitchen as he resumed his pacing. "She wants to talk. Says I owe her an explanation. Which, I reckon I do. But honestly, I'd rather throw myself into oncoming traffic."

"What sort of explanation is she after?" Hew asked casually.

Britt's expression tightened. "She wants me to explain why, despite the fact that I can't get her out of my head, despite the fact that I can't seem to stop following her around like a damned dog, despite the fact that I think she's the most wonderful woman on earth, and despite the fact that we have wild chemistry—"

Hew lifted a hand. "Spare me the details of your wild chemistry. I heard everything I needed to at the cabin."

Ignoring him, Britt barreled on. "She wants me to explain why, regardless of all that, I refuse to consider starting something with her that will inevitably end in heartbreak."

Confusion made Hew slow-blink. "Who says it'll end in heartbreak?"

"In my life, I've seen love come in two forms." Britt's jaw tightened. "The first is a brilliant, gleaming gift. The other is tragedy in the making. Both are equally likely. And I'm not a risk-taker."

"Bullshit! You *live* to take risks."

"Not like this. This is too terrifying."

Hew chewed his last bite of cheese thoughtfully, letting the moment breathe before he spoke. His tone, when he finally did, held none of its usual sarcasm. "Here's how you beat fear, my friend. You live a life so full of love and happiness that there's no room for it. Fear looks for holes, for emptiness. So you just make sure it can't find any."

Britt stopped pacing so he could adamantly shake his head. "You make it sound so simple."

"It is." Hew shrugged. "You just have to grow a pair and heal all that hurt inside you, all those gaping wounds. Because if you don't heal them, you'll bleed all over the people who never cut you. And that's not fair. To them *or* to you."

"I think I like you better when your nose is shoved in a book and you're keeping your thoughts to yourself."

Hew chuckled, picked up his paperback, and strode toward the stainless-steel trash can in the corner. When he turned back after tossing his empty cheese wrappers, it was to find Britt had quit the room.

Go ahead and run, he thought with a fond shake of his head. *If you run fast enough, maybe your demons won't catch up with you.*

He was halfway to the kitchen door, intent on finding a quiet corner to read, when he collided with Sabrina.

"It's like running into a freight train." She laughed after stepping back.

His breath strangled in his lungs for reasons that had nothing to do with the collision.

The first thing he noticed—always the first thing—was how good she looked. Her hair was healthier than when she'd first arrived at BKI. The overhead light showed how the dark strands glimmered. And her face… that face that was emblazoned on the backs of his eyelids when he closed his eyes at night…had filled out. The sharp hollows had been replaced with soft curves and a rosy glow. But it was her eyes that tied his tongue. Large, luminous, and alive in a way they hadn't been before.

He'd always thought she was pretty. But now?

Christ! She's so beautiful that it hurts to look at her.

"What did you do to Britt?" Her tone was a mix of amusement and curiosity. "He ran out of here like a scalded dog."

And god help me, that accent!

Britt spoke with the same lilting cadence and round vowels, but somehow, it all sounded softer and sweeter coming out of Sabrina's mouth.

"I fed him some hard truths." He shrugged one shoulder. "I don't think he cared much for them."

Her lips curved into a small smile that he would swear did something diabolical to his heart. Then she settled her hand lightly on his forearm.

Her fingers were soft. Her skin was cool. And even though her touch was simple, it sent a jolt of electricity racing up his spine.

"You're a good friend, Hew." Her voice was soft and sincere. "Even if Britt doesn't see it right now, I do."

Friend.

The word hung in the air between them like an anchor. It seemed to sink into the tender, hollow place where his most secret hopes resided.

She'd clung to him like a lifeline in the months since she'd joined BKI.

He got it. Their shared grief, loneliness, and individual traumas had fused into a mutual bond. Now, he was her safe space, the person who never pushed, the one who listened without judgment.

As she stared up at him, her dark eyes full of affection and trust, he knew with a gut-deep certainty that friendship was all she felt for him.

Which is my bad luck, he thought wistfully. *Because I feel so, so* much *more for her.*

CHAPTER 34

Julia O'Toole's house

Britt stood at Julia's front door, his finger hovering over the doorbell like it was the detonation button on a bomb.

"Grow some balls," he repeated Hew's advice.

His finger shook when he pressed the bell. The chime had barely sounded before chaos erupted inside.

Ren's deep, booming barks rattled the windows. Chewy's shrill yapping joined in. And then, of course, there was Gunpowder. The parrot squawked twice before bellowing his favorite phrase: "Dick breath!"

Britt groaned. *So much for our retraining sessions.*

"I'm coming!" Julia called. Her voice—that sharp Chicago accent mixed with her low, husky tone—made his knees weak and almost sent him back down the walkway. But he stood his ground and nearly ground his teeth to dust in the seconds before the door flew open.

The first thing to greet him was Ren. The three-legged pitbull mix enthusiastically licked his hand. Chewy, the pint-sized sewer rat lookalike, clawed at his leg like he wanted to scale him. Binks sat on the back of the sofa and, in the way of cats, simply offered him a slow blink of disinterest as if to say, *Oh. You again.*

And then there was Julia.

She wore a soft, purple lounge set that looked cozy and unassuming—until he realized how it skimmed her curves. Her honey-blond hair was loose, cascading over her shoulders, and her dark eyes sparkled with amusement.

Britt's pulse skyrocketed. His throat tightened as his gaze dragged over her. His body had no shame when responding to her, so it went predictably hard.

"Come in out of the cold!" Her voice was warm and welcoming as she waved him inside. At the same time, she nudged Ren's snoot away. "Stop licking him, you goof. He doesn't want to smell like your stinky dog breath."

The house looked the same but somehow different. It was warmer and more alive since it was filled with her effervescent presence. Thanks to the fire that glowed in the hearth, it smelled faintly of wood smoke.

His mind flashed to another fire, another night, but he shoved the memory away and focused on a subject sure to keep his mind off more salacious things. "How's the shoulder today?"

She pulled the neck of her shirt down over her shoulder to show him. Her wound was pink and still healing. But it was clear she'd had a much better surgeon than he had. With time, it would fade to little more than a smooth, dime-sized scar. "Same as it was yesterday. Almost completely healed."

"I'm really glad you're okay." He swallowed convulsively. "I can't remember if I told you that yesterday."

The amusement in her eyes glittered brighter and he realized how awkward he was being. He latched onto the first thing he could think of. "Here." He thrust the plastic container of brownies at her. "Brownies. From Eliza."

She took them with a smile, her fingers brushing his for the briefest moment. But it was long enough for him to feel like he touched a live wire. "Tell her thanks. I'm guessing these are the ones I mentioned I really liked?"

"Probably," he mumbled, suddenly unsure what to do with his now-empty hands. He shoved them into his coat pockets and his fingers bumped against the small plastic figure he'd tucked there.

He'd scoured the internet in the days and weeks following his stint as her pet and house sitter. At the time, he'd told himself he was curious about her collection and what, exactly, might be missing from it. But when he'd found the mint condition Sand Person on eBay, he'd plugged in his credit card information before he'd even stopped to think if he'd ever get the chance to give her the toy.

It'd been in his coat pocket for months. Now, he pulled it out and held it toward her. "This is from me," he said quietly as Chewy continued to paw at his jeans.

Her face lit up when she took the figurine from him. "Britt! This is—oh my god, it's a Tusken Raider! Where did you find it?"

The joy in her voice opened up an ache in his chest in the general vicinity of his heart.

"It's amazing what you can find on the World Wide Web." He hoped for a joking tone but wasn't sure he managed it.

Her arms looped around his neck, and her soft, warm body pressed against him as she whispered, "Thank you."

He wanted to freeze the moment, hold on to it, hold on to *her*, but she pulled away.

"I have the perfect spot for this." She motioned for him to follow her.

After bending to pick up Chewy, he trailed her into the small dining room like a man caught in a spell. Silently, he watched as she opened the china cabinet and carefully placed the Tusken Raider next to the Admiral Ackbar figurine.

After closing the door, she stepped back to admire her handiwork. "What do you think?"

She turned to him with a smile so radiant, so full of joy, he had to fight not to lift a hand to shade his eyes. Instead, he petted Chewy's bony little head and was rewarded with a neck lick.

"I think you're gorgeous when you're happy," he said before he could stop himself.

A sly grin tugged at her lips. "That wasn't what I meant, Sergeant Rollins."

"But that's what I wanted you to know, Agent O'Toole."

Her expression wobbled and then turned serious when she glanced past him. "Binks!" She snapped her fingers. "Stop it!"

Britt glanced over his shoulder to find the cat had caught the cord on the front blinds and was doing his best to cut it in half with his razor-sharp teeth.

"Jar Jar Binks!" She clapped her hands. "I will take away your catnip if you don't quit chewing on that cord right this minute."

The cat dropped the cord. But in answer, and to make sure Julia understood his kitty disdain, Binks lifted his leg behind his head and started bathing his own butt.

Unperturbed, Julia rolled her eyes and returned her attention to Britt. "Where were we?"

He opened his mouth to return them to their previous conversation. But he decided to latch on to the distraction Binks had provided instead. "Chewy is short for Chewbacca. Binks is short for Jar Jar Binks. And Ren is short for..." He narrowed his eyes. "Kylo Ren?"

She nodded, still shooting censorious glances toward the cat should he decide to go back to the cord. "Of course."

"I don't know how I'm just now putting that together."

She made a face. "I know. I'm a one-trick pony." Then she motioned toward him. "Here. Let me take your coat."

He hesitated, his hands instinctively tightening around the Chihuahua.

"This isn't my attempt to get you naked, Britt," she added with an eye-roll. "I promise to stop with the coat."

Feeling like an idiot, he transferred Chewy from hand to hand as he shrugged out of his jacket. She walked it to the coat-tree by the front door and carefully hooked it over a peg.

Ren had run into her bedroom. His claws clicked against the hardwood floors as he raced back down the hall with a stuffed rabbit flopping in his mouth. In his excitement to bring Britt the toy, he overshot his mark and slammed into the standing lamp beside the bookshelves.

"Cockwaffle!" Julia and Gunpowder screeched at the same time as Julia lunged to keep the lamp upright.

Despite his nervousness, despite his heartache, Britt found himself biting the inside of his cheek. Julia's house was chaos. Warm, wonderful chaos. It suited her to a tee.

"Can I get you a drink?" she asked after she'd saved the lamp and rejoined him in the dining room. "I have beer, wine, and whiskey." She headed toward the rolling bar cart in the corner.

"I probably shouldn't." He ran a hand through his hair and realized he'd caused his cowlick to stand up when her gaze flicked to the top of his head. Self-consciously, he patted it down before adding, "It's too cold to ride the bike, and I didn't want to blow my paycheck on an Uber. So I'm driving Becky's car. Best if I stay sober."

She grabbed a bottle of red wine and two glasses without missing a beat. "One won't hurt you." She poured expertly and motioned for him to grab a seat at the table. "And maybe it'll calm your nerves. I swear, Britt, I usually can't tell what you're thinking. You have an amazing poker face. But right now, it looks like you think I might pull out a box with Gwyneth Paltrow's head in it."

He blinked at her. "What?"

"*You know.*" Her tone was she said, her tone teasing as she made dramatic motions with her hands. "*SE7EN*? 'What's in the box? What's in the *box*?'"

He stared for a moment and then burst out laughing, the tension in his chest finally breaking loose completely. But three seconds later, he sobered because…

Toast.

Cooked.

Completely dunzo.

In that moment, he realized that despite every defense he'd built, despite every promise he'd made to himself, he'd gone and done the stupidest thing ever.

He'd fallen in love with Julia O'Toole.

CHAPTER 35

"**D**o you love me?"

Julia asked the question as soon as they both took a seat. She'd decided her best bet was bluntness. Not only was she no good at beating around the bush, but she was done trying to wade through all the words that seemed to lay unspoken between them.

Time to put all my cards on the table and let the chips fall where they may.

Britt went completely still. The only things that moved on him were his rapidly blinking eyes. "Why would you ask me that?"

"Oh, I don't know." She rolled her eyes. "Maybe because you did the one thing my family most needed when I was in the hospital. You took care of my house and my pets." She motioned over her shoulder toward the cabinet. "Or maybe because you took the time to figure out which *Star Wars* action figures I'm missing. Or maybe because you've been stalking me for months."

Britt's face twisted into that half-frown. "I don't like to think of it as stalking."

"No?" She raised an eyebrow. "What would you call it then?"

"Covertly observing?"

"Bullshit," she scoffed, intentionally using one of his favorite words. "Try again."

"Fine." He sighed heavily. "I *was* stalking you. But only to make sure you didn't go and fall for some asshat the likes of Chaz of the double-shot espressos. How was your date, by the way?"

"Why do you care who I date?" She avoided his question.

"Because I *like* you. I want what's best for you. *Chaz* doesn't fit that bill."

"I don't need another older brother looking out for me," she told him with a sniff. Silently, she added, *I just need you, you big dolt. Can't you see you need me too?*

"How was your date?" he asked again. The jealousy in his voice was undeniable. It almost made her smile. *Almost.*

"It was nice." She drew the last word out just to see him squirm. She could be a sadist when she wanted to be. "Chaz is a decent guy despite his annoyingly perfect looks. Unfortunately, when he kissed me good night, there wasn't even the hint of a spark."

Britt's face darkened. "He kissed you?"

"Stop changing the subject and answer my question." She pointed a finger at his nose. "Do you love me?"

She watched his jaw tighten, the muscles working overtime. His lips pressed into such a thin line that it occurred to her he might choose not to answer her at all.

Maybe I was wrong. Maybe I should have taken a more circuitous route instead of getting right to the point.

But then Britt spoke, and his words left her breathless.

"I've spent so many nights wishing I was different. Wishing I wasn't afraid of love. But I am. And that fear, as much as I hate it, will keep me from taking the steps I know you need a partner to take. You deserve more than hesitation and doubt, Julia. You deserve a love as boundless and fearless as your heart."

He loves me, she thought, a kind of wild relief filling up all the empty spaces inside her. He hadn't *said* it. Not outright. But his words revealed what was in his heart, nonetheless.

He loved her. And yet, fear held him back from accepting that love.

She drew in a shaky breath, forcing her emotions under control. Her biggest question had been answered. But his response left her standing at the edge of a new one.

Tread lightly, she silently coached herself, feeling like Britt was a wild mustang—all raw power and deep scars. If she weren't careful, she'd spook him, and he'd bolt. If that happened, she might never get the chance to catch him again.

"You know," she started slowly, "one of my mom's favorite sayings is that if your dreams don't scare you, they're too small."

A forlorn smile played at his lips. "Your mom is something else. I can see where you get it from."

"Get what?"

"All that toughness and tenacity. The way she bosses around your father and brothers is something to see. And the way they jump to do whatever she tells them tells *me* that, despite the men in your family looking like they could each bench press a Buick, she's the one with the real strength."

It warmed her heart that he'd quickly homed in on the truth of her family dynamic. But she wasn't surprised. Britt was highly perceptive.

He's also highly skilled at changing the subject.

"Why are you afraid of love?" She was careful to keep her tone calm and gently curious. "In the alley yesterday, you said you know what it's like to love someone and lose them. You said you know what it's like to be the *reason* they're gone. What did you mean by that?"

He swallowed jerkily and smoothed Ren's silky ears when the dog, having sensed Britt's sadness, laid his big blockhead on Britt's lap, slobbery stuffed rabbit and all.

Britt's voice, when it came, was filled with pain. "My mother died in childbirth with me."

Julia had to fight to hold back her gasp of surprise and horror. His file indicated he'd lost both parents at a young age. But it'd been light on the specifics.

"How awful," she whispered.

"She had an amniotic fluid embolism," he continued. "That's when some of the amniotic fluid leaks out of the placenta during birth and enters the mother's bloodstream. It causes all sorts of problems. But in my mother, it caused cardiac arrest."

It took everything she had not to reach for his hand. Not to rise from her seat so she could fold him into a hug. But she couldn't make a wrong move. She couldn't do or say anything that might make him run.

So all she did was tell him sincerely, "I'm so sorry, Britt," even though the words seemed too small to encompass the depths and breadths of her sympathy.

The pain she saw in his eyes when his gaze found hers was enough to have her gripping the stem of her wineglass so hard she thought it a wonder it didn't shatter. "You know the layman's phrase for amniotic fluid embolism?" he asked.

She wasn't sure her voice would work over the lump in her throat. So she simply shook her head.

"Anaphylactic syndrome of pregnancy. My birth caused her body to have a deadly allergic reaction."

"Britt—"

"My dad did his best to step up," he continued as if he hadn't heard her interruption. "He tried to be the father *and* the mother to me and Knox. But he was a man's man, rough around the edges. Even though he loved us with everything he had, he mostly left us to run wild. That's probably why Knox and I are the way we are—thrill-seekers and risk-takers. Without the gentling influence of a woman, we never developed our softer sides."

That's not true, she wanted to tell him. She'd *seen* his softer side that night at the cabin. She'd never had a more tender, thoughtful, *thorough* lover.

But she didn't want to interrupt him now that he was sharing. So she took a slow sip of wine to drown the words perched on the back of her tongue.

"I prided myself on being a daredevil. I loved highlining and dirt biking and bungee jumping. When I was fifteen, I broke my arm trying to impress a group of girls at the skate park. It was a bad break. A compound fracture."

He lifted the sleeve on his T-shirt—this one was army green, snug around his biceps, and printed with a black Avengers logo. He pointed to the white scar on the inside of his upper arm.

"It took a trip to the ER and an emergency surgery to set it," he continued. "My dad was a dockhand who worked at the harbor. Health insurance was hit-and-miss for us. And it just so happened we were in a *miss* year. Dad had let the policy lapse so he could afford Knox's college tuition."

"How much?" she asked, knowing where this tale was headed. No one could deny the problems with the American healthcare system no matter which side of the political divide they landed on.

"Twenty-four-thousand dollars," Britt said.

"Good lord." She breathed, shaking her head at the injustice of it all.

"Anyway, fast-forward a few weeks, and Dad starts feeling sick. He loses his appetite, and his skin is itchy. But he doesn't go to the doctor because we can't afford it, right?" The agony on his face had her heart cracking right in two. "A year later, he was dead."

"What was it?" Her voice was hoarse.

"Pancreatic cancer."

She closed her eyes as the air leaked from her lungs. She's read how wretched that disease could be.

"I'm so sorry, Britt," she said again. And again, the words seemed too trite.

"Knox quit college to come home and take care of me," he continued. It was like, now that he'd determined to give her details, he wanted to get through them as quickly as possible. "He said he'd rather have his bare nuts dragged across hot asphalt than let me go into the foster care system. But money was scarce, and rent was expensive. He ran into a guy who told him he could make some quick cash by stealing a car and the rest"—his eyes once more met hers; she had to grit her teeth not to flinch at the pain she saw in them—"is history."

Ren whined pitifully. He was such a sensitive little soul. Britt looked down to find the dog's melting brown eyes glued to his face.

"I know, pal." He fluttered the pitbull's floppy ears. "It's a sad tale."

"Bye, bitch!" Gunpowder squawked from his perch on the coat-tree.

Britt's lips twisted and he shook his head. "Is that my cue to leave?"

Julia ignored his question as she arranged her thoughts. As she carefully worked through all he'd told her and all the ways she could convince him that his past didn't have to be the reason he didn't grab onto his present with both hands.

"So…" she started slowly. "You feel responsible for your parents' deaths and your brother's path in life? You feel like—" She stopped and tilted her head before continuing. "What? You feel like everyone you love comes to a bad end, so it's better just not to love?"

His bearded chin bobbed. "Pretty much."

"Well, that's just boloney."

He blinked, taken aback by her bluntness.

"Women die in childbirth all the time, Britt. Pregnancy and birth are inherently dangerous. Surely you don't blame *other* infants for what happens to their mothers, right? So why would you blame yourself?"

"I—"

She barreled on, refusing to let him interrupt. "Pancreatic cancer is almost always fatal. From everything I've read, most people don't realize they have it until it's in its advanced stages. It wouldn't have mattered if your dad had gone to the doctor when he first started feeling sick. His fate was already sealed."

"But—"

"And as for your brother," she continued despite his attempt at protest. "Maybe he got into a life of crime out of desperation to keep food on the table and keep you out of foster care. But he continued doing it because he liked it. Because something about it feeds his need for speed, so to speak. And that has absolutely *nothing* to do with you."

He breathed quickly, his eyes wide on her face as if it were the first time anyone had ever told him these truths. As if it were the first time he'd even *contemplated* them.

As a talented interrogator—*even if I do say so myself*—she knew when to press her advantage.

"We cannot protect ourselves from pain, Britt. We cannot protect ourselves from loss. To live is to suffer and lose. But the *love* we experience, the *people* who come into our paths and make our journeys sweeter, *that* is what life is all about. It's the *reason* for living."

His Adam's apple bobbed in his throat.

Her voice was softer, gentler, as she continued. "You think you're not brave. But do you know what kind of courage it takes to say all the things you just said? To admit your fears out loud? Most people don't even have the guts to face them, let alone speak them."

He shifted uncomfortably in his chair, his fingers still absently stroking Chewy's dome. "It's not the same. Words are easy. Actions…that's where I fall short."

"Not true." She leaned forward, her elbows resting on the tabletop. "You've shown me love in a hundred ways without even realizing it. The little things you've done, the way you've been there when I needed you, when my *family* needed you…those aren't the actions of someone who falls short."

He shook his head, his jaw tightening. "That's not enough. You deserve someone who can give you everything. Someone who doesn't hold back."

She bit her lip, considering her next move. She couldn't let him keep retreating into his doubts, but she also couldn't push too hard. He was like a puzzle—complex, intricate, and worth every second it took to figure him out.

"I don't need *everything*, you big idiot," she said quietly. "I just need you. Flaws, fears, and all. You think I've got it all figured out? I haven't. I'm scared too. Scared of taking a chance on something real, something that could hurt if it goes wrong. But I'm more scared of not taking that chance. Of letting you walk away because you think you're not enough when you're everything I want."

His eyes met hers then, and she saw the conflict there—the hope battling with the doubt, the love warring with the fear. He looked like a man standing on the edge of a cliff, unsure whether to leap or retreat.

It was time for the finishing blow. "I love you, Britton Daniel Rollins. I think I've loved you since the moment I walked into Eliza's ER suite and you sneered at me and Dillan and said, 'Oh, joy. The fuck-up fairies are here.'"

He winced. "You heard that?"

"Hate to be the one to break it to you, but your voice carries." She wrinkled her nose. "And I don't think you were actually trying to keep your opinion to yourself."

"Julia..." he began, his throat thick with emotion.

She cut him off by standing and walking over to his chair. Placing a hand on his shoulder, feeling the muscles automatically tense at her touch, she said, "Don't. Don't talk yourself out of this. Out of us. Because if you think I'm letting you walk away without a fight, you don't know me as well as I thought."

For a moment, the room was silent except for the crackle of the fire in the hearth and the *click-clack* of Ren's claws on the hardwood floor as he vamoosed himself into the living room, having determined Julia was ready to take his place as Britt's comforter.

"Do you love me?" she asked again. "Just answer the question honestly."

Slowly, tentatively, Britt reached for her hand. His grip was warm and steady despite the storm of uncertainty she knew raged inside him.

"I love you so much I can barely breathe. But I'm terrified," he admitted, his voice hardly above a whisper.

"So am I." She squeezed his warm, callused fingers as her heart grew three sizes. "But let's be terrified together and see how it goes. What do you say?"

"Hew told me if I don't heal all that's hurt inside me, I'll bleed out on those who didn't cut me." His tone was tinged with desperation. "I don't want to bleed out on you."

"The only person you're bleeding out on at the moment is yourself. And as for healing the hurt inside? Let me help you. Let me *show* you how good life can be when you let love in. When you let it fill up and smooth over all those empty and wounded places inside you."

For the first time that night, she saw a spark of something other than fear in his eyes.

It was hope. *Tentative* hope. But hope all the same.

CHAPTER 36

Britt lay on his back, his chest heaving as he tried to catch his breath. His skin was damp with sweat, his muscles pleasantly sore. Beside him, Julia was equally breathless as she turned onto her side, her flushed cheek resting against the pillow.

"Wow." He raised his eyebrows in approval. "That last move you did was…" He searched for the right words, couldn't find them, and settled on, "It was really something."

Her kiss-swollen lips curved into a mischievous smile. "You'll find I'm full of promises." She wiggled her eyebrows.

He chuckled, feeling lighter than he had in years. "Luke? *The Empire Strikes Back*, right?"

Her expression shifted to amused intrigue as she propped herself up on an elbow, gazing down at him. "You've really brushed up on your *Star Wars* trivia."

He reached out to gently run his thumb over her bottom lip, marveling at how soft it was. How it fit perfectly against his when they kissed. "I wanted to impress you."

Her eyes sparkled as she lifted the covers, glancing down his body. "It's not *Star Wars* quotes that impress me."

"Oh, yeah?" he teased, his grin widening as he tackled her onto the mattress. She let out a squeal, her laughter lighting up the room as he pinned her beneath him. She didn't fight back—instead, her arms wrapped around his shoulders, and her body molded to his. He couldn't help but take a moment just to feel—her warmth, her softness, the sheer *rightness* of being here with her. The thought that he might get to feel this way for the rest of his life filled him with something dangerously close to happiness.

"So." He brushed a strand of hair from her face. "When do we get to start trading *Marvel* movie quotes?"

She scrunched her nose. "I have to admit. I've never gotten into the *Marvel* universe."

He blinked, utterly baffled. "Why? Superheroes are just star-fighters with better costumes."

She laughed, the sound like music to his ears, and reached up to smooth down his perpetually unruly cowlick. Her fingers lingered in his hair, and he closed his eyes, luxuriating in her touch. "Maybe because nobody ever took the time to introduce me to the finer attributes of the franchise."

"Well…" He wiggled his eyebrows. "We're going to have to remedy *that* immediately."

Her smile softened. "So you're planning to stick around?"

The question made his heart stutter. There was still so much to consider. He'd have to tell her the truth about BKI. If they were really going to do this, he refused to keep secrets from her. But that would come later.

For now, he gave her the simple truth, "I want to. I'm scared of the thought of loving you and losing you. But now I think *not* letting myself love you is even *more* terrifying."

"Good answer," she whispered, tilting her head to kiss him. Her lips were soft, her tongue eager. "Right answer," she added before crossing her ankles behind his back and wiggling her hips against him in a way that made his body surge with renewed desire.

As he moved with her in that age-old rhythm, his thoughts slipped away from fear and into something else entirely.

Boss was right all along. So was Taylor Swift.

From the beginning, some invisible string had been pulling him and Julia together. He'd tried to fight it, tried to stretch it until it broke, but it was stronger than him. Stronger than her.

It was the strength of *them*. Together. And *that* was the biggest adrenaline rush he'd ever known.

EPILOGUE

Washington D.C.

The snow drifted softly against the windows of the hotel suite like a curious visitor.

Bishop leaned against the glass, gazing out at the Capitol. Colorful Christmas lights adorned the buildings and shimmered through the flurries.

To most, the sight would be a symbol of hope and seasonal joy. To him, it was a pretty façade that covered a cracked foundation that would crumble to dust soon enough. And oh! How he longed for the day.

Behind him, a soft knock announced the arrival of his visitor. He didn't call out as he hit the remote that automatically closed the blinds and blocked out the view of the city.

Let him wait, he thought maliciously. *The strong control the clock. The weak merely watch it tick away.*

"You're late," he said after taking his time to open the door and then motion for the operative to come in.

The man shifted uncomfortably, his leather shoes scuffing against the polished wood floor as he stepped into the room. "Traffic."

Bishop snorted, brushing past the man on his way to the seating area. "Such a quaint excuse. As if you haven't been trained to overcome obstacles. But let's not waste time with apologies."

"I brought what you asked for." The man set a leather satchel on the low coffee table. "Every digital correspondence, logs of all encrypted calls, and videos of every virtual meeting. All the evidence you'll ever need to expose the whole thing."

After sitting in one of the plush armchairs, Bishop's sharp gaze roved over the young operative. It was clear the man was still raw. He had a nervous energy that made Bishop itch.

"If you'd like my help leaking it to the press, I can—"

"No," Bishop interrupted, his tone flat and final. "This isn't about exposing them. Not now. It's about understanding the entirety of the board before making the final move."

The operative frowned. "But if the public knew—"

Bishop slammed his hand down on the coffee table. The sound was sharp and decisive, like a gunshot in the quiet room.

"The public knows what they're told to know. And I'm telling *you* that the timing must be perfect. Or this information will do nothing but scatter the pieces. I don't want chaos. I want a controlled demolition."

The man swallowed, nodding quickly. "Understood, sir."

"Good." Bishop reached for the glass of scotch on the end table and swirled it idly, staring at the amber liquid. "The cracks are spreading. People are angrier and more divided than ever. Fear is rising. It's all going according to plan."

"And in the meantime, you just let Black Knights Inc. continue to operate with impunity?"

Bishop smiled, but the cold curve of his lips never reached his eyes. "They're a minor nuisance. Like Madam President herself. They'll all fall in time." He swirled the liquid in his glass again, his eyes gleaming with dark purpose. "But only when I say so."

AUTHOR'S NOTE

As time and society progress, we become aware certain words and phrases that are part of our everyday lexicon actually have problematic origins or can be used to further marginalize already vulnerable readers.

As a writer and a lover of language, I strive daily to educate myself on outdated, offensive terms and stereotypes and work to eliminate them from my novels. (We're not talking swear words here, people.) But I'm still learning. And if I screw up, I'd love to be educated and allowed the opportunity to correct any mistakes. Because I truly believe the pen is mightier than the sword.

Or, in simpler terms, *words matter*.

ACKNOWLEDGMENTS

Major thanks to "The Asheville Crew" for keeping me hiking, laughing, and karaokeing. You all save me from atrophying behind the keyboard by forcing me (sometimes unwillingly) out of my pajamas and into the real world. Glad to be on this part of the journey with all of you.

As always, props to the people who do the unsung work of getting a book into readers' hands: Marlene Roberts, proofer extraordinaire, Jennifer Johnson, formatter for the stars, and Erin-Dameron Hill for the beautiful cover.

And last but certainly not least, thank YOU, dear readers, for coming back for more Black Knights Inc. I hope you all had as much fun jumping back into the world of motorcycles and mayhem as I did.

OTHER BOOKS BY JULIE ANN WALKER

BLACK KNIGHTS INC.

Hell on Wheels
In Rides Trouble
Rev It Up
Thrill Ride
Born Wild
Hell for Leather
Full Throttle
Too Hard to Handle
Wild Ride
Fuel for Fire
Hot Pursuit
Built to Last

BLACK KNIGHTS INC: RELOADED

Back in Black
Black Hearted
Man in Black
Black Moon Rising

DEEP SIX

Hell or High Water
Devil and the Deep
Ride the Tide
Deeper than the Ocean
Shot Across the Bow
Dead in the Water

In Moonlight and Memories

In Moonlight and Memories: Volume One
In Moonlight and Memories: Volume Two
In Moonlight and Memories: Volume Three

ABOUT THE AUTHOR

A *New York Times* and *USA Today* bestselling author, Julie loves to travel the world looking for views to compete with her deadlines. And if those views happen to come with a blue sky and sunshine? All the better! When she's not writing, Julie enjoys camping, hiking, cycling, fishing, cooking, petting every dog that walks by her, and... reading, of course!

For more information, please visit:
https://julieannwalker.com

facebook.com/julieannwalkerauthor

instagram.com/julieannwalker_author

tiktok.com/@julieannwalker_author